I0557928

The Ramtalans
Origins: Book One

The Ramtalans, Origins: Book One

Copyright © 2024 Sofia Diana Gabel. All rights reserved.

Sofia Diana Gabel asserts her moral right to be identified as the author of this book.

Without limiting the rights under copyright reserved above, no part of this book may be reproduced in any form or by any electronic or mechanical means, including information storage and retrieval systems, without prior permission in writing from the publisher, except by a reviewer who may quote brief passages in a review.

This is a work of fiction. Names, characters, places, and incidents either are the product of the author's imagination or are used fictitiously, and any resemblance to actual persons, living or dead, events, or locales is entirely coincidental.

Previously published by Escargot Books and Music as Two Brothers: Origin by Sofia Diana Gabel.

ISBN: 979-8-9893356-5-7

Printed in the USA by Sofia Diana Gabel

This book is dedicated to three of the most amazing women in my life: Alexandra, Olivia, and Andrianna.

Chapter 1

Mojave Desert, Palmdale, California-Four Months Ago

The dim, brick room was sticky-hot. The feeling of malevolence that permeated the room would send chills through an ordinary person. But there were no ordinary people here.

A voice—distant, harsh, pained—emanated from the depths of a wavering red light, "I need those boys. I've waited too long. My strength is almost gone. No more stalling or delays. If you cannot do your job, then I have no more use for you." A pause, then the voice grew louder, more forceful, "Bring them to me now! They are the key to ending this madness. I created you for this singular purpose. Do not disappoint me."

Ari swallowed and drew in a calming breath. "I'm doing the best I can. It's not easy getting past their Guardian. Give me a little more time."

"Do whatever you have to do to get them. I will not wait much longer."

"I understand. I won't fail you. They will be with you soon." Ari wiped his brow and lowered his eyes. He'd succeed. He had to.

PALMDALE, CALIFORNIA-Present Day

This would be a good day with no trouble. Argus had said that over and over again all morning, but now that he was standing at the school attendance office counter, right under an irritating flickering light, he had his doubts. He gripped the pen and filled in his information on the enrollment form:

Name: Argus Dachel

Age: 17

Previous school: Home schooled

His stomach fluttered and he wiped a trace of sweat off his forehead. What was he doing? How could this be a good day? He didn't belong. High school was where normal kids went. He and Tai, his twin brother, weren't exactly normal. They had special abilities that they weren't allowed to use in public, and some sort of rare blood disease that kept them away from other kids. How much weirder could they get?

They were in their senior year and their guardian, Aunt Celeste, said they should go to a public high school to be around other kids. She seemed a bit hesitant, like she wasn't quite sure about it, but in the end said it was for the best. How? How was going to a school filled with regular kids for the best? She said other kids didn't have super strength or the ability to dissolve and reappear, so what was the point in being around normal teens?

He'd spent most of his life secluded in their house in the middle of nowhere, and that's how he liked it. He had freedom at home to do what he wanted, without restrictions like he had now. Now it was all, *no using your abilities at school, no getting hurt or cut, no telling anyone about anything.* Secrets. And that sucked.

He glanced sideways at Tai as he filled out his own paperwork. Tai was an inch taller at six foot one, with blue eyes and sandy blond hair. Yeah, Tai would do all right with his all-American California teenager look. He was probably exactly what every high school girl wanted. Argus put the pen down. All he had to offer was wavy dark brown hair that wouldn't lie flat and chameleon-like hazel eyes that changed color to match the clothes he wore. Freaky, but nothing special. It wouldn't matter that he was better at math and science than Tai. What girl would care about that?

The frazzled school secretary dropped another bunch of papers onto the counter and said simply, *fill these out.* Aunt Celeste stared at the papers and let out a sigh. At over six feet, she was taller than either him or Tai.

Argus licked his dry lips and wished he'd brought his lip balm. His chest tightened, and he couldn't breathe. "Aunt Celeste, I'm not sure..."

She pointed to the only two chairs in the office waiting area. "Everything's fine, Argus. You and Tai might as well sit down while I complete this paperwork. They want every detail of your schooling and health information. This will take a while."

He went over to the chairs. They were red plastic. There were no hard plastic chairs at home, only comfortable, soft furniture. He glanced around and realized that he didn't know anything about a real high school. He sat. As he thought, plastic chairs were uncomfortable.

He looked toward the main door and noticed that a few of the kids coming in didn't seem happy, in fact, they seemed depressed to be back at school. He wanted to commiserate and say to them, *Hey, I understand. I'm not happy to be here either.*

As a couple of kids ran by like they were trying to get away from something, Argus noticed a guy about the same age as him shove a skinny boy in the lobby right near the counter. Argus started to get up but stopped. He should go and help the skinny kid, shouldn't he? That was the right thing to do. With one punch, he could knock the bully across the room, if he was allowed to use his strength.

The tough guy was big, broad at the shoulders and maybe as tall as Tai. He was very tan with black close-cropped hair and a scowl. He didn't look like he wanted to be friends with anyone. When the skinny kid slipped away and ran through the lobby, the tough guy noticed Argus watching and glared with his eyes squinted, drawing his finger across his throat. Great, the first day of school and he'd already made an enemy. Every movie he watched about high school, and he'd watched a lot lately preparing for today, had bullies bent on causing trouble.

"Arg," Tai whispered, "Stop looking at that creep. He'll think you want to fight him."

"Really?" Argus turned to Tai. "What makes you think that? I didn't do anything, not yet anyway. Do you really think he's going to want to fight me?"

Tai smiled. "Maybe. I read somewhere that bullies are like wild animals. If you look 'em in the eyes, they think you're challenging them. Then the only way to fight them off is with a chair and a whip."

A joke. Tai always joked when he was nervous. But this wasn't a joke. There was nothing funny about high school or bullies. Argus nudged his brother in the ribs. "Ha, ha. You know I don't want to be here. What if I can't control myself and I use my abilities? I want to use them right now and punch that kid in the mouth."

"I wouldn't suggest that. Aunt Celeste would pull us out of here and I happen to want to be here. Relax." Tai rolled his eyes, a habit of his. "I'm psyched, bro. Did you see all the girls when we came in? Girls everywhere. Every shape and size. I think I'm going to like high school."

"But this is crazy. We're not like everyone else. I don't know how to behave like a normal kid."

"Sure you do." Tai smirked. "We've watched every possible movie and TV show about high school kids. What about all of those vampire and werewolf teenager shows and books? Those guys aren't normal, and they fit in. Sort of."

"That's fiction, Tai."

Argus looked around. The bully was gone. He watched Tai as he winked at a passing girl. Tai was so confident and sure of himself, maybe a little too sure. He wasn't afraid of anything. That sort of overconfidence could get him in trouble someday.

Argus sighed. He and Tai had been raised by Aunt Celeste their whole lives. They'd never spent any time apart. Now they'd have different classes and wouldn't see each other for most of the day. It would be strange not having Tai around constantly, but maybe it was time to grow up. Maybe that's why Aunt Celeste enrolled them.

Argus watched a couple of girls stroll by the office, giggling. They probably had a normal life, with parents and sleepovers and school dances. His life had never been normal. His parents died when he and Tai were babies and Aunt Celeste had been their guardian and their teacher ever since. And their nurse. She told them about the blood disease and said it would cause "catastrophic results" if they got an infection due to a cut. That's why they weren't allowed to play rough sports with other kids. Although they did play tackle football outside whenever Aunt Celeste left them alone for an hour or so to go shopping. Not that he'd ever tell her that.

Tai nudged him. "Hey, bro, don't look so scared. It's only high school."

Argus swallowed a lump that had settled in his throat. "I guess. But what about that guy? What am I supposed to do if he does want to fight?"

"Seriously, Arg? If he comes at you, take him down. Aunt Celeste said we're not to get hurt. You're stronger than twenty men."

Argus nodded. "Yeah, I guess. But I'm not going to use my abilities unless I have to, which means you can't go and disappear in front of anyone unless you have to."

"Well, duh, I know that. And trust me, Arg, I'm not dumb enough to dissolve in public. I have self-restraint." He smirked again.

Tai with self-restraint? Not likely. Argus watched Aunt Celeste at the counter filling out page after page of enrollment forms. She had her blonde hair tied back in her usual long ponytail that seemed to swish and come alive every time she moved her head. It was strange, but she never seemed to age. She must be around forty but looked more in her twenties. Weird. "I don't think she meant for us to showcase our abilities, Tai."

Tai shrugged. "It's not showcasing if it's a necessity."

A small, thin girl with wavy reddish-brown hair halfway down her back came into the lobby and went straight to the counter like she was on a mission. Argus couldn't take his eyes off her. There was something about her. The way she moved, graceful, feminine, yet strong and confident. She wore slightly baggy jeans and a tee shirt with frayed sleeves and when she turned around, he was breathless. She looked right at him with deep green eyes that caught the fluorescent light, and her smile, that incredible smile, lit up her entire face. She was amazing.

She stared at him for a moment. "Hi, I'm Lola McCreary." Her voice sang like the prettiest music. "Are you the new students?" She came over and extended her hand.

Argus jumped up and took her hand in his and kissed it. That was his first reaction. His second reaction was embarrassment when her green eyes widened, and she retracted her hand.

"I'm sorry," he mumbled. That move, ill-fated as it was, had been straight out of an old movie he'd seen. Guys didn't kiss girls' hands these days, he knew that. Mistake number one.

Instead of laughing at him, Lola smiled and her cheeks blushed red. "Wow, that's the nicest thing I've ever had anyone do to me. So, are you the new students?"

Tai, obviously trying to suppress a laugh, but not quite doing it, nodded. "Yeah, I'm Tai and this is Argus. I hope you don't mind if I don't kiss your hand. My brother seems to have that gallant move covered."

Argus wanted to die. He'd never been so embarrassed. First girl he meets, and he's humiliated beyond belief. *Thanks, Tai.*

Lola smiled and shook her head. "No, that's all right." Her eyes locked onto Argus's. "Anyway, I'm like the welcoming committee of Highland High. I'll help orient you and take you to your classes, show you the cafeteria, the gym, where the best bathrooms are and what not to do."

Argus cleared his throat before talking so his voice wouldn't come out sounding like he was going through puberty again, "What do you mean by what not to do?"

"Oh, like don't cross the football field during lunch or you'll risk getting trash-canned by the super-seniors. That's their turf." Lola twisted a strand of her hair.

Argus was still lost in her eyes. *Don't stare, Argus.* He glanced away. "What are super-seniors?" He had an idea what they were but wanted to keep her talking. Whenever she spoke, his body tingled, and he really liked that feeling.

She shrugged casually. "The kids on their second time round as a senior. You know, been kept back another year."

"Oh." Argus looked over at Tai. "Why don't you see how much longer Aunt Celeste will be?"

Tai rolled his eyes again. "Sure, no prob, bro." He got up with a grin and went to the counter.

Lola sat down in Tai's chair. "So, Argus is it?"

Argus felt hot and had to wipe his forehead. "Yeah."

"I like that name. Unusual, but nice. I was told that you were home schooled. That must have been great."

Argus nodded. "Yeah, but lonely." His heart raced. He'd love to take Lola's hand and put it over his heart, so she'd know that she made it race like that. But that would be incredibly worse than the hand kiss. He'd never met a girl before today, and he liked it.

She twisted her hair again. "I don't think I'd be lonely if I were home schooled. No teasing, no shoving in the lunch line. It'd be a relief."

"Well, if anyone ever shoves you, you let me know." He felt protective, like a clichéd white knight defending a princess. She deserved to be protected and he'd do whatever he could to keep her safe.

"Okay, deal." She smiled and got up. "Let me go find out if I can show you around now."

"I'll be right here." Argus sighed and watched her hike up her loose jeans as she went to the counter beside Aunt Celeste. Were the jeans hand-me-downs or did she buy them a size too big? And her hair was messy, like she didn't particularly care. Everything about her was fascinating. He couldn't wait to find out more.

It was great to have a friend, his first friend in high school, and a girl at that. He'd had some friends growing up, but they were other home-schooled kids. None of them had been girls.

She turned and gave the okay sign with her fingers and came back. "You're all mine now."

Argus blurted, "What? Really?" Did that mean she liked him, too?

She tilted her head. "What? Come on. I'll show you and Tai around. The bell won't ring for about ten minutes, so we'll have a little time."

Okay, Argus, you're acting like an idiot. She didn't mean anything by that. Get a grip. He watched her as she opened the office door. She's the welcoming committee like she said before. It's her job to be nice to new students. Then again, she did say she liked it when he kissed her hand.

Aunt Celeste spun around, her ponytail swishing. "Argus, Tai, be careful. Call me if you need anything or if you notice any...you know. Do you have your cell phones?"

Argus knew exactly what she meant by "you know". Their abilities were increasing and becoming more pronounced. She told them, under no uncertain circumstances, to tell her right away if they noticed any changes or new abilities. She'd never explained completely why they had to keep their abilities a secret, only that it wouldn't be good to let anyone know. She said she'd explain it all later.

Tai rolled his eyes. "Of course we have our phones, Aunt Celeste. Can we go now?"

She nodded. "But remember, call or text if anything goes wrong. Anything." She stared at them for a few seconds before getting back to the paperwork.

Argus glanced at Lola. He should say something, so it didn't look like he and Tai were a couple of wimps who needed a nurse maid. "Um, my aunt is overprotective. She means well, but..."

Lola shrugged. "I think that's nice. My dad doesn't really care...I mean, he does, but he doesn't...ah, never mind." She seemed to force a smile.

Was she hiding something, or maybe she meant her dad was too busy to pay any attention to her. Another thing he'd have to find out. She motioned for them to go through the doorway leading to the rest of the school. Argus went first but froze when an endless stream of kids hurried by. How were there that many kids in one place? Even at the mall during the holidays he'd never seen so many people.

Whispering in his ear, Tai said, "We're not in Kansas anymore."

"Kansas? This is another planet." Argus watched two girls in matching cheerleader outfits skip by arm-in-arm. Their skirts were so short he could see their underwear or shorts or whatever they were. Their legs were long and tanned and they both had short blonde ponytails. He couldn't take his eyes off them.

"This way," Lola ordered in a loud tone very different from before.

"Easy, bro," Tai whispered, "I don't think your little girlfriend likes you staring at those hot cheerleaders."

Tai was probably right, judging by the way Lola stomped down the hall in the opposite direction to the cheerleaders. Mistake number two. Could she be jealous? He didn't do anything but look. Okay, looking at other girls upset Lola, so no more looking. Except maybe when she wasn't around. He jogged to catch up. If she was upset, then she must really did like him. There was so much to learn about girls.

Lola stopped suddenly at a door with a placard above that stated Boys Locker Room. She pointed to the sign and continued down the hall, dodging her way through the throng of kids. Uh-oh, she wasn't as friendly as before. Something was definitely wrong. Argus would have liked to look in the locker room, but Lola was almost out of sight.

Tai nudged him. "Our tour guide's leaving. You know, you don't have to settle for plain little what's-her-name. The school's full of babes."

Argus frowned and stepped into the flow of bodies. "Don't say babes. I like Lola, Tai. But I didn't mean to piss her off."

"Well, you did."

Everyone passing by had a backpack and almost everyone was texting on their phones while walking, occasionally bumping into other kids. Argus felt out of place without a backpack, but at least he'd picked out clothes that blended in; new dark jeans and a gray tee shirt. A guy, staring at his phone, bumped into him and muttered an *I'm sorry*. It was chaos, but an exciting chaos.

He caught up to Lola and was going to apologize for whatever he might have done, but she stopped at a set of double-doors with a placard that said Cafeteria. This time, she turned. "If you buy lunch, try to get in line early or you won't get served in time. The super-seniors come in about ten minutes after the lunch bell rings and...well, you'll find out." She wasn't smiling anymore.

"Lola, did I do something wrong?" Argus glanced at Tai, who pretended he was looking around.

"I'm sure I have no idea what you mean." She frowned and twisted a curl of hair. "I think we have time to check out a couple of your classrooms." She took a slip of paper from her pocket. "Argus, you have physics first period with Ms. Montgomery, same as me. And Tai, you have English. The English room is down that hall a bit." She pointed to another hallway at an intersection. "And the science class is that way." She pointed in the other direction.

Tai nudged Argus. "Hey, why don't I go and wait in the cafeteria? I can get a juice or something."

Argus nodded. *Thank you, Tai.* "Yeah, okay, good idea." He waited until Tai vanished through the double-doors of the cafeteria. "Hey, Lola, can you show me where the science lab is, so I don't get lost?" Now that he had her alone, he could find out more about her.

"I guess." She walked fast, not stomping like before, although she didn't exactly look relaxed. She came to a door with a windowpane in the center that was smudged black. "This is it."

"What's that all over the window?" Argus touched the glass, but the smudge was on the inside. It didn't look like paint, more like soot.

"Oh, that's from when Justin Jones blew up the lab last year in chemistry. Ms. Montgomery told everyone not to ignite any flames because they were collecting hydrogen, but Justin lit a cigarette lighter anyway." As she talked, her brow pinched, and her eyes didn't sparkle as much. "His lab partner lost his eyebrows and Justin got suspended for a week. That black smoke stuff is embedded in the glass."

Argus touched the glass again. "Nobody got hurt? Other than the eyebrows, I mean." He peered in through a tiny clear spot in the window. The classroom was made up of stools in front of long counters filled with microscopes, Bunsen burners, and glassware. Almost as good as the makeshift lab Aunt Celeste made for them in their kitchen. He turned back to Lola.

She shook her head. "Amazingly, no. But Ms. Montgomery was told by the school board not to do anything with flammables anymore." Now she looked sad. "I love science class, but now all we get to do is stupid boring experiments."

"That sucks. I like science, too."

She peered up at him. "You do?" Then she looked down. "I thought you were a jock."

Why would she think that? Argus wanted her to look up again so he could see her eyes and try to figure out what she was thinking. "Really? How come?"

Her eyes were still cast down. "Because you're so tall and...muscular...and, you know, you seem so cool."

Cool? Him? Seriously? He was anything but cool. And what did she mean by cool? What made someone cool? She didn't even know him. Was coolness an attitude or the way you looked? He didn't have an attitude and he certainly wasn't anything special to look at. So what was it?

All he could say was, "Oh." *Okay, Argus, talk about something else, she's embarrassed.* "Well, science is one of my best subjects. I once built a Jacob's ladder. You know what that is?"

She finally made eye contact and smiled again. "I saw a video of one. It looked really amazing."

"What the hell. Science geeks!" came a harsh voice above the sound of kids rushing around.

Lola's expression changed, she looked scared. Argus turned and saw the same guy who'd been staring at him through the office window, pushing past a few kids who quickly turned the other way and ran off. What did he want?

The guy came up to Argus, stood too close, and looked him up and down, and shook his head. "I knew you looked like a geek. What's your name, geek? Poindexter?"

"No, it's Argus." Argus moved in front of Lola. He was her white knight after all.

"Fart-gas? Ha! Well, fart-gas, where you from? I haven't seen you around."

The guy stepped to the side and only then did Argus see there were two other, smaller guys hanging back a bit. What were they, his entourage?

"Don't answer, Argus," Lola whispered.

"Is that Lola-Lola-belongs-in-a-stroller?" The guy gave Argus a shove out of the way and glared at Lola. "It is! Look, boys, it's baby Lola."

"Shut up, Justin." Lola ducked behind Argus, holding onto his arms. "Leave us alone."

"You gonna cry, baby Lola?" Justin pushed Argus again. "Are you her bodyguard, fart-gas? Are you a tough guy?"

That was it, Argus had had enough. He took a step forward. "Look, I don't know what your problem is. We're not bothering you."

"Yeah you are. You're breathing and that bothers me." Justin puffed out his chest. "You wanna go? I'll give you one free shot."

Argus shrugged. "Go? Go where?"

"Fight, fart-gas."

Oh, that's what he meant. A fight? In the middle of the hallway? What was this kid thinking? Argus shook his head. "I'm not going to fight you." *Cause if I did, it wouldn't end well for you.* He watched Justin ball up his fists. Apparently he wanted a fight even if it was one-sided. *Bad move, Justin.*

As Justin hauled back to throw a punch, Argus intercepted by grabbing his fist. Justin was strong, but no match for Argus's strength. It didn't take much effort at all to hold onto his hand and slowly force him to the ground by rotating his arm so he had no choice but to drop. *Told you it was a bad move.*

When Justin grunted in pain, Argus let go. He glanced around. He shouldn't have made such a public show of his strength. He'd left imprints of his fingers on Justin's hand. Not good. Luckily, it didn't seem like anyone but Lola, Justin, and his buddies saw.

"Hey, I'm sorry." Argus extended his hand, but Justin slapped it away and got to his feet. "I said I was sorry."

"Asshole. Think you're better than me, do you? You got lucky, that's all. I tripped. Right, guys? I tripped." Justin looked at his buddies. They stood there open-mouthed and nodded.

Argus turned to Lola. "Are you okay?" She looked a little frightened.

"Argus, look out!" she shouted.

Caught off guard, Argus didn't have time to get out of the way and got a punch right to the mouth. It stung. He staggered to the side and tasted blood. It only took a second to recover. He quickly prepared to fight Justin, but something was wrong. Justin wasn't gearing up for another hit. Instead, he was stumbling around, shaking his hand furiously like it was on fire. There were tears in his eyes! What was going on? One punch couldn't have broken his hand. A group of students started to gather around, and one girl screamed.

Justin fell to the ground on his butt and stared at his hand. Argus wiped his mouth and saw a smear of blood on his fingers. He looked closer at Justin's hand. What the hell? There was a quarter-sized area on his knuckles that looked like the skin had been melted away. Yeah, not a good first day.

Chapter 2

Argus backed away. Did he do that to Justin's hand? If he did, how? Before he had time to say anything, Tai appeared out of nowhere and stood by him. Thankfully nobody seemed to notice. Typical Tai, using his shared-sight to see what was going on and then dissolving and reappearing. It was a cool ability, but he sometimes abused it. Argus remembered one time when he was on the Internet looking at pictures of girls and Tai appeared in his room, laughing, and making fun of him. They got into a fight over that.

Tai looked from Justin to Argus, and kept his voice low, "You okay, Arg? I had a feeling you needed help and turned on shared-sight, but I didn't see everything. What the hell happened? Did that guy hit you?"

Argus wiped his mouth again. "Yeah, he did. But I'm okay, no big deal." He really didn't want Tai butting in. Especially not with Lola around. Tai was better looking and if he seemed like the hero, Lola might...

Lola placed her hand on Argus's arm. "It is a big deal."

He turned his head and saw those green eyes staring into his. She squeezed his arm slightly. Okay, what did that mean? Did she like him, was she angry at him, worried, annoyed, scared?

Tai wrinkled his nose. "Yeah, I think it's a big deal, too. Arg, that patch on his hand looks like...like raw meat. Did you do that?"

"Of course he did!" Justin shook his hand and glared at his buddies. "You gonna just stand there?" Now he glared at Argus. "What did you do to me, you freak? My hand's on fire!" He blew on his hand.

Argus stepped away from Lola so she wouldn't be in the line of fire if Justin or his gang decided to fight. "Me? *You* hit me, Justin. I didn't do anything but bleed. You need to go to the hospital and get your hand looked at."

Justin turned to his buddies again. "You saw him, he had acid or something. Look at my hand. He poured acid on me. You stole acid from the lab!" He pointed to the classroom. "You're gonna pay, freak. You're gonna pay." He ran down the hall, followed by his minions trotting after him like loyal dogs.

Tai raised an eyebrow. "Arg, you didn't use acid on him, did you?"

"Seriously, Tai. No, of course I didn't. Um, Lola, can you wait in the classroom? It's not safe out here. Justin might come back." Argus opened the door for her. He really needed a minute with Tai, but also wanted her to see how much he cared about her. That was chivalry, wasn't it?

Lola frowned. "I can take care of myself."

Uh-oh, is she mad again? Argus opened the door wider. "I'm sure you can, but I don't trust Justin and I don't want to be responsible if you get hurt. Please." He motioned for her to go inside.

"Fine." She stomped into the classroom.

Yep, she was mad. Argus grabbed Tai by the arm and pulled him down the hallway and out of the way of several guys playfully shoving each other. "Listen, Tai, I don't know what happened, but when he punched me, his skin...melted."

Tai raised an eyebrow. "Damn. I guess that's another ability you have. Melting hands."

"Not funny. I hurt him. I feel like shit. We're supposed to tell Aunt Celeste if anything new happens. But I don't want her to pull us out of school anymore. And I bet Justin's going to try to fight me again."

Tai nodded. "Yeah, I'd say that's a fair assessment."

Argus sighed. "So what should I do? I thought maybe I could feel normal for once in my life, but now—"

"Bro, you're not normal. Neither am I. Neither is Aunt Celeste. *Normal* is only a word anyway. Stop stressing over *normal*. I like being different."

Argus didn't need to be reminded that they were special. Being *special* is what had kept them away from other kids. "But I want to *feel* normal. Can't you understand that?"

Tai rolled his eyes. "Not really. You need to stop feeling like a freak. Don't worry about Justin. If he thinks you can melt skin, he'll stay the hell away from you. And if he doesn't, pummel him into hamburger."

"I can't do that." Argus sighed again. Whatever happened to Justin's hand was his fault. He had no idea how, but it was. It was like that time a few years ago when he was at the mall and accidentally bumped into a little kid in a shoe store and sent the kid flying into a display, all because of his abnormal strength. The kid's mother wanted to call the police, but Aunt Celeste pulled her aside and must have convinced her not to. But it didn't change the fact that he hurt a little boy.

Tai had a look of sympathy. "Look, seriously, don't worry about it. We'll fit in. I know we will. I'm going to go and see if I can find my class. Hang out with what's-her-name and relax, have fun."

"Lola. Her name's Lola." Argus knuckle-bumped Tai. "I don't know if I can relax or have fun, but I'll try."

With a grin, Tai spun around and jogged down the hall. Argus waited for a moment, standing to the side as another group of guys hustled by and several kids filed into the science room before going in himself. Lola waved him over to a stool next to her. There was one microscope in front of them that only a single eyepiece. Theirs at home was a binocular microscope. And the Bunsen burners on the counter looked old with burn marks all around the top. Aunt Celeste always had brand new instruments and equipment. Obviously you had to take what you could get in public school. Guess that was another thing he'd have to get used to.

Lola looked at him. "You look...worried. Is everything all right? What happened to Justin?"

She wasn't angry now. Good. He'd have to make sure not to tick her off again. But how do you do that? Lola's mood seemed to change by the minute. He shrugged to appear casual. "I think he's going to get first aid. I've never been in a fight before, that's all."

"Oh. Okay. What do you think Justin did to his hand? It looked awful." She rubbed her own hand. "You didn't do anything. I'll swear to that if I have to."

"Thanks. I'm not sure what he did." Argus wanted to grab her hand and kiss it again. Feel his lips on her skin. *Come on, stop daydreaming!* "I think he's going to blame me, though."

"Yeah, he's a jerk. I'm glad he hurt his hand. Maybe he won't pick on anyone for a while." She glanced around the room. "I know most of these kids. I can introduce you after class if you'd like."

Argus nodded. "Sure. That'd be great."

A couple kids looked in his direction and did a chin thrust as a greeting. He did it back, feeling a little weird and awkward. Did Tai feel the same way? Probably not. He'd be sitting in English with a handful of hot girls around him. And he'd love it.

Argus leaned on his elbows and concentrated on his brother. If he concentrated hard on a person, he could, for a brief few seconds, see what they were doing a minute before they did it. It was like watching a scene in a movie. Not quite Tai's shared-sight which was in real time. Future-sight was great to get an overall perspective of what was going on in the very near future. And right now, he wanted to see what Tai was doing. Problem was, his ability drained him and he was weak for a while after. That sucked, but it was worth it. Aunt Celeste said it was because he hadn't completely grown into the ability yet.

He breathed in slowly and thought of only Tai. When the image of Tai began to come into focus, Argus concentrated even harder. He saw Tai with his hand on a classroom doorknob, but when he stopped suddenly and turned around, Argus saw Justin was right behind him.

Argus broke his concentration and drew in a deep breath. He couldn't let Justin fight with Tai. He hopped off the stool, but his knees buckled. Damn it, too weak to stand yet. It'd take about half a minute before he got his strength back properly.

"Argus, what's wrong?" Lola got off her stool and grabbed his arm. "You okay?"

"Yeah. I must have twisted my ankle or something." He sat down and took a few deep breaths.

His head spun and his arms felt heavy. He rested his head in his hands and tried to concentrate on Tai. No use, he was too weak to focus. He checked the clock on the wall. Class would start in only a few minutes.

Lola let go of his arm. "You don't look so good."

He shook his head. "No, I'm fine, but I have to leave. My brother needs me."

Lola wrinkled her brow. "Huh? What do you mean? He's probably in English already. What makes you think...oh, you're twins. I've heard that twins have a connection or something. But isn't that only for identical twins?"

When the door opened, Argus turned. Tai walked in, glanced around, came to him, and whispered in his ear, "Arg, your buddy, Justin, isn't going to leave you, or me, alone."

Argus put his feet on the ground and stood up carefully. He was strong enough to stand. "What did you do?"

Tai rolled his eyes. "Nothing. He called me a few unsavory names and said he'd be waiting for us after school. I thought I should let you know."

Argus pulled him aside and whispered, "You didn't dissolve in front of him, did you?" *Please say you didn't.*

Tai smirked. "What do you take me for? I wanted to, but I didn't. But I'll tell you this, I *will* be waiting for him after school."

"Tai. You can't do that. You saw what I did to his hand. We've got to be careful. Don't be stupid."

Tai narrowed his eyes. "I know what I'm doing. Don't ever call me stupid, *bro*."

"You are being stupid. We have to act normal." Argus checked the clock. "The bell's going to ring any second. Go to class. I'll see you at lunch."

"Don't try to boss me around, brother." Tai's posture relaxed a little. "Just because you're three minutes older than me doesn't make you the boss of me." He turned and hurried from the room.

A loud mechanical chime rang out in the hallway. Still feeling slightly weak, Argus sat on his stool and waited. The students were noisily chatting and pulling notebooks from their backpacks. Oh, crap. He didn't have a backpack or a notebook. Why didn't he remind Aunt Celeste to buy supplies? Because he was too nervous, that's why. He couldn't think of anything the past few days except trying to fit in. Now how could he fit in when he didn't even have something as basic as a notebook?

He stared at one of the cheerleaders who sat a few stools down from him. She was wearing the cheerleader uniform; tight red shirt, short skirt that rode way up her thigh, and lacy white socks with matching white sneakers. She was cute, really cute. Was it a prerequisite for all cheerleaders to be cute? She looked at him and smiled. Wow.

He felt Lola tap him on the shoulder. He turned away from Cute Cheerleader and noticed that Lola's green eyes seemed sad. She said quietly, "Hey, what was up with your brother?"

"Um, he wanted to tell me that Justin said he'd be waiting for us after school." That was the truth.

Lola nodded. "Oh." She motioned discreetly to the cheerleader. "That's Mariah Gomez. I can introduce you if you'd like."

"What? No, that's okay." He was mortified. If Lola saw him staring at Mariah, who else might have? He'd get a reputation for staring at cheerleaders. He didn't want to be labeled as anything on the first day. Plus, staring at cheerleaders seemed to really upset Lola. He didn't want that. "I don't think she's my type. I...like...smart girls with red hair who like science." Cool, that was a great line. He smiled.

"Oh." Lola's cheeks burned red, and she looked down at her ratty backpack on the counter. She pulled a few loose sheets of paper out and mumbled, "We don't have much money, so I've used the same backpack since middle school. And loose paper is cheaper than notebooks. I...don't like to waste money."

Why was she apologizing for not having much money? Argus wanted to wrap her in his arms and tell her he didn't care, but that would be another kiss-the-hand move. "Hey, I don't have a backpack *or* paper, so you're better off than me."

She perked up. "We can share."

"It's a deal." Argus faced front when the teacher, Ms. Montgomery, came in and went to the front of the room. She was probably close to Aunt Celeste's age, around forty, but she looked so much older. Ms. Montgomery's hair was streaked with gray, and she had thin lips and a sharp nose, almost birdlike.

Scanning the class, Ms. Montgomery cleared her throat. "Argus Dachel? Who's Argus Dachel?"

Argus had a sinking feeling in the pit of his stomach. He glanced around and put his hand up. "I'm Argus Dachel." He could feel everyone's eyes on him.

Ms. Montgomery pointed to the door. "Mr. Dachel, you're wanted in the principal's office."

As if being the new kid and getting in a fight wasn't bad enough, now he was being sent to the principal. And it was the first class of the first day.

How much worse could it get? He slid off the stool, kept his head down, and hurried to the door, looking back at Lola as he left.

Chapter 3

Max Jackson, special investigator for the Astronomical Urgent Recovery Administration, AURA, sat in his cramped basement office in the Los Angeles headquarters building regretting how little he'd actually accomplished in his life when his energy sensor beeped. He spun his chair around and stared at the computer.

It had detected an energy alert in the Palmdale area again. It couldn't be a glitch or a random surge in a transformer as his boss insisted because the sensors were set to record spikes from organic sources. No, this had to mean something. He added the data to his graph and saw a pattern. The surges were all within a ten-mile radius. This recent one, though, was coming from a local high school. Hmmm, curious.

The phone rang. Max held his breath for a moment before letting it out. He was not looking forward to answering it. He picked up the receiver. "Max Jackson here."

"Jackson, my office. Now."

"Yes, sir. On my way." Max printed out the graph and slipped it into a manila folder crammed with photos and notes and headed off down the hall to the office of AURA's Chief of Operations, Lawrence Stone.

Stone was the kind of guy who never minced words, never accepted an excuse for failure, and never smiled. Max rubbed Stone the wrong way, probably because Stone's daughter had divorced Max six months ago claiming he'd made her an alcoholic and had ruined her life. She always said he cared more about chasing aliens than he cared about her. As much as he hated to admit it, she was right.

He placed his hand on the doorknob to Stone's office and hesitated. It wasn't like he didn't have any evidence. It was because he didn't have any *hard* evidence. Unfortunately, that's exactly what Stone wanted. Max opened the door.

Stone was sitting upright and stiff at his large, hand-carved oak desk, with a scowl on his face. Max stepped into the office and slid the folder onto the desk.

Dropping his eyes to the folder, Stone dragged it closer with his index finger. "This looks pretty thin, Jackson."

"I think I might have—"

"Think? Might? Those aren't words in my vocabulary, Jackson. If you haven't found anything significant in nearly a year of surveillance, then you've wasted not only your own time, but my time. And a bunch of taxpayer's money." Stone opened his desk drawer and took out a large envelope. "This is your new assignment. A nine-year-old girl in Tacoma, Washington."

Max took the envelope. "But sir, I'm onto something. I know I am. Like I was about to explain, if you'll look at the latest data, there have been more than ten energy fluxes in a matter of months, all coming from—"

"Energy fluxes, Jackson? I never thought you to be one to make something out of nothing. What else do you have?" Stone flipped open the folder and leafed through the documents.

Max waited until Stone looked up, then pointed to the graph that was now lying on the desk. "As you can see, sir, I've plotted the occurrences. Most of the surges come from a remote location outside of the Palmdale area and today there were three blips, close together, originating from Highland High School. There's no way to explain that, sir. The power grids for the remote location and the school are different. And the sensors focus on organic sources that are much higher than human or animal."

Stone closed the file and placed his palm on top. "What's your plan? What are you hinting at?"

"Well, I think it's time for contact."

"Contact? You don't even know the source of the surges." Stone kept the graph on the desk, staring at it. "What's your directive?"

"My directive?"

"Your directive."

There was no way to avoid it, he'd be fired for sure if violated the directive. "The primary directive for all special investigators is to observe, document, and investigate....unseen....unless prior approval and authorization has been given."

"That's right, Jackson. I don't recall giving you approval and authorization. Or am I mistaken?"

"No, sir, you're not. But I would like to officially request authorization to take a pool car to Palmdale and contact the inhabitant or inhabitants at the remote location."

Stone sat there, nodding slowly. He slid the file across the desk toward Max. There was a slight hint of smile. "You're going to fail and I'm going to enjoy watching you fail. Consider this official authorization. You have thirty days to bring me solid, indisputable evidence of extra-terrestrial intelligence on Earth or you'll spend the rest of your career in the mail room. Understand? Thirty days to prove you're worth a shit or you'll be out of my hair permanently." He slid the Tacoma file back into his drawer. His lips curled up into a full-blown smile. The first smile Max had ever seen.

Max managed a quick nod, scooped up his folder and graph and hurried out the door. He stood for a moment in the hall. It went better than he'd hoped. At least he had another month to dig up something tangible. He'd have to step up his game and do whatever he had to do to find something. Hard evidence is what he needed. He couldn't let Stone win. The last thing he wanted to do was end up in the mail room, or even worse, chasing after false leads in Tacoma. Palmdale is where he had to be, there was something going on and he'd find it.

Chapter 4

A rgus turned the corner and saw Aunt Celeste pacing outside the main office. She looked more worried than angry. Even though he hadn't done anything wrong, he felt guilty. He didn't want to let her down. He'd promised, over and over, that neither he nor Tai would get into any trouble. How could he have been so dumb to think he'd ever fit in?

Aunt Celeste sighed. "What happened, Argus? I got a call to come back to school for a meeting with you and the principal. I was just briefed."

Briefed? She always sounded like she was in the military. He shrugged. Who could have told her? Not Justin, because he said he'd be waiting after school. "I didn't do anything. Really, I didn't."

She opened the office door. "That's not what I heard. According to what the secretary said, a boy named Justin told some other boys that you burned his hand with acid. One of those boys went to the principal and reported it. I know you didn't have acid, so I want to know exactly what happened."

Time for the truth. Argus drew in a breath. "That guy, Justin, hit me with a sucker punch. Then something weird happened to his hand and he said I splashed him with acid, which I didn't."

"Wait." She held up her hand, closed the door and peered closer at him. "You were hit? Where?"

After explaining every detail, including the burn on Justin's hand, Argus waited while Aunt Celeste paced again. She seemed to be thinking things over. Did that mean she was considering whether or not to take them out of school? *Please, no.*

She stopped and put her hand on his shoulder. "All right, I'll do damage control. Come on."

He followed her into the principal's office where Justin and his two minions were sitting. Justin had a bandage around his hand. How did he have time to go to the hospital? Maybe there was a nurse at the school. The principal, an older man with grayish-white hair, thick glasses, and deep lines across his forehead, motioned for Argus to sit in the only remaining chair. Aunt Celeste stood behind him. It was like being on trial.

"Mr. Dachel, I'm Dr. Hector Chavez, the principal here. As I understand it, there was an incident in the science lab with acid. Is this true?"

Argus shook his head. "No, sir, it's not."

"Ah huh. Then how did Mr. Jones get a burn on his hand? I saw it and it's definitely a burn. His father is picking him up to take him to the ER." Dr. Chavez kept his eyes on Argus. Intense, dark eyes.

Argus squirmed. So did Dr. Chavez put the bandage on? Did it matter? No, it didn't. All that mattered was that Justin was hurt. "I don't know how his hand got burned, sir." He didn't know what else he could possibly say. He wanted to say that Justin got mad because he'd been forced to the ground, but he couldn't. Plus, Justin would deny it anyway.

Aunt Celeste came forward. "Dr. Chavez, I'm sure this is a misunderstanding." She glanced over at Justin, who appeared to cower slightly. "It's possible that Mr. Jones burned his hand with a cigarette."

Dr. Chavez nodded. "I suppose, but I got a report from another student that said Mr. Dachel is responsible. Mr. Jones, would you like to tell your side?"

Justin was staring at Aunt Celeste, looking small and timid. "Ah, yeah, it happened like that. A cigarette. I, ah, blamed fart...I mean Argus."

Aunt Celeste turned and looked at Argus. "Argus, is that what happened?"

What was going on? Argus stared at Aunt Celeste. She wanted him to lie. Why was Justin going along with it? Oh, well, time to lie to the principal. "Yes, he somehow burned it with a cigarette."

Dr. Chavez now looked at the minions. "What about you two? Is that what happened?"

Each, with gaping mouths, nodded quickly.

"Fine. Then we don't appear to have an issue except for underage smoking and lying." Dr. Chavez got up. "Let me make this clear, gentlemen, we have a zero tolerance for bullying, so I don't want any of you involved in bullying. If I find either of you are, both of you will be expelled. Zero tolerance. I'd suggest all four of you get back to your classes."

"Yes, sir." Argus stood and followed Aunt Celeste into the hallway. Okay, that was the weirdest thing.

She leaned down and whispered, "Do not use your abilities. Do not get into any fights. If you do either of these things, I'll know, and you'll finish your education at home. Understand?"

"Yeah. I mean, yes. But I told you it wasn't my fault. That guy's got it in for me." Argus sighed. "I didn't mean for him to get hurt."

Aunt Celeste nodded. "I know. Do your best to stay away from him. I want you to report in every few hours, so I know you're all right. This isn't negotiable. Understand?"

Argus groaned. "Yes. Can I go now?" Report in every few hours? What, was he in kindergarten? She was being way too overprotective.

She straightened and tossed her ponytail so it snaked down her back. "Go back to class, Argus."

He'd be glad to get back to class and away from the principal, Justin, and Aunt Celeste's mind tricks. "Okay. Thanks for whatever you did back there."

She pointed down the hall. "Go to class."

He jogged through the empty halls toward the classroom, but stopped a few doors down to send Tai a quick text to let him know what was going on:

> *I was called to the principal, but when Aunt Celeste looked at Justin, he said he burned his hand with a cigarette. Weird. She's got more abilities than she's told us about. See you at lunch.*

When he looked up, Justin was heading his way, alone, no minions anywhere in sight. Great, now what?

"So fart-gas, we gonna do this or what?" Justin sneered.

"Do what? What's your problem, Justin? I don't want to fight you. I don't even want to talk to you. You heard what Dr. Chavez said, so move."

Justin puffed out his chest. "Dr. Chavez? What the hell are you babbling about, freak? You won't be so ballsy when I tell everyone how you poured acid on my hand."

What was going on? Didn't Aunt Celeste make him lie? Argus took a step back. "What are you talking about? We were in the principal's office, and you said you burned..." he stopped mid-sentence. Justin didn't seem to be fooling around, he looked dead serious. Didn't he remember what happened a few minutes ago?

"I just said what, fart-gas?" Justin narrowed his eyes like a gunfighter in a Western movie.

"Nothing. Look, I have to get to class." Argus stepped around him.

"I'll be waiting for you, fart-gas! Your face won't be so pretty by the time I'm done with you!"

Argus ran the rest of the way to the lab but stopped and turned around. Justin was walking away. Good. He texted Tai again:

I think Aunt Celeste really messed with Justin's mind. He doesn't remember that we were just in the principal's office. Weirder and weirder.

What did Aunt Celeste do exactly? Did she erase Justin's memory with a look? Was that possible? She never talked much about her abilities, but she never denied having them. Like the time she fell off the brick wall at home when she was installing one of the security cameras. She didn't get hurt because she drifted down slowly and floated above the ground like a balloon. She never hit the ground at all. Simply put her legs down and stood up. All she said was that she had some abilities too. There'd been no further explanation after that. He always wanted to ask her, but every time he was about to ask, she'd change the subject or left the room.

He opened the door to the classroom and took his seat by Lola. She looked so small sitting on the tall stool. She glanced at him and smiled. In front of him were a few sheets of paper and a pen. He was glad he'd met her. Now all he had to do was not make any more mistakes around her. And stop looking at cheerleaders. That was evidently very important. She gave him another smile. Maybe the day was going to be all right after all.

Chapter 5

Max piled his computer, notes, and graphs into the motor pool car and drove out to Palmdale. The morning traffic was light, which let him exceed the speed limit the entire way. The government plates on the car must have helped keep the state cops off his ass.

His GPS led him right to Highland High. He circled the block, his computer scanning for any energy blips. After a few minutes and no surges, he pulled up to the curb and parked at the side of the school. It was quiet. He checked his watch. Only 10:44. Class was still in session.

It had been so long since he'd been to high school, he'd forgotten how bad it was. He thought back to his senior year, not a good year by any means. He'd contracted mono after a particularly amorous make-out session with Erin Lichvar in the back seat of his dad's new Volvo. That one night, as great as it was, cost him two months at home right after Christmas break. After that, he never seemed to catch up and got mostly Cs. His dad got on him about how he'd never get into college with grades like that, and his mother seemed oblivious to anything except tending her orchids. She treated those damn plants better than she treated her family.

A loudspeaker blasted an electronic chime that brought him back to reality. He looked at the computer. Still nothing. Hunkering down in the car, he watched a parade of students pour out of the school behind the chain-link fence and head in different directions. Could one of them be the cause of the energy surges? What did aliens look like? Most of the kids looked panicked, like they were in survival mode, just trying to get through the day. He remembered that feeling all too well.

One guy stood out among the rest. He was a good-looking kid with dark hair, walking slowly with a small, frail, red-headed girl in baggy jeans. He was taller than most of the other boys and was built like an athlete. His tee shirt couldn't hide his biceps and abdominals. Damn, how could a teenager have muscles like that? Must be a football player or weightlifter.

Max checked the computer again and noticed a very slight rise in energy coming from the school. It wasn't a surge, but a steady, gentle increase. It leveled off at three degrees above the normal range. Anything above normal was suspect. Yep, there was something going on at the school. Since the energy increase didn't happen until the students came out, it had to be one of them. Cool.

He waited until the students all disappeared back into the classrooms and another bell chimed. He took his hand-held energy sensor, the Organic Energy Emitting Device or OEED, and got out of the car. There wasn't any type of security other than the surrounding chain-link fence, so he had no trouble walking into the school's lobby.

This area of Palmdale, with its' newer houses and precisely trimmed lawns, was different than most of the Los Angeles schools with their metal detectors and police officers. Must be nice for the kids to feel safe without campus police. He sneaked through the lobby when the secretary was busy, her head down and a frown etched on her face. As he passed by one classroom, he heard the teacher explaining the grading system and how many points the various tests were worth. Poor kids. He didn't envy them one little bit.

When the OEED beeped, he stopped and looked at the sign above the door: Boy's Locker Room. How was he going to get inside there without being accused of being a pedophile?

"Think, Max, think," he mumbled to himself.

He held the OEED close to the door and noticed the same three degree increase in energy. Whoever was causing the small spike was definitely inside the locker room. There were voices, kids' voices, chattering and then a man's voice telling them to hurry up and get dressed.

Max had an idea. Maybe not the best idea he'd ever had, but it would get him into the locker room. He pushed open the door and looked around. Half-naked boys were goofing around; shoving each other, throwing gym socks over the lockers, and mocking the skinny kids. It was exactly like he remembered.

Off to one side, standing with his back against the wall, was the same good-looking guy that he'd seen before walking with the red-headed girl. His shoulders were stooped and while everyone else was putting on their gym clothes, he stood alone, fully clothed. With no friends hanging around to interfere, he was the perfect person to approach for a little Q & A session.

"Excuse me," Max said softly as he came up to the guy, "I'm a sub. Never been to Highland before. I have no idea where I'm supposed to go. I heard voices and thought someone in here could help me out."

The guy shrugged. "Oh, ah, this is my first day. I'm not really the best one to ask. The gym teacher's right over there." He pointed out a middle-aged man in snug-fitting shorts and a tight blue tee shirt, with a whistle dangling from his neck. "I'm sure he can help you. Welcome to Highland High, sir."

Max genuinely liked this kid. He wasn't obnoxious or full of indifference and angst like most other teens. "Thanks. My name's Max."

"Argus." The kid extended his hand politely, not like other teenagers who'd probably recoil at the sight of an adult.

Max shook his hand. "Okay, well guess I'd better check with…" Max stopped mid-sentence when the OEED in his pocket beeped. It beeped again and again.

Argus motioned to Max's pocket. "I think you've got a text."

"Yeah, okay, um, thanks again." Max glanced around but didn't see anything out of the ordinary, except for Argus. Whoever was making the sensor beep was close by. Could it be Argus? Or maybe the gym teacher? He looked at the kid again. Nothing said aliens had to be adults.

Max ducked behind a bank of lockers and checked the OEED. The energy levels had spiked, not near as much as during the surges, but enough that it couldn't be an anomaly. First day in Palmdale and he was already onto something. He edged closer to the gym teacher to check him out, but the level decreased. Rule out the gym teacher.

"Hey! What are you doing in here?" The gym teacher shouted in a gravelly voice that sounded like he'd smoked too much for too many years.

Max looked up and shoved the OEED in his pocket. "Sorry, I'm a sub and I didn't know where to go. I…"

The gym teacher groaned. "Well, unless you're a substitute gym teacher, you don't belong in here. Go to the office for God's sake." He turned away, shaking his head.

"Sorry." Max looked around, but Argus was gone. Damn. He hurried out of the locker room.

So if it wasn't the gym teacher creating the surges, it had to be Argus. Then again, what if it was coming from machinery or a bad circuit in the building? He thought for a minute. No, that wasn't possible. He'd designed the sensor so it would only pick up variances caused by organic molecular compounds above the normal range of humans, animals, and plants. It was a life form with abnormal energy fluctuations. An extra-terrestrial.

He took out his wallet and found an old ID card that said he was a credentialed teacher in the state of California and had passed the necessary background checks to sub. The teaching credential was real, but not current. Hopefully it'd be good enough to get him into the school.

The main office was empty except for the secretary who was busy rifling through an old metal file cabinet. She turned around when he knocked on the counter for attention.

"Can I help you?"

Max flashed his ID card. "Um, I hope so. I'm a sub, but I'm not sure where I'm supposed to go."

She took a quick glance and shrugged. "Haven't seen an identification card in a long time. I didn't know anyone called for a sub. I don't remember hearing about any teachers being out today."

He smiled. "Well, someone called me in."

"Okay, let me check the call log." She flipped open a manila folder.

The OEED suddenly started beeping like crazy. There was no reason for it to go off. It must be broken. Damn it. Max slipped his hand into his pocket but couldn't find the off switch fast enough.

"Is that your cell phone? You'll need to put it on vibrate." The secretary said without looking up.

He found the switch and turned off the OEED a second before an attractive, tall woman with a long blonde ponytail and athletic build swept into the office and went right to the counter.

The secretary shut the folder. "Oh, Ms. Apodaca, did you need something else? You already filled out all of the enrollment forms."

The woman hesitated, turned her head, and stared at Max. Her light blue eyes were intense, piercing. He was uncomfortable. It was like she was looking into his soul.

In one quick move, she extended her hand. "Celeste Apodaca," she said as an introduction.

He shook her hand and felt a tingly sensation in his fingers. "Max. Nice to meet you. Have we met before?"

"No, we haven't." She released his hand and faced the secretary again. "I wanted to check on the boys."

With a smile, the secretary nodded. "I understand. But trust me, they're fine."

Celeste glanced at him again. She didn't blink. "I hope they are. Are you a parent, Max?" Her voice was accusing, probing.

"No, a teacher. Substitute teacher." He couldn't shake the uncomfortable feeling that had settled over him.

"Hmmm," she said and then strode out into the hall without another word.

He watched her walk past the window. There was a mysterious presence about her. "Wow. Who was that?"

The secretary didn't answer. Instead, she put her hand, palm down, on the manila folder. "Nobody called for a sub today. Must have been one of the other schools. You really should pay attention to which school calls."

"Yeah, my mistake." He gave a quick smile and rushed out of the office, but Celeste was gone.

He took the OEED from his pocket and turned it back on. Nothing. He had to find Celeste and see if she was the one he was looking for. Of course she wasn't in the locker room. Could there be two aliens? His assignment might be completed in one day, not the thirty days Stone had given him. That could mean a promotion. A big promotion. If he found an alien, or two, he'd be famous. That'd show his ex-wife that he wasn't worthless and that his obsession with aliens was well founded. And Stone would finally have to admit that he knew what he was doing.

He ran to the parking lot. No sign of Celeste, but that didn't mean he couldn't track her down. She'd said she wanted to check on "the boys". Now all he had to do was find out which boys were hers. It was a high probability that Argus was one. Just a matter of time now. Soon, he'd find them all.

Chapter 6

Argus had to sit on the bench by the track in PE, because he didn't have gym clothes. He would have participated if the teacher had let him, rather than sit alone while everyone else ran warm-up laps. Oh, well, maybe it was best to sit out the first day anyway, to get a feel for what PE was really like. He watched the guys run. A couple of them were fast.

He couldn't wait for it to be lunch so he could sit with Lola. And Tai of course. Lola promised to give him the "low down" as she called it, on the super-seniors and the cool crowd. So far, the only real trouble he'd run into was from Justin, and that seemed like it was all over and done with.

"Dachel!" called the gym teacher and football coach, Coach Smith. "Get over here!" He waved from the track where he was standing with a scrawny kid.

Argus got up off the bench and ran to Coach Smith. "Did I do something wrong?" How could he, he was only sitting on the bench?

"What? No. I figured you could help Dave carry the equipment." Coach Smith pointed to the skinny kid, the same kid who'd been in the hall getting shoved by Justin when Aunt Celeste was filling out the enrollment papers. "Dave, this is Argus Dachel. Show him where the equipment is stored." He grabbed his whistle and blew it several times.

The students stopped running and walked the rest of the way around the track while Coach Smith motioned for them to go to the bleachers.

Dave, lanky, short hair, and a crooked smile gave a brief wave. "Hi. Argus? Cool name. Follow me."

"Hey, Dave." Argus returned the smile.

Dave walked toward the locker room with a slight limp, looking back to make sure Argus was coming. Once they were inside, Dave went to a small closet and opened the door.

"This semester we're doing flag football, so we'll need that box over there with the flags in it and that canvas bag of footballs." Dave dragged the canvas bag out of the closet with a grunt.

"I can carry those," Argus offered.

"Hey, man, I'm no wuss."

"I didn't say you were." Argus stepped back and let Dave drag the bag all the way out. It looked heavy, but if Dave wanted to prove he wasn't a "wuss", why not let him.

"Well, most people think I'm weak because my ankle never healed right after I broke it in ninth grade. I have a limp, in case you didn't notice. Coach Smith doesn't make me run. He's cool. He's always looking for potential football players though, so of course I limp a little more than I have to, so I don't have to do PE at all. I'm not good at sports." He grinned. "Um, if you still want to carry the bag, you can."

Argus smiled and took the bag. He liked Dave. "Hey, Dave, you know a guy named Justin Jones, right?" He slung the bag over his shoulder like he was Santa carrying a bag full of toys.

"Justin? Ah, man, I hope you don't run into him. He's a super-sized jerk. A mega, gigantic, atomic jerk." Dave grinned again and picked up the box of colorful flags. The box didn't look heavy, but Dave still struggled with it.

Argus waited until Dave had a good grip before heading toward the door. "You know, Justin wanted to fight me this morning. He hurt his hand and was trying to blame me."

Dave stopped smiling. "Man, he's an ass. Dr. Chavez, the principal, knows it, too. Everyone does. Stay away from him. Justin's always looking for a fight. He mostly leaves me alone because of my limp. Another reason I limp a little more than I have to. Be careful, cause Dr. Chavez has this zero-tolerance policy against bullying, so if he catches you fighting or picking on the freshmen, you'll get suspended."

"Thanks for warning me." Argus had no doubt that Dr. Chavez was tough. He sure seemed like he wasn't fooling around.

On the way back to the field, Argus pretended the bag of footballs was heavy so he wouldn't hurt Dave's feelings. "Wow, Dave, these balls feel like they're made of lead." Hopefully that sounded believable.

"I think they are!" Dave laughed. "These flags aren't exactly light either."

As soon as they were within sight of Coach Smith, Dave's limp became more exaggerated as he made his way to a bench and put down the box. How could you not like a guy who faked a limp? It was one of the coolest things Argus had ever seen anyone do. He almost laughed out loud but managed to stop himself. He'd tell Tai all about Dave at lunch.

Coach Smith motioned for Argus to put the bag of footballs on the grass beside the bench. "Okay, you two can retrieve the balls when these meatheads throw them too hard. Go sit on the bleachers."

Argus deposited the bag on the ground and followed Dave to the bleachers. Retrieving balls didn't sound very exciting. "So, Dave, what do we do, wait to chase after the footballs?"

Dave shook his head. "Nah, not chase. Nobody can throw a football worth a damn. They can tackle, but they can't throw. The balls won't go far! We'll have it easy for the rest of class." He sat down on the lowest level and stretched out his legs. "Hey, where are you from?"

"Right here in Palmdale. I've lived here my whole life."

"How come I've never seen you around?" Dave dodged a football when it bounced right at him. "Dang, throw the ball the other way!"

Argus really didn't want to talk about his personal life in case Dave thought he was an outcast. He seemed like a straight-up guy, but what if he didn't want to hang out with a not-so-normal guy who'd never been to a real school? Only one way to find out. "My brother and I were home schooled."

"Really? I've never known anyone who was home schooled. You must have a stay-at-home mom. My mom's divorced and has to work. Must be nice to have your mom home."

Argus watched the other students attempt to throw the footballs. Dave was right, they were awful.

Dave spoke again, "Hey, man, did I say something wrong?"

Argus sighed. He didn't want Dave to think he did anything wrong. Okay, time for more personal info. "Um, both of my parents are dead. I live with my aunt."

Dave sat up straighter. "Oh, shit! No kidding? I'm really sorry, man. I didn't mean anything. Let's change the subject. Ah, do you like sports?"

Argus nodded. "Yeah, I like baseball and football. My brother and I practice in the backyard."

Without a word, Dave jumped up and rifled through the half-empty football bag. He came back and handed a football to Argus. "Let's play catch."

Argus took the ball. "Are you sure? We won't get in trouble?" The last thing he wanted was to get sent to the principal's office again.

With a grin, Dave pointed at the coach. "Coach Smith is busy yelling at the meatheads. He won't even notice. Come on, let's see what you've got."

Argus turned the football over several times. It felt different than the football at home. This one was a bit lighter and made of plastic or vinyl not leather. He gripped it with his fingers over the laces like Aunt Celeste had shown him. There was never any talk of how she knew the correct way to throw a football, but she could hit a target every time, so he paid attention to her instructions. Might as well toss it and see if he could make it fly straight.

He hauled back and searched out a target to aim for. "Dave, I'm going to try to hit that goal post about ten feet off the ground."

"Yeah, right! That goal post's about a million miles away."

Argus shook his head. "More like sixty feet." Sixty feet was nothing, he'd hit targets at about eighty feet several times.

Dave shrugged. "It might as well be a million miles."

Argus made sure nobody except Dave was watching and then let the ball fly. As it left his fingers, it arced gracefully in the air, a perfect spiral, and hit the goal post exactly where he'd aimed. He smiled and turned to Dave, who was staring with his mouth gaping.

When Dave finally blinked, he mumbled, "You hit it. You freaking hit it. How?"

With a shrug, Argus smiled. "Practice." And his secret strength, not that he'd share that little tidbit of information.

"Hey!" shouted Coach Smith.

Argus tried to look innocent, glancing around whistling. Did that really look innocent or was that only how actors in movies pretended to look that way? Guess he'd find out.

Coach Smith stormed over to the bleachers. "Which one of you clowns threw that ball? We don't have a big supply budget, so if you destroy a ball, your parents are gonna replace it. Got it?"

Dave waved his hands around. "Argus threw it, Coach Smith. You should have seen it. He said he'd hit the goal post, and he did. Right where he said he'd hit it. It was amazing. You should put him on the—"

Shut up, Dave. Argus interrupted, "Okay, Dave, I don't think Coach Smith is interested in..."

Holding a hand up, Coach Smith shook his head. "Wait. You threw the ball from here. From the bleachers?"

"Ah," Argus wanted to smack Dave for opening his mouth. "Ah, no...yes...um, a lucky shot."

"Can you make that "lucky shot" again, Dachel?" Coach Smith grabbed another football from the canvas bag and held it up.

"I don't think..." Argus shook his head. "I'm not really into sports." Oh, no, this wasn't good. This would fall under showcasing their abilities, exactly what he warned Tai about.

Coach Smith shoved the ball at Argus. "Well, if you can throw a football and come within five feet of your target, you're on the varsity team. These guys are great at tackling and running, but nobody on the team can throw a ball worth a damn."

"Told you," Dave snickered.

All right, throwing a football wasn't really showcasing, was it? Lots of guys could throw a ball. He looked at the football in his hands. What would it be like to be a football star? Cheering crowds, adoring fans, cheerleaders. Well, maybe not cheerleaders. He'd had enough trouble simply looking at them. Wow, it would be pretty sweet to be on the football team. He positioned his fingers on the ball and threw it as hard as he could toward the goal post again. Oh, no, he'd thrown the ball too hard. It zipped through the air and impacted the goal post with a hard thump, bending the post a few inches.

Coach Smith extended his hand. "Welcome to the team, Dachel. I'll order your varsity jacket and letter and take care of the paperwork. Jacket costs two hundred fifty bucks, so tell your parents." He walked away, shaking his head, and chuckling slightly.

"Ah, man, Argus, making the varsity team on your first day of school." Dave looked at the ground. "Can we still be friends?"

Argus watched Dave. He looked embarrassed or sad. Why? What was going on? "Of course. Why'd you ask that?"

He didn't look up. "You know."

Argus didn't know. Did teenagers change friends every few minutes or something? "No, I don't know what you mean." He sat down on the bleachers. Was Dave having second thoughts about being his friend?

"You're gonna make me come out and say it? Fine. I'm not popular, Argus. I'm like a popular kid repellent. Nobody who's anybody wants to be seen around me."

Now Argus felt bad for making him explain. "You're my first friend, Dave. Well, guy friend. Friends don't abandon one another over something as dumb as football."

Dave grinned. "You mean it?"

"Sure do. You want to come to my house and hang out sometime?" Argus really did like Dave and couldn't wait to introduce him to Tai. They could all play football in the backyard. That is if Aunt Celeste would let Dave come over. Maybe he should have run it by her first before inviting him.

"Yeah! Wow, my first in-crowd friend." Dave beamed.

It was a good feeling to see Dave so happy. No wonder people liked having friends. They made you feel good. When Argus looked up, he saw the substitute teacher who'd come into the locker room walk onto the field, looking at a cell phone or something, very determined. He glanced around and locked eyes with Argus. Argus had an uncomfortable feeling about the way the guy kept looking down at the phone and back up, right at him. What was he doing?

"Hey, I know that guy," Argus mumbled. "I think his name's Max. Said he was a sub."

Dave squinted. "What's he doing? Is he coming to you or me? What's that he's holding? A GPS? Look, it has a small antenna. Phones don't have antennas anymore. What is that?"

Argus took a deep breath and focused on Max. He used his future-seeing ability. In a few seconds, Max would come right to the bleachers with the device. And it definitely wasn't a cell phone. The device came more into focus. It had a display of a graph with a rising measurement line, almost like the heart monitors he'd seen on TV. It was detecting something. Max smiled and as the wind caught his jacket, Argus saw a holstered gun on his hip. Substitute teachers didn't carry guns. In fact no one on campus would be allowed to carry a gun.

Argus broke his concentration. The hairs on the back of his neck prickled. His instinct told him to get away, that he was in danger. Aunt Celeste always told him to pay attention to his instinct and leave any situation that made him uncomfortable. This was a situation like that. Max got closer, striding more purposefully now. Argus felt weak and sure enough, when he stood, his legs buckled. He needed a little time to get his strength back. Damn it, he had to get away.

"Dave, I need a distraction to delay that Max guy. I don't trust him. I have to get out of here. Can you help me out?"

Dave snorted as if to say, "you don't have to ask". "No problem, friend. I've got your back."

Chapter 7

A rgus gritted his teeth and struggled to stand. Dave limped to the canvas bag of footballs, plucked one out and tossed it toward Max as he was looking down at the device.

Only then did Dave shout, "Heads up!" He turned and winked at Argus.

Max ducked and dodged as the football flew right at him. "Hey! Watch it!" He glanced at the football as it bounced and wobbled in random directions on the field. He wasn't watching as Dave threw another ball that bounced directly off Max's head.

Dave snickered. The distraction worked better than expected. Max dropped the device and clasped his hands over his head, mumbling a few words that weren't appropriate for a supposed substitute teacher. That should be enough time. Argus took a few steps. Yes! His strength was back. As fast as he could, he went around the back side of the bleachers and made his way to the locker room. *Thank you, Dave*!

Of course, now Dave could be in danger. Argus groaned. He sure didn't want that. He peeked out the locker room door to make sure Dave was all right and watched as Max recovered and picked up the device. He looked around and stomped his foot, then put the device in his pocket and strode off the field toward the campus. Yes! Dave was fine, in fact, he was pumping his fist in the air like he'd won a gold medal at the Olympics.

As Argus turned, he bumped into Tai. "Damn it, Tai."

Tai raised an eyebrow. "I'm here to help. If you need help that is. Who is that guy? What's that Geiger counter thing he's holding?"

"No idea what it is, but it's not a Geiger counter. It was like he was tracking me, like the device led him to me." Argus looked around. No sign of Max. "Hey, did you dissolve in front of anyone?"

"Course not. I went to the bathroom. I got the idea from these slacker kids I met. The undesirable crowd I presume from the way the other kids look at them. They sneak off to the bathroom all the time to smoke. Can you believe that? They don't care. They have no fear of—"

"Tai. Come on. Smoking? What if Aunt Celeste finds out? She'll ground you or whatever parents do."

"She's not our real parent or did you forget that? Anyway, she won't find out anything unless you tell her." He raised his eyebrow again. "I'd never smoke. My body's my temple, bro, and it's for the ladies to worship at." He thumped his chest like a gorilla in a zoo. "I'm not about to mess it up with nicotine. Anyway, I saw that you were in trouble, so I asked to be excused and then I dissolved. And here I am. Ta-dah!" He winked. "You're welcome."

"Yeah, thanks. Everything's fine. But this isn't a game, Tai. We should be careful. That guy's not a substitute teacher like he told me."

"You spoke to him?"

Argus shook his head. "Not exactly. He came into the locker room before PE and said he was lost. I suggested he go to the office. Said his name is Max. He seemed okay, but now I don't—"

"Damn, Arg. What if he knows about our abilities? Could he know? Is there any way he could?" Tai paced.

Argus shrugged. "I don't think so. But listen, I saw a gun under his jacket. He was measuring something with that device, that's for sure. Maybe he's doing safety checks on the campus, looking for hazardous...something." That explanation didn't even sound realistic to him.

With another raised eyebrow, Tai cocked his head. "Really? Pretty sure substitute teachers don't go around looking for hazardous chemicals or whatever and carry firearms. Should we tell Aunt Celeste?" He peeked out the door. "Hey, I think the gym teacher's looking for you."

Argus looked out. Coach Smith was talking to Dave, who was shrugging and feigning like he didn't have a clue. Yeah, Dave was shaping up to be a good friend.

"Okay, Tai, get back to your class. We'll keep this our secret for now and only tell Aunt Celeste if we need to. I don't want to stay home with her every day for the rest of my life. And I'll tell Coach Smith I had to use the bathroom."

"Hey, that actually sounds good. We're turning out to be fairly decent liars." Tai smirked and dashed from the locker room.

Huh, Tai was right. They really hadn't lied much at all before, and now all of a sudden, they were accomplished at lying. Not much of a skill or talent. But throwing a football was. He smiled. That was a real talent that would make him popular. He ran back to the field. "Sorry, Coach Smith, I had to use the—"

"You don't go anywhere without asking first. Understand?" Coach Smith was angry, his cheeks were flushed. "You're going to be my star quarterback and I don't want you getting suspended before we start our first practice." He calmed down. "Understand?"

"Yes, sir." Argus glanced at Dave and mouthed a thank you. Dave beamed.

"Good. Now I want you and Dave to toss a ball around. Well actually, Dave, you can retrieve the balls and Argus, you can practice throwing. Work out that arm of yours." Coach Smith nodded like he was pleased with the arrangement and strode back toward the rest of the kids.

"Hey, Argus, nobody suspects a thing. Ah, man, that Max guy was pissed!" Dave laughed. "Did you see I hit him square on the head? My aim's not so bad."

Argus couldn't help but smile at Dave's enthusiasm. "Thanks. You nailed him for sure. I appreciate your help. I want to find out more about Max. Want to help me?" Argus already knew Dave's answer.

"Duh!" Dave rubbed his hands together. "This is so cool." He picked up a football and tossed it to Argus. "So, what do you want me to do?"

"Keep your eyes sharp and your ears open. If you see Max, follow him, discreetly. Don't let him know you're following him. Know what I mean?" Argus felt like an Army commander or something, giving orders. It was kind of cool.

Dave nodded several times. "Yep." He rubbed his hands together again. "Better throw the ball, Argus, Coach Smith is watching."

Argus positioned his fingers and threw the ball across the field, not at any particular target. He heaved a couple more and waited for Dave to bring them back. What was it going to be like to be the quarterback of the varsity team? He'd never really played any sports, aside from the rare backyard games with Tai.

Oh, no. What would Aunt Celeste say? She won't like it, that's for sure. But would she forbid him to play? Hopefully not. She'll stress that he shouldn't do anything that puts him at risk of getting hurt or cut, and probably give him that look of hers that's halfway between a scolding parent and a sympathetic parent. Damn the blood disease, whatever it was. He took a ball from Dave but hesitated before throwing it. Whoa. What if his blood burned Justin? Could it do that? How could it? Guess Tai was right, neither of them was normal. Maybe being like the other kids was overrated and didn't matter. Maybe.

Chapter 8

Max sat in his car and stared at the OEED. That sudden surge at the school track sure wasn't an anomaly. The source had to be caused by the kid in the locker room...what the hell was his name? Angus, Artie, or something like that. If that other scrawny kid hadn't thrown the damn ball and whacked him on the head, he would have asked Artie-Angus-whatever some questions.

"Damn it," he mumbled.

The school bell rang. Lunch time. He'd have to keep up the ruse of being a sub. He could do that. He'd taught middle school math and science for three years before joining AURA. How much different could it be to teach high school students?

He let out a long sigh. He knew what he'd have to do. To get into the school, he needed help from his boss. After dialing Stone's number, Max sat back and massaged his forehead. He had a raging stress headache. Every time he had to talk to Stone, along came the headache.

On the third ring, "Stone."

"Ah, Chief, I need to infiltrate Highland High School." Max massaged a little harder. "Palmdale."

"Oh, really? This better not be your way of trying to get a little action with a bunch of teenage girls. Is that the real reason my daughter divorced you? You got a thing for the under aged?"

What! Max pulled the phone away from his ear and stared at it. Did Stone really think he was that depraved or was he trying to get under his skin? *When I deliver you a gift-wrapped alien, you'll take back everything you ever said.* He cleared his throat. "I'm onto something, sir. I need a cover as a substitute math or science teacher."

"I thought you *were* a math teacher. Elementary school, wasn't it? Or kindy-garten?" Stone's voice was mocking as hell.

"Middle school. Junior high. Can you arrange it?" Max kept his tone flat, professional. Not easy to do around Stone, that's for sure.

There was a faint sound coming from the other end, like teeth grinding. Finally, Stone came back on. "Yes. Time's ticking, Jackson. Results in 29 days. Solid results. I want tangible proof or...." he didn't finish the sentence.

Max knew full well what the "or" was. Mail room or Tacoma. Damn. "Yes, sir. Solid results."

"Hold on." Stone was gone for a couple of minutes, then came back, "All set. You'll be replacing a Ms. Rubio in math."

"And what's happened to Ms. Rubio?" Max asked, not really wanting to know. There were rumors that Stone could make anyone disappear if he wanted to. But they were only rumors, weren't they?

"Not your concern. Called away on a, ah, family emergency. She's out of the picture, that's all you need to know. Report to the office secretary. She's expecting you. Tangible proof. Now, if you'll excuse me, I've got to call my daughter and make sure she's receiving her spousal support from you in a timely manner." He hung up.

Of course she was. Max frowned. Stone had the money taken straight from his paycheck every two weeks. *So you want tangible proof? I'll get you tangible proof, you piece of shit.*

Max waited in the car for a few minutes to collect his thoughts. He watched the students through the chain-link fence. They were wandering around the campus munching on sandwiches, sitting in groups laughing, sitting alone looking scared. Yeah, high school is such a challenging time for teens. How anyone makes it to graduation without permanent psychological scares is anyone's guess.

He took a last look at the OEED. Slightly elevated levels, but nothing significant. He dropped it into his jacket pocket and got out of the car, taking his time to get to the office. There were a few stares as if being an adult was taboo, but mostly he was ignored.

The secretary glanced up and smiled, then her brow creased. "You're back?"

"Yes, I got a call that I'm to sub for Ms. Rubio, math teacher." Max handed the secretary his credentials again.

She waved him away. "Already seen your ancient ID card." She looked at the call log and shrugged. "Yep, she was called away on a family emergency," she muttered. "Room 152. Lunch is over in ten."

"Thanks." He strolled into the hall and looked up and down. Where was room 152? He had to dodge a couple of skater kids racing through the hall on their skateboards, but after a couple wrong turns, he found the room and went in. There were textbooks already on each desk. He grunted. Calculus. He taught algebra. Middle school algebra. How do you teach calculus to high school kids? Did they already know the basics? Damn it. He poked around the desk and found the teacher's edition of the textbook.

After spending the rest of lunch reading through the first chapter of the textbook, the bell rang and a throng of kids ambled into the classroom, not looking very excited to be there. Max stood and wrote his name on the board and waited until everyone took a seat. When the final bell rang, he smiled.

"I'm your sub while Ms. Rubio is out. Ah, that's my name, Mr. Jackson." He pointed to the board and a couple students chuckled like he was an idiot. "You can call me Max."

He picked up the roll sheet and read off a few names, but stopped when he came to a name he recognized. Argus. It was Argus, not Artie or Angus. That's right, now he remembered. "Argus Dachel?" he said.

From the back of the room, a hand went up slowly. "Here." Argus stared straight at him. The scrawny kid from PE was sitting next to him, too.

Max tried to hide a smirk. Seems he was always running into this kid. Coincidence or fate? Good luck is what he called it. Maybe now he'd get the opportunity to talk to him, find out if there was anything to go on. He'd ever only interrogated one man before, but the guy turned out to be a postal worker, not an alien. But how hard could it be to question a kid? Easy peasy.

Chapter 9

Argus's heart pounded. He couldn't believe it, why was Max in the classroom and where was their regular teacher? His class schedule said Ms. Rubio was the math teacher. He looked away, but he could still feel Max looking directly at him.

Max spoke, "So, this is calculus. Anyone know anything about it?"

Dave raised his hand. "Cosines. And sines." He bumped Argus on the shoulder. "That's all I know. I hope I impressed that dude with my extreme knowledge," he said with a goofy grin.

Argus smiled briefly, too, but went back to looking at Max. Was he really a sub? No, he couldn't be. He must still have that device somewhere. It would be great to get a look at it. But how?

Max nodded at Dave's answer and finally turned away. "Good. That's a start. Open your books to the first chapter and read it."

While Max leafed through the math book, Argus took out his cell phone and sent a text to Tai.

Max is a sub in my math class. He's got to be following me. Why?

"Mr. Dachel," Max said loudly. "No texting in class. Put your phone on my desk."

The last thing Argus wanted to do was give up his phone. It was his lifeline to Tai. "Sorry, Mr. Jackson. I wasn't texting, I was checking the time. I don't wear a watch and the clock on the wall seems to be wrong." That sounded reasonable.

"There's no need to check the time, Mr. Dachel, class has started. Is there somewhere else you have to be?"

The class giggled and when they settled down, Argus's cell phone chirped with an incoming text. Why didn't he put it on silent? He glanced at the phone as Max approached with his hand extended. The text was from Tai.

Want me to dissolve and come there?

There was no time to text back or delete the message. Max grabbed the phone, looked at it, pinched his brow for a moment, and smiled. The phone went right in his jacket pocket. Argus glared at Max. He had to get the phone back.

Max glanced at Argus. "No cells in class. Okay, we'll start with the basics. Calculus is about angles...and curves."

When the door opened, a few whistles, "whoo-hoos" and one "that's what I call curves" erupted as several guys pointed at a blonde-haired girl in a short cheerleader outfit as she bounced into the classroom and took a seat up front. Argus saw why she got the attention. She was very curvy, a lot more than Lola, but that didn't matter. There was something about Lola that made him want to be with her. It was weird because he hardly knew her. Was it the way she looked at him with those green eyes, the way she twisted her hair or how she didn't try to be someone she wasn't? Or was it all of that? All he knew is that he felt good around her. He glanced up and saw that Max had a frown on his face.

"That's enough." Max slammed his textbook on the desk. "You're here to learn. Read the chapter because there'll be a quiz tomorrow."

Now everyone groaned, including Argus. A quiz? On the second day of school? Even Aunt Celeste wasn't that heartless. Although when she did quiz him and Tai, one wrong answer would result in five additional questions. Okay, maybe she was heartless after all.

Dave poked him on the arm. "Hey, Argus, are you good at math?"

"Yeah." Argus flipped open his textbook. It was all pretty familiar. Aunt Celeste had taught them calculus last year, although Tai didn't quite get the concept, which meant the lessons ended up being very, very long.

"Cool. You can help me then. Not my best subject." Dave opened his book and grunted. "It's like another language to me."

"It is another language, Dave," Argus whispered. "It's not hard once you get the basics down."

"Mr. Dachel!" It was Max, coming down the aisle. "Are you going to be the troublemaker of the class? Perhaps we should talk out in the hallway."

That was the last thing Argus wanted to do. Being alone with Max probably wouldn't end well for either of them. He shook his head and glanced at Dave, who was smirking. It wasn't funny. Max had seen Tai's text.

Argus's cell phone chirped again from inside Max's pocket. Damn.

Max reached into his pocket, took out the phone, and read the incoming text.

"Can I have my phone back, sir?" Argus grabbed the phone out of Max's hand and turned it off, but not before checking the incoming message from Tai.

Everything ok w/Max?

Max looked shocked. "You can't...give that back." He snatched the phone but couldn't turn it on because it was password locked.

Argus smirked. *You're not going to read my messages.* "That's my personal property, Mr. Jackson. How would you like it if I took something of *yours*? Like that device you were using."

"What?" Max glared. "Kids shouldn't have phones in school." He tried to turn the phone on again. "You can get it after class." He shoved the phone in his pocket. "Your teacher's syllabus said you'll be reviewing this week. Now read the damn chapter!" He spun around, leafed through the teacher's textbook, and sketched out the formula for slope on the blackboard.

Argus knew the formula. This was going to be an easy class. He unfolded one of the pieces of paper that Lola gave him and wrote the formula, although he had it memorized already.

rise/run = y2-y1/x2-x1

$= (x+a)^2-x^2/(x+a)-x.$

$= x^2 + 2ax + a^2 - x^2/a$

$= 2ax + a^2 / a$

$= 2x + a$

Right when Max finished writing, a chirp came from *his* pocket. The class ohhed and ahhed and a kid grumbled, "okay for the sub to use his cell phone, huh?" Max reached into his pocket.

"Shut up and copy that down," he said, motioning to the board.

While Max droned on about circumferences and pi, Argus pretended he was looking at his book, but instead, he concentrated on where Lola was. He needed a distraction, or he'd fall asleep for sure. Her image appeared after a few seconds. She was in PE, in the gym near a basketball hoop. As the image got clearer, he saw basketballs lying unused on the polished floor. Lola stood by herself, all alone. A tall girl behind her held a basketball and looked around. A second later, the girl threw the ball at Lola's head.

"No!" he shouted, jumping from his seat.

Lola was about to get hurt. He had to stop it.

Chapter 10

Argus collapsed back into his chair, drained. He was out of breath, like he'd run a couple of laps. Seeing Lola about to get clobbered by a basketball was too much. He had to stop it from happening. He had to protect her.

"Mr. Dachel!" called Max. "Are you normally this disruptive?"

Argus caught his breath. "I...I have to...can I be excused?"

"Argus, you okay?" Dave whispered. "Man, you're pale and sweating. Kinda like you were at the bleachers."

Max came closer. "Are you ill? You weren't sick a minute ago."

What should he say? Faking illness would get him out of the classroom and if he hurried, he might get to the gym before Lola got hurt. But what could he do? He couldn't barge into the gym.

"Mr. Dachel?" Max sounded impatient.

Argus placed his hands on his desk and pushed himself up. "Yes, sir, I'm not feeling well."

"I don't believe you. You're not going anywhere." Max motioned for him to sit back down.

Dave spoke up, "But he's sick."

Max glared at Dave. "This isn't any of your business. Take a seat, Mr. Dachel."

Argus sat and stared at Max. Great, Max obviously wasn't going to let him leave. "Then can I have my cell phone back?"

Max shook his head. "After class." He smiled and went back to the board.

Argus put his elbows on the desk, rested his head on his hands and closed his eyes. It was weird how much he wanted to protect Lola. It was almost as if he couldn't turn off the feelings. Was he only because she'd been the first girl to ever pay attention to him?

He concentrated on her again to make sure she was okay. His heart thumped hard, and he felt uncomfortable, uneasy, like his skin irritated him. He had goose bumps on his arms and his hands trembled. What was going on? In a split second, Lola's image came into view. The girl was poised to throw the ball. His skin was prickly, and he couldn't catch his breath. What was happening? Maybe he really was sick.

The girl took a final look around and was about to throw the ball. No! Don't throw it! The scene shimmered and when it came back into view, the girl put the ball down and walked away.

What? He drew in a deep breath and felt calm. He lost his concentration and the scene vanished. Did that really happen, or did he dream it? If it happened, then he'd done something to stop the girl. He'd never done anything like that before. He opened his eyes and looked up. Max wrote more formulas on the board.

Dave tapped him on the shoulder and whispered, "Argus, you awake? Damn, you were really out."

"I was? Did anyone notice?" He felt good, like he'd woken from a nap. He wasn't weak at all.

Dave smiled. "Nah, half the class is asleep. The sub's boring everyone. Is he really a teacher?"

Argus shook his head. "I don't think so."

Max tossed the teacher's textbook on the desk with a thunk! that woke the rest of the class up. "Bell's going to ring. Memorize those formulas I put on the board. Quiz tomorrow, remember?"

In less than a minute, the bell rang, and the kids got up and shuffled out of the room. Argus went to Max. "My phone, please." He held out his hand.

"Sure." Max got the phone from his pocket. "Oh, Mr. Dachel, who did you text and how were they going to dissolve?"

Argus took the phone. "It's a joke. People can't dissolve." He slipped the phone into his own pocket. "What's that device you have?" *Take that, Max!*

"If there's something you'd like to tell me, I'm listening." Max covered his pocket with his hand. "Like you, I have a cell phone. It's not a device, it's a phone. So, anything you want to tell me?"

Ah, Max wanted to play games. Argus smiled as politely as he could. "I don't think I have anything to say to you, Mr. Jackson. I'd better get to my next class." He turned to go, but Max grabbed him by the sleeve.

"I'll be watching you, Dachel."

Argus pulled free and hurried from the room. Confirmed; Max was *not* a substitute teacher. Argus jogged down the hallway. He wanted to get as far away from Max as he could. He kept walking as he texted Tai.

Hey, meet me in the student parking lot. Got news. Hurry.

It wasn't very hard to get lost among the other students hurrying to their next class, but when he made it to the lobby, he had to rush through the main doors before the secretary saw him, and went right to the parking lot, which thankfully was deserted.

A moment later, Tai came out. His eyebrow arced up. "Parking lot? Are we ditching already?"

"No. Well, yeah. I don't want that Max guy to find me. That's part of the news I have."

Tai looked around. "Max Jackson? Okay, spill."

Argus explained about Max reading the text and about the new ability of mind-control. Tai seemed impressed judging by his wide eyes.

Tai leaned against a faded green Honda Civic. "We'd better be careful about texting. Hey, that ability's like the coolest ability ever."

"I know. Maybe it's the same ability Aunt Celeste has for mind control. I can't believe it, I wasn't weak after I did it. Do you think that means I'm getting more used to my abilities?"

Tai straightened. "I guess. What did you do? I wonder if I can do it."

"I don't know if you can. It was weird. I was watching Lola with future-sight and saw that some girl in PE was going to throw a basketball at her. It pissed me off. I don't understand why I care so much about Lola, but I do. Anyway, when I had the image in my head, I thought of the girl not throwing the ball, and she didn't. I think it's telepathy or mind control or mind influencing."

Tai looked dumbstruck. He nodded. "You know what that means? You can tell every teacher to give you an A."

"Is that all you can think of? Try to think a bit bigger than school, Tai. I can tell heads of state to stop fighting, make sure nobody hurts anyone. There'll be no more wars. This is way beyond cool." He sure didn't feel powerless anymore. "If this is being abnormal, it's not so bad. What if we're like this so we can change the world?"

"Seriously? I don't think we're global saviors or whatever. I think we're more like mutants. Cool mutants, but mutants. Are you going to tell Aunt Celeste?"

Argus felt a chill settle down deep. He couldn't tell her. "I can't. She'll know I used my abilities at school."

"Yeah. Well, it'll be our secret." Tai smirked. "I wonder if I'll get a mind control ability, too."

Argus shrugged. "Who knows? But one thing I do know is that Max knows something. I don't think he has a clue what dissolving means, so we should be safe. We should use code when we text, in case he gets my phone again."

Tai nodded. "Agreed." He leaned against the car again. "You know, I like the freedom of being around other kids."

"Freedom? You mean being able to talk about things without an adult hanging around?"

"Exactly." Tai laughed.

The bell rang and they hurried back inside with the other students. Argus went to his next two classes and practically counted the minutes until the final bell rang. He didn't see Max anywhere until he got outside. There was Max, standing out front. He smiled at Argus.

Tai came up behind Argus. "Yep, he's definitely stalking you. Hey, there's Aunt Celeste."

Argus waved as Aunt Celeste pulled up in her black SUV. "Let's get out of here."

"Hey, Arg, how do you think he knows about your abilities? Who is he?"

"I don't know. He didn't see me throw the football, which you will not tell Aunt Celeste about. I want to find out more about him." Argus looked around to see if Lola was anywhere but didn't see her among the kids heading to the buses, parents' cars or their own cars in the student parking lot. She must have left already.

When they were both in the back seat of the SUV, Aunt Celeste started the engine, but didn't pull away immediately. She turned. "How was your first day?"

Argus glanced at Tai and shrugged. "Nothing special."

Aunt Celeste's eyes narrowed slightly. "Since neither of you texted or called, I presume there were no issues. Are you sure you don't have anything to tell me?"

Argus gave another shrug. "Nope. I mean no. No trouble. Other than this morning." He wanted to ask her about the mind control thing she did to Justin but wasn't sure if he should. She never seemed open to talking about her own abilities. Oh, well, might as well give it a try. "Aunt Celeste, can I ask you something?"

Her eyes were fixed on his. "Yes, Argus, I have the ability to alter thoughts. I'm sure you've suspected that by now."

Confirmed. Argus nodded. "So you can control and—"

She nodded slowly. "Hear your thoughts? Yes."

Argus swallowed again. All thoughts? Could she *hear* everything? What about all of the things he thought when he was alone, his personal, private thoughts. Oh, no, *everything*?

She shook her head this time. "No, Argus, I can't hear everything you think. Thoughts in the back of your mind are cloudy and I stop listening if your thoughts are too...personal. Only when you're actively thinking of something can I hear it clearly. Plus, I need to be close. Anything else?"

"No. Well, yes," he continued. "Does everyone have different abilities?"

She sighed. "We've talked about that, Argus."

Tai blurted, "No, we really haven't. All you said was that we have to keep our abilities secret. That's a pretty non-specific answer. So that must mean not everyone can do things like we can. Right?"

"Yes, Tai," she paused and turned forward, looking in the rearview mirror. "You and Argus are special. This is why I was not in favor of you going to public school. I'm honoring your mother's wish that you attend with other teenagers, otherwise I would never have allowed it. It's too dangerous." She released the parking brake.

Argus watched her reflection in the rearview mirror. Her eyes were on the road ahead. She was calm, giving no hint of irritation and no hint that she was going to explain why it was too dangerous.

"Wait, Aunt Celeste," Argus started. "Why are we different? I can understand that we have something wrong with our blood, but that doesn't explain why we have these abilities. You have them, too, and you're not our real aunt. So what makes the three of us special?"

She pulled into traffic and accelerated down the road. "This isn't how I'd planned to explain our situation. Perhaps it is time, though. You two are almost eighteen, you should know. You've been sheltered enough."

Know what? Sheltered? And what "situation" was she talking about? Argus looked out the window at the kids walking home. Now he was even more curious to know what made him and Tai so different.

The rest of the trip home was in silence. They lived way out in the desert, away from every other house, with a huge eight-foot brick wall surrounding their spacious home, with security lights and cameras at each corner. It never seemed strange before, but now it bothered him. His perspective had changed. Nobody else in town had an eight-foot wall and nobody else had abilities. They *weren't* normal kids, but why not?

Aunt Celeste pressed the remote and opened the heavy gate at the driveway and pulled the SUV into the three-car garage. She shut off the engine. "I hope you're ready to hear this. Some find it very difficult to hear," is all she said before getting out and going into the house.

Chapter 11

Max tidied up the classroom, picked up gum wrappers and scraps of notebook paper, and went to his car. How do teachers do this day after day? It was different when he taught. Younger kids were cleaner and eager to learn. Well, most of them were. Overall though, the Highland High students were reasonably well-behaved and listened, but the few who were disruptive made the day drag on and on. Thank goodness this wasn't his real job, only a temporary gig so he could gather intel. Maybe he shouldn't have confronted Dachel so soon. He could be on his guard. Oh, well, too late now.

He drove around looking for a motel and found one a little out of the main section of town. It'd do. Nothing fancy but looked comfortable and clean. Once he checked in and got settled, he downloaded the data from the OEED into his computer database and created a graph. There, staring at him on his computer screen was a bar chart showing every surge he'd detected today. True, it wasn't exactly the tangible proof Stone wanted, but it was a start. Something was going on at Highland High and Dachel was at the heart of it. Now all he had to do was get real proof. If it meant taking Dachel to LA and presenting him on a silver platter, then so be it.

The download from the OEED indicated conclusively that the energy surges were from an organic source as expected and not electrical, as Stone insisted. So far so good. First day and he'd already recorded several surges. He'd also encountered a couple of suspects, the attractive woman in the office and of course Argus Dachel. Both of them would have to be questioned at length at some point, starting with the kid.

He leaned back in the uncomfortable motel-quality chair and lay out his maps of Palmdale and the Mojave Desert. If there was a correlation between the city of Palmdale and alien beings, he'd find it. Now that he'd infiltrated the school, he'd have the opportunity to poke around and talk to students as well as teachers. He wasn't about to stop with Dachel. There were probably more aliens around. He laughed. He'd round 'em all up like a cowboy herding cattle.

After examining the maps for a while, he decided to go out for a drive to soak up the local scenery. With no particular destination in mind, he drove to the outskirts of the city. It was a nice day, a bit too hot, but the sky was a brilliant blue that made the stark sandy brown desert look really bland. Yeah, the desert wasn't for him.

As a kid, he'd gone camping with his dad in the desert and it was fun then. They rode their dirt bikes, went hiking, and gazed up at the stars at night. His dad was always fascinated with astronomy and got him thinking about other life forms out there. Locating aliens was a nagging desire implanted by his dad.

After he got married right out of college, his wife put an end to his "silly fantasy" as she called it. That's how he'd met Stone, his wife's father. Stone never liked him and right at the altar suggested to the minister that the wedding get postponed. Stone was a jerk then and had never changed. His new wife made him get a job teaching, although his heart was never in it.

He drove out a bit further, away from the houses and buildings and pulled the car off the road as much as he could. A walk is what he needed to clear his head. There was a small hill a short distance to the west that would give him a great view of the area. He trudged through the desolate landscape, kicking up little clouds of sandy dust that stuck to his clothes, and climbed up to the crest of the hill. He was sweaty and dirty by the time he made it to the top, but the view was worth it.

There really wasn't much untouched desert left. It was losing ground to sprawling communities. Years ago, Palmdale wasn't much of a town at all. He shielded his eyes from the blaring sun and peered in the distance. There was some sort of large structure or house, all by itself with nothing else around it. Looked almost military with a huge wall surrounding the entire perimeter. It didn't look like a normal house, more like a secured building, a fortress. The structure was large, maybe three or four thousand square feet. Too big for a single house in the middle of the desert. He squinted and saw what looked like security cameras placed on the walls. Strange. It didn't show up on his aerial map, he would have remembered. What was it? If only he had his binoculars. But they were in his suitcase at the motel.

His curiosity drove him forward and he slid down the other side of the hill toward the structure. Damn, he'd left the OEED at the motel as well. Stone always said, "be prepared for field work or don't bother going". Okay, so in this case, Stone could be right.

He stopped and looked back toward his car. Maybe he should go and get the OEED. No, not yet. It could be a military stronghold or something, nothing to do with aliens. No harm though in a quick recon to see if there was anything worthwhile around it.

He stopped. What if it was a secret government structure that emitted the energy surges? All of the data he'd collected before would be worthless. Stone would have a field day mocking him and demote him right away. His career would be ruined. He'd end up a middle school math teacher again. He shuddered at the thought.

On the other hand, if it wasn't government, and there was something significant, he'd make Stone look like an idiot for not supporting him in the past. He kept that thought in his head as he sneaked up closer to the wall.

Chapter 12

Argus opened the car door. The garage was quiet and dark, except for the fluorescent light hanging from the rafters right above the SUV. For some reason, it seemed ominous. It never had before.

He looked at Tai. "I'm kind of scared to know what Aunt Celeste's going to tell us." What could it be? Was their blood disease fatal? Was that it?

Tai nodded. "Me too, bro. I'd suggest we don't think about Max or your new ability, in case she reads our minds. One thing's for sure, we can't sit in the garage all afternoon."

"No, we can't." Argus got out, followed by Tai, and found Aunt Celeste in the kitchen making a couple of sandwiches. Sandwiches? Really? Like that was going to make it easier to hear whatever she had to say.

She finished and handed them each a plate with a turkey and cheese sandwich. "I thought you'd be hungry. In movies, I always see kids eating after school. Let's go into the living room."

She seemed nervous, which was not at all like Aunt Celeste. She drew the curtains in the living room and paced for a minute. Argus sat on the couch with Tai and turned on the nearest lamp since the house was dark with the curtains closed. Their living room was big, but felt small now, like the walls were closing in.

"Okay, boys," Aunt Celeste said. She stood in front of the couch and looked down at them. "I don't really know how to start, but as I've received permission to tell you, I figure this is as good a time as any. I've been preparing for it your entire lives, but now that it's time, I can't find the words."

Argus glanced at Tai and then back at Aunt Celeste. "Just say it, Aunt Celeste. You don't usually have any trouble telling us exactly what's on your mind." *Don't make us wait any longer.*

She looked away. "All right. But this is different. Very different." She drew in a deep breath and sat down in the easy chair across from the couch and extended her right arm, palm up. A softball-sized blue light rose up from her hand and hovered in the air a few inches above her palm.

Argus leaned forward. What the heck was happening? What was that light? He looked at Tai, who was staring, wide-eyed.

Aunt Celeste gestured to the front door with her left hand. The ball of light floated toward the door, then changed direction when she pointed to Tai. The light came over and hovered right above his head. Argus was speechless. It was bright, glowing and wasn't solid. In fact, it was transparent.

Tai shifted in his seat and tried to move away from the light, but it followed his every move. Argus reached out and tried to touch it, but his hand went right through. There was nothing solid to touch, but the air felt warm.

He got up, his heart thumping. "Aunt Celeste, what's going on?"

She blinked and the light came to her like it was a trained bird. It vanished into her hand. "First of all, neither of you have any sort of disease, rare or not. You are both in perfect health. I'm your Guardian, as you know, but I'm also..." she hesitated. "I'm not exactly like...other people...humans."

Tai got off the couch and stood with Argus. "No kidding. What was that thing?"

She drew in a breath. "That's my energy source. It resides within me inside this host body and provides me with life. I can project it when I tap into the energy."

Argus stared at her. Host body? What was she talking about? Energy source? What sort of energy? "Aunt Celeste, I don't think you're doing a very good job at explaining things."

"I know. I apologize." She blinked and her eyes glowed brilliant blue, the same color as the ball of light. "I'm a Guardian, appointed to watch the two of you to make sure you learn the ways of...humans."

There's that word again. Humans. Argus's legs felt weak. He flopped back onto the couch. "What are you talking about? We're as human as everyone else. You said we weren't sick, so what do you mean?" His head spun. What sort of explanation was this? She wasn't telling them anything. Well, nothing that made sense anyway.

She continued, "You're technically half human. But your non-human genetic traits are dominant, so it's my job to make sure your true half doesn't over-power the human half and that no one finds out who you really are. Integration is critical to survival. Boys, you are part of a cosmic experiment that's more than fifty thousand years old."

Tai laughed out loud. "Cosmic experiment? Right. I sure don't feel fifty thousand years old!" He shook his head.

Aunt Celeste wasn't laughing. "No, you're almost eighteen. The experiment is fifty thousand years old. You two are evidence of its success. It started with twenty pairings fifty thousand years ago. Only the hardiest of the early humans were chosen for the experiment. Over time, our experiment expanded. You should be proud. Your abilities are increasing and show great promise."

Argus couldn't believe what she was saying. Why would she make up a crazy story like that? Of course he was human. He didn't have a weird blue light coming out of his hand. He thumped his fist on the coffee table and cracked it in half. "Ow. This is BS, Aunt Celeste. You're telling us we're...I can't even say it. This is ridiculous."

Tai stopped laughing. "Arg is right. I know we're not aliens, Aunt Celeste, so ha ha, very funny. I don't know how you did that magic trick with the blue light, and it was cool and all, but I don't understand why you're saying these things."

She got up and flipped her head, so her ponytail slithered down her back. "This isn't a joke, boys. I was almost recalled as your Guardian because a government agency has been detected snooping around and we can't risk your exposure. Both of you are too important."

Argus went to the front window and peeked through the curtains. All he saw was their expansive front yard and the brick wall. No government men sneaking around. What Aunt Celeste said was absurd. Yes, they could do things that other kids couldn't, but did that mean they were from another planet? And what about the blood disease Aunt Celeste said they had. Why would she say that if it wasn't true?

Aunt Celeste came up behind Argus. "I know this seems like a fantasy, but it's not. You boys are the future of our race."

He turned around. "What do you mean we're the future? Why us? What about you?" Maybe she was related to them after all. But why not come out and say that?

She placed her hand on his shoulder. "No, I'm not related to you. Not directly anyway."

Oh, yeah, she could read his mind. Argus closed his eyes. "I don't understand. What do you mean?" He opened his eyes and stared at her, waiting for an answer.

She squeezed his shoulder gently. "I'm a pure-form." She motioned for him to sit back down on the couch. "I have no human DNA. Guardians have been around since the beginning of the experiment to nurture the new race. Your race. Pure-forms are flawed due to a genetic mutation on our home planet. It's not something we can fix. We cannot reproduce."

Argus shook her hand off his shoulder. She was lying, she had to be. But why? "None of this can be real."

Aunt Celeste continued, "It's all real. You know you and Tai are different. How many humans have shared-sight or can see things a moment before they happen? Or Tai's ability to dissolve and reanimate somewhere else. And your incredible strength. These aren't human traits."

Argus sat down on the couch again. She was right about that, but he couldn't wrap his head around what she was saying. "Okay, so we can do things, which doesn't mean we're aliens. And what about the whole blood disease thing?"

"It's partially true, but you're not ill. Your blood is toxic to humans." Aunt Celeste shrugged. "It's a side-effect. Like all living things, there are spontaneous mutations in the genetic code. As your race evolves, there are certain mutations. The beneficial ones include intelligence and good health. The main genetic traits that are passed down are your abilities."

It was hard to believe that any of what she was saying was true, but it made sense in a really twisted way. Argus now felt horrible that Justin's hand had been burned simply because he came in contact with blood. Alien blood. "So how many aliens are there here?" He felt stupid saying alien.

"Argus, we don't like the term alien. It's distancing. We refer to ourselves, the pure-forms on Earth, as Settlers. There are twenty thousand Settlers on Earth and over half a million New Breeds."

Tai spoke up, "Half a million? Like us?"

"Well, not exactly like you." Aunt Celeste began to pace around the living room. "You boys are very special. The New Breeds are beginning to...fail. There aren't any New Breeds, except for you two, that have lived past 16-years-old. Our medical personnel discovered that the blood has a new component in it that becomes toxic not only to humans, but to the New Breeds as well during the teen years when hormones increase."

Argus watched Tai turn pale. The way Aunt Celeste came out and said their blood was toxic was like she was explaining why the sky is blue. A simple fact, no sorrow that they could die, just a fact. "I don't understand. I've touched my own blood, and it didn't burn me."

She nodded. "That's because it's toxic to you on the inside, on a cellular level, not the outside. Other New Breeds or pure-forms can't be burned with contact, but humans can."

Argus stayed close to Tai. He needed him for support. This was all too much to take in. "So, are you telling us we're going to...die?"

Her expression changed, now she looked sympathetic, caring. "We hope not. If you've made it this far, it seems like both of you have beaten the odds. Now that you know the truth, you'll be examined to find out what's different about the two of you."

Argus wiped his forehead. Now he was feeling sick. "You make it sound so clinical. We're not experiments, you know." He sat quietly for a while, trying to process everything. Actually, according to her, they *were* experiments. "How did our parents survive? You said every...New Breed...dies at sixteen."

She still looked sympathetic. "*Your* generation, Argus. Your mother was a New Breed, and your father was human. The Citadel was against the marriage because such a pairing had only been allowed twice before in fifty thousand years and both of those produced New Breed DNA that was so diluted that the offspring had no abilities and became sick and died in infancy."

Tai interrupted, "What's the Citadel?"

"Our command center on Earth. Like I was saying, when we first settled, the *Homo sapiens* race was still very primitive and our DNA was dominant, our traits of hardiness and of course the abilities were passed to the offspring.

And now after so many spontaneous mutations, the offspring have stopped thriving. The Citadel has done autopsies but can't find the reason the blood component is lethal at around sixteen."

"Then we're all going to die, and you can't do anything about it? Why'd you tell us this?" Tai grunted and threw his plate across the room.

Aunt Celeste stared at the broken plate. "Mind your temper."

Tai took a breath. "I would prefer to have kept living in ignorant bliss."

Argus knew his brother. "No, you wouldn't." Tai always had to know everything, there was never an ounce of ignorant bliss. "What if we're the last of our kind, Tai? Don't you want to find out why?"

He shook his head. "Not if it means I'm going to die before I graduate high school. Who the hell wants to know they're going to die? Not me, that's for sure."

Argus went back to the window and looked out. Everything he'd known, or at least thought he'd known, was a lie. Then again maybe it wasn't even true, and Aunt Celeste was playing a prank. Although she'd never played a prank before, not even on April Fool's Day. In fact, she'd never even told a joke. Was it possible that aliens had lived on Earth for fifty thousand years and nobody knew about it? A dark thought crossed through his mind. What if Max knew? What if he was searching for evidence? What if others were as well?

Chapter 13

Argus wasn't sure what he felt. Confused? Lost? Angry? Alone? Definitely alone. There were no other New Breeds on the planet over the age of sixteen. He still might die. He'd started making friends, real friends. He didn't want to be different. Especially not alien-different. Sure it was great to have abilities, but somehow it only seemed cool when he thought he was human.

He watched Tai, who had his face covered with his hands. What was he thinking? The same things probably. Aunt Celeste sure dropped a bomb. Argus turned his attention to her. She was standing there, looking at them both.

He tried to swallow the lump in his throat again. "Okay, say I believe that we're aliens...half aliens. What does this mean? What's the point in going to school?"

"Argus," she said softly. "You and Tai must lead as normal a life as possible. I told you, you must integrate into human society. Long ago, the early humans interpreted the New Breed abilities as miraculous and...most myth is rooted in fact."

Tai uncovered his eyes and raised an eyebrow. "And? Where are you going with this?"

She continued, "Mythology began. The humans considered New Breeds to be gods. That was all right for a while, in fact it was beneficial to the New Breeds because they didn't have to hide their abilities and they were treated with respect, but recently, during the Dark Ages, things changed. Society became repressive and suspicious. New Breeds were hunted and persecuted as demons. That's why it became necessary to assign Guardians to each New Breed instead of simply monitoring the experiment. We are responsible for integrating them into human society and teaching them to hide their abilities."

Argus sighed. "That...sort of makes sense."

"Yeah. We're gods!" Tai pumped his fist in the air.

Aunt Celeste shook her head. "No, you're not gods. You're New Breeds. You have to be cautious though. Even with a Guardian, you cannot allow humans to see your abilities. There's something else, too. As you grow and your hormonal levels fluctuate, you will acquire different abilities."

With a loud groan, Tai blurted, "You already told us that. It's like going through puberty again. I hated that the first time around."

Aunt Celeste paused for a moment. "There's nothing that can be done, Tai. Your body changes. This is why the Citadel has been trying to get me to bring you two in for study. There is something special about you two, something that has made you overcome the fatal defect."

Argus closed his eyes. *Make it all be a dream.* There was too much information shooting through his brain. He opened his eyes. *Nope, not a dream.* "Aunt Celeste, I want to be like everyone else."

Aunt Celeste looked sympathetic again. "You're not like everyone else. You're not even like other New Breeds. You're different. That's a simple fact, Argus."

He glanced at Tai. Nothing was a simple fact at this point. "Why don't we go to...what's our planet called?"

"Earth." Aunt Celeste sat down beside him. "Earth is your planet. Ramtala is mine."

"Ramtala?" Tai asked.

She nodded. "Ramtala is in the Milky Way galaxy, but on a different spiral arm than Earth. Ramtala has a similar atmosphere as here, although our climate is more extreme. We're closer to our sun, so we are warmer overall. We chose Earth because of the similar conditions and because of the early *Homo sapiens* that were already established. It was a decision based on solid scientific fact."

Argus tried to process everything he'd heard so far. It was crazy, but fascinating at the same time. "You said pure-forms can't reproduce, so how are you here? I mean, are you...fifty thousand years old?"

She smiled, finally, taking a bit of the tension away. "I'm glad you were paying attention. I'm here to answer any questions you might have, always remember that. I am one of the pure-forms born of the last generation that could reproduce. When our learned ones discovered the genetic defect, they gathered together all the viable Ramtalans and used them to, ah, seed Earth with our DNA. That was the generation prior to mine, the ones who could still reproduce. My generation can't reproduce."

Argus shook his head. "I don't understand."

She paused. "In your terms, Argus, I am approximately fifty thousand planetary years old. Our energy source fades over time, sort of like aging in human terms. It takes a long time though and dissipates into the surrounding environment, absorbed by other living things. On Earth, our host body wears out, so we acquire a new one. When we could reproduce, part of our energy would pass to our offspring and they would absorb more as they grew, leaving the parents with less energy. Ramtalans didn't live as long as my generation does now. These days we aren't sharing our energy with any offspring. Things aren't like they used to be. I wasn't always on Earth, boys."

Tai perked up. "You weren't? When did you come here?"

"I've been a Guardian on Earth for nearly 1,000 planetary years. Before that I was assigned as a monitor back on our planet." Her smile faded. "I'd much rather be a Guardian. Monitoring is tedious. I like Earth."

Tai held up his hand. "What are planetary years?"

Aunt Celeste explained, "The years as measured on Earth. Our time is measured differently on Ramtala."

Tai sighed. "Okay. I get it. I think."

Argus wanted to know more now. A lot more. He was a New Breed. Half alien. Wow. Holy shit! How incredible was that? Scary, but incredible. Maybe being different wouldn't be as bad as he thought. "What's our planet like? I mean, your planet. How different is it? Can we see it?" He'd always enjoyed astronomy. He even had a telescope his dad left him but hadn't looked through it in years because it never seemed to work right. The image was cloudy. There was no way he could get rid of it though. It was all he had from his dad. His dad was an astronomer, but that was all he knew. Other than what Aunt Celeste said about both of his parents dying in a boating accident.

"Use your telescope, Argus." Aunt Celeste smiled gently. "You can see Ramtala for yourself. Your father wanted you to see where half of your genes are from."

"I was thinking about my telescope." Oh, that's right, she'd read his mind again.

She looked at him, still smiling. "Argus, I don't *have* to hear your thoughts. Pure-form telepathy can be turned on or off at will. If you want me to turn it off for you so I don't invade your privacy, simply say so."

He nodded. "Okay, I don't want you reading my thoughts. Ever."

"Hey!" Tai shouted. "What about me? I don't want you reading my mind either."

She nodded. "All right. No reading minds for you either, Tai."

Argus sighed. He felt a little better now. At least he could have personal thoughts around her now without worrying about her knowing everything. "Aunt Celeste, my telescope doesn't even work. The lens is bad or something. Besides, I have no idea where to look for Ramtala."

She shook her head. "It's not a bad lens. You might not know where to look, but the telescope does. I can activate it for you now that you know the truth. It was your father's idea to wait until you knew about our history before activating it. Point the telescope to the east, press the red button on the side of the eyepiece twice and the green button once and the telescope will locate Ramtala for you. Your father designed it. Well, with help from the Citadel."

"Really?" So that's why it never worked. It wasn't activated. Argus smiled. "Our dad made it? That's cool. Really cool." Now he couldn't wait until it was dark to try it out. But he still wanted to know more. "You said our parents died."

She turned away. "In a boating accident. You know that. We believe they were being followed and tried to get away but ran aground. A tragedy." Her voice sounded odd, like she was hiding something.

Tai stood and shook his head like he wasn't sure if he believed everything. "Can we go to Ramtala sometime?"

Aunt Celeste turned and brought her ponytail around over her shoulder. "It's not likely. Pure-forms can make an intra-galactic leap by shedding our host body and projecting our energy source around our natural body. You don't have that luxury I'm afraid."

"Wait." Argus thought back to what she'd said a moment ago. "Aunt Celeste, you said you were a monitor on Ramtala. What did you monitor? Earth?"

Her expression changed. Serious again. "Boys, I have to explain something else that might be difficult to hear."

Argus groaned. Something else that was difficult to hear. "Like what? You've already told us we're the oldest New Breed aliens on the planet and you have a blue energy ball inside you. I'd say we're handling that okay so far. I don't think there's anything you can say now that'll shock either of us."

Tai nodded. "Yeah, go for it, Aunt Celeste. What the hell." He went over and finally picked up the broken plate he'd smashed and set it on the coffee table. "Sorry about the plate."

She motioned for him to leave the plate. "I didn't tell you everything because I wanted to gauge how well you could absorb the basic information. There have been instances where New Breeds had psychotic episodes when they learned the truth. But you two are handling this very well. It's hard for me to bring up this next topic. It's unpleasant to say the least." She pointed to the couch. "Please sit."

Argus sat, not sure if he really was prepared or not. What could it be? When Tai sat down next to him, Aunt Celeste faced them and closed her eyes for a few seconds as if she was gathering her thoughts.

She opened her eyes. "Boys, I'm officially known as Guardian 647. I was your mother's Guardian as well and her father's. I've taken an oath to protect my New Breeds. While on Ramtala, I was a monitor, like I told you. My time was spent glued to satellite and inter-space monitors, looking for Invaders. On Earth, I still monitor, but mostly for AURA infiltrators."

Argus leaned forward. What? "Hold on, what's AURA? And who are Invaders?"

She sat on the edge of the coffee table. "AURA stands for the Astronomical Urgent Recovery Administration. It's been around for about fifty years or so." She drew in a breath. "This is so distasteful to talk about, but you need to know. Invaders are the lowest sort of being. They're violent, ruthless, self-serving, and ethnocentric. They believe New Breeds are an abomination. Invaders are Ramtalans, but persist in their view that the pure-form race can be saved without inter-breeding with humans. On

Ramtala, we try to track and identify Invaders, but they maintain a low profile. Invaders might have been tracking your parents." She stopped talking.

Argus felt like his head would explode. He couldn't absorb it all. Did she say these Invaders thought he was an abomination, and they might have caused his parents' deaths? That thought left him cold. He was an orphan and an abomination. His stomach knotted up. This certainly wasn't the sort of news he wanted to hear. Too late to take it back though.

"Are you boys doing all right? Shall I stop?" Aunt Celeste asked softly.

Tai shook his head. "I guess I'm okay. And Arg hasn't run screaming from the room, so I think it's safe to say you can keep going. What else is there?"

That's exactly what Argus was thinking. How could there be any more?

She continued, "The Citadel wants to recall me and bring you two in for study, as I said, and for protection. I've delayed them for the last two years, but they're becoming insistent, especially since you've both passed beyond the New Breed failure age. Being recalled is to fail. I don't like to fail at anything. I failed once when I couldn't save your mother. She trusted me and I don't want to disregard her wishes that you two remain among humans and live a normal life. It's the least I can do for her at this point."

Before she could say any more, her cell phone chirped. She got off the coffee table and picked up the phone off the desk in the living room. She didn't answer it right away, but instead looked at Argus and Tai.

"What is it, Aunt Celeste?" Argus got up. "Do you want privacy?"

She shook her head. "No. This isn't only a cell phone, it's my communicator as well. This is how I contact the Citadel."

"So they're calling? Now?" Tai groaned. "I don't want to be a lab rat."

Neither did Argus. He didn't want to be studied. He wanted to be a senior in high school and go to Prom and play football and hang out with Lola and Dave. Only one day in school and he already knew he wanted to be around other kids.

Aunt Celeste held out the phone/communicator. "They can't take you without my consent. As your Guardian, I have to relinquish my protection of you, and I won't do that. Not now anyway. I'll put it on speaker so you can understand what's going on. You should be included in all conversations relating to you." She pressed a button on the communicator. "Guardian 647 here. You are on speaker with my New Breeds listening in."

A low-pitch man's voice responded on speaker, "Understood. Welcome Argus and Tai. Guardian 647, the Citadel has detected some movement within AURA. An agent has been dispatched to your location. You are advised to take extreme caution. Again, the Citadel recommends you bring the two brothers in. Not only are you risking them, but you risk being exposed yourself. You can be reassigned at the Citadel or back on Ramtala. Your choice. Our only concern is the safety and well-being of the brothers."

Argus felt sick to his stomach. He glanced at Tai. Would they end up as test subjects, locked away at the Citadel, wherever that was, to be studied and probed? They'd be prisoners. What sort of life would that be?

Aunt Celeste spoke again, "I can control the situation. If there's an AURA agent in Palmdale, I'll track him down and make sure he finds nothing."

The voice was louder, "Guardian, I know you have a responsibility to the brothers, but they need to be protected and tested."

She objected, "No, you know how important it is for them to live as they were intended, as humans."

The voice on the other end of the phone softened, "Celeste, I know you need to complete this mission." There was a pause. "You are an excellent Guardian, therefore I will issue a directive to allow you to use whatever qualities you feel are necessary to keep the brothers safe, but only if you do not risk exposure."

She glanced at Argus and Tai, "I understand. Thank you."

"I'm not finished," there was another pause. "Understand this. While you will have leniency using your qualities, the brothers will not. I want a complete breakdown on what qualities they have developed up to this point. They are not to use their qualities unless in complete privacy and secrecy. Report back to me every week." The call was disconnected.

Aunt Celeste put the communicator away. "Do you boys understand what you heard?"

"Um, I think so." Argus nudged Tai. "Did you understand all of that?"

Tai shrugged. "I don't know. What are qualities?"

She smiled. "Your abilities. Your special...talents."

Tai nodded. "Okay."

Argus admired Aunt Celeste's effort to keep them at home. She always seemed to know what they needed and wanted to be happy. He looked at her. "So the Citadel is giving you permission to use your abilities to keep us safe?"

"Yes, but only if necessary."

He thought for a second. "We're in danger. Is that right?"

"Not necessarily." She ran her fingers through her ponytail. "AURA is always snooping around. Both pure-forms and New Breeds emit a low-grade energy pulse that AURA has detected. They know the energy range is from an organic source but haven't located the source...yet."

"How come?" Argus glanced at Tai, who was as interested as he was. The energy source had to be what Max was tracking. Not good.

She smiled again. "The Citadel transmits random bursts of energy all over the planet, so AURA can't figure out exactly where the energy is coming from."

Tai leaned forward. "But the Citadel said an AURA agent was in Palmdale. Aren't you worried?"

"Moderately," she said.

Argus slumped against the couch cushions. Did that mean Max was the AURA agent? "So what should we do?" If Max was the agent, he really should he tell Aunt Celeste. She should know. But if she did, they'd be sent to the Citadel for sure. No, he could handle Max, throw him off the trail, and only bring in Aunt Celeste if things got out of hand.

She stared right at Argus. "Don't use your qualities...abilities, or AURA might pick up the energy surge that it causes. For us pure-forms, that's one of the ways our energy is dispersed over time. If we use our qualities a lot, we...use up our energy at a faster than normal rate. We...die...sooner than we would if we lived without using them. Do you understand?"

Tai nodded, but Argus was confused.

He got up. "Wait a minute. Does that happen to us, too? The New Breeds? Will we die early if we use our abilities?" Not a good thought, not a good thought at all.

She shook her head. "No. Because your DNA is conjoined with human DNA, your energy is locked up tighter than ours. It's hard to explain, but I can if you want."

"No, that's all right." He wasn't so sure he wanted to know the specific details, not yet anyway. He needed time for everything to sink in. "Maybe later when my head's not spinning."

"Yeah, same here," Tai agreed. "I'm still trying to get used to the fact that I'm half alien and my aunt is a full-blooded alien." He smirked.

Argus watched his brother. It seemed like he'd already accepted Aunt Celeste's disclosure. That was good because it might stop him from always trying to push boundaries. By knowing he had to be careful not to bring attention to himself, he might not be so reckless.

Last summer, Tai had climbed to the roof of the house when Aunt Celeste went shopping, because he said he liked the sun to beat down on him. Then he dissolved into the desert about a half mile from the house. He came back on the roof about an hour later, only a few minutes before Aunt Celeste got home, and said he saw a rattlesnake and threw rocks at it. The danger of getting bitten apparently didn't even enter his mind.

But Argus never told on him. At the time it didn't seem so bad, but now, knowing about AURA and the Invaders, it was a dumb and reckless thing to do. For some reason, Argus always felt like the big brother, trying to keep Tai under control.

With a deep sigh, Aunt Celeste clapped her hands together. "Well, now that that's taken care of, how about we celebrate by going into town for dinner and some shopping to get you school supplies? I noticed that all the other kids had backpacks and notebooks."

"Yes, they did. We're all going?" Argus smiled. They rarely went into town and hardly ever went to a restaurant. At least he could pretend to be a regular kid at a restaurant. And if they got supplies, he could repay Lola with a ream of paper.

Aunt Celeste smiled warmly, the smile that made it feel like she really was their aunt. "You boys deserve it. First day of school, learning about your heritage, and being the longest surviving New Breeds on the planet. I'd say that's cause for celebration."

That last part of her list made Argus lose his smile. He didn't want to be reminded of that. What if he and Tai didn't live much longer? Was that thought going to hang over their heads forever? Any minute they could die? Aunt Celeste said no one knew why they'd outlived the other kids. The fact that no one, even advanced aliens, had any idea why they were still alive wasn't very comforting.

Argus went to his room to change out of his school clothes. He ran a comb through his hair, washed his face, and put on a clean white tee shirt and his favorite pair of jeans. Considering all that he'd learned, he was really excited about school tomorrow. Especially at the thought of seeing Lola again. He should ask her for her phone number or email or friend her on social media or whatever.

"Boys, are you ready?" Aunt Celeste called from the kitchen.

By the time Argus made it to the kitchen, Tai was already there waiting, wearing a black tee shirt and matching black jeans, his blond hair tousled like he didn't care what anybody thought. Nobody would guess they were twins. Aunt Celeste dangled the SUV key fob from her fingertips.

She winked. "Which one of you wants a driving lesson?"

They'd both gotten their learner's permits on one of their rare excursions to the outer world months ago. Even though they had their permits, Aunt Celeste didn't let them drive much because she insisted it was too dangerous because of their condition. Obviously it wasn't their fictional blood disease she was worried about, it was AURA or Invaders or whatever.

Argus grabbed the fob a second before Tai did. "Me first!"

Tai frowned for a moment, then said, "I get to drive home."

Once settled into the driver's seat, Argus pressed the remote, opened the garage door, and started the SUV. It was always an incredible feeling to sit behind the wheel. He was the driver, in charge. It was awesome.

He eased out of the garage and rolled slowly down the driveway. The gate automatically slid open when he got close and ran over the sensors in the driveway. Aunt Celeste gave him a few words of caution; *don't go too fast, accelerate smoothly, use your blinkers.*

When the gate was fully open, he started to accelerate, but slammed on the brakes when he saw a man who'd evidently been standing at the gate turn and run off into the desert. There was flash of recognition. He looked like Max.

Chapter 14

Max ran as fast as he could from the gate of the mysterious structure after he was almost run over by a black SUV. He only dared look back once from the crest of the small hill near where he'd left his car. He dropped to his stomach and peered at the SUV as it sat in the driveway right outside the gate. Why weren't they moving? Did they see him?

It looked like a regular SUV without government plates, which meant he'd almost trespassed on private property. There was no way they'd know who he was, so he should be in the clear. The side windows of the SUV were tinted, which made it impossible to see who was driving. It was curious why someone would live outside of town surrounded by walls and security cameras. Probably one of those kooks who didn't trust the government and tried to live off the grid. Good thing he got out of there as fast as he could, or he might have found his butt peppered with shotgun pellets.

He slid down the back side of the hill and got into his car and took a minute to think about what sort of person, or people, would hide behind walls. The distrusting types. Government haters. He chuckled because he knew damn well the government couldn't be trusted. He'd order surveillance of the house to make sure the inhabitants weren't anyone to worry about. Ha! That'd show 'em. *Try to hide from us and we'll watch you from space, from the air, and from the ground.*

Arriving back in town, he stopped at the nearest restaurant for a bite to eat; a pizza joint with a crowded parking lot and a faded sign that said *Marco's Pizza*. It didn't seem like an overpriced tourist restaurant, but more like a local hangout. Exactly what he was looking for. That was the best sort of place to gather intel.

He climbed out of the car and wiped his brow. How could anyone live in the desert? It was almost five and still about ninety degrees. Miserable. He hurried inside. *Marco's*, thankfully, was good and chilly from the air conditioning. Nice. He sat in a booth and in less than thirty seconds, a young waitress, Sandra according to her name tag, was by his table asking what he wanted.

It was noisy with all the chattering going on, so he had to raise his voice to be heard, "What would you recommend, Sandra?" He raised an eyebrow.

"The EBTKS pizza is good. Oh, that's 'everything-but-the-kitchen-sink'." She gave a thin smile.

"Great, bring me a medium. And a beer." He watched her walk away. Ah, to be a teenage boy again. He settled back in the booth and checked the place out.

There were groups of school kids gathered around the four video game machines off to one side, and almost every seat was filled with teens gabbing about the first day of school. Yep, a popular hangout. It made him feel a little out of place.

He discreetly turned on the OEED and took a reading. Nothing out of the ordinary. Next, he checked messages on his phone. Hell, a voicemail from Stone. He put the phone to his ear.

Jackson, I expect daily reports emailed to me. And a breakdown of expenses. You're on a tight leash. One screw up and...and I'm really hoping you screw up.

That was all. Max put the phone and OEED away when the pizza arrived. It was huge, stacked with meats, onions, mushrooms, peppers, globs of cheese and ample quantities of diced garlic. When an adult came with his beer, he had a long drink. He tugged a slice of pizza free, strings of gooey cheese stretching apart, and took a bite. When he was married, his wife would never let him have pizza.

After eating a couple more slices, the noise of the place started to give him a headache. He asked for a to-go box, but before he got up, three people walked in. He tried not to stare, but one was the attractive woman, Celeste somebody, from the school office, and another was Argus. He didn't recognize the other boy. So Argus was one of the "boys" she'd referred to. Interesting.

They walked past his table. Argus turned and looked right at him with a frown but kept walking. *Yeah, kid, it's me.* Max flinched when the OEED chirped. He plucked it from his pocket. An energy spike. A big one. Okay, now he knew for sure that Argus or Celeste or both had to be causing the spikes. He watched them as they went to the back of the restaurant and took a booth. They didn't look like aliens. Then again, what would aliens look like? AURA hadn't actually found any. Not until now anyway. This was going to be the find of a lifetime.

Chapter 15

Argus slid into the booth at *Marco's Pizza* and peeked over the top of the menu at Max. He was following them. Yeah, it must have been him sneaking around at the house. Argus nudged Tai who was sitting beside him.

Tai grunted. "Ow, what?"

"Let's play a video game," Argus said softly, hoping Tai understood he wanted to talk.

"We haven't ordered, Arg." Tai grabbed the menu. "I want to order everything on the menu. How often do we get to come here? I'm not missing out—"

"Video game. Now." Argus tugged on his brother's sleeve.

Aunt Celeste looked at him with her suspicious, unblinking eyes. "I saw him, too, Argus. He's an AURA agent."

"I knew it!" Argus shouted louder than he'd intended. He lowered his voice, "How do you know?"

"How do you anything at all about him?" Her eyes brightened.

"Oh. I saw him at school, acting weird. How do you know?"

"I shook his hand at school and...saw things." She turned slightly and looked in Max's direction. "I'm not sure if he suspects us or if this is a coincidence."

"Coincidence?" Tai let out a breath. "Aren't we the only New Breeds in Palmdale? And didn't the Citadel say an AURA agent was in Palmdale? That can't be coincidence. He's here for us."

She watched Max. "I need to verify that before drawing absolute conclusions. I've been exceptionally cautious when it comes to protecting our identities, so I don't know how he could have discovered us. Our home is protected with a field of disruptive ionic pulses." She paused, but continued a moment later, "That's a method of hiding objects from satellites or other means of detection. Our home is virtually invisible from electronic sources and the walls and cameras give me more protection from land invasion."

"Invasion?" Argus said softly. So that's why she had all of the security around the house. What sort of invasion was she talking about? Tanks, paratroopers?

Aunt Celeste grew quiet. She sighed. "Perhaps a poor choice of words. I should have said surveillance from the ground. Is that better?"

"Not really," Tai mumbled.

Now Argus knew he should have told her about Max earlier. Although she evidently already knew about him. *Time to spill it, Argus.* "Aunt Celeste, I think maybe Max is spying on me."

"Excuse me?" Her eyebrow jerked up. "Why do you say that? And how do you know his name?"

"He's a sub in my math class. And I saw him in PE, twice. I used my vision to see he had a device that measures something. I got away, so don't worry about that." He took the menu away from Tai and peeked behind it at Max again.

"You should have told me that." Aunt Celeste's face gave no hint if she was angry, although her mouth was held tight, and her eyes were bluer than normal. "I told you boys to call or text if anything happened."

"Nothing happened," Argus tried to sound casual, but his voice cracked a little.

She lowered her voice, "He's AURA, Argus. AURA wants evidence of Settlers or New Breeds. They haven't a clue what they're looking for, but they're aware of our energy levels. That's why the Citadel said not to use your abilities. That device he has must be an Organic Energy Emitting Device, OEED. The Citadel got their hands on one a few months ago. They're working on a way to circumvent it."

Argus felt his stomach sink. "So he knows?"

What would happen if the government knew for sure they were aliens, half-aliens? He didn't want to spend his life hiding, or worse, as a prisoner to be studied by the government. This was starting to look like a choice between being a prisoner at the Citadel or the government. After spending his whole life secluded at home, hardly ever allowed outside the walls, he didn't want to go back into hiding. He'd tasted freedom and liked it. And what about Lola and Dave? They were his potential friends and Lola had to be protected from Justin and anyone else who might try to hurt her.

Tai groaned. "I don't want to be hounded by that guy."

Argus nodded. "Same here. I've made friends. I can't—"

Aunt Celeste drew in a breath. "Don't overreact. AURA doesn't have any conclusive evidence. Not yet anyway. My job as your Guardian is to make sure they don't get any."

A waitress came over to the table. She smiled at Argus and didn't take her eyes off him. "Hi, I'm Sandra. What can I get you?" She seemed to be ignoring Tai and Aunt Celeste. "I've seen you in here a couple times, haven't I?"

Argus smiled back. She had dark eyes, shiny brown hair, and red lipstick that made it hard to stop looking at her mouth. "Yeah, I'm Argus. This is my brother, Tai, and my aunt. Do you go to Highland?" Why did he ask that? He didn't want a conversation. It sort of came out.

She blushed a little. "No, Palmdale High. I work here after school. I haven't seen you at any of the games. You go to Highland?"

A trickle of sweat dripped down his back. "Yeah. A senior." *She probably guessed that, stupid.* "Enrolled for senior year. Home schooled." Why was he talking in short sentences? Because his brain wasn't working right and he couldn't stop looking at her, that's why.

Those red lips of hers formed another smile. "Cool. Um, are you ready to order?"

Aunt Celeste spoke up, "Yes. Large cheese pizza, three salads, two Cokes, and a water for me. Thank you, that's all." That was her not-so-subtle way of dismissing Sandra.

"Oh. Okay." Sandra spun around and went through the double swinging doors into the kitchen, turning once to look back at Argus.

Tai laughed. "She's got it bad."

Argus ignored him and turned his attention to Aunt Celeste. "You didn't have to be so abrupt. That was rude."

She took out her cell phone/communicator. "It wasn't rude. You don't have the luxury of flirting right now."

Tai raised an eyebrow and let a snicker escape. "Yeah, bro. Besides, I don't think your little Lola would be any too happy to see you with Sandra."

"Who's Lola?" Aunt Celeste narrowed her eyes.

"A girl at school. And I wasn't flirting." Or was he? He wasn't sure. He'd never flirted before. Sandra was cute though, there was no denying that. She affected him the same way that Lola did; made him feel warm and gave his stomach the jitters.

Aunt Celeste dialed a number on her cell phone and kept her voice low. "Guardian 647. I need a tracker put on AURA agent Max Jackson. I want to know every move he makes. No, the Commander does not need to be informed. Out." She slipped the phone in her jacket pocket. "Mr. Jackson is an agent in the Los Angeles AURA office. He'll now be tracked and his whereabouts will be transmitted to my communicator."

Wow, really? Argus was blown away by how authoritative Aunt Celeste was. Of course she'd always been like that to him and Tai, but watching her boss other people around was kind of cool. He was grateful to have her around.

He thought back to what Tai said about Lola. He didn't want to make her jealous, but he knew nothing about girls. Nothing at all. And it seemed like it was easy to make them jealous.

He leaned forward. "Hey, Aunt Celeste, you met Lola in the office at school. Remember? I don't know how...I mean...I don't know what to say or how to act around her."

She reached over and touched his hand. "Do you want to know what thoughts I heard from Lola?"

What? Did he? Argus glanced at Tai and then to Aunt Celeste. "Um, no. I don't think I should know. I mean, then it's like I would be invading her privacy."

Aunt Celeste nodded slowly. "Very gallant, Argus. I'm sorry, but you'll have to learn about human girls on your own. She likes you, I can tell you that much." She smiled briefly, turned, and watched Max. "You boys are not to interact with him, other than as a student to a teacher. Since he's undercover as a teacher, you will need to go along with it until I find out what he's up to. Understand?" She finally turned around again. "This could be an excellent way to find out what AURA knows, if anything."

Argus wasn't sure if it would be an excellent way to find out anything. It could be dangerous if Max knew about them. When Sandra came with a tray of food and drinks, Argus instinctively got up to help her. He took the tray and placed it on the table. She smiled sweetly at him and put the pizza, salads, and drinks on the table, then said *thank you* and retreated to the kitchen. He took a sip of Coke, but before he had time to eat, Max started their way, winding past a few people who were leaving. What the heck was he doing?

Max waved when he was close. "I thought that was you, ah, Argus, right? And if I'm remembering, Celeste?"

Aunt Celeste put on a smile. "Yes."

He continued, "So these are your boys?"

"Nephews," she corrected. "Why don't you two go play some videos?" She handed Tai a ten.

That was their cue to leave. Argus scooted out and waited for Tai. The video games were on the other side of the room, but they had a good view and watched as Aunt Celeste motioned for Max to sit. That was unexpected. Argus smiled. *She* was investigating Max. She looked so calm and in control. *You picked the wrong pure-form to mess with, Max.*

"Hey! It's fart-gas!" Justin called out from behind a small crowd of people at one of the games.

Oh, no. This wasn't a good time to have to deal with Justin. Argus moved away, but it was no good, Justin made a bee-line to him. Tai blocked the way.

Argus looked around his brother. Justin's hand was wrapped with a thick wad of gauze. What an idiot, trying to pick another fight after getting his hand burned with alien blood. "Justin, we don't want any trouble."

"Where's baby Lola? In her crib sucking on a pacifier?" He laughed, a deep, hoarse laugh.

Why did he keep calling her baby Lola? It obviously upset her, but she never said anything about it. Argus took a few steps back and glanced at Aunt Celeste, but she was focused on talking to Max. "Leave her alone, Justin." He whispered to Tai, "Go and get some tokens for the video games."

"Bro," Tai said quietly, still staring at Justin.

Argus turned away from Justin. "I'm not going to do anything. Not with Max twenty feet away."

"Don't turn your back on me, fart-gas!"

Before Argus could do anything, Justin lunged at him and pushed him to the ground. He landed hard with a thump to his head. His eyes were blurry for a few seconds, but when they focused, he saw that Tai had Justin pinned against the wall, punching him in the face. Justin swung as well but missed more times than he hit. Struggling to his feet, Argus pulled Tai off Justin. Tai's lip was bleeding and like before, Justin flailed his unbandaged hand in the air. A crowd gathered, moving in for a better look at what had happened.

"Great," Argus mumbled. "We've got to get out of here, Tai."

"No shit." Tai grabbed a napkin off the nearest table and dabbed at his lip. "Sorry, I saw red and jumped on him."

"What the hell!" Max shouted as he jumped up from the booth holding the OEED.

Aunt Celeste glared at Tai, then got up and blocked Max with an outstretched arm. Argus's head throbbed and his vision was clouding over. He must have hit his head harder than he thought. This wasn't good. He felt Tai's arm around his shoulders.

"Come on, bro," Tai said in Argus's ear as he led him out of the restaurant.

Argus couldn't walk straight, his feet felt heavy. He shuffled more than walked. Thank goodness for Tai. The hot sun outside made him feel worse. There were shouts coming from the restaurant. Shouts to stop, shouts of call the police. Where was Aunt Celeste?

They made it to the SUV. Tai grunted and slammed his fist against the door. "The keys! Arg, will you be all right for a minute? I'm going to dissolve and get the key fob from Aunt Celeste."

The question must have been rhetorical because Tai was gone before he could stop him. As he leaned against the SUV, Argus closed his eyes and concentrated on Max. The scene wasn't clear, probably because of the bump to his head, but he could make out Max as he darted around Aunt Celeste and ran right into Tai.

Chapter 16

In a minute, the scene Argus had seen would happen. He had to stop it, prevent Tai from literally running into trouble. He opened his eyes and took a step, immediately collapsing onto the ground, whether from his concentration or the bump on his head, he didn't know. Either way, he was powerless to help Tai.

"Hey, Argus!" called a familiar voice. It was Dave.

"Dave! Help me up." Argus groaned as Dave grabbed his hands and yanked him upright.

Dave supported him. "What's wrong, man?"

"A fight. With Justin...again. Inside. Smacked my head. Can you help me get back in there? My brother's in trouble."

"You stay here, man, I'll go and make sure he's okay." Dave didn't go until Argus was leaning on the SUV.

He took a few deep breaths and followed after Dave. He wasn't as dizzy anymore and could see clearly. He assessed the situation. Max was about to get around Aunt Celeste, who looked like she wanted to kill him. Argus found Tai, grabbed him by the sleeve, and pulled him to the side as Max got away from Aunt Celeste. Max stared at the OEED, pointing it toward Tai.

"Arg? How'd you get here?" Tai asked.

"Max was going to run right into you. He's looking at that OEED thing. He knows."

Tai shrugged. "Maybe not. Could be Justin he's tracking."

Argus let go of Tai's arm. "Really? You don't believe that, do you?"

Tai frowned. "No. Now Justin's other hand is burned. That dick got me hard on the lip."

Aunt Celeste came over to them. Her mouth tight. Argus prepared for a scolding. Couldn't something, anything, go right for a change?

"Aunt Celeste..." Argus started but was cut off.

She held up her hand. "Another fight? Really? Now Jackson knows something for certain. His OEED spiked when Tai got involved. Your anger must have caused an energy burst. I hadn't realized an emotional connection to your energy fluctuations. We must leave right now."

Leave? Argus didn't like the sound of that. Did she mean leave *Marco's* or leave Palmdale?

"Hold on!" Max called, coming back toward them.

Aunt Celeste sighed heavily. "I need to disarm this situation. Boys, take the SUV and go straight home."

"But we only have permits," Tai said.

"Go home." She tossed the key fob to Argus. "Now."

Argus and Tai ducked down and hid behind some other kids as they made their way out of the restaurant. At the door, Dave caught up to them.

"Hey, what's going on? Oh, you found your brother. What happened to Justin Jones?" Dave pointed to Justin, who was sitting in a booth with his hand pushed into a glass of ice water.

There wasn't any time to explain much to Dave. They had to get out of there. "Um," Argus motioned to Max. "That Max guy is here, and we have to leave. Want a ride home, Dave?"

Dave nodded. "Ah, sure. Will you tell me what happened?"

"Yeah, but later." Argus hurried outside, unlocked the SUV, and slid behind the wheel. Hopefully he wouldn't get pulled over by the cops. He'd drive extra carefully.

Tai got into the passenger seat and Dave got in the back. Argus drove at exactly the speed limit and slowed to a perfect stop at a red light. He glanced in the rearview and saw Dave drumming his fingers on the door.

Argus accelerated gently when the light turned green. "Dave, it wasn't anything, really. Justin picked another fight and Tai jumped in. That's all." He accelerated a bit too fast and made the SUV lurch forward, throwing them all back into their seats. "Sorry."

Dave leaned forward. "It's okay, man. I don't mean to butt in."

Argus slowed the SUV a bit to keep it at the speed limit. "No problem. We're friends, we're supposed to talk about stuff like this." He didn't want to admit that he didn't know what friends did because Dave might think he was stupid, and he didn't want to lose the budding friendship. He stopped at another red light. "Dave, where do you live?"

"Ahh, back in the other direction." Dave shrugged with a lopsided smile. "Guess I should have told you that before, huh? I got caught up in the...what's it called? Intrigue?"

Tai chuckled. "Yeah, intrigue. Give me your address."

When Dave said where he lived, Tai typed it into Aunt Celeste's GPS. Luckily they didn't have to go past *Marco's*, but turned down another street that went behind the restaurant. They went over the railroad tracks and ended up at a mobile home park. The homes were nice, not as nice as a real house, but not run-down either.

"That's my house." Dave pointed to a large mobile home painted dark blue with a small porch out front covered with fake green grass. "My dad doesn't live with us, we don't have much money," he said quietly, apologetically.

It was weird how Dave and Lola seemed to think they had to apologize for not having money. Why was that important? "It looks like a great home." Argus smiled.

Through the rearview, he saw Dave smile, too, sit up and nod. "Yeah, it is. Do you want to come inside? My mom's not home from work."

Argus shook his head. "No, our aunt wants us to go straight home."

Tai took off his seat belt. "Arg, come on, let's go inside. Nobody'll know we're here."

He considered it for a moment. Tai was right. Aunt Celeste would keep an eye on Max, and she did say they were supposed to integrate with the humans. "Yeah, okay, but only for a few minutes." No harm in a quick visit.

Leading the way, Dave unlocked the door and ushered them in. It was comfortably cool inside because the window air conditioner blasted even though no one was home. When a yapping puppy bounded out from a bedroom, Argus understood why the air conditioner was on. The puppy was small and brown with floppy ears.

"You have a dog?" he asked, jealous. Aunt Celeste said no to pets. Even goldfish. "What's his name?"

"Pudgy." Dave knelt and gathered the wriggly puppy in his arms. He brought Pudgy over. "He won't bite, but he might lick you to death."

Argus reached out to pet Pudgy and got a slobbery lick like Dave said. He laughed and held the puppy when Dave offered. After a few slurps to his face, he handed off Pudgy to Tai who was more than happy to accommodate.

"So, Argus, want to play my video games?" Dave went to a TV set where the controllers were.

"Sure. We've got a few games, too. What games do you have?" Argus watched Tai wrestling with the puppy and laughed again. How great would it be to have a dog. When he got home, he'd ask Aunt Celeste again for a pet and see if she'd change her mind. Then again, maybe this wasn't the best timing to bring up a pet. She had enough to worry about.

Dave inserted a game into the console. "You'll like this one. You have to shoot down aliens before they get to Earth."

"What?" Argus felt the color drain from his face. Shooting aliens? Playing the game didn't sound like much fun now. "Um, maybe later." He wanted to change the subject. "What does your mom do?"

Abandoning the game, Dave flopped down in a worn easy chair. "She's an admitting clerk at the hospital. Swing shift. How about your aunt?"

He wasn't prepared for that type of question. In fact, he'd never considered where Aunt Celeste got her money. She never went to work and was always home, except for the infrequent shopping trips. They went on a few short vacations, so where'd she get the money? They'd been to Santa Cruz, on the coast of California, once, and to New Mexico, but that was it. So how did Aunt Celeste have enough money to live?

"She works from home," Argus said, then, to get the conversation away from Aunt Celeste, "Hey, do you know a girl named Lola?"

Dave sat up and grinned. "Lola McCreary? Yeah. I've had a crush on her since ninth grade."

"Oh?" Argus felt a tinge of jealousy. How could he be jealous? He'd only just met her.

Dave continued, "She's like a genius. Cute, too. Why?"

"She showed me around this morning and Justin Jones made fun of her. Called her baby Lola. It upset her." Argus gritted his teeth at the thought of Lola being hurt.

"Justin's a jerk. Lola can take care of herself, you don't have to worry about that." Dave laughed and grabbed Pudgy as he ran by.

Argus watched the puppy lick Dave's face. "She can?"

Tai went to the game console and inserted a game.

"Yep. I told you, she's smart." Dave shrugged and let the puppy go.

"So why does he call her baby?"

"Oh, because she's only sixteen. She skipped a grade because she's so smart. She was the only one who was nice to me in ninth grade when I broke my ankle. She signed my cast."

Argus played back what Dave said before. "Wait, you were in ninth grade together? If you were in the same—"

Dave smiled. "She was in the same grade because she skipped eighth grade. They wanted to let her graduate early in high school, but she didn't want to. She told me once that she doesn't want to feel different. I wouldn't care. *I'd* graduate early if I could."

"Yeah." Argus understood exactly what Lola was feeling. No wonder they connected.

Tai turned off the game and motioned to the SUV outside. "Hey, Arg, we probably should get going. Should we go by *Marco's* to see if Aunt Celeste needs a ride? How's she going to get home? The bus?"

With a sad look on his face, Dave said, "Ah, man, I hope you don't get in trouble for coming here."

"I don't think we will." Argus hoped he sounded convincing because he had a bad feeling that he would be in trouble. He turned to Tai. "We should go home. Aunt Celeste is probably waiting. I'm sure she found a way home because she told us to go home."

"Okay, but I get to drive this time." Tai held his hand out for the key fob.

At the door, Argus thanked Dave for his hospitality, even though it appeared that he didn't exactly know what the word hospitality meant. "See you at school tomorrow, Dave."

"Yep. See ya." Dave waited on the porch while they drove away.

Tai drove too fast. He screeched the tires when he accelerated out of the mobile home park and skidded onto the road. He grinned and headed down City Ranch Road past the landfill toward their house while Argus held onto the dashboard. When they were about fifty meters from the house, the gate slid open and Aunt Celeste stood to the side, waving them forward. Her eyes were bright blue. She looked angry.

Tai brought the car into the garage but didn't get out. "What should we say?"

"The truth. She'll know if we're lying." Argus opened the passenger door and scooted out.

"Where were you?" Aunt Celeste said, her voice raised to a pitch that definitely meant she was angry. "I've been home for twenty minutes."

Twenty minutes? Okay, time to tell the truth. Argus knew it was the right thing to do. "We drove my friend Dave home and he invited us in. I didn't want to be rude, Aunt Celeste, he's my friend."

She said nothing for a moment, making the tension worse. At last, she nodded slowly and her expression eased a bit. "Yes, you do need friends. But you must tell me where you are. Why do you think you have cell phones?"

"How come you didn't know where we were?" Argus closed the passenger door. "I thought you could read minds and, well, whatever else you can do."

She sighed. "As I said before, I can only hear thoughts when I'm close to a person, and, if you remember, I agreed not to use telepathy on you or Tai. You have cell phones, use them. I was about to trace the GPS in the car. I must know where you are at all times. I'm your Guardian."

"Sorry," Tai mumbled, but Argus saw he had a slight smirk on his face. He always enjoyed testing limits.

"Go inside." Aunt Celeste closed the garage door and ushered them into the house.

Argus had to know what she did at the restaurant. "Hey, what happened with Max? And Justin?"

Her face darkened. "I couldn't alter Mr. Jackson's thoughts because it would only cause more suspicion, so I tried to manipulate his memory enough to throw him off."

Tai sat at the dining room table and picked up an apple. "What does that mean?"

She continued, "I created a block in his memory. Every time when he noticed a link between his OEED and one of us, I inserted a false trail. Now he'll think the OEED spiked when he was in his car, at the motel he's staying in, and in the teacher's bathroom at school. There's no connection to us. That should hold him off for a while. That said, we've got to be more cautious when he's around."

"Why don't we, you know, off him?" Tai asked with his smirk getting bigger. "We've got all sorts of abilities. We're better than humans."

"Tai!" Argus shook his head. "I hope you're not serious."

His smirk dropped. "Damn. Why'd I say that?"

"Tai." Aunt Celeste went to the table and took the apple from his hand. "You will never talk like that. Humans are not to be hurt intentionally. Ever. Remember, you're part human. Our qualities are not something to be trifled with, boys."

"I don't know why I said that." Tai got up and went to his bedroom, shaking his head as if he was confused.

Without Tai around to cause problems, Argus decided to talk to Aunt Celeste and find out more information. "Can I ask you a couple of questions?"

She nodded. "Of course. If you want to know about Justin, his other hand is burned now. I'm going to have to do something about that. I can't make him believe he burned it with another cigarette, not when there were witnesses."

"Um, okay, but that wasn't what I wanted to ask. Where do you get your money from?" he blurted, taking her by surprise.

"Oh." She paused for a few seconds. "The Citadel provides all Guardians with whatever is needed."

"They give you money? How much?" It was funny, but he'd never wondered about money until Dave asked about it.

"Whatever is needed." Aunt Celeste tilted her head slightly. "Why are you asking? Do you need money?"

"No. Well, I need school supplies. We still didn't get any."

"That's right. I was going to take care of that tonight, but...I can go out later I suppose, now that Mr. Jackson is taken care of. Did you have another question?"

He did. It was bothering him how money seemed to matter so much. "Yeah, I mean yes, I do. Why does everyone think money is so important? Lola said she doesn't have much money and neither does Dave. I don't care. I like them both."

"In this society, there is a stigma about being less than affluent. In the past, not all societies revolved around a monetary system, but these days, if you have money, you have power. Without money, you're limited. It's that limitation that creates the gap between the affluent and the less affluent. And that gap creates a stigma where the wealthy enjoy being at the top and promote themselves as being better because of it. They have access to things that poorer people don't. Better medical care, food, houses, cars. Those without money suffer and are looked down upon. Do you understand?"

He sort of did. "So it doesn't have anything to do with the sort of person someone is, but whether or not their bank account is loaded? That's dumb. What good does it do to have money in the bank if you're a terrible person? I'd rather hang out with poor people who are nice or give my money to people who need it."

"A noble thought, Argus. But money is still needed to function in society. I have to buy food and clothing. And your supplies for school."

"I know. So where's the balance?" He sighed. It was easier when he didn't think of money.

"That's the hard part. Finding the balance between needing money and wanting money. Those who want more and more become greedy and greed is dangerous. All right, enough questions. Do you have any homework?"

"Ah, no. Do you think I can use the telescope? I'd love to see Ramtala."

The telescope used to keep him company when he was little. He'd keep it by his bed every night. It was almost like having his dad right there. And to think that his dad helped design it. What a great man he must have been. It would be awesome to have a dad, not that Aunt Celeste didn't give them everything they needed, but she wasn't loving like a parent would be. He missed that. She'd never even given him a hug.

"Are you all right, Argus? You seem...lost."

"I'm fine. Just thinking of my dad. What was he like?" He sat down at the table.

"Physically he was tall, almost six feet two inches. That's why you and Tai are tall. His intellect was admirable for a human. Your mother loved him very much." She paused. "Is that enough?"

"I don't think it'll ever be enough. What else? Did he like sports, did he have hobbies?" Argus couldn't even remember his dad, not his voice or his smile. Nothing.

"You've seen the photographs. I've already told you about him. Why the sudden interest?"

"I don't know. My friend Dave only has a mother and I guess it got me thinking about my family. Not that I'm not grateful to have you here, especially now that I know the truth, but I don't even have a mother. At least Dave does."

"Don't let the past cloud your future." Aunt Celeste came over and sat beside him. "Give me your hand."

It wasn't like Aunt Celeste to want to hold his hand, but he held it out anyway. She grasped it tightly in her own and gazed into his eyes. His hand tingled, not painful tingling, but like static electricity tingling. Aunt Celeste's eyes were bright blue, intense, he was drawn to them. She gripped his hand harder and immediately a flood of images popped into his head.

A wedding with a couple standing under an arch of white flowers by a lake. A mountain cabin surrounded by tall pine trees. The man in hip-waders standing in a lake fly-fishing. A picnic; blanket on the grass, wildflowers everywhere. The same couple lying on the blanket, embracing, looking so much in love. Next, the woman, very pregnant, in a wheelchair in a hospital. The images came fast, as if they were a movie that was fast-forwarding. A house, a car, a boat, then...an explosion...a woman's body, burned, washed up on the shore of a lake...

"Argus! Let go!" Aunt Celeste shouted.

He hadn't realized he was squeezing her hand. He let go. Her eyes weren't as bright anymore.

"You weren't meant to see those last images," she said softly, shaking her head.

"Were those...my parents? And my mom? On the shore?" There was a lump in his throat. Nobody should see their mother dead. Worse, burned. "What happened to her? And my dad?"

Aunt Celeste placed her arm around him. "I told you, a boating accident. I got there too late to help your mother. Your father's body was never found.

There was nothing I could do. I was watching you and Tai so they could have some time alone."

Argus jumped up and slammed his fist on the table, causing the wood to crack. "But you're a pure-form! Why couldn't you save them?" The memory was still fresh, like it had only happened. Like he'd just lost his parents. It hurt.

"Please calm down. Our qualities can't change the natural course of life. I could have repaired some of the damage to your mother if it wasn't so severe and if I'd arrived in time. I *am* sorry. This is a memory that I live with every day, but it was never intended for you."

Well, maybe it wasn't intended for him, but now he had the images planted in his brain. The charred body of his mom would haunt him forever. "I'm going to bed." He shuffled to his bedroom next door to Tai's and looked out the window at the beginning of the sunset. The sky was already a light pinkish orange. He turned away and sat down on the bed. Thank goodness Tai didn't see those images. No point in both of them seeing death.

So much had happened in one day, one single day. What if it all was a dream? This is one dream he'd love to wake up from. He lay down, closed his eyes, and repeated over and over, *this is a dream*. But, when he opened his eyes, he was still lying on the bed, and nothing had changed. His parents were dead and he was a New Breed. Maybe it would have been better if Aunt Celeste never told him the truth. But isn't the truth supposed to be a good thing?

There was a series of knocks on the door; two followed by three knocks. "Hey, bro, can I come in?" Tai asked quietly.

"Yeah." Argus sat up.

Tai opened the door and walked in with his shoulders stooped slightly. "Arg, I can't stop thinking about how I felt back in the dining room. I really wanted to kill Max. I felt it deep down, almost like a compulsion. That's how I felt when I attacked Justin. I'm still freaked out." He shut the door. "I still kind of have that feeling. I can't shake it."

"What, like you want to kill him? Shhh." Argus jumped up and pressed his ear to the door listening for footsteps. Everything was quiet.

"Yeah. I can imagine my hands around his neck, squeezing. Look, my hands are shaking." He held out his hands. "What's wrong with me?"

Argus shook his head. "I don't know. Try to relax, think of something else. Think of Pudgy."

Tai sat on the floor at the foot of the bed and took a deep breath. "Pudgy, Pudgy, Pudgy," he mumbled, wringing his hands together. He let the breath out slowly. "Okay, I think that worked."

"Good. I was excited at first that we're New Breeds, but now I wish we didn't know. I don't like being different. I want to be like everyone else." He peered out the window again. The pink in the sky was deepening to red.

Tai stood beside him. "I don't know, I think I like being different. I mean, I don't want to think about killing people, but it's cool knowing we're half alien. And I like my abilities."

Aunt Celeste knocked on the door. "I'm going out to pick up school supplies. Will you boys be all right? I don't want you to leave the house right now."

"We'll be fine," Argus called out. "Can you get us backpacks like the other kids have?" At least they would *look* like normal teenagers.

"Of course. I won't be long. Do not leave the house."

Argus watched out the window as Aunt Celeste drove down the driveway and through the gate. He couldn't get rid of the images of his parents. He needed a distraction. "Tai, I want to try to see what Lola's doing."

"Okay. Better do it now so you'll have plenty of time to recover before Aunt Celeste gets home." Tai stretched. "While you do that, I'm going for a walk in the desert. I've got to clear my head."

Argus nodded. There was no use trying to stop him. "Be careful. It's almost dark. Make sure you get back before Aunt Celeste does. If you see Max sneaking around, get back here right away."

Tai smiled. "I need some air, stretch my legs. See you in a few, bro." He dissolved from the room.

For some reason Argus thought he was going to use the door and actually walk.

He looked in the mirror above his dresser and ran his hand through his hair. He'd love to do that to Lola's hair. He really wanted to see her, to see what she was doing, or about to do. Was she eating dinner, doing homework, chores? He sat on the bed again, shut his eyes and concentrated on her.

Before long, the scene opened up and he saw her standing in what had to be her living room. Her face was wet from tears streaming down her face. Why was she crying? The view pulled back more to show a man standing beside her, red-faced and yelling. Argus broke his concentration and opened his eyes. He had to go to Lola, to stop the man. His need to protect her felt like what Tai was talking about, a compulsion, something he had to do. He forced his body off the bed and stumbled to the bedroom door.

He grabbed the doorknob and stopped. Aunt Celeste had the car. But Lola was in trouble, he had to get to her. But how? He let go of the doorknob and felt a jolt to his entire body. Before he knew it, he was in Lola's living room.

Chapter 17

Max was lightheaded. He sat in his car outside his motel room with the air conditioner running full blast, trying to remember what had happened in the pizza restaurant. Hell, he couldn't even remember driving back to the motel. There'd been some sort of commotion, but he couldn't remember what it was. It was as if he'd blacked out and lost time. But why, how? Was he drinking? He didn't feel drunk. His memory was muddled, tangled, events all blurred together.

Did he even eat? He checked his watch. Six. The sun was going down. How long had he been sitting in the car? He shut off the engine and went into his room. It must be the heat that made him foggy. What else could it be? He lay down and tried to reconstruct the last couple of hours.

After school, he...did what? He'd been looking for clues. The OEED! He pulled the sensor from his pocket and checked the data. There were several instances of spikes, although he vaguely remembered those happened in the teacher's bathroom and in the car. No aliens were in his car, that's for sure. Damn, maybe it was malfunctioning. One day down and he'd gotten nowhere.

He put the OEED on the nightstand as his cell phone rang. He'd have to recalibrate the sensor later. He grabbed his phone. "Hello?"

"Jackson, Stone here. I hope you don't think you're on vacation. AURA is footing the bill for this."

"I know, sir." Max got up and paced. Of course he knew he wasn't on vacation.

"Any information yet? Found any little green men?" Stone's voice sounded like he might have been trying to hide a laugh.

"It's only been one day, sir. I did get a few readings, but they turned out to be nothing. If there's an alien presence here, sir, I'll find it." Max flipped the phone the bird.

"Uh-huh. Well, carry on. Oh, one of the mailroom clerks was promoted, so there's an opening. Entry level."

"Yes, sir." Max wanted to throw the phone across the room. He'd find evidence and rub it in Stone's face. Maybe it'd be Stone who'd end up in the mail room. Oh, what a great thought.

Thankfully Stone hung up without another word. The last thing Max wanted to do was get into a verbal battle. He picked up the OEED and went to his laptop. He might as well download the data in case Stone insisted on seeing what he'd collected. He plugged in the USB cable and watched as the day's information downloaded and a graph formed.

It was strange how he hadn't found anything useable, even though there was data on the OEED. Oh, well, tomorrow would bring another day of possibilities. When the download was complete, he studied the graph. There was something wrong. It showed that all of the day's data was from organic sources, which meant the OEED wasn't broken. He brought up a map of Palmdale and plotted the surges. He stared at the results. It didn't make sense. They were at the high school *and* the pizza restaurant. That wasn't right. What was going on? Was he somehow misreading the results? Why did he think the surges happened in his car?

He thought back to the last thing he remembered. He was at the pizza restaurant after driving into the desert and sneaking up on the walled house. Ah, the restaurant. He saw that kid Argus and his aunt. After that, everything was fuzzy. What happened in the restaurant?

He had to get Argus alone. In some way, he was the key to the mystery. There had to be a link between the energy surges, the loss of memory, and Argus. Maybe the kid slipped him a mickey so he wouldn't remember what happened. Did kids even know what a mickey was?

"Sorry, kid, but you're my new target."

Chapter 18

Argus stood in Lola's living room right across from her, holding his breath. She was acting like he wasn't there. She stared straight ahead, directly at him. There was no way she couldn't see him. He let out his breath. Why didn't she scream or something? Wouldn't that be the normal reaction if someone appeared in your living room?

He watched her to see what she'd do. She was so still, like a scared animal afraid to move in case there was a predator close by. He waved, but she didn't move until a loud man's voice shouted, then she flinched.

"Where's my dinner?" the man screamed. The man, the one Argus had seen in his vision, came from the hallway and stomped right up to Lola. He stood behind her, towering over her. It had to be her father. Why was he yelling? He grabbed her backpack off the coffee table and rummaged through it.

Argus took a step forward, prepared to do whatever was necessary to get her out of the situation. So why didn't her father notice a stranger standing in the living room? It was weird the way they ignored him.

Her father shouted, "I gave you ten sheets of notebook paper and there's only two left! What did you do with it? Write love notes? You got a boyfriend, Lola? I knew I shouldn't have let you skip a grade. Stupid girls like you are easy pickings for older guys." He stopped yelling and came around to face Lola.

It was the scene Argus had already witnessed. Lola was crying. If he'd known how angry her father would be about the paper, he never would have taken a few sheets from her. It was only paper. Why was he so mad?

"Excuse me!" Argus called out, but neither Lola nor her dad seemed to pay him any attention. What was going on? How was he standing there, invisible? A new ability like Tai's? Well, not quite like Tai's because Tai was never invisible. Was it even possible to be invisible?

If he was invisible, how could he use this ability? What could he do? He walked to Lola's father, reached out, and touched him on the shoulder. The man spun around, his eyes wild with fury.

"What the hell? Who did that?" He turned back to Lola. "What did you do?"

Lola looked down at the ground. "Nothing, Dad."

"Yeah, I bet." Her dad continued his rant, "So, you have a boyfriend? Are you on birth control?"

"No, Dad. I don't even have any friends." Lola never looked up.

Argus got close to her. "Yes you do, Lola. Me. I'm your friend. Please stop crying."

Her father kept on, "That's because you're a dumb girl. Ugly, too. Just like your worthless mother. Should have drowned you at birth. You're nothing but trouble."

"I'm not dumb, Dad. I get good grades. I—"

"Shut up! Did I say you could talk?"

That was it. Her father had no right to talk to her like that. Argus grabbed him by the shoulders and pushed him to the ground. Lola stood there, shocked, her hand clasped over her mouth.

Argus stepped back. What did he do? He can't attack an adult. That was a violation of Aunt Celeste's rule of never harming humans. But what was he supposed to do? There was no way he could stand by and let Lola's father berate her like that. She didn't deserve that. Nobody did.

Without a word, her father got off the floor, looked around and glared at Lola. He stormed out of the house, and slammed the door. A moment later a car screeched out of the driveway. Argus walked to Lola and wanted to hold her but knew he couldn't. The last thing he wanted to do was scare her. At least she wasn't crying anymore. Did she have a small smile on her lips? He got a little closer. She did.

He whispered in her ear, "I won't let him hurt you, Lola."

She didn't hear him, which was probably a good thing because she'd undoubtedly be creeped out if she could hear him without seeing him. So, how was he supposed to get home? He closed his eyes and thought of being in his bedroom. He visualized his bed, his bookshelves, his weight set, his awesome video game set up. But, when he opened his eyes, he was still in Lola's house.

This wasn't good. If no one could hear him, or see him, how could he call for help? It wasn't like Aunt Celeste could find him because she said she wouldn't read his mind anymore. If he was able to transport to Lola's, why couldn't he transport back home like Tai did? He could touch things, which meant he could open the door and leave. Well, that was something.

"Bye, Lola. See you at school tomorrow," he whispered, knowing she couldn't hear him.

To avoid scaring her, he waited until she left the living room before opening the front door. He was quiet and managed to open and close the door without making much sound at all. Unfortunately, he had no idea where he was. The neighborhood wasn't familiar at all. The houses were nice with neat lawns. But he'd never been there before. The sun was getting low. Damn it, he had to get home.

He sat on the stoop and concentrated on Tai. "Come on, Tai, use your shared-sight. Come and help me."

The vibration from his cell phone broke his concentration. He reached into his pocket and looked at the caller. Aunt Celeste. He answered the phone, "Aunt Celeste, can you hear me?"

"Hello? Argus, are you there? Argus?" She sounded worried.

"Yes, I'm here. Aunt Celeste?" Damn it. She couldn't hear him either.

"Hello? Argus? If you can hear me, Argus, say something." Her voice was almost frantic.

"Aunt Celeste!"

She disconnected the call. Okay, so he was invisible and not even Aunt Celeste could hear him. But he could feel and touch things. He'd be excited about this new ability, if only he understood how to control it. What if he'd be invisible forever? If he couldn't change back? His heart thumped hard.

"Arg?" It was Tai. "Where are you, bro?" He sounded strange, distant.

Argus jumped up and saw Tai, doubled-over, on the lawn. His face pale and he breathed hard.

"Tai! I'm right here!"

"Arg? Where the hell...are you? I'm in trouble, bro."

Argus went to him and put his arm around his shoulder. "Tai, what's wrong?"

"What the hell!" Tai straightened and lashed out with his hand, striking Argus on the jaw. "Who's there? What's going...on? Is that you, Arg?"

Damn it! Still invisible. And that hit hurt. He let go of Tai right away. "Tai, it's me."

"Oh, there you are. Where'd you come from?" Tai stared at him.

"You can see me?"

"Ah, yeah, now I can. How come I didn't see you before? That was you who touched me?" Tai doubled-over again. "Ow."

"Tai, what's wrong? I was invisible. I have a new ability. I can dissolve and turn invisible and...never mind, what's wrong?" He helped Tai sit down on the grass. He looked awful.

Tai groaned again. He was very pale and sweaty. "I went for a walk in the desert, but a rattlesnake came out of nowhere. I swear, it wasn't there and then it was. It bit me. On the calf. I don't feel well at all."

"Why didn't you dissolve and get to the hospital?" Argus looked around. What could he do?

"You needed me. I felt it. I figured I could help you...first. Why didn't you dissolve back home? Arg, I can't breathe." Tai's breathing was more of a gasp, as if he couldn't fill his lungs.

He grabbed his phone and dialed Aunt Celeste. "Tai, I did try to dissolve home, but it didn't work." This time Aunt Celeste would hear him. It only rang once before she picked up.

"Argus, why didn't you answer when I called?"

"I did. I tried. We need help. Tai was bitten by a rattlesnake. I'm at Lola's house, but I don't know the address."

"Hold on. All right, I've traced your phone location. Stay there, I'm on my way." She hung up.

Argus tried to remember everything he knew about snake bites. Stay calm, don't get excited or the venom will spread faster, stay warm to prevent shock. "Lie back and breathe slowly. I'm going to see if Lola can help."

He ran to the front door and rang the buzzer about ten times. He heard footsteps inside and then the door flung open. Lola's eyes were wide.

"Argus? What are you doing here?" She glanced past him and saw Tai. "What's wrong with your brother? He looks terrible."

Argus blurted, "Bitten by a rattlesnake. Do you have a blanket?"

Lola looked around. "There's a snake here? Where?"

He shook his head. "No, in the desert. A blanket?"

"Oh, sorry." She vanished inside, returning a few seconds later with a fleece blanket. "I'm calling 9-1-1."

"No! My aunt's on her way. She'll take us to the hospital." He knelt beside Tai and placed the blanket over him, then rolled up his pants and saw where the bite was. It was swollen and red with two distinct fang marks. "Damn it, Tai."

Tai forced a smile that quickly disappeared. "Sorry, bro. Trust me, I'm definitely having regrets about leaving the house. And getting anywhere near rattlesnakes."

Argus stayed beside Tai until Aunt Celeste screeched to a stop and skidded the SUV on some loose gravel. She didn't say anything, but opened the rear door, hurried to Tai, lifted him up with no effort, and put him gently across the back seat.

"Get in the car, Argus." She nodded to Lola, got into the driver's seat, and accelerated once Argus was in.

He looked out the window at Lola as they drove off. How was he going to explain to her why he was on her lawn with Tai? He'd think of something. "I'm sorry, Aunt Celeste." He turned around and watched Tai. "How are you doing?"

Tai had his eyes closed. "I'm still alive, so I guess not too bad."

Aunt Celeste glanced in the rearview. "No jokes, Tai. This is serious. We'll talk about your blatant disregard for my rules later. That goes for both of you. For now, we need help."

Argus faced forward. "Can't you heal him? I thought you—"

"I don't have miraculous healing abilities, Argus. I can do limited treatment, but not for something like this. He needs a real doctor." Her eyes were bright blue and her hands gripped the wheel so tightly that her knuckles were white.

Facing Tai again, Argus assured him, "It's going to be all right. We'll be at the hospital soon."

"Argus, turn around," Aunt Celeste spat the words. "You and your brother have New Breed blood, remember? It's not so easy to have either of you treated at a hospital. I will have to handle the situation with help from the Citadel. I don't want either of you to answer any questions or speak to anyone. Understand?"

Argus nodded even though he really didn't understand what was going on or why he couldn't talk to anyone. But if Aunt Celeste said not to, then he'd do as she said. Not a good idea to cause trouble right now. And what did she mean by getting help from the Citadel? Was that bad? Would he and Tai get in trouble for disobeying her? It was the Citadel that wanted them brought in after all. He took a quick look at Tai. Why didn't he stop Tai from leaving the house? Could he have stopped him? Probably not. But he should have tried anyway.

The SUV turned sharply into the emergency entrance of the hospital. Argus stared out the window at the large building. He'd never set foot in the hospital before. It was imposing, situated at the top of a hill overlooking the town. A cold chill settled over him. What if Tai died? *No, no, no, push that thought away. Don't think like that.*

Aunt Celeste moved incredibly fast and parked the SUV, opened the rear door, scooped up Tai, and hurried through the ER doors. Argus had to run to keep up with her. Once inside, he stopped and shivered. It was cold. Not only from the air conditioning, but from the white-washed walls and antiseptic smell. He was scared.

"I have a boy bitten by a rattlesnake about 15 minutes ago," Aunt Celeste called out to a nurse behind a desk marked Triage.

The nurse, a man maybe in his late thirties, ran to her, looked at Tai, and motioned to a set of double-doors. "Right through here." He pushed a large square silver button on the wall and the doors swung inward exposing a white tiled corridor on the other side. He yelled, "Snake bite!"

Argus followed along, feeling slightly queasy. There was nothing he could do to help. The nurse ushered them to a room with glass sliding doors and a blue curtain surrounding a bed. Aunt Celeste put Tai on the bed and stood back. Tai wasn't moving anymore. He was sweaty and his breathing was slow, very slow.

A man with gray hair and black-rimmed glasses, wearing a white coat with a stethoscope around his neck, rushed in with two women, one in blue scrubs and one in a white jacket. The man, the doctor, felt Tai's head and listened to his heart with the stethoscope, while the woman in scrubs checked his arms and legs.

The woman in the white jacket stood with Aunt Celeste. "How long ago was he bitten?"

"About 15 minutes," Aunt Celeste said, sounding a bit unsure. She looked at Argus.

He nodded. At least he thought it was about 15 minutes ago. "It was a rattlesnake. I might have been a bit longer than—"

Aunt Celeste glared at him. He shut up. Why didn't she want him to speak? It wasn't like he was going to tell them Tai dissolved and appeared in the desert.

The doctor gave orders to the woman in scrubs; blood tests, antivenom, antibiotic IV. Argus wanted to do something to help Tai, but what could he do? Nothing. He had to watch while doctors and nurses poked his brother with needles and stripped off his pants and shirt, and dressed him in a thin blue and white hospital gown.

Once the IV was hooked up, Aunt Celeste motioned for Argus to follow her into the corridor. She leaned down and whispered, "I know you're worried. I'm worried too. A representative from the Citadel will be here any second to intercept the blood samples."

What did that mean? How would they intercept the blood samples? When did she contact the Citadel? And how could anyone be there any second?

"I shouldn't have let him go," was all Argus could manage to say.

"Shhh. I said no talking."

"Why? I don't understand."

She glanced back toward the room. "I don't want you to accidentally say anything that might draw suspicion. Best to keep completely quiet. You're upset and might not think before speaking. I don't mean to sound harsh, but I can't have you endanger yourself or Tai. Now, don't say anything else. If you want to ask me something, give me permission to use telepathy on you and I'll hear your thoughts."

Wow, she had to ask his permission. He nodded. "Yeah, go ahead. I don't care. Is Tai going to be all right?"

Her expression was hard to read. Her eyes weren't as bright, she looked calm, but with a severity underneath. Then it struck him. She didn't know if Tai would be all right. Her eyes flashed brightly for a moment, then dimmed again.

"Argus, I have attuned to your thoughts now. And no, I don't know how Tai is. When you no longer want me to use telepathy, simply say so. There's a waiting room over there, go and sit down. I've got to go to the lobby to meet the representative. You can explain to me later how you got to Lola's house." She peeked into the room again, turned, and went down the corridor and through the double doors.

How could a representative come from the Citadel so fast? Was the Citadel close by? As usual, there wasn't an explanation from Aunt Celeste. She never divulged much. He'd accepted it growing up, but now it was annoying as hell. He went to the waiting room that wasn't really a room at all, but an area where there were seats arranged in three rows. Two women sat together, talking about someone who'd had a heart attack, and a man and woman paced around looking very nervous. He didn't want to wait there. Instead of going into the waiting area, he sneaked to the double doors leading to the lobby and pushed on one to open it a few inches.

There was Aunt Celeste, standing with a very tall, thin woman dressed in a dark gray business suit. The woman had to be well over six feet tall. Her dark hair was bundled loosely on top of her head, making her look even taller. Was she a pure-form, too? There didn't seem to be any way to tell. After a couple of seconds, the woman glanced around and strode off down another corridor with a sign on the wall that pointed to the *Lab* and *Radiology*.

Aunt Celeste went down a different corridor with a sign that said *Pharmacy*. What was she going to do? Argus crept into the lobby, making sure Aunt Celeste didn't see him, and peered down the corridor. He watched her open the door and walk into the pharmacy.

"Can I help you?" said a man's voice behind Argus.

Argus spun around, startled. A security guard stood right behind him. Not good. "Oh. Ah, no. My brother's in the ER. I..." Aunt Celeste said not to talk to anyone. "No, I'm fine."

The guard took out a small notepad and pen. "What's your name?"

There wouldn't be any harm in giving his name. That wasn't a secret. "Argus Dachel."

After jotting down the name, the guard continued, "And you said your brother's in the ER? Where are your parents?"

"Um, my aunt...can I go back to my brother now?" Argus felt beads of sweat spring up on his forehead. *Aunt Celeste, can you hear me? I need you.*

"Your aunt what?"

"She's...in the bathroom. I'm waiting for her." Hopefully that sounded reasonable.

"There's a bathroom in the ER. Why are you skulking around out here?"

"I'm not *skulking*. I told you, my brother's sick. I came out here for some fresh air." *Fresh air?* In the lobby? Where was Aunt Celeste?

"Okay, kid, you're coming with me until you decide to tell me the truth." The guard grabbed him by the sleeve and pushed him in front. "This isn't the place to goof around. People come here for help."

"Code blue, ER. Code blue, ER. Code blue, ER," came a voice from the speaker system.

Argus froze. Tai! He shoved the guard out of the way and ran back toward the ER. At the double doors, he turned and saw the guard slide across the polished white floor and slam into the far wall. He wasn't moving. But there was no time to worry about the guard, he had to get to Tai.

Chapter 19

Max looked out the motel room window as the sun completely descended beneath the horizon and plunged Palmdale into darkness. Even though his memory was spotty, he remembered being suspicious of the kid, Argus.

He logged into the school's academic records, which was surprisingly easy as a sub, and found Argus's home address. Damn, the address wasn't on any map. It simply didn't exist. Hmmm, a bogus address? If it was, then that meant the boys' aunt must have lied on the paperwork. But why? What was she hiding?

Tomorrow he'd tail them and find out where they really lived. Then it'd simply be a matter of timing to get into the house when they weren't home. He'd find the hard evidence Stone wanted.

He opened the door and stepped outside. It was cooler, but still too warm for his liking. His phone vibrated in his pocket. He looked at the caller ID, not a number he recognized, but it had a Palmdale area code. "Hello?"

"Mr. Jackson?"

"Yes, this is he."

"This is Hector Chavez, the principal at Highland High. As you must know, we have a zero-tolerance policy for bullying at Highland, so I'm personally calling our teachers, and the subs of course, to let you all know that there's been an incident with one of the students."

"Oh, really? What's happened?" Max wasn't particularly interested, but he had to make it sound like he was to avoid suspicion.

"One of our seniors, Justin Jones, has received severe burns to both hands. At first he claimed he burned his own hand, but he recanted and now he's saying two new students, the Dachel brothers, did it. Argus Dachel is in one of the classes you're subbing. Anyway, we're having a staff meeting in the morning before school starts to address this sort of violence. 6:45."

"Ah, yeah, okay. I'll be there." Max let out a whoop of joy when he hung up. So, the Dachel brothers were involved in a fight that injured another kid. Interesting. Argus had seemed like a good kid, but he must have a darker side. Everything kept pointing to that family. He whooped again.

A couple going into their motel room stared at him, muttering about how rude it was to shout. Max didn't care. For heaven's sake, it wasn't late or anything. He went back inside, enjoying the chill from the air conditioning, and review his files on his laptop. He'd researched the city of Palmdale for the past fifty years, so he'd have a little background history. Most of the information was unreliable, coming from kooks claiming they saw strange lights in the sky, abduction tales, the usual. However, one story stuck out.

About twenty-five years ago, a miner working a small claim in the desert said he saw a weird bluish glow over Palmdale. Of course, Palmdale was smaller then, not as sprawling as it was now, but the glow stayed over the city for about 24 hours, causing blackouts, then dissipated. AURA had noticed an increase in energy readings around Palmdale at the exact same time. Back then, AURA didn't draw any conclusions, but now, it was obvious to Max that there was a correlation between the glow and the increased energy. He was definitely in the right place.

He jumped when someone knocked on his door. Oh, what now, was he in trouble for shouting after sunset? He closed the laptop and opened the door. Two men in Air Force uniforms stood outside. They were the same height and build, both with short-cropped hair and serious faces. They looked almost like clones.

"Can I help you gentlemen?" Max tried to sound as casual as he could.

"Are you Max Jackson?" the one on the left asked.

"Yes."

"We're here on official business from Edwards Air Force Base. You're an AURA agent, correct?" the one of the right asked this time.

"Yes. What's this about?" Max wanted to slam the door on them, but Stone would probably throw a fit because he didn't exercise professional courtesy.

The one on the right took a step forward. "Making contact, sir. You're in our jurisdiction. I'm Lieutenant John Franklin."

"Jurisdiction? I'm here on an intel gathering mission. This isn't a jurisdictional issue." Max put his hand on the door, ready to shut it.

Franklin positioned himself in the doorway. "Exactly what intel are you gathering, sir?"

"That's none of your business." Max closed the door a little, but Franklin was in the way.

"Personally, sir, we think of AURA as a joke, but we were given orders to investigate."

"Investigate? Me?" Max groaned. It had to be Stone's doing. Why couldn't he leave well enough alone? "There's nothing to investigate. I'm looking into energy surges, that's all."

Franklin glanced behind him at his cohort and turned back with a smirk. "Energy surges? You are aware, aren't you, sir, that there are nearby wind turbine farms and solar energy collecting stations right outside city limits? Those, sir, are your energy spikes."

"Maybe so," Max started, "But I have to collect data." No point telling the truth when a well-worded lie would do. "That's all I do. Collect data and compile it, go back to the office, and make a pretty graph for my boss. That's it."

Taking a step back, Franklin nodded. "Sounds dull as hell, sir."

"It is. It really is. So, is there anything else you gentlemen need?"

Franklin nudged his buddy. "A drink. You know a bar around here?"

A drink sounded good. It would also be an excellent opportunity to find out what the guys knew. "Yeah, I think I passed by a bar not too far from here. Mind if I tag along?" Making friends with the Air Force was a good strategy that would hopefully pay off. Max got his car keys off the desk.

Franklin and his buddy stood aside. "Lead the way, sir."

Max drove his car with the Air Force guys pacing him in their plain white military pool car. He pulled into the *Desert Rose Bar*, not exactly a high-quality place. Half of the sign's lights were burned out and the front door's paint was peeling. Didn't matter, booze was booze. With any luck, the guys would get loose-lipped after a couple of drinks and spill what they knew about the mysterious happenings around Palmdale. Max smiled as he walked into the dingy bar. He'd soon have reliable information to report to Stone.

After settling onto a barstool, Max turned to his new friends. "First drink's on me."

Chapter 20

Argus was almost to the ER double doors when he was grabbed from behind and thrown off balance, making him fall against the doors. It was another security guard, a bigger man holding a wooden baton in his left hand.

"Hold it right there!" he yelled, pointing the baton at Argus.

Recovering, Argus considered ignoring the guard, but knew he wouldn't get far. Where was Aunt Celeste? He gave her permission to use telepathy. Unless she was too far away. Hadn't she said she needs to be close?

He pointed to the doors. "I have to check on my brother. He's in the ER. Please."

The guard shook his head. "You're not going anywhere. You committed assault. I'm placing you under arrest." He reached around the back of his belt and unclipped a pair of handcuffs.

This couldn't be happening. Argus backed up until he bumped against the doors, but they didn't open. He glanced at the button on the wall. There was no way to press it without the guard stopping him.

"Don't make a scene, kid." The guard approached, grabbed Argus's right hand, and clamped one of the handcuffs around his wrist.

The metal was cold, and the guard had put it on too tight. Instinctively, Argus pulled away and reached with his free hand toward the door button. He was only a few inches away when the guard tugged on the handcuffed hand and brought him to the ground.

"Argus!" shouted Aunt Celeste, running through the lobby. "Get your hands off him!"

The guard spun around, keeping his grip on Argus. "Get back, lady!"

"Release him now," her voice was controlled, firm, angry. Her eyes were bright.

"Aunt Celeste!" Argus pulled again, careful not to use all his strength, but was held tight. He wasn't going anywhere. "I heard them announce code blue in the ER. Is Tai okay?"

She looked toward the double doors, then back at the guard. "This is unacceptable. I heard the announcement, too. It is Tai." She waved her hand, and the handcuffs broke in pieces, freeing Argus.

He pushed the button and opened the doors. He didn't bother to look back. Aunt Celeste would handle things. He ran straight to Tai's room, but couldn't get in. The room was crowded with doctors and nurses, carts on wheels with monitoring machines and a defibrillator. He knew what a defibrillator was from television. And it meant that Tai's heart had stopped.

The doctor held the paddles above Tai. "Again," he said harshly.

The paddles were depressed against Tai's bare chest and a moment later, his body arched as the electricity shot through his heart. Argus watched as the doctor handed the paddles to a nurse and checked the monitor. The line was still flat.

"You can't be in here," said a young man in scrubs. "You can wait outside."

Argus had no intention of leaving. His place was with Tai. "I'm his brother. He needs me." He felt tingly all over. He looked into the young man's eyes. "Please, he needs me."

The young man slowly nodded and moved aside. Argus came into the room. That was easy enough. Tai was pale and still. The heart monitor line was still flat. Tai was dead. How could that be? He was alive a few minutes ago. No, he couldn't be dead. He couldn't!

Argus pushed in between two nurses and stared down at Tai. "You're not dead, Tai. You can't be. Wake up. Wake up now!"

"Excuse me," one of the nurses said. "You can't...whoa, what's going on? Why are your eyes like that? Are you all right? Doctor."

What was she talking about and why was she staring at him? Argus looked around. Everyone was staring at him, including the doctor. "Stop looking at me and help my brother."

The doctor stared for a few more seconds, then got back to the defibrillator and pressed the paddles to Tai's chest again. Still no change in the monitor. Argus wanted to scream and throw something, anything. Tai couldn't be dead. That was his brother, lying there, without life.

"Argus, stand aside." It was Aunt Celeste.

She placed her hand on his shoulder and guided him a few steps to the side. He didn't want to leave Tai even though there wasn't anything he could do, but he trusted Aunt Celeste. She could fix him. She had to. Right behind her was the tall woman from the Citadel. The woman strode past them and went to the bedside.

The doctor didn't seem to notice her. He glanced up at the clock. "Time of death—"

"He's not dead," the tall woman said like it was a command. "Your monitors are malfunctioning."

Now the doctor noticed her. "Who are you?"

"I'm his private physician." She took out a syringe from a small leather bag hooked to her belt. "It's an allergic reaction. He needs this."

"You're not injecting anything..." the doctor objected, but when the woman's eyes brightened like Aunt Celeste's, he backed away without another word.

The woman pulled a cap off the end of the syringe, squirted a trace of liquid into the air and plunged the needle into Tai's chest. She placed her hand over his forehead and closed her eyes. Argus watched the clock tick the seconds away; ten, twenty, thirty seconds. Everyone in the room was quiet, not objecting, not moving. It was eerie, like he was watching a weird movie.

Then there was a beep, followed by another and another. He couldn't believe it, the flat line on the cardiac monitor fell into a regular rhythm.

Tai was alive. Argus let out a relieved breath. Whatever the woman injected into Tai brought him back to life. She removed her hand and opened her eyes. How had she done that? Not only did she help Tai, but she obviously had power over everyone. The doctor and nurses all stood around the bed, staring into the distance, appearing like they were waiting for instructions.

The woman stared right at Argus. "Argus, I presume," she said in a silky voice. Her eyes dimmed to a normal blue, darker than Aunt Celeste's.

He nodded, about all he could manage at the moment. Aunt Celeste was near the doorway, quiet and solemn. Was she in trouble? It looked like it by the way her head was drooped down slightly. Argus swallowed. Uh-oh, that couldn't be good.

The woman continued, "Argus, none of this is your fault. Your brother will recover shortly. I understand from Guardian Apodaca that you understand your true heritage. That's good. It's something that should have been disclosed many years ago." She shot Aunt Celeste a harsh look. "Are you and your brother in the habit of disobeying your Guardian?"

Argus shook his head and cleared his throat. "No, ma'am. I mean, we'd never do anything to...well, we did, but I mean..." He glanced at Tai to make sure he was still breathing, which he was. His color was back, too and his hand twitched. "How did you bring him back?"

She smiled. "There is much I can do. You too, apparently." She tilted her head. "Your eyes. I've only seen that on two other occasions."

Argus touched his eyelids. What did she mean? "I don't understand." There was nothing wrong with his eyes.

From the same leather bag that held the syringe, she took out a small mirror and handed it to him. "Look for yourself."

He peered in the mirror and gasped. His eyes, normally hazel, were black. Completely black. What the hell? He could see through them as clear as ever, but there was nothing there except black.

"Guardian, take Argus into a private room until his eyes revert back to normal while I stay with Tai."

Aunt Celeste nodded and motioned for Argus to follow. He really didn't want to leave Tai, but when Aunt Celeste motioned again, he gave in and followed her down the corridor into an empty room. What was happening?

As soon as the door closed, he blurted, "Aunt Celeste, what's going on? What did she do to Tai and what's wrong with my eyes?"

"Calm down. Galena is a pure-form with special qualities. She can bring New Breeds back to life if they were deceased for no longer than about five minutes, but only..." Her face darkened.

"But only what?"

"Only by altering...do you really want to know, Argus?" Aunt Celeste paced around the room.

He hesitated. What the hell did the woman, Galena, alter? He couldn't stop his body from trembling from too much adrenaline, like he'd run marathon or something. "Of course I do. Is Tai going to be okay?"

"You need to calm down, Argus. And yes, Tai's recovering. Galena uses an enzyme tracer to locate the human DNA nucleotides in the cells. Once the nucleotides are identified, she...alters some of them." She placed her hand on Argus's shoulder.

He took a few deep breaths. "What do you mean by alters? Did she do something to Tai?" Argus slumped into a chair. "What did she do to my brother?"

Aunt Celeste's expression softened. "He's still your brother, Argus, except now he has approximately three quarters Ramtalan DNA. It was the only way to save him."

What? How could that be? You can't change someone's DNA. Well, humans can't. But Galena is a pure-form, like Aunt Celeste said.

"Okay, but how did she do it? Was the enzyme in the syringe?" He thought about the biology lessons Aunt Celeste gave them. She'd taught them about genetics. "How did she recombine Tai's DNA with Ramtalan DNA? I don't see how she could do that without extracting it from the cells and then—"

"Galena is the only Settler with healing qualities like that. Her touch transmits healing, whether it's by altering the genetics, as in this case, or by repairing organs, cuts, broken bones. It was fortuitous that she was nearby. Very fortuitous." Aunt Celeste had an expression like she wasn't so sure it was luck that Galena happened to be close. "Argus, Galena wants both of you to stay at the Citadel. She's insistent."

Argus held up the hand mirror and checked his eyes again. They were changing, not quite all black. "I don't want to go anywhere. What's wrong with my eyes? Am I sick? Is this what happens to all of the New Breeds? Am I dying?" He could hardly breathe. He didn't want to die.

"Not at all." She pulled up a chair and sat in front of him. "You and Tai are still developing your qualities. Each generation develops abilities at different rates and like with any type of evolution, there are mutations. The other New Breeds of your generation never had the chance to develop theirs fully, so we've not been sure what the potential is. Until now. We've seen the black eye color change several times before over the past few thousand years." She paused and took his hand in hers. "You're what's known as a protector.

You have an instinctual need to protect those close to you. The eye color change means your ability to protect is accelerating."

He withdrew his hand. "That's BS, Aunt Celeste. I couldn't protect Tai. He died. His heart stopped and I didn't do a thing to help. I don't have any ability to do anything."

"Perhaps not right now, but soon."

He shook his head. "I don't believe that. Not for a second." He leaned forward.

"Argus, you're already exhibiting the trait. When your ability to protect takes over, your eyes change color. Similar to when I, or Galena, exercise our abilities. Did you see Galena's eyes change when she seized control of the humans in Tai's room? That's because she tapped into her energy source to apply, ah, mind control."

"Mind control? That's what you did to Justin in the principal's office. Wait, so I can tap into my energy source?" He tried to absorb it all. Aliens, mind control, telepathy, black eyes.

"No, not quite. You're half human, you don't have the same energy source that pure-forms do. Your ability is genetic, passed down by your parents. Or in your case, by your mother. She must have had powerful abilities that we didn't know about and now you're developing them. It's quite extraordinary, Argus."

Extraordinary? It wasn't extraordinary. He really was a freak. Freaks weren't extraordinary, they were just freaks. "Are you sure I'm not dreaming all of this? Yesterday I was a normal teenager who couldn't wait to attend school and now I'm a half-alien with eyes that turn black."

"You're still a teenager."

"Yeah, but not a normal one." He jumped up when he remembered the security guard. "Oh, shit!"

"Watch your language, Argus."

"Sorry, but I hurt a security guard. Did you see him in the lobby? I shoved him. That's why that other guard tried to arrest me."

"Galena took care of it. You must learn to regulate your strength. That guard had a concussion, two cracked ribs, and a broken wrist. Your protective instincts will overpower your reason at first. As your ability increases, you're going to have to practice control, or you'll do a lot worse than break a few bones."

Argus sat back down. He could have killed the guard. "How can I control it? I don't even know how to control my other abilities."

"I'll help you. But for now, we need to concentrate on Tai...and Galena. It's too much of a coincidence that she happened to be right here when I needed her. If she insists on bringing you two in, there's nothing I can do. Your mother was adamant that you be brought up as humans. She never wanted the Citadel to interfere. In fact, she lodged a formal complaint to the Ramtalan Council when the commander at the Citadel first refused to allow her to marry your father. I delivered the complaint and made a plea on her behalf. They agreed, but only after your father went through a complete screening performed by Galena herself." She sighed. "Your mother was never one to give up. So, as your Guardian, I will do everything within my power to uphold her wish that you stay in human society. I'm on your side, Argus."

Deep down he knew she was. She'd always given them everything they needed. He looked at his hands, turning them over and over. On the outside, he looked like a human. "You know, at first I was excited when you told us we were New Breeds, but now, I'm not so sure. I can hurt people. I've already hurt Justin and now a security guard. What if Lola finds out? I really like her. She's great. Funny and smart. But if she finds out I'm half-alien, she'll probably hate me. And what if I accidentally hurt her?"

Aunt Celeste got up. "If she's as nice as you say, she'll understand. And you're a Protector, you won't hurt her. Perhaps you're attracted to her because you have a need to protect her. But, Argus, you are not to disclose your true identity to her. It's dangerous. AURA is actively seeking us out. We mustn't let them find anything significant. I can only do so much to confuse Max."

"What about Galena? Can't she stop him?" Argus wanted Max out of the way. Permanently.

Aunt Celeste shook her head. "Argus, I'm still hearing your thoughts. Don't let Max cloud your reasoning. I will deal with him. Harming him will only make AURA more suspicious."

"Okay. So what about Galena? Isn't there anything she can do to get him off our trail?"

"She won't step in unless he actually attempts to capture you. Galena would prefer to take you and Tai to the Citadel rather than deal with AURA. I don't know what she's up to, so we must be very careful to keep Max at arm's length. I don't want to give her any reason to take you away." She let out a long breath. "Perhaps I shouldn't say that. After all, she did save Tai. She exchanged Tai's blood samples before tests were run and she's controlling the lab techs, the doctor and nurses, and the security guards. And I took care of the pharmacist so he wouldn't issue any drugs that would interfere with Galena's healing."

Argus watched Aunt Celeste. She seemed worried. She didn't trust Galena. "So, Aunt Celeste, how do you control someone's mind? Can I do it?"

She shook her head. "No, I don't think any New Breed has the capacity to use a technique like that. Pure-forms can implant memories, exchange memory or muddle memory, and of course seize control of a human's mind temporarily. It's complicated and not all pure-forms can perfect the technique. Galena is more advanced and skilled in this than I am."

Wow, someone with better abilities than Aunt Celeste. That was hard to imagine, considering the things she was able to do. He looked in the mirror again. Finally, his eyes were hazel again. So he was a protector. That did explain why he felt like Lola's white knight.

It was still hard to imagine that there were aliens, pure-forms, living on Earth. Other than the abilities and the weird glowing eyes, they didn't look any different. He closed his eyes and imagined what it would be like to go to Ramtala and see how the pure-forms live and what they did every day. Did they work at regular jobs, live in houses, have cars? Were there teenagers who didn't fit in with the rest of society? He'd always wondered if there was life on other planets, now he knew.

"It is *very* different on Ramtala, Argus. No cars or freeways and our homes are underground. And teaching is done through implanted thoughts from the parents, no schools." She sighed. "I do miss it, although I love it here on Earth."

Oh, yeah, the mind reading thing. Argus opened his eyes. "Um, can you stop with the telepathy now? I want to keep my thoughts to myself. Hey, why can't Galena fix the genetic problem back on Ramtala so pure-forms can reproduce? If she can alter genes, then why..."

Aunt Celeste brought her ponytail over her shoulder and ran her fingers through it. "It's far more complicated than replacing a few human nucleotides. Human DNA is easily replaced, but Ramtalan DNA is...difficult to handle. There are defective genes in pure-form DNA that if replaced, removed, or altered, kill the Ramtalan. We've tried, Argus, for more than fifty thousand years. Galena still experiments when she can...with volunteers."

Volunteers? Wow, Ramtalans volunteered for experimentation. That must take a lot of guts. Or maybe it was desperation. Would he be that brave? Probably not. Of course, he wasn't given the choice if he wanted to be part of an experiment. "Fifty thousand years of failed experiments? That really sucks. I don't want to think about this anymore. Can we go back to Tai?"

She peered at him. "Since your eyes are back to normal again, we can go." She got up and opened the door, motioning for him to follow her. "But try to stay calm so it doesn't happen again."

Was she kidding? It wasn't like he did it on purpose. He nodded and followed her to the room. Tai was sitting up, leaning against a couple of pillows, looking pale and weak, but he was alive. Argus smiled. His brother was alive. Galena sat on a stool by the bedside, her mouth in a serious flat line and her eyes not blinking. The doctor and nurses were still standing to one side, saying nothing. Argus watched them. They could have been wax figures except they were breathing and blinking their eyes. It was weird, really weird.

Tai waved, jangling the IV tubing coming from his arm. "Hey, bro. I feel like crap. But for a dead guy, I guess I shouldn't complain."

Argus glanced at Galena and went to Tai. "So you know what happened?"

Tai nodded. "Yeah. I'm really sorry, Aunt Celeste. I shouldn't have gone into the desert. I like to get away by myself once in a while. It's peaceful in the desert."

With a smile that looked forced, Aunt Celeste looked quickly to Galena. "It is peaceful, but you are never to leave the house without my authorization."

Galena stood. "Guardian, Tai Dachel is under my personal protection now. His care is under my jurisdiction from here on."

The smile on Aunt Celeste's lips dropped. "I am Guardian for both boys." Her eyes lit up.

Mirroring Aunt Celeste's eyes, Galena's shone bright. Argus backed away. What was happening? Galena placed her hand on Tai's shoulder. "He is under my protection, Guardian 647. I will permit him to continue to reside with his brother since it was his mother's wish, but should there be one more incident involving either of them, I will return and bring them both in. And you will return to Ramtala. I have authorization from the Commander."

Whoa. Argus didn't like the sound of that. He wasn't going anywhere with Galena, no matter what she said. Who the hell was she to say what would happen? He went back to Tai's bedside.

Aunt Celeste's eyes dimmed to their normal pale blue. "Understood." She turned and strode from the room.

Argus didn't know what to do or where to go. Should he follow her or stay with Galena and Tai? Galena had a cold, almost detached expression. It wasn't fair of her to humiliate Aunt Celeste like she did. It wasn't Aunt Celeste's fault that Tai left and got bitten by a snake. Tai chose to dissolve and go into the desert. It was his fault.

Argus looked into the hallway, but Aunt Celeste was gone. Galena went over to the doctor and nurses, stood in front of each one for a moment and came back to the bed.

Her expression hadn't changed. "Boys, I cannot allow either of you to come to any harm. You are too important to our race. I respected your mother and will honor her wish that you lead as normal a life as possible, however, should there be danger, I will know, and I will come for you. Celeste is a good Guardian, an excellent Guardian in fact, but if you continue to disobey her, not only will you relinquish your place among the humans, but she will too. I cannot take you from your Guardian without good cause, so don't give my cause to do so. Enjoy your lives...carefully. I must return to the Citadel now."

"Wait," Tai leaned forward so he was off the pillows. "You said you made me stronger so my body could fight the snake venom. What did you do? I don't feel any stronger."

Argus sneaked a look at Galena and noticed a slight frown. She hadn't told him the truth. Didn't she want to tell him? Or maybe she wasn't supposed to rearrange his genetic makeup. Tai deserved to know.

She touched Tai again on the shoulder. "I gave your immune system a boost. It's not important." She glared at Argus.

Why was she staring? A warning maybe to not tell Tai the truth about his new DNA. But why not? Argus sighed. He didn't like keeping secrets from Tai, it wasn't right. He turned away from Galena. "I'm glad you're better, Tai. You scared the shi...heck out of me. Um, Galena, what's going to happen to them?" He pointed at the doctor and nurses.

"Once I leave, they'll reanimate and will believe the doctor successfully resuscitated Tai. Go along with it or it'll cause them undue stress. It was a pleasure meeting both of you." She smiled and nodded to each of them. "Make Ramtala proud, do well in school. We'll meet again." Her smile got broader. She strode out of the room without looking back.

Argus stood in the doorway and peered out. She was gone, but Aunt Celeste came down the corridor. She brushed past him and looked around the room.

"Argus, stay where you are and look concerned. Don't move too much. Tai, lie down. We don't want them to notice any time lapse."

"But the clock." Argus pointed to the clock on the wall. "The doctor was looking at it when he called the time of death...um, he knew what time it was."

With a wave of her hand, the clock hands went back about 15 minutes. "Follow my lead. They'll animate any second now."

Argus waited by the door and sure enough, the doctor drew in a breath and blinked, as if he'd woken up from a nap. The nurses did the same. It was like watching a weird science fiction movie.

Aunt Celeste put on a smile. "Thank you, doctor, for saving my nephew's life."

The doctor walked to the bed. "Oh, ah, yes." His eyes went to the defibrillator on the cart and then to the clock. "Mark the time of resuscitation at 1827."

One of the nurses jotted down the time in the chart, checked the IV and wrote a few more notes. Argus caught Tai's eye. Was he any different now that his DNA was altered? He had the same face and eyes and hair. Tai smirked and rolled his eyes. Yep, he was still the same Tai, nothing could change that.

After the doctor checked Tai and told Aunt Celeste that they would keep him overnight, he excused himself. The nurses messed around with the IV, packed away the defibrillator, and said Tai would be taken to a room as soon as one was ready.

Once alone, Tai let out a breath of air. "Overnight? I don't want to stay here."

"It's only one night." Aunt Celeste sat on the edge of the bed. "I'll stay with you. Argus, will you be all right at home by yourself?"

By himself? He'd never stayed home alone. Of course he'd be all right. He was almost eighteen, practically an adult. "Sure."

"Good. Keep your phone on you at all times. Drive the car home. I trust you because you did a reasonable job before. Don't draw any attention to yourself since you only have a permit. I don't want to have to come to the police station."

"Yes, ma'am." His heart raced at the thought of driving home to an empty house. He could watch TV all night, play video games, anything. Maybe even have Dave over. Or Lola. Would she want to come over?

She handed him the key fob. "Be careful. Text me as soon as you get home. Lock all of the doors and set the security alarm. You have school in the morning, so get to bed before...eleven."

"Yes, ma'am. Tai, let me know if you get a cute nurse to sponge bathe you." Argus raised an eyebrow.

Tai laughed. "My luck I'll get a dude."

Aunt Celeste got off the bed. "All right, that's enough. Argus, straight home." She escorted him to the door. "I mean it."

"I will. Don't worry. I'll be fine. Nothing's going to happen." He gave Tai a chin jut and headed out to the parking lot.

It felt strange sitting behind the wheel with no one else in the car. Strange, but liberating. This had to be the freedom normal teenagers felt. He liked it. He drove out of the parking lot, down the hill to the main road and accelerated. He wound the windows down and turned up the radio, and sped up a bit over the speed limit because there weren't any cops around and

Aunt Celeste would never know. He stopped at a traffic light, but instead of turning onto City Ranch Road, he made a right turn. *Marco's Pizza* was only a couple blocks away and he could use a soda and maybe some breadsticks. It wasn't really disobeying Aunt Celeste because he'd go right home after he ate. He'd be extra careful not to draw anyone's attention. It was only a small detour.

Chapter 21

With an alcohol-induced fog settling over him, Max ordered another pitcher of beer for his new Air Force friends, John Franklin, and Angel Flores. They were stand-up guys, but it sure was taking a long time, and a lot of beers, to get them drunk.

Angel excused himself and went to the bathroom while John poured another mug of beer. It was hard to tell in the poor lighting, but it sure looked like John's eyes were getting glassy.

"So, John," Max started, "How long you been at Edwards?"

John held up his hand to say *hold on* while he downed the entire mug of beer. He licked his lips. "About three years."

"You like it out there in the desert?"

John shrugged and stared into his empty mug. "Yeah, I guess. The stories are...enter...enter...taining."

"Oh? What stories?" Max filled John's empty mug.

"You know." He leaned forward on his elbows. "Aliens," he whispered.

"Really? Aliens? I haven't heard any stories about aliens."

John let out a chuckle. "You've missed out then, man. I guess aliens must like the desert or something. Area 51 is in the desert outside of Las Vegas, did you know that? And Roswell, too, I think, but that's in Mexico...New Mexico. But we've got our own...um, our own..." he paused and seemed to be searching for the word.

"Aliens?" Max offered.

John slapped his hand on the table. "Yeah! Aliens." He lowered his voice and leaned across the table, "We caught one once."

"What? When? Where?" Max couldn't believe what he heard. Why didn't AURA know about this?

"About fifty...sixty...no, fifty some-odd years ago. I think." John leaned back when Angel returned and plopped down in his seat. "I was telling Ma...Man..."

Max smiled. Finally, John was drunk. "Ah, Max."

"Sure! Max. Angel, I was telling Max about the alien at Edwards." John closed his eyes for a moment and swayed slightly.

With a raised eyebrow, Angel stared at his friend. "Why'd you tell him that? It's a secret, stupid."

"Oh, yeah. But he's with the government, too." John slugged back some more beer.

Max knew he'd better say something to keep them talking. "I already know about the alien. I'm sure I don't have as much information as the Air Force though. But your superiors probably didn't tell you anything else, you know, you two not being high echelon."

"We know more than you think," Angel said with a smirk. "Like how the alien could use his mind to control people and to disappear."

This was fabulous. Well worth the cost of three pitchers of beer. Max turned all his attention to Angel because John had passed out with his head on the table. "What happened to the alien? Do they still have him?"

Angel shook his head. "Nah. They locked him up and tried to keep him doped up so he couldn't use his mind control and when they had him prepped for brain surgery, he snapped out of it and killed them all. Nobody's seen him since. Creepy." He shivered.

"No shit. Here, you might as well finish the beer. Doesn't look like John's having any more." Max poured the rest of the pitcher into Angel's mug and waited while he drank half. "You don't happen to know where I can find the data on the alien, do you? You know, for research."

"Classified." Angel drank the rest of the beer. "But I know the file name." He blinked and gave a lopsided smile. "They don't know I know but I know. You know?"

"I don't believe it. You couldn't possibly know anything about the file."

"I do. It's Jared XTRA 1963. Ha, see? Told you I know it." Angel put the empty pitcher to his mouth and let the last few drops trickle down his throat. "You're cool, Max, for an AURA agent." He dropped the plastic pitcher onto the table, leaned back and passed out sitting up.

"I know I am. Oh, and thanks for the info, boys." Max got up, left a ten-dollar tip for the waitress and went to his car. Finally he was getting somewhere.

Now he had to find a way to hack into the Edwards database and find the Jared file. How tough could that be? He had a Secret level security clearance which would hopefully be enough to gain access into the computer system. If not, he'd work a deal with a computer hacker friend. That would be his last option, however, since they'd had a falling out several years ago. But, if necessary, he'd swallow his pride and do what was needed.

He got in his car but didn't want to go to the motel. He was hungry. Maybe he hadn't eaten before when his memory got foggy. He craved pizza: mushroom, onion, and pepperoni. Beer wasn't a meal. Not by a long shot. He drove to the only restaurant he knew in Palmdale, the pizza place *Marco's*.

Chapter 22

When Argus pulled into *Marco's* parking lot, a flash of guilt shot through him for disobeying Aunt Celeste. Again. If Galena found out, it wouldn't be good for anyone; not Aunt Celeste and certainly not for him or Tai. What was he doing? He was acting more like Tai.

He looked in the rearview mirror and saw the reflection of a seventeen year-old, a normal teenager, not a half-alien New Breed who could become invisible and appear in a girl's living room. It wasn't wrong or defiant to want to grab a slice of pizza and a Coke. He had to admit, he wasn't really all that hungry, but he wanted to *feel* normal and normal kids went to *Marco's*. If he didn't stay long, Aunt Celeste would never know.

"Okay, Argus, you drove here, so you might as well go in," he said to his reflection. He smoothed his hair and took a deep breath. "Just don't get caught and everything will be fine."

It was crowded even though it was almost seven. Most of the people were kids hanging around the video games or sitting in booths with their friends. They were having fun, all smiles and laughter. This was exactly where he wanted to be.

"Hey, Argus!"

He turned and saw Dave at the drink dispenser. "Hi, Dave." He wound his way around the tables. "You came back?"

Dave pressed his cup against the dispenser lever. "My mom's on her girls' night out with her friends from work, so she drops me off here to play video games. I'm sitting over there with a couple of my friends. Want to join us? Unless you're here with your aunt and brother."

"Nope, I came here alone." Argus smiled at the thought. He really was alone. And it felt good.

Dave stuck a straw in his drink. "Sorry, man, I forgot your brother's name."

The image of Tai lying in the hospital bed with no heartbeat popped into Argus's head. "Tai. His name's Tai."

"Didn't he want to come?"

"No, Dave, he didn't. He was bitten by a rattlesnake. He's in the hospital." Argus didn't mean to sound rude. "Sorry, but it was tense for a while."

Dave scrunched up his face. "Ah, man, no, I'm sorry. I hate snakes. Hope he's okay. Where was he when he got bit?"

"In the desert. He likes to hike in the desert. He won't be doing that for a while though. My aunt was pissed." *And so was Galena, but I can't tell you that, Dave.*

"I bet she was. My mom would have grounded me for a year if I did something like that." Dave went to a booth where two other guys were sitting. "Argus, this is Mike and Scott." He pointed to each one as he said their names. "This is Argus. He's our new quarterback."

Argus had completely forgotten about being made the quarterback. He nodded to Mike—straight shoulder length hair that was between blond and brown—and Scott, who had very short reddish hair. "Nice to meet you."

Mike smiled. "Damn, the quarterback? I tried out in the summer but couldn't hit any of the targets with the ball. I didn't see you at the try-outs."

Dave shook his head. "He wasn't. Coach Smith sort of declared him quarterback after Argus threw the ball at the goal post, hit it exactly where he said and dented the shit out of it." He laughed and sat down.

Since Mike and Scott were on the same side of the booth, Argus slid in next to Dave and picked up a menu. "I got lucky, that's all. My brother and I toss a football around at home."

"No, you're good, Argus, you're really good." Dave waved to the waitress, Sandra.

She waved back and came over. "Hi, Dave. Your mom's girl's night? Oh, hi, Argus. You're back." Her cheeks blushed pink.

"You remember my name?" Argus smiled. His stomach was fluttery. Sandra sure had a beautiful smile. Actually, all of her was beautiful. Her short hair was glossy, light brown and sort of curled under her chin. She had smooth skin with a natural glow and her hazel eyes sparkled in the light. He'd never met a girl with hazel eyes like his.

She kept smiling. "I have a good memory. So you and Dave are friends?"

Argus nodded. "We have PE and math together."

"Oh, no," she said with a roll of her eyes. "Dave, are you going to make Argus limp like you do to get out of sports?"

Scott and Mike burst out laughing. Dave frowned. He took a sip of his drink. "My ankle never healed right, Sandy, you know that. Besides, Argus is our new quarterback, he doesn't need to get out of playing sports."

"Really?" Sandra touched Argus on the sleeve. "Congratulations. The new quarterback. That's really cool. Would you like a soda? I can get you one for free."

Dave grunted. "You never get me a soda."

She shot him an angry glance and looked back at Argus. "You got Coke earlier, right?"

"Ah, yeah." Argus could see that Dave was upset or embarrassed. Did he like Sandra?

"Be right back." She tossed her head and went to the dispenser.

Dave sighed and slumped in his seat. "Okay, man, I've got to know how you do that?"

Argus shrugged. "Do what?"

"Get all the girls. I guess if I was as tall and ripped as you, and on the football team, I'd have a shot." He slumped down a little further.

So Dave did like Sandra. And Lola. He'd already admitted that. Argus folded his arms across his chest and shrunk down to look smaller. He'd never thought of himself as *ripped* or tall. He'd ever only compared himself to Tai, who was taller and better looking.

Sandra returned with a large Coke and an order of fries. "We had a basket of extra fries." She placed the fries and Coke in front of Argus. "Let me know if you want anything else. Um, I get off at nine if you maybe want to hang out or anything." She blushed, turned, and hurried to the kitchen.

When Mike and Scott excused themselves to play video games, Argus pushed the basket of fries over to Dave. "There are a lot of fries here, Dave, you'd better have some."

"I'm off at nine," Dave mocked, batting his eyes. "Sheesh, how obvious can she be?" He sat up straight and grabbed a couple of fries. "Girls."

"Are you mad at me, Dave?" Argus hoped not. He sure didn't mean to do anything wrong.

"Nah. It's Sandy who's putting it out there. How can I be mad? If I stick with you, I'll get free fries." He grinned.

After finishing the fries and his drink, Argus went with Dave to play the video games, but his cell phone vibrated before he had the chance. He looked at the incoming text message from Aunt Celeste.

Make sure all the doors are locked and the alarm is set. Tai will be discharged in the morning. Come to the hospital at seven with a change of clothes for Tai and I'll drive you both to school. Have a good night.

He really should go home. "Hey, Dave, I better get going. Can I drop you off at home?"

Dave shook his head and fed a five-dollar bill into the token machine. "Nah, my mom will come by in about an hour. You really have to leave? Come on, one game. My treat. Well, my mom's treat."

He checked his watch. It was still early. "Okay. One game won't hurt." He accepted a few tokens and dropped them into his favorite game, ironically a space alien game.

They played the one game and then another. Mike and Scott left, but Dave had to stay and wait for his mother, so Argus agreed to wait with him. Even though *Marco's* was noisy with kids laughing and music blaring from the old-fashioned jukebox, it felt great to be a part of it. He felt like a regular guy. They were on their third game and about to save Earth from the aliens when a man burst in through the front door. Argus turned in time to see him grab Sandra as she walked by.

"Give me the money in the register or the girl gets hurt!"

Chapter 23

Max was lost. He'd driven in circles for half an hour. Maybe he should call it a night. It was getting too late for pizza anyway. He'd probably end up with a raging heartburn that'd keep him up all night. He shouldn't be driving anyway after having a couple of beers. Not that he was drunk, but he had a nice buzz going.

He did a U-turn and sped off down the street toward the motel. What the heck? Straight ahead on the right was *Marco's Pizza*. How'd he miss it? Maybe he was a bit more than buzzed. Oh, well, he'd sober up after pizza and wings.

There was one parking spot left. He pulled in and stood by the car for a minute to make sure he had his footing. If someone reported him for being drunk in public, Stone would demote him to the mail room for sure. He drew in a deep breath and took a step. Yep, he was okay. He looked around. The owner of *Marco's* must be rich judging by the full lot. He walked by a black SUV and stopped. It was the same model as the SUV that almost ran him over at the walled house.

Reaching into his pocket, he took the OEED out and switched it on. Three degrees above the normal range. Yes! He jotted down the license plate and went inside. Crowded with teenagers again. Didn't they ever go home? They all stared at him, and someone yelled *watch out!* a second before an unseen assailant knocked him on the side of the head with something hard.

He stumbled and fell against the door and dropped the OEED. It only took a moment to assess the situation. A robbery in progress. The gunman held Sandra the waitress at gunpoint. Max had his service revolver in his holster on his hip, but there was no way to do anything yet. Best to wait until the robber was on his way out.

The robber shouted, "The money! Get me the money now! And if I see one person on their cell phone, I'll open fire."

"Take it easy. You don't want to hurt anyone," Max said as calmly as he could.

"Shut up. You think I'm bluffing, old man?" The robber waved the gun in the air as if to make his point.

Old man? Who was he calling old man? Max was only 45, that wasn't old. But, if the robber thought he was old, it could work to his advantage. He wouldn't expect an old to have a gun and be trained in hand-to-hand combat.

"Come on." The robber dragged Sandra through the dining room and behind the counter.

The cashier opened the register and put the money on the counter. The robber grabbed a paper bag and made Sandra scoop the money into it. He smacked the cashier with the gun and grabbed the bag.

He leaned close to Sandra as she struggled. "She's coming with me, in case any of you heroes get it in your head to try anything stupid."

"Let her go!" shouted someone from within the crowd.

"Argus, no!" Sandra screamed.

Argus? The kid from school? Max looked around but couldn't see him. This was beyond coincidence. From the floor, the OEED beeped. Where was it? Over there, under a table. *Oh, yeah, Argus, you're the one.*

"What the hell is that?" the robber yelled, peering under the table. "I said no cell phones." He raised the gun to Sandra's head.

"I said let her go." Argus appeared right in front of the robber.

Before the robber could react, Argus's brother came out of thin air, dressed in a hospital gown, and grabbed the robber's hand, twisted it, and wrestled the gun free without a single shot being fired. A hospital gown? What the hell was going on? Max watched, amazed as Argus pulled Sandra to freedom and his brother held the gunman's arms behind his back.

What had happened? How could two teenage boys disarm a gunman and rescue a hostage? And how'd they get there so fast? One moment they weren't there and the next they were. The OEED beeped like crazy. Argus turned and glared at Max. Oh, shit. The kid's eyes were black, pitch black. *Now I got you, Argus. You're mine.*

Chapter 24

Argus looked away from Max. From his expression, Argus knew his eyes must have gone black again. Now what? And why did Tai have to appear? That only made things worse. It would be impossible for Aunt Celeste to muddle everyone's minds.

"Tai," Argus whispered in the dead silence as the patrons watched, open-mouthed. "We've got to get out of here."

"You think? I'm standing here in this ridiculous hospital gown. Sorry for using shared-sight, but it's good that I did." Tai held tightly to the robber's arms. He called out, "Did anyone call the cops?"

Dave came forward, holding a cell phone in the air. "I did." He went to Argus. "What's wrong with your eyes, man? How'd your brother get here so fast? You said you were here alone. Wasn't he in the hospital? I'm confused. I mean really confused, man."

"Don't worry about it, Dave." Argus had to think of something to explain what happened. But what? How do you explain black eyes, a brother that appears out of thin air, and an OEED that was beeping out of control? The OEED!

Argus ran forward and slid under the table at the same time Max did. They collided.

"It's you, isn't it?" Max asked, his head bleeding from where the gunman hit him. He grabbed the OEED and held it out of reach. "You're an extraterrestrial. I knew it, I knew it."

"I don't know what you're talking about. That crack across your skull is making you hallucinate." Argus scooted out from under the table.

"Wait." Max scrambled out as well and blocked the way to the door. "You're not going anywhere." He smirked. "You're what I've been looking for. Your eyes...I've never seen anything like that before. You're coming with me."

143

Argus backed away. Great. How was he going to get out this? He turned to Tai, who was holding the robber. But before either of them could do anything, the door opened.

"It's a medical condition." Aunt Celeste came in, her eyes bright and her mouth in a frown. She reached out and took the OEED, dropped it on the floor and crushed it under her heel.

"That's government property...I mean, personal property. And that's no medical condition." Max sidestepped to get out of her way. "Look, we should talk."

Aunt Celeste took a step forward, letting the door close behind her. "Are you a licensed medical professional, Mr. Jackson? I thought you were a schoolteacher. It *is* a medical condition. Ocular refractive disorder. The pigmentation varies depending on stress levels. I would guess that Argus experienced a stressful situation. Am I right, Mr. Jackson?"

He nodded and narrowed his eyes. "Sure. Considering your nephews disarmed a gunman without anyone getting hurt. However, it doesn't change the fact that you destroyed my...tape recorder for no apparent reason."

"Tape recorder?" Aunt Celeste turned to Argus and shook her head. "What part of *go straight home* didn't you understand?"

"Not now, Aunt Celeste, not in front of everybody." Argus glanced at Sandra. "Are you okay, Sandra?"

She nodded and wiped away a tear. "Oh, God, thank you. I don't know...I don't...thank you."

Argus grabbed a napkin off the closest table and handed it to her. A siren grew louder and louder, then stopped outside the restaurant. There was no way to get out of *Marco's*. And now everyone, including Max, had seen the spectacle. Argus looked down at the ground so no one else would see his eyes. Was there a chance they'd believe Aunt Celeste's explanation?

Two uniformed policemen burst in, looked around and went to Tai when a dozen people pointed at him and said he had the robber. They took over and Tai received a round of applause. He bowed and grinned, obviously loving every minute of the attention. At least he had underwear on under the hospital gown. Not that he seemed to care either way.

"Tai, you'd do well to remain humble," cautioned Aunt Celeste. "Both of you, get in the car. Now."

Argus tugged on Tai's sleeve to get him moving, although he didn't want to leave. Once outside, Tai couldn't settle and kept pacing.

"Arg, I feel alive, I mean, really alive. My heart's racing. This hero stuff is fantastic. And did you see the girls? They would have come home with me if I told them to. I can have any girl I want. I'm a hero."

Argus grabbed him by the arm. "Tai, listen to yourself. You're out of control." What if the genetic alteration Galena did was changing him? "Let's wait in the car." Argus unlocked the SUV and got in the rear seat with Tai.

"You don't get it, bro. We're better than these humans. We're like superheroes." Tai drummed his hands on the back of the seat. "Your eyes are kind of freaking me out, Arg."

Argus peered in the rearview mirror. The streetlights were bright enough to let him see that his eyes were solid black. How was he supposed to control his ability? Now everyone thought he had an eye condition as well as a blood condition. He was a freakish weirdo. He sat back and held his hand over his eyes.

"You don't have to do that." Tai was settling down. He took a few deep breaths. "Oh, man, I feel exhausted. Was that the OEED that Aunt Celeste smashed?"

Argus nodded, keeping his hand covering his eyes. "Yeah. I don't know how we're going to get out of this."

"Hey, I know I said sorry for using shared-sight but let me say it again. Sorry. I didn't mean to spy on you. I was bored in the hospital. I know that's no excuse, but I was jealous that you got to go home."

"Don't worry about it. You dissolved at the hospital, in front of Aunt Celeste. That takes balls, Tai." It really did, especially when he was recovering from a snake bite and had his DNA altered.

Tai laughed for a second, then turned serious. "Maybe, but I bet we're about to get grounded by a pure-form Ramtalan for me being so ballsy."

There was no doubt they were in trouble. Argus watched the door, but Aunt Celeste didn't come out. "What do you think she's doing in there? Mind-controlling everyone?" Could she do that? Galena had controlled a lot of people in the hospital, but Aunt Celeste said Galena had better abilities.

Tai shrugged. "Who knows." He closed his eyes.

"Tai, what did Galena tell you about what she did in the hospital?"

He shrugged again, but kept his eyes closed. "That she's some sort of healer Ramtalan. Oh, and that's she's my Guardian now. I don't know what that really means because we're still with Aunt Celeste. Galena's very...intense."

"Yeah, she is. Um, do you feel any different? I mean, from Galena's healing." Argus wasn't sure what being more alien would feel like. Maybe there wasn't any difference. What if there was? Tai already had feelings that he was better than humans. What if the Ramtalan DNA made those feelings even worse?

Tai opened his eyes and stared at Argus. "Hey, bro, your eyes are back to normal. Aunt Celeste said your ability makes your eyes change color. And no, I don't feel any different. Should I?"

Aunt Celeste came to the car, her body stiff and her lips pressed together. She wasn't happy. It didn't take a genius to figure that out. She climbed in and held her hand out for the key fob. Argus dropped them into her palm and put his seatbelt on. Even without her saying anything, he felt like a scolded child. She always made him feel like that and he was getting sick of it. He was almost eighteen.

The only thing he'd done wrong was go to *Marco's* instead of home, but that turned out to be a good thing. He'd saved Sandra and Tai stopped a dangerous robber. They were heroes, like Tai said. Aunt Celeste was overreacting. Everything could be explained by convincing the people that they were in shock and saw things that didn't really happen, like Tai appearing out of nowhere. Tense situations always caused people to be confused about events. At least that's what he'd heard.

When they were almost home, Tai leaned forward. "Aunt Celeste, did you mind-zap everyone? Are we in the clear?"

She pulled to the side of the road and turned around. "I don't *mind-zap* people. And I cannot muddle memories of that large a group. I did my best to do damage control, but I'm sure Max didn't believe a word I said. No more school for either of you." She accelerated, skidding in the soft sandy-dirt on the shoulder.

Argus flinched. It was like a punch to his stomach. No more school? That meant no more Lola, no more football, no more freedom. They were heroes. Everyone at school would hear about what they did at *Marco's*. He slumped in the seat. She'd messed with Max's mind before, so it should be no big deal to do it again. Was this really the first and last day of high school? No, it couldn't be. He'd have to do something to convince her that everything would be all right.

Chapter 25

After talking to the cops and rescuing the remains of his OEED from a maintenance guy at *Marco's*, Max went to his motel room and booted up his computer. No more Mr. Nice Guy. He was onto something and no matter what spin Celeste Whoever put on the situation, he knew better. Argus wasn't a regular student at Highland High and he sure as hell didn't have an eye condition. No high school kid acted the way he did, and no high school kid could make the OEED spike like it did. The brother had to be investigated as well. Max smiled. It looked like he'd fallen into a nest of aliens.

He got into the secure military database and did a preliminary search for Jared XTRA 1963. Nothing. Not surprising, but it would have been nice to get at least one hit. Next, he tried logging in under his Secret security clearance. Two hits this time.

He clicked on the first link and waited as a photo downloaded onto his screen. It was from a military newspaper and showed an Air Force general standing in front of an airplane hangar with a tall man—white hair, wearing a lab coat. There was a short article below the photo.

> *General Jared Daniels, retiring after 35 years in the Air Force, attended the unveiling ceremony of the XTRA-A1 Super Stealth Bomber, accompanied by civilian aerospace engineer Dr. Argustine Lenox. Lenox, well known among military personnel for his advanced technological developments in war craft, made a brief speech proclaiming the XTRA-A1 to be decades ahead of its time.*

Max closed the article and clicked on the next link. Another photo with only a caption. The photo was of the man wearing the lab coat in the previous photo. He was handcuffed and being led to a military police Jeep. The caption read simply:

Dr. A. Lenox, arrested for espionage and sentenced to life in prison.

There were no more articles. What had happened to Lenox? And what did General Daniels have to do with...wait a second. Max went back to the first article. Dr. *Argus*tine Lenox. Argus.

"Whoa. There's the connection I was looking for." He jumped up and pumped the air with his fist. "Yes!" There had to be some sort of link between Argus Dachel and Argustine Lenox.

Thank you, John Franklin and Angel Flores for your drunken blabbing. But this was only the tip of the iceberg, or maybe tip of the alien iceberg was more appropriate. There was more information, he could feel it. It was time to call in a favor with his hacker friend.

He dialed the number and waited. And waited.

On the thirteenth ring, Gretchen Manheim answered, "What?"

"Gretch, it's Max. Max Jackson."

"Max Jackass? Why would you call me at this hour? Scratch that. Why would you call me at all?"

"As charming as ever, Gretch. I need a favor."

"No. I don't work for AURA anymore. Not since they busted me for hacking into the retirement fund and fattening my account, which I deserved for all the hard work I've done over the years."

Max had to get on her good side. He needed her. "You're a civilian. You didn't have any right to the retirement...water under the bridge, Gretch. I kept you out of jail. Don't you remember that?"

"Sure, but I also remember you stood before the judge and said I should pay a fine instead. A forty thousand dollar fine, Max. And now I'm supposed to repay the *favor.*"

Whoops, she was still pissed about that. "That was the only way to keep you out of jail. The judge wasn't going to let you go without any punishment. So, yes, I need your help getting into the Top-Secret files at Edwards."

She laughed. "What, so I can get caught and go to jail this time? No thanks."

"Gretch, listen. I'm on to something, something big, but I can't pull any more data on a particular file. I've only got a Secret clearance. I need you." That should stroke her ego.

Silence. Footsteps, the faint sound of a refrigerator opening and footsteps coming back. Silence again.

"Gretchen?"

A long, drawn-out sigh and the unmistakable pop of a can opening. "Fine, give me the information."

Max provided her with the file name, General Daniels, and Argustine Lenox's names, and asked her as nicely as he could to contact him as soon as she had anything. She grunted and hung up, which for Gretchen was her agreeing. With that task handled, all he had to do was wait. Oh, and prepare for the next school day.

If Argus Dachel had anything to do with Argustine Lenox and if Argustine Lenox knew something about alien life, then Argus Dachel had to be seriously interrogated. *Too bad kid, but you're of interest to AURA, and me.*

Max shook the paper bag that held his broken OEED. It would be impossible to repair it at this point, not that it mattered much. He'd made sure to turn on the automatic data logger so that everything was transmitted wirelessly to his laptop as soon as it was collected. Guess Celeste Whoever didn't know that. He smiled. It seemed pretty easy to fool these aliens.

He might have to drive to LA on the weekend though and pick up one of the older prototype sensors that was in the development lab, but other than that minor inconvenience, he'd made excellent progress in only one day. Nothing was going to stand in his way now. Nothing.

Chapter 26

The rest of the trip home was awkward with nobody saying a single thing. Argus went straight to his room and sat at his desk to search for Lola on every social media account he could think of. He wanted to let her know what happened and explain about how he rescued Sandra before she heard it from the rumor mill.

If he couldn't get Aunt Celeste to lighten up, then maybe he could get her to let Lola and Dave come over. At least then he'd have his friends to talk to. It wouldn't be the same though. He'd miss the freedom most of all. That small taste of it he'd had was enough for him to crave it even more. He hadn't felt like a prisoner before because he didn't know any better. But now he did and the thought of being trapped at home was driving him crazy.

It took over an hour for him to realize that Lola evidently wasn't on any social media sites. He had to contact her and tell her everything. Well, maybe not everything. If he didn't, she might think she'd done something to make him not want to come to school anymore. He had to get a message to her.

He lay down on his bed and closed his eyes, clearing his mind of everything except Lola. Slowly, her image came to him. She was lying on her stomach on her bed, wearing cute PJs covered in pink bunnies, writing in a book, a journal. He focused on the journal, getting closer and closer.

Dear Diary,

Today was awesome! I met a new guy, Argus Dachel, who's incredibly hot and tall and has amazing eyes. He's smart and nice and I think he likes me too. He's into science, can you believe that?????? And the best part of today was when Dad was yelling at me, again, and I did something. I don't know how, but I made him fall down! I can do things with my mind! It's late, so I better get to bed. I can't wait to see Argus tomorrow. I don't know if I should tell him about my powers

or not. He might think I'm a freak. Maybe when I know him better.
I hope I dream about him tonight.

Argus smiled. She wanted to dream about him. So now he knew for sure that she liked him. He opened his eyes and gasped. He was standing at the foot of her bed. Oh, no, not again. He really had to learn to control this ability. Well, he might as well snoop around a bit. There had to be a way to communicate with her without scaring her. At least she wasn't upset about seeing an invisible force throw her father to the ground, because now she thought she had powers. That wasn't bad though, was it? Better than thinking she had a ghost in the house, or a New Breed. He walked around the room while she wrote in the diary, looking for...what? What could he use? Then he saw it. How stupid not to think of it first.

Her cell phone was sitting on her bedside table. They could talk and text every day. But he needed her number. Carefully, he picked up her phone while she wasn't looking and searched for her number. He typed it into his phone and started to put her cell back onto the table when she gasped.

"Oh, my God! I'm doing it again." She slid off the bed and reached for the phone that to her was suspended in mid-air.

He let go of the phone and it fell onto the table before she grabbed it. She picked it up and smiled. That smile of hers lit up her whole face. She was so pretty.

"I like it when you smile, Lola," he whispered.

He should get back home before Aunt Celeste noticed he was gone, but how? Last time Tai came, although that didn't exactly work out. He watched her dance around the room with her cell phone clasped in her hand. If he could materialize in one place, why not reverse the process?

When Lola finally settled down and crawled into bed with a book, he sat on the floor and closed his eyes. He thought of his bedroom, his bed, his curtains, his desk, his lamp, his computer, but nothing. Why wasn't it working? He extracted his cell phone from his pocket and texted Tai. Hopefully a text would work.

I'm stuck at Lola's. Help!

A few seconds later, a return text:

Are you freaking serious, bro? After all that happened, you pay your little girlfriend a visit??? Tell me what you want me to do.

Argus thought for a second and texted back:
You have to drive the car over here.
Tai's response:

Steal the car?!! You don't think Aunt Celeste will hear me drive away? Anyway, I can't get out. I'm under lock and key. She keeps coming to my room to make sure I'm ok. I wasn't supposed to be home until tomorrow.

Aunt Celeste wasn't taking any chances with Tai. Argus didn't blame her. She probably didn't want to give Galena any reason to get involved again.

Tai, I really need your help. Dissolve into the garage, push the car down the driveway and come here ASAP!

Tai's immediate response:
What's the address?
Damn. He didn't know the address. Last time Aunt Celeste traced his cell phone to find the house. There had to be something in Lola's room with her address on it. He looked on her desk and found an envelope with a greeting card half out of it. Lola wouldn't notice anything; she was reading her science textbook. He carefully picked up the envelope, turned it over and sliced his finger with a paper cut. Ow. Her address was on the front.

"Argus! What are you doing here?" she screamed, covering herself with a blanket.

His mind was blank. Completely blank. Why did he turn visible? How could he explain anything? He dropped the envelope on the desk. "Ah, hi, Lola." Well that was stupid. *Come on, Argus, think of something.*

"How'd you get in my house? Did my mom let you in? You can't be here, Argus. If my dad finds out..." She pulled the blanket up higher.

"Lola, I...I had to see you." Okay, that wasn't bad. "My aunt is going to keep home schooling us and I wanted to tell you in person."

"Oh." She looked toward the bedroom door. "I didn't hear you come in. Why didn't you knock?"

"I was...ah, I was...going to surprise you. Surprise. Now that I think about it, that probably wasn't a good idea. I didn't mean to scare you. I should go." Yes, he should. And now, before her parents heard him.

"Yeah, I don't think it's a good idea for you to be here. If my dad catches you here..."

The door flew open, and her father stomped in with his hands stiff at his sides and his fists balled up. "What the hell is going on? Who's this pervert? Think you can bring guys into my house and do God knows what right under my nose?" His voice boomed and his face got redder and redder as he spoke.

Lola shrunk down under the covers. "Dad, it's not what it looks like."

"Sir, it's my fault," Argus explained. "I wanted to tell Lola something in person. I didn't mean to disrupt you or frighten her."

Her father came closer, beads of sweat covering his forehead. "Did you defile my daughter? Did you?"

"What? No!" Argus backed away. How was he going to get out of this? Her father evidently wasn't about to listen to reason. "Sir, I'll leave, but don't be angry with Lola. She had no idea I came here."

"You should be worried about yourself, not her. You trespassed into my home. By all rights, I can kill you."

As Argus continued to back away, her father passed by the desk, grabbed a lamp, and smashed it to the floor. He unbuckled his belt, slid it out of the loops and wrapped it around his hand. What was he going to do? Argus could hardly breathe. He bumped against the wall; his heart was thumping. He was trapped. If only he'd had time to text the address to Tai.

Lola's father continued to come forward. He kicked Lola's backpack out of his way and punched his belt-wrapped fist into his other fist. If he was trying to be intimidating, it worked.

"Dad! Stop it!" Lola got out of bed. "I didn't want to do this, but I can use my mind to do things. If you don't stop, I'll hurt you and throw you to the ground again."

Her father stopped and glared at her. "You didn't do anything. I tripped and fell. You've always thought you were so smart and different. Because you could read early and add two and two doesn't make you smart."

"Yeah, it does." Tai stood behind Lola's father. "Lola, come over here behind me."

Her father spun around. "What the hell? Get outta my house!"

Lola spoke in a timid voice, "Tai, I can do things. I really can. I don't want you or Argus to get hurt because of me. Let me handle it."

Argus shook his head. "Lola, go ahead and get behind Tai. I'll take care of this. Please."

She hesitated for a moment but scurried behind Tai. A terrible thought filled Argus. He was hoping that her father would try something. He wanted to hurt her father and he could see that Tai did, too. What was going on? They were turning into monsters.

Her father moved to the side so he could see them both. "I don't know what you punks think you're doing, but you're trespassing. Lola, call the cops."

She peeked around Tai. "No. Leave my room, Dad."

"Hell no." Her father brought his belt-wrapped fist up and swung at Argus.

Argus was too quick and ducked in time to avoid the blow. His skin tingled and his heart raced. Her father smashed his fist into the wall, crashing through the drywall. He cursed and made another attempt to hit Argus. *No way, old man, you'll never get me.*

"Oh, that's enough," Tai blurted as he grabbed Lola's father from behind and tossed him across the room into the desk. "You don't attack my brother. Argus, take Lola out of here."

Argus was still fired up, feeling an amazing amount of energy that had built up. "What are you going to do, Tai?" He went to Lola to make sure she was okay. Other than trembling, she wasn't hurt.

Tai's eyes flashed bright blue. "This human needs to be taught a lesson."

Argus watched Tai. He had the same eye color as Aunt Celeste and Galena. What did that mean? He was like them now? "Tai, watch what you say." He put his hand on Tai's shoulder. "Let's go home."

Tai turned, his eyes a steady blue glow. "No. You go home if you want, but this human must understand that he is weak and powerless. I am..." He blinked and his eyes dimmed. "What was I saying?"

"Are you all right?" asked Lola, reaching for Argus's hand. "Was that me again? Did I do something?"

Argus squeezed her hand. "No, it wasn't you. Tai, we need to go." Maybe he should let her think it was her so she wouldn't suspect they were aliens. What was he saying? *Aliens* probably wouldn't even cross her mind.

Lola's father got to his feet, his eyes darting from Tai to Argus. "Get the hell out of my house," he growled.

Argus was not about to leave Lola in the house with her father. He took a pink robe off a hook on the back of her bedroom door and handed it her. "You can stay at our house tonight."

"She's not going anywhere with you!" yelled her father.

There was no point in arguing. Argus held her hand tightly and took her into the hallway while Tai stood in the doorway blocking her father from coming out. Lola was scared and still trembling. Argus put his arm around her.

She looked down the hallway. "My mom's in her room. I can't leave her. My dad might..."

Her mother's door opened. "I'm here, Lola. I won't let him hurt us anymore." She came into the hallway, a gun in her right hand. "No more, no more, no more."

"Whoa," Argus mumbled. "Um, ah, this isn't...you can't...Tai!"

Tai stepped out of the room, looked at the gun and smiled. "Way to go, Mrs., ah, Mrs. Lola."

"It's going to be Miss after tonight." She raised the gun higher. "Step aside."

Argus was close, so he got in front of Lola's mother. "I don't think you need the gun. We'll make sure your husband leaves." His heart still thumped a mile a minute. What a great feeling. He was strong, empowered, in charge. He was a hero.

Lola ran to her mother and took the gun. "We'll be okay, Mom." She looked back at Argus. "Are you sure you don't want me to do whatever it is that I do?"

He shook his head. "No, Lola, that's okay. Let us handle things. Go in your mother's room and wait."

Lola nodded, took her mother's hand, and pulled her back to the room. Argus was hyper-alert, like he could hear the slightest sound, which was a creak from inside Lola's room. He went into the room along with Tai as Lola's father picked up a heavy-looking stone bookend off Lola's shelf.

"Drop it," Argus said in a deep voice he hardly recognized.

"You can't push me around, punk." Lola's father grasped the bookend in both hands.

Rather than retreat, Argus advanced. "I said drop it." He was invincible; at least that's how he felt. His adrenaline was surging through his body. He could do anything.

After a short pause, Tai spoke up, "Here's what's going to happen, old man. You'll drop the bookend, pick up your belt, leave this house and never return." His eyes were bright again. "You're only a human. You're no match for me. Leave or you'll regret it."

Lola's father shook his head. "You're freaks. That's what you are. What are you going to do? Two against one, eh? Well, freaks, I used to box in the Army. You really want to take me on?"

"I do. I really do." Tai stepped forward, raised his hand, palm toward Lola's father. A split-second later, a burst of blinding white light shot from his hand and struck Lola's father in the chest, throwing him backward against the wall where he crumpled to the ground.

What was that? How did Tai do that? Argus put his hand on Tai's arm. "Tai? I think that's enough."

Tai glared at him with intense blue eyes. "Really, brother. I don't think it's enough." He turned back to Lola's father. "Is it enough, old man?"

Lola's father groaned and struggled to his feet. He wobbled and staggered past Tai and Argus, mumbling under his breath about wanting to leave anyway. When he made it to the hall, Tai raised his hand again and shot another blast of light, striking Lola's father square in the back and sending him flying about five feet. He got to his feet and took off.

Argus drew in a deep breath and felt his heart slow down. "That's enough, Tai."

"Is it?" Tai blinked and his eyes were normal again. "Holy...what's happening to me?"

"I, ah, I don't know." Argus had a good idea what was happening. Why didn't Galena tell Tai what she did and why? Maybe she didn't realize he'd develop new abilities.

Tai stared at this palm. "What did I do? Let's get the hell out of here."

Argus nodded and ran down the hall and knocked on Lola's mother's bedroom door. "It's all right. He's gone."

Lola opened the door. "Really? Is he coming back?"

"I don't think so." Argus glanced at Tai. "Did you see him go?"

Tai smiled. "Yeah. Right out the door. I heard tires screeching from the driveway."

Lola wasn't smiling. She was upset, afraid. "Thanks, you guys. I'm really embarrassed that you had to see that." She turned away.

Argus put his hand under her chin, so she'd look at him. "Don't ever be embarrassed. Your father needs help. You did nothing wrong. I don't think you and your mother should stay here tonight though, in case he does try to come back."

"Argus," Lola said very softly, "We can't afford a motel and we don't have any family around here. We'll be okay."

Argus glanced at Tai, but Tai held up his hand and took out his cell phone. He let out a breath. "I'm ahead of you, bro. You realize that Aunt Celeste isn't going to let us ever forget this, don't you? We'll be grounded until we're forty."

"Yeah." Argus held onto Lola's hand. Whether they got grounded or not, Lola was safe, and that's all that mattered.

Chapter 27

Max got up early so he'd make it to school for the absurdly early staff meeting. He was still groggy from the effects of last night's beer extravaganza, but somehow he managed to get to the principal's office a few minutes before 6:45.

Everyone turned and stared at him as he came in. There was a lumpy, old couch against the wall closest to the door and ten plastic chairs arranged in front of the principal's desk. All were full. It seemed like it was best to come early to staff meetings. Max decided to stand near the door so he wouldn't block anyone, and he could be the first to leave.

Hector Chavez, a man of about forty-five or fifty with graying hair and dark eyes, nodded to Max and started the meeting. "I know it's early and I appreciate you all showing up on time. Okay, we need to address a serious matter. One of our students who you all probably know by now, Justin Jones, was involved in an incident where he received burns to both hands. His parents are threatening to sue the school, the city, and the guardian of the Dachel brothers, the boys he's accusing."

From one of the chairs, a woman with her hair drawn back into a severe ponytail spoke, "Are we certain these brothers are to blame? I think we all know what Justin's like."

There were a few other comments about Justin's bad attitude and bullying, but when one of the teachers questioned the behavior of the newcomers Argus and Tai, Max got an idea.

He took a step forward and cleared his throat. "I've met Argus Dachel a couple of times, he's in my class. Seems like a stand-up kid. Why don't I talk to him and see what I can find out before we go off half-cocked?"

"Half-cocked?" Chavez raised an eyebrow. "We never accuse anyone of anything until we have all of the facts, Mr. Jackson."

Chavez was a smart cookie. Max stepped back again. "I didn't mean to imply otherwise. I'll ask Argus to stay after class today and feel him out."

Chavez nodded slowly. "Good. Who has Tai Dachel in one of their classes?"

A teacher on the couch raised his hand. "I do. English."

"Then you can ask him a few questions." Chavez sighed. "Don't make it obvious why you're questioning the boys. If we need to investigate further, we'll make it official. I've got a meeting with a representative from the school board tomorrow. They'll be meeting with Justin's parents. We all need to be proactive when it comes to bullying, so be on the lookout for trouble during breaks and in between classes. All right, now let's talk about the student parking situation."

As Chavez and the teachers droned on and on, Max grew impatient. He was an expert at interviewing suspects and drawing information out of the most closed-mouthed types, so he'd get intel from a teenager for sure. He took out a bottle of Ibuprofen and popped two into his mouth to help his hangover.

By 7:05, the meeting was over, and Max slipped from the room before anyone could talk to him. He was not in the mood for idle chit-chat about the lunch menu or homework. On the way to his class, he stopped by the attendance office to check in and fill out his substitute's timecard. His mind wandered a bit, and he wondered if he would actually get paid from the school district or if Stone would step in and stop the payment. Knowing stone, he'd be on top of it. No double-dipping.

"Oh, Mr. Jackson," the secretary called from a small desk with a telephone and a stack of folders.

"Yes."

"Since you're here, I'll tell you instead of sending you a memo. You have Argus Dachel in your class, and we got a message last night that he and his brother are being withdrawn from school already by their aunt. Guess she's going to home school them again. Poor kids probably couldn't hack the social nightmare of high school."

"Wait, what? Withdrawn? Seriously? On the second day? Damn it!" He thumped his fist on the counter and knocked over the tin can filled with pens. His only way to contact Argus was as a sub, and now that was gone.

The secretary glared at him. "Please pick up those pens. I'll have to have Dr. Chavez confirm it, but the message said that due to a medical issue with the boys, it was safer to keep them home."

Medical issue? There was no medical issue. Max scribbled his name on the timecard for yesterday and went straight to his car. No point in hanging around the school if the Dachel brothers weren't there. He knew where he had to go and what he had to do. He couldn't let Argus Dachel slip through his fingers. He squealed his tires as he burned out of the school parking lot and drove toward the walled house in the desert. It had to be their house.

Chapter 28

Once they got home, Argus offered to sleep on the couch so Lola and her mother could have his room, but Aunt Celeste insisted they take her room. The other two spare rooms in the house also belonged to Aunt Celeste. One was her study, and the other was a locked room she called her workroom. It was obvious that she wanted to be in the living room, to guard the household to make sure Lola's father didn't try to break in.

Tai crept into Argus's room around midnight, and they stayed up for hours talking about Tai's weird ability to throw balls of light and how Aunt Celeste didn't seem to be all that angry at them when she came to pick them all up at Lola's house. By morning, they'd had only a few hours of sleep and had to be roused by Aunt Celeste knocking on the door.

Argus climbed out of bed and nudged Tai where he was asleep on the floor. He tried to go back to sleep by putting a pillow over his face until Argus gave him another nudge.

"Tai, get up. I want to make sure Lola's all right."

"Of course she's all right. She's in a household of Ramtalans. Now let me sleep," The pillow muffled Tai's voice.

Argus gave up and left the room. He smelled pancakes and eggs. Aunt Celeste stood at the stove, but turned when he came in.

"Sit down, Argus," she said softly. "Lola and Patty will be out shortly."

Patty? Lola's mother obviously. He sat on a stool at the breakfast bar, practicing what to say over and over in his head. He wanted to apologize for going to Lola's in the first place but wasn't sure if Aunt Celeste would accept an apology.

"Pancakes?" she asked casually as if nothing had happened.

"Um, yes, please." He took a deep breath. "I'm really sorry about last night. I like Lola and wanted to see her. I honestly had no idea that there'd be any trouble."

She came over and put two fluffy pancakes on a plate in front of him. "I know, Argus. I'm not angry." She sat beside him and smiled. "You're very much like your mother. When she was about your age, she sneaked out all the time. That's how she met your father. She was twenty-two when she first met him at a bar of all places. Like you, she wanted to be like everyone else. She was proud to be a New Breed, don't get me wrong, but knowing the truth made her...feel odd."

"Really? What was she like? I mean really like." All he knew of his mother was what Aunt Celeste told him; that she was tall, intelligent, funny, and loving. He had no memory of her at all. What he'd seen in the vision from Aunt Celeste wasn't how he wanted to remember his mom.

"Argus, your mother was a wonderful woman. The day she turned 21, we went to her favorite place to celebrate."

Argus picked at the pancakes. "Where?"

"The Acoma pueblo. We lived in New Mexico at the time, and she loved to visit Acoma."

Argus remembered how Aunt Celeste took Tai and him to Acoma once when they went on a short vacation to New Mexico. It was a Native American Pueblo built high up on top of a hill. People still lived up there, although most of the tribe lived elsewhere. Wasn't New Mexico where Roswell was? He didn't remember going to Roswell.

She continued, "She said it made her feel at peace. I never understood what she meant, but that was her special place, so I didn't question it."

"I think I know what she meant. When I'm with Lola, I feel happy and like I don't want to be anywhere else." Argus stopped talking when Lola and her mother walked into the kitchen.

Lola's eyes were red and puffy, and her mother looked barely awake. Had they stayed up most of the night, too? Aunt Celeste motioned for them to sit at the table and poured a cup of coffee for Lola's mother.

"Would you like pancakes and eggs, Patty?" Aunt Celeste held up the frying pan of scrambled eggs.

Patty shook her head. "No, thank you. I'd better call for a cab. I am so sorry to be an inconvenience."

"You're not an inconvenience. In fact, it's very nice to have visitors. As you see, we're quite isolated out here."

Argus smiled. Aunt Celeste was a gracious hostess. It felt like they were an actual family. She scooped out a pile of eggs for Lola and her mother, regardless of the previous objection.

Argus took his plate to the table and sat next to Lola. "Were you able to sleep?"

She shook her head. "Not really." She reached under the table and took his hand and lowered her voice, "Your house is so big and nice."

Argus liked holding her hand. Every time she was close to him, his stomach felt jumpy, but in a good way. "You know, you can stay here as long as you like." He glanced at Aunt Celeste. "I mean, if that's okay."

"Argus, I'd like to speak to you." Aunt Celeste motioned with her head for Argus to follow her.

Oh, no. Was he going to get in trouble now for...well, for everything? He followed her to the living room. It would be a lecture for sure. Of course she didn't reprimand him last night because Lola and her mother were there. But now she had the opportunity. Great.

She pointed to the couch. "Sit down, Argus."

Yep, this was it. She'd already taken them out of school, so what was left. Permanent grounding? He should have stayed in bed.

She smiled gently and kept her voice low, "I'm not angry with you, if that's what you're worried about. You acted very gallantly last night. As a protector, you not only have a need, but a duty to protect. I understand that. Protectors are valued among Ramtalans. So are defenders. Tai is a defender." She glanced around. "Tai's Ramtalan abilities are taking over his New Breed abilities. This is good and bad, as you can imagine. I will have to explain his new genetic composition to him very soon. You're his twin, do you think he can handle the news?"

Argus sat and tried to absorb what she said. A defender? Yes they were twins, but after Galena's treatment, Tai wasn't like he used to be. And not only on a genetic level. His attitude was different. He was changing constantly.

"I'm not really sure what Tai can handle. He keeps saying things like humans are weak and his eyes glow like yours and Galena's. I feel like I'm losing my brother." It was embarrassing, his eyes were tearing up. He blinked in an effort to stop them.

"He'll always be your brother, but both of you are different now. It's natural for him to pull away."

"Natural? My brother's changing right before my eyes, and you call that natural?" Argus leaned forward and rested his elbows on his knees. There was nothing natural about what Galena did.

There was a quizzical look on Aunt Celeste's face. "It is natural. Think of the rearrangement of his DNA as a spontaneous mutation. Mutations are natural occurrences. That's all I'm saying. You understand genetics. We went over it extensively."

"I know, but this isn't a lesson from a book, this is my brother we're talking about. And it wasn't a natural mutation. Galena did it to him. It's killing me that I can't tell him."

"Argus, please understand, it was the only way to save him. He was reckless going into the desert alone and this is the result. We'll deal with it. Galena or I will tell him when it's the right time. I haven't reported to her what happened last night, but if Tai doesn't learn to control his new abilities, she will find out. Neither of us wants that, do we?"

Argus shook his head. He'd be happy never to see Galena again. "Hey, if Galena can add more Ramtalan DNA, why can't she reverse it and put in the human DNA again?"

"Not possible. She has control of Ramtalan DNA, not human. She's attempted to recombine Ramtalan DNA to fix the sterility issue, but each time she adds in human DNA, the host dies. I thought we already covered this?"

"We did, but..." Argus saw Tai wander into the living room, his hair mussed. The conversation would have to wait.

Tai sat next to Argus. "What are we talking about?"

"Lola and her mother," Argus mumbled.

Tai nodded and yawned. "Hey, did you tell Aunt Celeste about my, ah, my—"

"No. I figured you better tell her." Argus had a feeling she already knew Tai could throw light balls without having been told. It probably went along with being a defender.

Tai sighed. "I thought you would have. Ah, Aunt Celeste, I think I hurt Lola's dad. I don't know how I did it. I kind of knew I could do it and then I just did it. A burst of light came out of my hand and slammed into Lola's dad. What is it and how did I do it? I tried to do it again last night, but nothing happened."

Aunt Celeste nodded slowly and looked at Argus, then back to Tai. "It's called a photometric pulse. It's never been recorded in New Breeds. And not all pure-forms can produce a photometric pulse. Those that can, rarely learn to control it. It becomes a hindrance."

"A hindrance?" Tai ran his hand through his messy hair. "It sure came in handy last night. How can I learn to control it?"

"Practice." Aunt Celeste put her finger to her lips. "We can't talk about this now. Later."

"Okay." Tai yawned again. "Are those pancakes I smell?"

A red light above the front door flashed. That was the silent security alarm Aunt Celeste had installed a few years ago. She dashed to the front window and looked out. "Go in the dining room with Lola and Patty. I'll be in my study."

Argus got up. Aunt Celeste kept her security monitors in her study. So who was sneaking around their house? It had to be Max. Damn that guy. Didn't he have anything better to do?

Tai extended his hand, palm outward, toward the door. "Nothing. What good is it to have a photometric pulse if I can't use it?"

"Come on, Tai, I saw what you did with it. I'm glad you can't use it. That's a dangerous ability to have. Even Aunt Celeste thinks so. It's cool though, but only if you can learn how to control it."

"You're jealous, aren't you?" Tai smirked.

"No, I'm not." In truth, he was a little jealous. It was such an amazing ability, even if it was a dangerous one.

He went with Tai to join Lola and her mother in the dining room. After a minute or so, Aunt Celeste came into the kitchen looking grim. Her mouth was tight and her eyes had a darker tone to them.

She frowned and had her communicator clutched in her hand. "It's Max sneaking around the perimeter. But I have an idea."

Argus looked at Tai, hoping the defender in him wouldn't take over and do something stupid.

Chapter 29

It was only 7:45 a.m. and Max sweated in the blistering heat as he crept around the walls of the house. Why was it so damn hot? But, hot or not, he knew he'd find the evidence he needed.

All he had to do was scale the eight-foot walls and avoid the security cameras. No problem. He'd run obstacle and agility courses during training for AURA. Of course he was younger then, but he was still in good shape. He listened. There weren't any sounds coming from the house; the occupants were likely still asleep. Good, that'd make it easier to break in.

Sweat dripped down his face and off the tip of his nose. He wiped his hand across his forehead, took a deep breath, and found a foothold in one corner of the wall. He worked his fingers into the mortar between the bricks and pulled himself up. It was an arduous climb, and his shirt was soaked by the time he made it to the top.

He reached up and gripped the top of the wall. Whew, now he could take a breather for a second. A siren cut through the early morning quiet. He looked toward City Ranch Road and saw a marked police car zooming along. Probably after a speeder heading to Las Vegas.

He pulled his body onto the top of the wall and stopped. The police car turned down the road leading to the house. Huh? The cop headed toward the house. Damn it all to hell. Max weighed his options. One, get caught for trespassing, or two, gather whatever intel he could before getting caught. Either option meant getting caught, so he chose number two.

He climbed over and tried to lower himself but fell to the ground on the inside of the wall and twisted his ankle. The siren blared on the other side of the wall. Not much time. He half ran, half limped toward the house, snapping photos with his phone as he went.

The siren stopped. Max held his breath and smiled. Now the occupants would have to come out to talk to the cops and let them in. He let out his breath slowly and hid behind a bush where he could see the front door of the house. If Argus, Tai, or Celeste came out, his suspicions about their implication in the energy spikes would be confirmed. It was worth dealing with the local cops to get this sort of intelligence. Stone would have to bail him out of jail, but so what? Once Stone found out what was going on, he wouldn't complain.

The driveway gate opened, and two uniformed officers walked up the drive with their hands on the butts of their guns. Max heard the front door open and peeked through the branches of the bush. No, that couldn't be right. How could he have made a mistake like that? It was the girl, Lola somebody, from school. And a woman that wasn't Celeste. Her mother?

"Freeze!" shouted one of the cops as he took his gun out of the holster in one smooth and threatening motion and pointed it right at Max.

Well, damn. Caught snooping, and for nothing. Stone might not bail him out now.

Chapter 30

From inside the house, Argus watched through the living room window as the police handcuffed Max and escorted him to the patrol car in the driveway. There was something very satisfying about seeing Max hauled away like that. The car turned around and sped off to the main road with Max peering through the back window. *Have fun in jail, Max.*

Lola ran into the house, all smiles. "How'd I do?"

"Great." Argus got caught up in her exuberance and gave her a hug. Wow, she felt good.

She wrapped her arms around him and hugged him back. She whispered, "I'm really glad I could help you. Why is that sub harassing you?"

Argus shrugged. "I don't know. Maybe he doesn't think home schooled kids should go to an in-person school." Did that sound good?

"I guess." She let go of him.

Aunt Celeste closed the door when Lola's mother came in. "Patty, Lola, you did a terrific job. Very convincing. I appreciate your help."

Lola's mother let out a huge sigh. "I was nervous. I've never lied to the police before, but you know what, it's not that hard." There was a small smile. "You've been so nice to us, I'd do about anything for you at this point."

"Thank you, but I think that'll take care of our trespasser." Aunt Celeste put her communicator away.

Argus admired Aunt Celeste's sneakiness. She'd called the police and asked Lola and her mother to pretend they lived in the house. The lie worked and now Max was out of the way for a while, and he'd think Lola and her mother lived there. Tai walked by with his head down, looking upset or angry.

Argus tapped him on the arm as he passed. "What's wrong? Max is out of the way, there's nothing to worry about."

"I could have taken care of Max," he mumbled, his eyes growing a little brighter.

Uh-oh, Tai was getting all worked up again. "Easy. Why don't we go into my room for a minute?" Argus grabbed Tai's sleeve and pulled him through the living room and into the bedroom. "Tai, your eyes are glowing."

Tai looked in the mirror above the dresser. "Damn it. Arg, I keep having these feelings. I can't stop them. What's wrong with me?" He peered closer. "Cool color, though."

Argus spun him around. "Yeah, cool. Your feelings are an after effect from the healing that Galena did. At least that's what Aunt Celeste thinks." Hopefully that sounded reasonable. "Galena gave you an extra shot of energy or something. Try to relax and stay calm, maybe that'll help."

"I'm not doing yoga, if that's what you're hinting at." Tai smirked. "I have to admit, whatever Galena did to me has made me feel really great."

"Well, that's good. I'm glad you're doing okay." Argus sat on the bed. "I have this feeling way down deep that Max isn't going to give up."

"Glad you said it, bro. I didn't want to be the doom-and-gloom guy here. I have a plan, but I don't think Aunt Celeste will like it."

"Let me be the judge of that." Argus waited while Tai explained his plan, which wasn't much of a plan. He suggested they convince Aunt Celeste to let them go back to school if they learned how to control their abilities. They could keep an eye on Max. If it got them back in school, Argus would go along with anything Tai came up with.

"Boys!" called Aunt Celeste. They found her in the living room, dangling the key fob from her fingers. "Lola and Patty are ready to go home via the police station where Patty will file a restraining order against her husband and fill out a report saying that Max was sent by her husband to spy on her."

Really? Argus looked at Lola's mom. She had a blank expression. Did Aunt Celeste use her mind control or was Lola's mother going along with everything because Aunt Celeste had put her up for the night?

He whispered, "We'd like to talk to you later. About Max." He took the key fob when Aunt Celeste offered them to him. "I'm driving?"

"Yes. Tai, you can drive home." She pointed to the door leading to the garage. "Shall we?"

They all piled into the SUV and Argus drove as carefully as he could, obeying the traffic laws and staying under the speed limit, making several morning drivers angry. He'd rather burn out and tear through town to show Lola what a good driver he was, but with Aunt Celeste beside him, that wasn't possible. He glanced in the rearview a few times and saw Lola smiling. Okay, so maybe she liked careful drivers. He looked forward again when Aunt Celeste shouted at him to watch out. He'd almost ran a red light because he was watching Lola. Whoops. He pulled into the police station and sat in the car with Tai while Aunt Celeste went inside with Lola and her mother. Tai climbed over the seat and sat in the front. He turned on the radio and cranked up the volume.

Someone banged on the rear window. Argus turned and saw Justin Jones. He held up his hands, both bandaged. In an instant, Tai's eyes glowed bright blue and he was out the door rushing toward Justin.

"No! Tai!" Argus scrambled out as fast as he could and got in between them. "Stop. We're at a police station, Justin. Do you seriously want to do this here?"

Justin clenched his jaw, his breath ragged. He wanted a fight. "Get out of the way, fart-gas. This is between your dickweed brother and me. Nice contacts, moron." He darted around Argus and shoved Tai in the chest. "You're dead, dickweed."

"Tai, get in the car." Argus glanced around. There weren't any police around. No witnesses if Tai went off again. "Come on, Tai, don't do this. Justin, leave, get out of here."

Justin shoved Tai again. "What you going to do, dickweed? You scared?"

"Don't do that, Justin." Argus grabbed Tai's sleeve and tried to pull him back. No use, he wasn't budging.

There was a low, animal-like growl deep in Tai's throat. His eyes were burning blue, and his body was tense. This wasn't going to end well for Justin, and in an instant, Tai had him by the throat, lifting him off the ground a few inches. As hard as Justin struggled, he couldn't get loose from Tai's grip. Argus grabbed his brother's arm, but Tai smacked him across the face with his free hand.

Argus got knocked off his feet and fell hard to the ground. A gurgling sound came from Justin, who was now hanging limp in the air. He couldn't get any air; he was being strangled. Argus closed his eyes and concentrated on Aunt Celeste. After what seemed an eternity, he saw her standing at the counter in the police station. He concentrated harder, blocking out the strangled gasps from Justin. When he opened his eyes, he was standing behind her.

"Aunt Celeste?" he whispered.

She didn't hear him. He was invisible. There wasn't much time left. What could he do to get her attention? What did he do last time? He reached into his pocket and got his cell phone and typed a text as fast as he could:

Aunt Celeste, I'm invisible behind you. Tai is outside killing Justin!

He pressed send and paced. Aunt Celeste's phone chimed, and she read the text, spun around, nodded, and jogged out of the station. He followed, but by the time they got to Tai, Justin was blue and not moving at all.

"Tai!" Aunt Celeste's eyes flamed blue. "Put him down, now."

Tai raised his free hand and fired a photometric pulse at Aunt Celeste. She waved her hand and the pulse disintegrated in mid-air. He fired another pulse, but this time she ducked and fired one back that struck him in the leg. Tai crumpled and released Justin as he fell.

Argus couldn't do a thing. *Come on, Tai, stop it.*

For a moment, Tai looked like he was going to shoot another pulse, but his eyes dimmed, and he shook his head instead, dazed. "Ow."

"Sorry, Tai." Aunt Celeste went to Justin and felt for a pulse on his neck. "He's alive. Argus, are you here?"

"Yes." Damn, he was still invisible, she couldn't hear him. He sent another text.

I'm here, but I don't know how to turn visible.

She read the text and looked around. "All right. I wish you'd told me about this ability. I've never heard of invisibility in a New Breed before. Argus, if you can get into the car, do it. Tai, get in as well. We must leave right now."

"I think you broke my leg." Tai struggled to get up, holding onto the car for support.

"You'll be fine. Photometric pulses can't break bones." She opened the rear door. "Argus, text me when you're in."

He got in as fast as he could and sent her a text. Tai got in next to him, looking around and rubbing his leg. It all happened so fast.

Tai wound down the window and peered out. "I would have killed him, wouldn't I?"

"Probably," was all Aunt Celeste said as she started the car.

"I'm a murderer," groaned Tai.

"No, you're not. Justin is alive."

Argus reached out and put his hand on Tai's shoulder, but instead of comforting him, it made him jump and curse. Argus slumped in his seat. Invisibility sucked.

"Damn it, Arg. And that's only semantics, Aunt Celeste."

"Not semantics, Tai. A fact. You didn't kill Justin, therefore you're not a murderer. Argus, try to reverse whatever you did to turn invisible." Aunt Celeste pulled out of the parking lot.

"What about Lola?" Argus called out, but again, nobody heard. What was he doing right before he turned visible each time? The first time he was on Lola's lawn with Tai. What happened then? Tai hit him. And the next time, he was in Lola's room. But what made him visible? All he was doing was reading the envelope for her address...and got a paper cut. Could it be that easy? Pain?

He made a fist and punched the window hard enough to hurt, but not to break the glass, or his hand. Ow! That should do it, his hand hurt like hell.

"Arg?" Tai stared at him. "There's no way I'll ever get used to you popping up like that."

"You can see me?"

"Duh."

"Yeah, well, that's what you do every time you dissolve and reappear. Aunt Celeste, what about Lola and her mother? We can't leave them there?" Argus turned in his seat and looked out the back window.

"They're fine. Patty is a strong woman, she just never realized it. I implanted a small suggestion into her mind."

So she did use her mind control thing. "Suggestion?" Argus looked at Tai, who shrugged.

"Patty will take self-defense lessons and will never again tolerate an abusive relationship. Lola said she'll take self-defense as well."

Argus leaned forward. "Wait. You used your mind control on Lola?" He never wanted Lola's mind to be screwed around with. It didn't seem right. She'd never done anything to anyone. It was different somehow when Aunt Celeste did it to Justin or Lola's mom, but doing it to Lola was...wrong.

Aunt Celeste shook her head. "I didn't do anything to Lola. She decided that on her own."

"Oh. Okay. What about Justin? How can we explain what Tai did?" Argus glanced at Tai. Tai was playing a game on his phone. He didn't seem too fazed by what had happened back at the police station.

"Let me worry about him. We need to go somewhere right now." Aunt Celeste turned the car around and headed in the opposite direction of their house. Where was she going?

She drove for about twenty minutes and turned into the small parking lot at Elizabeth Lake. Why bring them there? It was a great spot to relax, but it was doubtful they were there to relax. The only interesting thing about the lake was that it lay right over the San Andreas Fault line. It was also secluded away from any houses at the far end. They'd had several picnics over the years at the lake, but this didn't seem like the right time for a picnic.

Argus watched Tai again. How could he be so calm? Didn't he realize that he almost killed Justin?

Tai looked up from his phone. "Stop staring at me, bro."

"Sorry." Argus turned away. "You hit me back at the police station, Tai."

"What? I did?" Tai frowned. "Why would I do that? Aunt Celeste, you've got to help me."

She parked. "That's why we're here. It's too early for anyone, except perhaps a few fishermen." She got out and scanned the area. "All clear. This has been a training area for Ramtalans and New Breeds for a number of years. It was easier before people started to build houses down the other end, but it's still a useable area."

Argus climbed out and stood beside Tai. Training area? What sort of training? Going to the lake had always been a fun time. It was a place where they were free to run and play and Aunt Celeste would never tell them to be careful. It was their magic place, at least that's what Argus used to call it. It sure seemed magical at the time.

"Over here, boys." Aunt Celeste pointed to a worn trail leading through the shrubs and sage brush. "This is the best space to practice."

"Why?" Tai shuffled over to her.

Argus followed. "Why is the lake special?"

She walked down the trail a bit and stopped, cocked her head, extended her arms, and turned in a circle. "Can't you feel it? The San Andreas fault is directly beneath us. There is a constant small leakage of energy from the tectonic plates below as they gently grind on one another. That energy, however small, camouflages Ramtalan energy when we practice."

Oh, so that's why they always went to the lake. It made sense now. Argus walked to the spot where she stood. He did feel something, a little tingle in his gut. Why hadn't he noticed that before? "Why can I dissolve and turn invisible, but then I can't turn visible unless I feel pain?"

Aunt Celeste looked at him like she was studying him. "Pain? I'm not sure. It's a wonderful ability to have. But the pain, well, it could be any number of things. Perhaps pain triggers a release of adrenaline and that breaks the force of the invisibility. Whenever you discover a new ability, tell me right away. Quite sure I've said that before."

"I know. So what do we do?" Argus looked around. They were somewhat in the underbrush, far enough away from the parking lot and the road so no one could see them.

"You practice. Tai, you work your aim with the photometric pulses and learn control of the pulses and of your temper. An ability is useless unless you know how to use it. Argus, you learn to manage your strength and your invisibility." She jogged back to the car and took out a folding chair, brought it to the spot and set it up. She sat down. "Practice."

Argus was confused. Something wasn't right. Didn't the Citadel say they couldn't use their abilities? "Wait. Aunt Celeste, when you were on the phone with the Citadel, that guy said you can use your abilities, but we can't. Does that mean they already know we've been using them? And if we use them here, will they know that, too?"

She nodded. "They know. But I received permission to give you lessons so you couldn't accidentally do something, like turn invisible and appear in Lola's house or lift Justin Jones off the ground and almost kill him." She was serious, not smiling.

Tai raised an eyebrow. "But Galena said if anything happened, she'd know and take us away from here. Why hasn't she?"

Now Aunt Celeste had a trace of a smile. "I went above her to get permission. I explained that you two are young and developing incredible abilities, and that as Guardian, I should be the one to train you."

"And they agreed?" Argus couldn't believe it. How had she done that without Galena finding out?

The smile stayed on Aunt Celeste's lips. "I have friends at the Citadel, and they support me, when I can get to them without Galena getting in the way. She won't be happy about this, but I'm your Guardian and once I have authority from the Citadel, she can't do anything about it. Now, practice your abilities."

Aunt Celeste was cool, awesomely cool. Argus walked away a bit and stared at the hills around the lake. It was pretty and serene, but he wasn't there to take in the view. He was there to practice, but he had no idea how to turn invisible at will. His strength also needed a bit of management. After all, he did dent the goal post at school and now that he was on the team, he'd have to regulate his strength. School! That reminded him of the plan he and Tai had about keeping Max on their radar.

He motioned to Tai. "Aunt Celeste, we sort of want to ask you something. We don't want to stay cooped up at home again. We want to go to school. I'm the new quarterback and I have my friend Dave and of course Lola. If we learn how to control our abilities, can we go back?"

After a moment, Aunt Celeste got out of the chair. "I do understand your desire to be *normal* as you put it, but with all that's happened in only one day, I don't see how it's possible to continue high school. There are too many variables to consider, even if you do control your abilities. And football? That's a rough game where you can easily get scratched. You know what your blood does to humans. If you're at home, Max will have to move on."

"Let me handle this," Tai whispered. "I was thinking, if we were among regular human teenagers, we could learn to blend in and behave like regular teenagers. Isn't that what the whole New Breed experiment is about? If we're segregated like outcasts, we can't possibly fit in and then where will Ramtala be? You said Arg and I are the only New Breeds of this generation to make it past 16, so we might be the last chance Ramtala has of preserving Ramtalan DNA." He winked at Argus. "How can our race survive if we're locked away like animals?"

Way to go, Tai. Argus watched Aunt Celeste's face for any sign of softening. As usual, her expression was unreadable. She paced back and forth in front of the folding chair, hands clasped behind her back, her ponytail slithering from side to side. What was she thinking?

"And I've seen the other football players wearing long-sleeved shirts. I can do that, so I won't get scratched up. Besides, I'm not going to let anyone sack me."

Finally, she stopped, brought her ponytail over her shoulder, and nodded. "See that you don't. All right, everything will depend on how well you do here over the next few days. If you make even the slightest mistake at school, presuming I do allow you to return to school, then you'll risk exposure, and the Citadel will step in. Now, practice." She sat down again.

Tai fist-bumped Argus. "Okay, Arg, I'm going to perfect my photometric pulse throwing."

"Cool. And your temper. You're one mean New Breed when you're pissed off." They fist-bumped again.

Argus sat on the ground and concentrated on the inside of the car. It took a while, but he ended up in the car and had to stop himself from laughing when Aunt Celeste jumped up and searched around for him. He still had to pinch himself to turn visible though.

They'd been practicing for a couple of hours when Aunt Celeste said it was time to go home. She let Tai drive the car, but he wasn't cautious on the road and went over the speed limit, blew through a red light, and hit the brakes too hard at a stop sign. None of it seemed to bother Aunt Celeste, but Argus hung onto the back of the seat the whole way. He didn't want to die from Tai's bad driving.

After two more days of practicing at Elizabeth Lake each morning and being bombarded with lessons about Ramtalan history, Earth history, math and science in the afternoon, and then stopping at the DMV to get their driver's licenses, Aunt Celeste gave the okay for them to return to school.

Argus had a pretty good handle on his strength and with some pointers from Aunt Celeste, learned to turn visible without using pain as the trigger. All he had to do was think of something painful and bam, he'd turn visible.

He spent his down time texting and calling Lola. On Friday, it was time for school again, and time for the first football practice right after the 3:00 bell rang.

"Argus, Tai, hurry up or you'll be late," Aunt Celeste called from the living room.

Argus raced Tai down the hall and beat him into the living room. There was something strange about the way Aunt Celeste waited by the front door. She smiled, looking pleased with herself about something.

"Boys, if you're going to be regular all-American teenagers, you can't have your aunt drive you around everywhere."

Oh, no, now what? She wasn't going to make them take the school bus, was she? Argus glanced at Tai, who looked equally horrified. Aunt Celeste must have noticed their expressions.

She laughed lightly. "Look outside."

Argus beat Tai to the window. Whoa. It can't be. In the driveway was a cobalt blue 1976 rebuilt Camaro. It looked exactly like the car, down to the color, on a poster that Tai had on his wall.

Tai nudged Argus. "Arg, am I seeing things?"

The jangle of keys made them both turn around. Aunt Celeste kept smiling. "It belongs to both of you. It's been converted into an alternative energy vehicle." Aunt Celeste handed the keys to Argus. "Argus, you'll drive to school. Tai will drive home. Straight home, at the speed limit. Pick up your brother after football practice. I've left a remote control for the gate and for the garage inside the glove compartment. Oh, and you have a parking permit for school."

When did she take care of all of that? And what exactly was an alternative energy vehicle? An electric car? After a quick good-bye, Argus raced Tai to the car. The Camaro was a thing of beauty, shiny blue and all theirs.

Argus turned the key in the ignition and the Camaro roared to life. Inside, the seats were soft leather, and the instrument panel was equipped with GPS and a weird panel with flashing lights. It was almost too good to be true. What a way to return to school.

He revved the engine a couple of times to get a feel of the car. "Tai, this is one of the best moments in my life."

"No kidding. Where do you think she got the car?"

"I think I know. The Citadel. She said the Citadel provides everything. This is so much better than driving the SUV. I didn't see any cars even half as cool as this in the student parking lot." He accelerated and eased the car down the drive to the main road, picking up speed to see how the Camaro performed. It handled great. Being an electric or whatever it was didn't slow it down one bit.

He reluctantly reduced his speed in town and pulled into the student parking lot behind several other cars, mostly old beaters or clunky cars that probably belonged to parents. As much as he knew he shouldn't, he felt proud of the Camaro and liked how the other guys standing around stared as he drove by. He pulled into a parking space and shut off the engine. Right away a bunch of guys came over.

"Cool car, dude."

"Damn! That ride is dope."

"Sick car, man."

It was amazing to get such recognition for driving a cool, dope, sick, car. Argus smiled. "Thanks. Want to look inside?" He wanted to show it off.

"Yeah!" said one guy with shoulder-length hair. He slid into the driver's seat. "So cool."

Argus looked at Tai again, who shrugged and motioned for a girl who'd joined the crowd to get into the passenger seat. While everyone fawned over the car, Argus looked around for Lola.

"Hey, Argus! I heard you were coming back today," Dave yelled from across the parking lot. "Man, is that your car?" He came over, his mouth gaping. "I didn't know you had a car. When did you get a car?"

Argus smiled. "My aunt gave it to us. It's sweet, isn't it?" It was more than sweet, but he was trying to be cool about it so he didn't seem like a show-off.

Dave nodded. "Ah, yeah. Mega-sweet." He peeked inside. "Your aunt picked this out? Your aunt?"

"Yes, she did." Argus had to do a couple of return high-fives and fist-bumps before he could shut the door and lock the car.

"Hey, you're the new quarterback, aren't you?" the guy with the shoulder-length hair asked.

"Yes." Argus nodded. It was almost time for the bell to ring and he didn't want to be late on his first day back. "We'd better get going."

"I'm a wide receiver. I hope you can throw. Name's Jake Reyes."

"Nice to meet you, Jake." Argus cringed; that sounded too formal. "Hey, what's up?" That was better.

Jake motioned with his head toward the school. "Is it true what you did to Justin Jones?"

What? How did he know about that? Argus didn't know what to say. He could feel his coolness level dropping. "Ah, what did you hear?"

"That you and your brother messed him up. That true?" Jake ran his hand over the hood of the car.

"Self-defense, Jake," Tai said, coming up behind Argus. "Justin picked a fight with the wrong guys." He grinned.

Jake nodded. "Yeah, I guess. Hey, did you guys hear there's an assembly this morning? Something about behavior or bullying. I'm sure it's because of Justin. His parents are talking about suing you guys. His dad's a cop, did you know that?"

A cop? Really? The school bully's dad was a cop. That would explain why Justin was at the police station. "Great." Argus's excitement took a nosedive. Well, right up until he saw Lola standing at the school's double doors. She waved and his heart picked up speed. "Excuse me, Jake." He jogged up to her. "Hi, Lola. How are you doing?"

"Hey." She handed him an envelope. "My mom and I are great. My dad hasn't come around at all."

"What's this?" He opened the envelope and pulled out a greeting card with a sad-eyed puppy on the front. Inside were the words:

Welcome back. I missed you.

"Thanks, Lola. I'm glad you and your mom are okay. And I'm looking forward to science class. My aunt's a great teacher, but I'd rather sit next to you." He slipped the card into his new backpack.

A blush flashed across her cheeks. "Me too. Oh, you won't believe this, but Mr. Jackson subbed in science yesterday and he's supposed to be here again today. He totally ignores me. It's weird. How did he get out of jail so soon? Isn't trespassing something that should have stopped him teaching?"

Did he hear her right? "Mr. Jackson?" Argus didn't know how Max was back to teaching. Even Aunt Celeste thought he'd be out of the picture for a while. First math and now science. Was he somehow getting rid of the teachers so he could sub? This wasn't good at all.

"Are you okay, Argus?" Lola tugged on his sleeve. "We'd better get to class, the bell's about the ring."

Argus hesitated. How did Max know they were coming back to school? Damn. Aunt Celeste hadn't anticipated this. He looked at Lola. Max had seen him with Lola. Now Lola might be in danger. Well, that meant he'd have to stick close to her to protect her. Not that he minded. He took her hand and together they walked to class.

They took their seats in the science room and Argus put his backpack filled with supplies on the floor. He got plenty of attention from a couple guys who slapped him on the back and said, "welcome back" and "cool car". He pulled out two spiral notebooks and slid one in front of Lola.

"Repayment for lending me the paper on the first day." He smiled.

"Really? You didn't have to repay me. It was a gift."

"I know. Oh, I almost forgot." He unzipped the small pocket on the front of the backpack and took out a little white box. "And this is a gift from me, for helping us." He'd gone with Aunt Celeste to a jewelry shop to pick up a thank you present, a pretty gold heart pendant on a chain.

She twisted a curl of hair and opened the box. "Oh...Argus...I can't...this is too...Argus, you shouldn't—"

"Let me put it on for you." He fastened the chain around her neck. The heart lay on her pale skin like it belonged there. "It looks really pretty."

The door swung open and Max strode in. He smirked at Argus. "Good to see you're back, Mr. Dachel."

Okay, confirmed. Max did know the Dachels were coming back to school. Argus had been practicing self-control all week. He could do this. He said calmly, "Nice to be back, Mr. Jackson."

Max dropped his teacher's textbook on the desk. "Pop quiz."

The students groaned, which seemed to delight Max. He passed out a one-page test and announced they had ten minutes to finish. When he walked by Argus, he said, "If you need help catching up, see me after class."

Argus's first reaction was to completely ignore the offer, but on second thought, it might be a good idea to see what Max was up to. He'd turn the tables on Max and investigate him instead. The test was easy, and Argus finished it in about four minutes, but didn't want to be obvious, so pretended he was still working up until Max said to put their pencils down.

"Aced it," Lola whispered.

"Me, too." Argus smiled.

While Max taught the class, Argus daydreamed about Lola and how they'd go to the Homecoming dance together. Well, maybe not a dance. He had no idea how to dance.

When the bell rang, he hung back. "Lola, I'll see you at lunch, okay? I want to talk to Mr. Jackson to see what I missed all week."

"Oh, sure. I can help you with that if you like."

He watched Max. "Yeah, but I also want to see if I can find out how he got out of jail so fast."

"Oh, okay. Be careful though." She touched the heart around her neck. "Thanks for the necklace. I love it." She slung her backpack over her shoulder and left.

Max was busy stuffing the test papers into his briefcase when Argus approached. "Mr. Jackson."

"Mr. Dachel." He shut the briefcase. "You missed three days of school, right?"

Argus nodded. "Right."

"All right, that's not so bad, but missing the first week of school can put you behind very quickly. If you'd like a little one-on-one tutoring, we can get together after school."

Argus shook his head. "Oh, sorry, I have football practice today." *What are you up to, Max?*

"That's right, you're the new star quarterback. Well, perhaps over the weekend. We can meet at your house."

So that's what he wants, to find out where they live, which means he isn't sure. Argus shook his head again. "Not sure that's a good idea. My aunt doesn't like company, even a tutor. What about the library or *Marco's Pizza*?" Both were public places.

Max's eyes narrowed ever so slightly. He wasn't happy, but put on a forced smile. "Great idea. How about *Marco's* tomorrow, noon. My treat. Ah, the EBTKS okay?"

Argus laughed. "You sound like a local already. Um, everything but the kitchen sink is a bit much for me. Just plain cheese pizza is okay."

"Whatever you like, Argus." Max picked up the briefcase. "Now get to your next class before you're tardy."

Argus grabbed his backpack and went to his next class. He felt good at how easy it was to talk to Max, not awkward at all like he'd expected. He could do this. But he wasn't about to tell Aunt Celeste he was meeting Max on Saturday. If he could get information out of Max, he'd prove to her, and Galena, that he was old enough to do things on his own and didn't need the Citadel interfering. He wasn't a child anymore and didn't need to be protected.

At lunch, he took Lola to the parking lot to see the Camaro, but Tai was already there showing it off to a couple of girls. Lola loved the car, although she didn't seem to like the crowd and suggested they go for a walk around the track. That sounded like a much better idea than hanging around a car while a bunch of girls giggled and Tai gloated.

They strolled around the track, hand in hand, but had to retreat to a shady spot under a tree when the sun got too intense. Lola sighed and looked away.

Was she upset about something again? It wasn't like he'd done anything this time. In fact, he made a point of *not* looking at any cheerleaders that walked by. Might as well find out for sure. "What's wrong, Lola?"

"I know you think I'm crazy, but I really can do things with my mind. I threw my dad to the floor and then I...what's the word...levitated my phone that night you showed up in my room. I have powers, Argus. Please don't think I'm a freak. I don't know how I do it. I'm like I was before, but now I have these powers."

He wanted to hold her and tell her everything would be okay. But he couldn't tell the truth. Although if he didn't say something, she'd believe he really did think she was weird. "I'd never think you're crazy or a freak. It doesn't matter what you can or can't do." Change the subject, that was the answer. "Hey, have you ever been to Elizabeth Lake?"

She shook her head. "No. My dad never took us anywhere. But I've always wanted to go."

He'd love to show her the lake. "It's a great place. Maybe this weekend we can rent a kayak. There's a guy there who rents kayaks out."

She perked up. "Really? That'd be so cool. My mom's going to a meeting for abused women on Saturday, how about then?"

"Okay. After lunch, maybe around two? I'll pick you up." He couldn't wait. It'd be so much fun being alone with her for a while. Maybe he could even find a way to convince her that she didn't really have any special powers.

"Well, why don't we have lunch first?"

He shook his head. "Can't. I have a tutoring session with Mr. Jackson at noon."

"Are you kidding? Why? He's creepy. Not to mention you're not behind at all." Lola frowned and played with the gold heart around her neck.

Careful, Argus, she thinks you're ditching her. "I know, but I want to see if I can find out why he was sneaking around our house and how he got out of jail. Otherwise I'd definitely take you to lunch."

She nodded and smiled. "Okay, I get it. So you're like a detective. Did I tell you that's what I want to be? Actually, a crime scene investigator."

"That's a great plan."

That's why she liked science. He couldn't believe how lucky he was to have a friend like her. She sure didn't seem like she was only 16. "Dave told me that you skipped a grade." Should he have said that? What if it was a sensitive subject for her? Too late to take it back now though.

"Yeah, I did." She kept fiddling with the heart. "Does that make me like, a nerd? I'm not a genius or anything."

"I told you before, you're not weird in any way." He reached out and took her hand.

"Yeah, but I have mind powers." Her eyes were glassy.

He gave her hand a squeeze. "Lola, I like you exactly how you are. I don't care if you skipped a grade, in fact I think that's really cool. And I sure don't care if you have mind powers. That's about the coolest thing I've ever heard." He wanted to say, *if I accept you, maybe you'll accept me for what I am.*

She wiped her eyes. "Why do you like me, Argus? I mean, you're the quarterback, you're hot, and you're rich. Why me?"

What? She thought he was hot? Really? Him? Hot? "Are you serious? I'm lucky that a girl like you hangs out with me."

She shrugged and let go of his hand. "I've seen you looking at the pretty cheerleaders. You could go with any girl."

Why did she say that? It had to be her dad that'd made her so insecure. What a creep. He had no right to treat her so bad. "Lola, I don't want any other girl. I like hanging with you. You're perfect. I wouldn't change a thing about you even if I could." He checked the time. Lunch was almost over. "Look, we'll go kayaking on Saturday. And maybe a hike on Sunday. I'll pack a picnic lunch."

She finally let go of the heart pendant and nodded. "Okay, deal."

The rest of school went by fast without a sign of Justin Jones or Max. Tai told Aunt Celeste that he'd stick around to watch football practice so they could go home together.

Practice wasn't what Argus thought. It was tough, extremely tough, because he had to control his strength. A couple times he got carried away and threw the ball too hard. Coach Smith whooped it up and mumbled about how they were finally going to win a game. Argus couldn't wait. It was going to be fun playing a real game against another school. Best of all, Lola would be in the stands, cheering him on.

After practice, he wanted to go straight home, but Tai insisted on cruising around first since it was his turn in the driver's seat. He was carefully driving this time and loving every second of the attention as everyone waved and pointed and gave the car a thumbs-up. Even Argus got caught up and waved back.

On the third lap around town, Argus received a text message from Aunt Celeste:

Home. Now.

Damn. Argus groaned. "Tai, time to go home." He waved to Sandra who was standing outside *Marco's* as they passed by.

Tai slowed down. "She likes you, bro."

"She's simply being friendly. People can be friendly, you know." He knew she liked him. And he kind of liked her, too.

"Not her." Tai laughed and sped up, burning a little rubber. "She likes you."

Tai drove home with a silly grin on his face. Once inside, Aunt Celeste placed a couple of sandwiches on the breakfast bar. It was almost like having a mother around.

"How was your first day back?" she asked.

Tai shrugged. "Not bad, nothing exciting or Earth-shattering to report. But Arg has two girls after him." He laughed and bit into his sandwich.

Argus shoved Tai. "I do not."

Aunt Celeste leaned on the breakfast bar. "I thought you liked Lola. You bought her that five-hundred-dollar necklace."

Argus choked on his sandwich. "Five hundred dollars? It cost five hundred dollars?" He pushed his sandwich away and downed half a glass of water. "I didn't know it cost that much. What if she finds out? She'll think I want to marry her."

Tai laughed so hard he spat out bits of his sandwich. "Can I be the best man at your wedding?"

Argus gave him another shove. "That's not funny, Tai. I don't want her to think that...well, I mean I really do like her, but...five hundred dollars."

Aunt Celeste raised her eyebrow. "I didn't realize money was an issue. My expense account from the Citadel is quite substantial. Do you want to take it back and get something less expensive?"

He shook his head. "I can't do that. Maybe she won't realize. Aunt Celeste, next time tell me how much something is when I pick it out."

"You didn't object to the car." She straightened.

"Well, ah, the car is..." Argus couldn't find the words. He loved the car. It was the most awesome car at school.

Tai however, could find the words, "That car is one pimped out set of wheels. It's a chick magnet."

"I presume that means good?" Aunt Celeste sighed. "I've got a lot to learn about slang among modern youth."

Argus pulled the sandwich closer again. "Never mind about the cost of the necklace. It's fine. Are we rich?"

Aunt Celeste nodded. "According to modern convention, we would be classified as the wealthy class. Is that a problem for you, Argus?"

He shook his head. "No. At least I don't think so. I don't want the kids at school to think I'm a snob or anything." Especially since everyone always seemed to apologize for *not* having money.

"Snobbery is a behavior, not a given." Aunt Celeste poured a couple glasses of milk. "Because someone has money, doesn't automatically make them a snob."

Tai finished his sandwich. "It sure makes some people assholes though. There's this one kid at school who drives a Beamer and he's the biggest dick I've ever seen."

"Language, Tai." Aunt Celeste shook her head. "I'll need a teen slang thesaurus if I'm to communicate effectively."

Argus smiled. Poor Aunt Celeste. Fifty thousand years old and she couldn't keep up. "Um, I want to take Lola kayaking at Elizabeth Lake tomorrow. Is that okay?" He watched her as she considered the proposition.

She tilted her head and slowly nodded. "I suppose so. Elizabeth Lake is definitely one of the better places, as you know. If Jackson is still monitoring us, you'll be virtually untraceable there."

Tai objected. "Hey! What if I want the car?"

Argus shrugged. "You can have the car Sunday. I have a date on Saturday, and you don't."

"Yeah, yeah." Tai wandered off to his bedroom.

Aunt Celeste cleaned up the dishes. "Promise me you'll be careful, Argus. Remember, Galena's looking for an excuse to take control of you both."

"I will. I won't give her any reason to come back here." He headed to his bedroom.

Aunt Celeste didn't need to know about his meeting with Max. If she did, she'd never let him go, and she sure as hell wouldn't let him go kayaking afterward. Besides, nothing would happen at *Marco's* this time because he knew how to regulate his abilities. Not to mention Max's OEED was smashed to bits. It would be a piece of cake to do a little investigation into Max and see if he had any real data or not. *Let's see how you like being checked out, Max.*

Chapter 31

After grading the science quiz papers, Max logged onto his computer and checked his emails. As expected, there was one from Stone.

Jackson,

The local PD will back off your little snooping arrest providing you don't get caught again. If you do...you're fired. Time's ticking for you to give me hard evidence. So far, you've done nothing except annoy a local family and bring disgrace to AURA. I put my neck out for you, and I won't do it again. Next time you're arrested, you'll rot. 25 days left, Jackson.

Stone

Max smashed his finger on the delete button and read the next email. It was from Gretchen. Hopefully she had something on the Jared file from Edwards.

You owe me big time, Jackass. I got into the file and decoded it. Took a while, but you know me, I'm the best. I'm attaching a ZIP file, password protected. At six pm your time, I'll text you the password. What do you want this info for? It's bizarre and more than a little intriguing. Oh, by the way, my bank account's depleted. See what you can do about that.

Gretchen

He knew she'd come through. A Top-Secret file would be worth dipping into his bank account to fatten hers. He checked the time. It was only 4:45. Another hour and 15 minutes before she'd text the password.

This was turning out to be a very productive day. The next email was from Hector Chavez, the principal of Highland High School.

Staff:

Update: Justin Jones will be back in school on Monday. His parents have filed a negligence suit against the school board. Be vigilant on Monday if you see either of the Dachel brothers in the vicinity of Jones.

Have a good weekend.

Dr. Chavez

Oh, yeah, the Jones kid. He'd forgotten about it. He should probably investigate it further to see if there was anything to Jones' claim that the Dachel brothers somehow burned his hands. It was an odd claim, but the more he thought about it, the more he knew he should check into it.

He looked at the time again. 4:55. Gretchen wouldn't be texting the password for an hour. That gave him plenty of time to find Justin Jones' medical records. With most medical records documented digitally now, it shouldn't be too hard to find information on the injury.

Max used his Secret clearance to log into the medical record database and did a search. Sure, it was illegal, but who'd know. Right away he hit gold.

Medical Record Summary

Patient: Justin Jonathan Jones

Age: 17

Diagnosis: Severe third degree burns to both hands, dorsal surface, over first and second knuckle, approximately 2-3 cm circular pattern. Appears to be through contact with caustic substance as stated by patient. Negative on electric burn.

Prognosis: Possible skin graft to repair major dermal damage.

"Wow," Max mumbled out loud.

If it was true, what did Tai and Argus Dachel do to Jones? What caustic substance did they have and where'd they get it? If these kids were playing with acid, it was serious business. Max read some more. Both hands burned in almost the exact same place. Jones claimed he'd punched both Dachel brothers at different times and received the same severe burn each time. How could the brothers splash acid on Jones' hands after he punched them? Burns to his face maybe, but not his knuckles. It didn't add up.

Max practiced throwing punches and then pretended to be on the receiving end of a punch, but no matter how he tried, he couldn't see how to splash or throw a caustic substance on the attacker's hand. It wasn't possible. That meant that Jones was probably lying to get the brothers in trouble. What an ass.

It was only 5:00, an hour to go. He shut down the computer and got into the shower, taking longer than he usually did, enjoying the cooling water as it ran over his body. The desert heat had sunk into his bones and the water was great.

He dried off, checked the time, 5:25, and switched on the TV. The 5:00 news was almost over, but it was better than watching some old sitcom rerun. He sprawled out on the bed and relaxed. At exactly 6:00, his cell phone chirped. He jumped up, grabbed it, and read the text:

Ssakcaj

He stared at it for a few seconds until he realized it was jackass backwards. Funny, Gretchen, real funny. He logged back into the computer, downloaded the ZIP file, and unzipped it with the password.

The file was huge. It included pages and pages of notes, photographic folders within the file, medical data, psych profiles, and weird calculations. Damn, it was going to take all night to read through even half of the data. But he had to because he wanted to find out if there was any viable link between Argustine Lenox and Argus Dachel before tomorrow's meeting at noon at *Marco's*.

He opened the photograph folder and saw General Jared Daniels with Argustine Lenox giving a presentation to a group of military personnel, General Daniels sitting in a military court chambers as a defendant, and a slightly blurry photo of Argustine Lenox in handcuffs sitting at a table in a white-washed room. The room looked like an interrogation room, so maybe the photo was from a camera or through a one-way mirror. What had happened?

He thought back to what the Air Force guys John Franklin and Angel Flores told him. An alien was captured, but when the scientists were going to do brain surgery, the alien killed everyone and escaped. What if Argustine Lenox was that alien? Having him arrested and tried for espionage would give the military access to him without the regular court system being wise to what they were up to. It was brilliant. So where did Argustine Lenox go?

Another photograph popped up. It was some sort of high-tech airplane, the XTRA-A1 Super Stealth Bomber. The caption said it was 1963. 1963? The plane looked futuristic, more so than the ultra-modern fighters they had today. Was Lenox using alien technology to build a superior aircraft? And if he was, why?

Next, Max opened a folder marked *Top Secret-Ramtala*. What on Earth was Ramtala? Another bomber prototype? The folder contained scanned copies of handwritten notes and more photographs. The first photo was disturbing to say the least. Argustine Lenox was strapped to a gurney, naked except for a sheet over his privates, his wrists in thick leather restraints, and his head shaved. There were three men in surgical masks, doctors maybe, standing beside the gurney. Lenox appeared to be unconscious. Damn, was this when they were going to attempt brain surgery?

He clicked on one of the handwritten notes:

September 12, 1963-Daniels

Lenox isn't cooperating with the military tribunal. I told him to play along, but he won't. They must know that the XTRA-A1 isn't really a bomber. How did they find out? Not from me and I guarantee not from Lenox. They have him drugged on Thorazine to stop him using his qualities as he calls them. I have to try to free him. I believe they know I've been helping him with the XTRA-A1 design and implementation. This was his only hope of returning home.

Max was stunned. It was true. Lenox was an alien. And the bomber was a spaceship. Holy hell! He clicked on the next file, another handwritten note, only this one was scribbled and hardly legible.

September 19, 1963-Daniels

I've been betrayed! How could I be so stupid? It's over, it's all over. Lenox escaped and killed 29 personnel. He'll come for me next. I don't care. What I've done deserves punishment. If anyone finds this, please know that I was in the dark. Lenox convinced me he was only trying to go home. Now I know that he built the XTRA-A1 to destroy something he calls New Breeds. I don't know what they are or where they are, but apparently he considers them enemies and wants to kill them. He'll stop at nothing and has no regard for human life. I tried to get him to go back to his home planet, Ramtala, but he won't. God help us all.

Max's felt like his heart would explode. That was the last note from Daniels. *Thank you, Gretchen!* He clicked on another file labeled: *Astronomical Data-Ramtala.* The information was way over his head, but he did manage to understand that Ramtala was a planet located on a different spiral arm in the Milky Way galaxy. Incredible.

He clicked onto several other files, one with a medical record of Lenox. Nothing notable except for a slightly elevated body temperature. However, a notation at the bottom of the record stated simply:

Body temperature level of prisoner Lenox in OR prior to disappearance was normal, at moment of disappearance, temperature increased to over 400 degrees F. Host body vaporized and prisoner presumed dead.

He read the notation again. Host body? Four hundred degrees? This couldn't get any better. Once Stone saw the file, he'd have to admit he was wrong.

"Oh, damn," Max muttered.

He couldn't show the file to Stone. It was Top Secret. Stone would want to know how he got into the database. He couldn't very well sell out Gretchen again. Or could he? Exposing the truth about aliens on Earth would be worth anything. He'd make it up to her somehow. But first things first. He had a meeting with Argus at *Marco's* tomorrow.

Argus was the key somehow. The key that would lead to the greatest discovery in history. That kid had to be taken into custody and questioned. No way was he going to get away like Argustine Lenox did. No way in hell.

Chapter 32

Argus hadn't slept well. Kayaking with Lola had his mind was going a mile a minute thinking of what to talk about. He'd also mentioned hiking with her on Sunday, if she was up to it, and since he promised the car to Tai, he'd have to ask Aunt Celeste if he could borrow the SUV. In the back of his mind, he thought about Max.

After showering and getting dressed, he ate breakfast, played some video games with Tai, started an essay for English and finished his math homework. At 11:30, he drove off toward *Marco's*. He probably should feel afraid or nervous, but he didn't. Not at all. In fact, he was looking forward to finding out what Max was going to say and what sort of probing questions he had in mind.

With little traffic on the roads, he got to *Marco's* with five minutes to spare. He turned on the radio and waited in the car. Only a couple minutes had passed when Max drove up and parked beside him.

Max waved and got out, came around to the Camaro and gave a thumbs up. "Very cool car, Argus."

Argus got out, locked the car, and nodded. "It is."

"I always wanted a Camaro. Ah, well. Shall we go inside?" Max led the way, holding the door open.

Sandra was working again and smiled widely when Argus came in. "Hey, Argus. You're getting to be a regular these days."

He shrugged and followed her to a booth near the front. "I come to see you, Sandra." That wasn't a good thing to say. Not at all. *Take it back, Argus!* "I mean, I come for the pizza. Do you work here every day? You're here every time I come in." Nice recovery, maybe.

Max was smiling as he sat down and picked up a menu. He promptly put it back on the table. "Oh, that's right, we'll have a large cheese pizza, a couple of Cokes and some garlic bread, too."

Sandra jotted down the order, smiled at Argus, and hurried off to the kitchen.

"You like her?" Max asked, still smiling. "I haven't seen her around Highland High."

Argus didn't feel like talking about Sandra. "She goes to Palmdale High. So, Mr. Jackson, I'm not behind in science, but if there was any homework I missed—"

"You only missed one lab assignment, but that was done in class, and you can't really make it up. Only worth ten points, so I think you'll be all right. We can talk shop and go over some scientific nomenclature or chat about any other topic. I want to get to know you better. Your choice."

"Um, I guess we should, what's that expression, break the ice?" Argus had no intention of breaking the ice, he wanted to get down to business and find out more about Max. "I'll start. How long have you been teaching?"

Max looked like he was taken completely by surprise. "Oh, ah, about...ten years. I taught English before, but science and math are my forté. You like science, Argus?"

He nodded. "One of my best subjects. So where do you live? I haven't seen you around town before?"

"I've recently moved here. Staying in a motel right now until I find a house. Your name. It's unusual. Family name?"

Argus waited while Sandra placed a basket of garlic bread and two Cokes on the table. She gave him a sweet smile and a wink. A wink? What could he say? He'd hurt her feelings if he told her he hadn't meant to say what he said before. Best to leave it alone for now. Lola would never know.

"Argus?" Max slid the basket of garlic bread across the table.

"Oh, sorry. What were...oh, my name. I don't know why my parents chose my name. I don't remember my parents."

"I apologize, I shouldn't have brought that up. It's just that Argus isn't exactly a California-sounding name. Were you born in California?" Max took a long sip of his drink.

These questions were getting annoying. What was Max up to? "Yes, born and raised in Palmdale."

"And your aunt? You mother's or father's sister?"

Shit. He hadn't anticipated questions about Aunt Celeste. She didn't look like either of his parents, at least not from any of the few pictures he had of them. "My father's sister."

"She seems like a lovely woman. Does she work from home? I mean, she home schooled you and your brother, so she must stay at home." Max smiled up at Sandra when she brought the pizza and placed it on a stand in the center of the table.

Okay, time for more lies. Argus shoved a plastic spatula under the pizza and placed a slice on one of the plates Sandra brought. "She does something with computers at home. Telecommuting. Now my turn for questions." Yeah, Max, time for you to be in the hot seat. "I heard a rumor that you were arrested for trespassing. Is that true? How'd you get out?"

The look on Max's face almost made Argus burst out laughing. The man was positively pale, and his eyes were wide, all deer-in-the-headlights.

Max took a drink of Coke and dabbed his mouth with a napkin. "How odd that you heard about that. It was all a misunderstanding. Since coming to Palmdale, I've developed quite an interest in landscape photography. The desert is beautiful. I was taking a few snapshots and accidentally went onto someone's property. I've got nothing to hide, Argus. I've got a clear record, not even a speeding ticket." He smiled, looking smug.

Argus nodded, pretending he believed him. *Oh, sure, Max, you accidentally scaled an eight-foot wall while taking photos without a camera.*

Max continued, "Tell me, Argus, what do you know about Argustine Lenox?"

Who the heck was Argustine Lenox? Sounded like a rock star or maybe a computer billionaire. But why would Max ask about a random rock star or businessman? No, there was a reason he was asking. Argus shook his head. "Never heard of him. Or her."

"It's a him. Are you sure? Think about it, your name is Argus and his name is Argus-tine. Similar, eh? What are the odds of that, do you suppose?"

This game was getting weird. Okay, the names were similar, but that didn't mean anything. Or did it? "Well, with that line of reasoning, you could have something to do with Mexican Emperor Max-imillian." He paused to let it sink in. "So, who is Argustine Lenox?"

"An aerospace engineer, a scientist. Worked at Edwards Air Force Base. Hey, look at that. Another coincidence. You're good at science as well. Sure you've never heard of Lenox?" Max leaned back and folded his arms across his chest. "I think you know exactly who he is."

Why the accusatory tone? Argus really wanted to know who Lenox was and what connection Max was looking for. "I'm not sure why you think I'd know anything about an aerospace engineer." Argus felt his cell phone vibrating in his pocket. It could be Tai or Aunt Celeste. He had to take the call. "Excuse me for a second, Mr. Jackson."

He opened a text message from Aunt Celeste:

Why are you at Marco's with Max Jackson?

Oh, great. How did she know? Of course, the Camaro. She must have a GPS tracker on the car, and she had the Citadel keeping track of Max's whereabouts. He replied:

I was meeting Lola and Max showed up. Everything's fine.

An instant reply:
Lola is still at her house. Now, the truth or I'll come there myself.

"Everything all right, Argus?" asked Max, leaning forward, trying to read the messages.

"Sure." Argus tilted the phone so Max couldn't see. He quickly typed:

Who is Argustine Lenox?

No response came for a few seconds.
Get away from Jackson now!

Wow, that was an extreme reaction to a simple question. Why didn't she want to tell him?

Aunt Celeste, who is Argustine Lenox? I'm not going anywhere until you tell me.

"Your pizza's getting cold, Argus." Max drummed his fingers on the tabletop.

"Sorry, I know it's rude to text, but it's my brother. He's stuck on a homework math problem."

Finally, the response:

Argustine Lenox is an Invader from Ramtala who allowed himself to get caught by the US government. Now get away from Jackson.

Argus felt his stomach drop. An Invader? He put the phone away and stood. "I have to go. Thanks for lunch."

"Whoa, hold on there, Argus." Max wriggled out of the booth. "We didn't have the chance to finish our conversation and you didn't even eat your food. Why don't you stay for a few more minutes? You can help your brother later, after all, it's Saturday, he's got all weekend for homework."

"No, I really need to go. See you at school." Argus turned, but after he took only a few steps, Max grabbed the back of his jacket.

"I really must insist that we finish our conversation. I also want to find out what you did to Justin Jones."

Argus felt a sharp jab into the side of his neck. Before he knew it, he couldn't see clearly and the sounds around him were muffled. He tried to concentrate on Tai or Aunt Celeste but couldn't focus on anything. His legs were heavy, and he was vaguely conscious of being dragged. It sounded like someone said, "he's sick" and "taking him home". Was it Max's voice? It was distant and garbled, could be anyone.

He wasn't unconscious, but almost. He was in the back seat of a car, maybe. They were moving, driving to who knows where. Was he really going home? His stomach clenched, he felt sick. The car stopped.

He was supported, half carried by someone, but his legs dragged behind him, he couldn't get them to move. No matter how hard he tried, he couldn't move and couldn't concentrate enough to dissolve. Again, his stomach turned. It was from panic, real panic. He'd never felt this helpless and afraid before.

Now he lay on a bed or couch; it was soft. And light, there was a bright light shining through his closed eyelids. He wanted to yell, scream, ask what was happening, but no words came out of his mouth.

"Argus, you with me? Argus?" It was definitely Max's voice, louder, clearer, closer.

Argus swallowed. "Yes." Finally, he could talk.

"Good. Don't worry, you've had a dose of liquid Valium. It's harmless. You'll be fine."

Even though his eyelids were still heavy, Argus forced them open. What was liquid Valium? "Where..." Through blurry eyes he saw that he was in a furnished room. Max's motel room?

"Keep quiet and this'll go easier. If you try to shout for help, your brother won't be treated near as well."

Did that mean he had Tai as well? "Why are you doing this?" Argus tried to move his arms and legs, but they were restrained.

"Oh, Argus, we both know why. I couldn't let you walk out of *Marco's* without getting any answers, now could I? Hold still."

Argus blinked and focused his eyes enough to see Max lean over him. A second later there was a sharp sting in his right forearm.

Max straightened. "I gave you an injection of Amobarbital. Truth serum. Now you'll tell me everything."

"I don't know any...thing..." Argus was drowsy again, lightheaded, removed. Was he floating, still on the bed, on the floor? He couldn't tell. He closed his eyes.

"Yes, you do. Tell me about Argustine Lenox."

"Argustine...he's an...aerospace eng..."

"Yes, yes, go on."

Argus couldn't feel his tongue. "Aerospace..."

"Did Argustine Lenox go back to Ramtala?"

"Ramtala. Spiral arm...Milky Way..."

"Uh-huh, and where is Lenox now?" Max's voice was very close.

Argus had the urge to speak, to keep talking, but he knew he shouldn't. But why not? What shouldn't he say? His mind was confused, twisted up in knots. "Aunt Celeste...no...no...photometric...Argustine..."

"Come on, Argus, we're getting nowhere. Okay, let's try this. What do you know about Ramtala?"

That was easy. Argus even had a telescope that would point to Ramtala. And Aunt Celeste was a pure-form from Ramtala, but he was a New Breed, same as Tai. Did he say that out loud? Was he supposed to? He swallowed. "Thirsty."

"You can have a drink of water when you tell me what I want to know. Again, what do you know about Ramtala. And what do you know about aliens?"

"Aliens? In Palmdale?" He swallowed again. His throat burned and his stomach hurt. Pain. What was it about pain? Pain was important. But why? He was sleepy.

"Argus? Argus, you still with me? Argus? Damn it, shouldn't have mixed the Valium with Amo. Argus?" Max shook him.

"Stop...it." Argus thought of Lola. They were going kayaking, weren't they? When? Today? What day was it?

"I'll stop it when you start cooperating."

There was a loud crack, like splintering wood. Argus opened his eyes. The room was spinning, but somewhere among the wobbling of the room, he thought he saw a figure, a tall figure. Aunt Celeste. Could it really be her or was he dreaming? He had no idea.

A stern shout, "Get away from him!"

A reply, "How did you...?"

A burst of brilliant light. A thump against the wall. Quiet.

"Argus? Argus, can you hear me?" it was Aunt Celeste.

"I...what...Valium...truth ser..." his words were slurred, heavy and thick.

"Hang on, Argus. I'm taking you home."

She picked him up. It was like he was floating. He was too tired to stay awake any longer. Sleep was all he could think of. There was a familiar smell around him. Leather? Was he in the SUV? It didn't matter, he needed sleep.

Chapter 33

Argus shivered. He opened his eyes. He was at home in his bed. Tai paced back and forth, and Aunt Celeste sat on the edge of the bed. His mind flooded with images and thoughts, but he couldn't put them in order.

"Argus?" Aunt Celeste felt his forehead. "Can you hear me?"

He nodded. "Yeah. What...happened?"

"I'll tell you what happened, bro. That damn Max Jackson, that's what happened." Tai stopped pacing and sat on the other side of the bed. "How are you feeling? I'm going to make him pay."

Argus struggled to site up a bit and pulled the blanket up to his chest. "I guess I'm okay. I'm cold."

Aunt Celeste placed a pillow behind his back. "You're coming off the drugs Jackson gave you. I think Valium and Amytal sodium from what you tried to say in the motel room."

Argus licked his dry lips. "Amobarbital I think."

"Same thing. I never suspected he'd stoop to that level. And what were you thinking?" Aunt Celeste held a glass of water to his lips. "Drink. You're dehydrated. I underestimated AURA. That won't happen again."

The water was so good. It trickled down his parched throat and revived him. The fragmented information in his mind began to sort itself out. "Max asked me about...um, Argustine...Argustine...Lenox."

"What?" Aunt Celeste put the glass down, her eyes widening. "What exactly did he say? Try to think."

"It's fuzzy, Aunt Celeste. He drugged me at *Marco's*. How could he do that? I can't believe nobody did anything."

"People see what they want to see, Argus." Aunt Celeste sighed.

Argus sat up. "I've got to call Lola. We were going kayaking at Elizabeth Lake." He didn't want to disappoint her.

"I took care of that, bro. I called her and said you were sick." Tai handed the water to Argus again. "Have some more water."

After finishing the glass of water, Argus swung his legs over the side of the bed. "Aunt Celeste, why is Max asking about Argustine Lenox? He thought I knew who he was. And I'm not sure if I'm remembering this or not, but I think he was asking about Ramtala."

"That doesn't surprise me." Aunt Celeste got up. "If he knows about Argustine Lenox, then he certainly knows about Ramtala."

"Who the hell is Lenox?" Tai asked.

"He's an Invader." She extended her hand and helped Argus stand.

Argus was unsteady on his feet, but it felt good to stand. "Wait, he *is* an Invader, or he *was* an Invader?"

"Is. He was on Earth in the sixties. Right here in Palmdale. He was captured by the Air Force at Edwards. Prior to his capture, he'd convinced a general that he had to build a craft to get back to Ramtala."

"It wasn't true?" Tai's eyes flashed blue.

Aunt Celeste shook her head. "No. Remember, I told you that pure-form Ramtalans don't require space craft to go from one planet to the next. We must revert to pure-form without our host bodies though. The true purpose behind the building of the craft isn't known."

Argus held onto the wall so he wouldn't fall. "How did Max find out about Lenox?"

"That's what I want to know." Tai paced. "If Max kidnapped Argus, there has to be a reason and Argustine Lenox is mixed up in there somewhere."

"Calm down, Tai," Aunt Celeste ordered. "I don't know what connection Jackson is trying to make or why he kidnapped Argus. But I do intend to find out."

Argus staggered to the window. It was dark outside. "What time is it?" He'd lost most of the day.

Tai joined him at the window. "Almost midnight. I don't know what happened, Arg, I couldn't feel that you needed help. I'm sorry. If I'd felt something, I would have used shared-sight earlier."

Argus drew in a breath and filled his lungs. His throat was still raw. "Earlier? You used shared-sight? When? Maybe it was the drugs he gave me. I couldn't even concentrate properly. I tried to get away, but—"

"Don't dwell on it." Aunt Celeste placed her hand on his shoulder. "Back to bed. You need to recover."

He did as she said because his legs were still shaky, and he really wanted to lie down. "How did you find me? Did you break the door down? I thought I heard a loud crash."

She frowned. "I know your car didn't move from Marco's, but Jackson's car drove away. You didn't respond to any of my other text messages or calls, so I knew there was trouble. That's when I asked Tai to use shared-sight, but your eyes were closed so he couldn't see anything. I tracked Jackson to the motel." She looked away.

"And?" Argus knew she wasn't telling the whole story. "There's more, isn't there?"

"The Citadel has him. I had to use a photometric pulse to subdue him. It's generally forbidden to use the pulse on humans, but it was an emergency. I was exposed and had to call the commander at the Citadel." She lowered her eyes. "We will have to talk about this, but only once you're better. Sleep now."

Sleep? How could he possibly sleep after all that had happened? He wanted to hear more and find out what the Citadel would do with Max, and he wanted to talk to Lola. "I can't sleep."

"You will, Argus. I'm still your Guardian."

Still? So that meant she wasn't being sent away. That was good. That was very good. "Aunt Celeste, what'll happen to Max?"

Somber, Aunt Celeste explained quietly, "He'll be questioned. As far as we knew, AURA was in the dark about Argustine Lenox, and we had no idea that Jackson would ever find out. It's Top-Secret information and Jackson only has a Secret clearance. This means someone provided him with information. The Citadel will find out and locate his source or sources." She looked sad.

Tai whistled. "Whoa. Is the Citadel going to kill him and his source? Will they really do that?"

A cold chill hit Argus. If he hadn't agreed to meet Max, the Citadel wouldn't have him and maybe kill him. "It's my fault if anything happens to him."

"Don't think like that. Jackson knew the risks when he joined AURA. You can't chase after aliens and not expect catastrophic results." She shrugged and frowned again. "That's a quote from Argustine Lenox."

"You're not telling us everything, are you?" Argus watched her. There was something wrong.

"I may be recalled to Ramtala. I have a meeting with a tribunal from the Citadel tomorrow. You two are to come as well." She brought her ponytail to the front and ran her hand through it.

Argus knew that was what she did when she was nervous. With his heart pounding, he leaned against the pillows and tried to relax. "Why do we have to go? Will we be allowed to come back home?" All he could think of was Lola. What if it was a trap and once they were at the Citadel, Galena would force them to stay?

Aunt Celeste's expression changed, less emotion and back to being unreadable. "It will depend on the tribunal's decision. It has always been the goal to keep New Breeds among humans in as natural a setting as possible. Removal is only done in the most urgent circumstances. If the tribunal is satisfied with removing the threat—Max Jackson—then they will likely agree to allow you two to remain here."

"And what if they're not?" Tai's voice rose in volume.

That was exactly what Argus wondered. Their lives would be determined by people, well, Ramtalans, who they didn't even know. He and Tai were almost eighteen, why couldn't they decide for themselves where they wanted to live? It was like they didn't have any rights at all.

Aunt Celeste continued, "If the tribunal doesn't agree, then you will live at the Citadel for your own safety."

"That's BS!" Tai's eyes glowed.

"Take it easy, Tai," Argus cautioned. "We don't know anything about this tribunal or about the Citadel." The thought of being a prisoner at the Citadel with nothing but pure-forms wasn't appealing at all. "Um, Aunt Celeste, where is the Citadel?"

She glanced at Tai. "Tai, you need to relax." She turned to Argus. "It's on a small island off the coast of Labrador in Canada. You learned about Canada in our geography lessons, remember?"

Tai nodded. "Yeah, there are hundreds of islands around Newfoundland which is in the Atlantic near Labrador."

So that's why Aunt Celeste drilled them on Canada and Labrador. "Thousands," Argus corrected. "Thousands of islands. But, I shouldn't go. I still don't feel well." It was worth a try.

"You'll be fine by morning." Aunt Celeste pulled the blankets up. "Go to sleep. We'll talk more tomorrow."

"When do we leave?" Tai grumbled.

"Two in the afternoon from Los Angeles. I have a flight booked to Labrador." Aunt Celeste pushed Tai out of the room and turned off the light. "Sleep, Argus."

He lay in the dark, staring into the blackness. He'd fly to another country tomorrow and he hadn't even spoken to Lola to explain things. That wasn't right. He had to call her before she thought he wasn't interested. It was late, but he couldn't leave without talking to her. He dialed her number.

"Argus?" she sounded anxious and fully awake. "How are you? Are you feeling better?"

"I guess." Partially true. "Sorry for calling so late. Did I wake you?"

"No. I couldn't sleep. I was...worried about you."

He hated lying to her. "Don't be. I'm fine. Ah, I wanted to let you know that we're going out of town for a while. I couldn't leave without talking to you. I'm sorry I missed our date."

There was a pause. "That's okay. We'll go some other time. No biggie. So where are you going? Is this something to do with you being sick today? Are you okay to travel?"

"Yeah. I'm fine now."

He wanted to be there with her in her room, to see her and hold her. The possibility of living at the Citadel without her was tearing him apart. This couldn't be happening. Why couldn't it all be a dream? Then he could wake up and he'd be a regular kid without alien DNA and special abilities.

"So where are you going?" Lola sounded sad, her voice flat and quiet.

"We're going to visit friends of Aunt Celeste's. Up north." He yawned, still slightly drowsy from the drugs. It was all Max's fault. If Max hadn't drugged him, none of this would be happening. Then again, meeting Max for lunch was a stupid thing to do. Part of them blame fell right on Argus's shoulders.

"I'm keeping you up. Argus, you can text me any time. You know that, right?"

"Yeah. I'm going to miss you, Lola. You can text me, too. Hey, maybe we can have breakfast in the morning. Our plane doesn't leave until two." Why didn't he think of that before? He had to see her one last time.

"That'd be great," her voice rose, and she sounded happy now.

"Cool. I'll call you know in the morning and come around to pick you up. Good night, Lola." He imagined her sitting up in bed, her journal by her side, those green eyes giving off a sparkle in the lamp light.

"Night, Argie." She hung up.

Argie? She called him Argie. A nickname. He liked it. Did that mean she was his girlfriend? How do you know when you have a girlfriend? Are you supposed to talk about it, come out and say it, or is it assumed? He held the phone gently, pretending it was her hand. Maybe Tai would know more about the boyfriend/girlfriend thing. He always seemed to know more about being a teenager.

Argus closed his eyes, phone in hand. A part of him was excited to see the Citadel and meet other Ramtalans, but the other part of him wished he was all human and never knew there were pure-forms, New Breeds, or AURA agents. If the commander at the Citadel decided to kill Max, wouldn't other AURA agents come looking for him? Argus swallowed. He'd be responsible for a human getting killed. Even Max didn't deserve to die.

If Max vanished, it'd cause more trouble. The Citadel wouldn't want droves of agents combing the streets of Palmdale looking for Ramtalans and New Breeds. They'd probably question Max and erase his memories or something.

Argus felt a bit better about things. Maybe he could speak to the commander and explain how much he, and Tai, wanted to remain in human society, and that killing Max would only bring more trouble. Then they'd let Max go and allow Aunt Celeste to stay as their Guardian.

He felt lighter, like the pressure on him evaporated. A good night's sleep is what he needed to clear his head. He placed the phone on the bedside table. In the morning he'd see Lola and maybe he'd get the nerve to give her a real kiss.

Chapter 34

Max felt pain. Nothing else mattered except for the pain. He tried to pinpoint it. His wrists, his ankles, and most of all, his head. Sharp, piercing, blinding pain in his head. What was going on? How could he make the pain stop?

There were phantom voices floating around him, first near his head, then to the side. Everywhere. He couldn't see, something covered his eyes. He wanted to talk, but his voice wouldn't come.

"Ah, you are awake, Mr. Jackson," came a smooth male voice that enunciated each word precisely. "You are probably wondering where you are. The location is secret, but I can tell you that you are at Ramtalan headquarters on planet Earth. I am Jampara, Settler Commander. I will have the endotracheal tube removed so you can talk. It will take but a moment."

Max trembled. Was this some sort of joke or dream or was it real? The extreme pain in his head wouldn't allow him to think about it for long. He had to make the pain stop. When the tube slid up his throat and out of his mouth, he coughed and almost vomited.

"Relax, Mr. Jackson. The tube is out. Did you wish to speak?"

"My head," Max said hoarsely. "My head hurts. Make it stop. Please."

"Oh, yes. We have probes inserted into your cerebellum. They are stimulating the pain receptors in your brain. It is an effective form of punishment for humans that leaves no permanent damage. The pain will cease only if you confess how you discovered the information about Argustine Lenox."

"I can't stand it. Make it stop!" Max shouted, his throat raw from the tube.

"Tell me about Argustine Lenox and the XTRA-A1. You received an email containing a Top-Secret file, but the sender has hidden their identity very effectively. There is no IP address from the email. Who sent you the file, Mr. Jackson?"

"I don't know what you're talking about. I'm a government agent, you have no right to torture me." Max struggled, but his wrists and ankles were held firmly in metallic restraints that bit into his skin. As he moved, he realized he was naked. "Let me go!" There was a hand on his shoulder, a warm hand that stroked his skin.

"There is a simplistic solution, Mr. Jackson. Tell me what you know, and I shall free you."

"Okay. I hacked into the file. All I know is that...Argustine Lenox was from Ramtala, but I...don't know where that is. He built a bomber and was put on trial for...ah...espionage. He died. That's all I know. Now please, stop the pain." Max felt sick, his chest hurt, and his stomach was in knots from the pain. "Please."

Silence. Then someone took off the covering over his eyes. Max blinked and saw a blurry figure over him, touching his shoulder. His eyes focused more, or maybe they didn't, because the figure was light blue, all over, looking more like a cartoon version of a ghost than a person. The figure had arms and legs, but they didn't look solid.

"I am Jampara, Mr. Jackson."

Jampara waved his hand over Max's head and in an instant, the pain stopped.

An immense sense of relief washed over Max. "Thank you."

"Oh, do not thank me quite yet, Mr. Jackson. I removed the pain so you can speak clearly without having a distraction to cloud your thoughts."

"What's going on? I'm a government agent. You can't—"

"Yes, you already said that. For your information, Mr. Jackson, I can do whatever I please. Besides, we are not in the United States. You will answer my questions accurately or I shall intensify the pain."

Jampara came closer and Max saw that his eyes were large, almond-shaped, and black. Black eyes. Where had he seen black eyes before? On Argus, that's where. "How did I get here?"

"No, Mr. Jackson. I ask the questions. Why have you been investigating the Dachel brothers? Of what concern are they to you?"

"The Dachel brothers?" Max had no intention of telling the truth. "I'm not investigating them. I'm undercover as a substitute teacher at their school, looking for evidence of a drug ring involving students. I've only just met the Dachel brothers."

Jampara leaned down close, those black eyes staring into Max's and the slit of a mouth opening slightly. "Mr. Jackson, with a touch, I can stop your heart." He placed his hand on Max's chest and immediately Max's heart started thumping harder and harder. "The truth or I shall destroy you. What do you know about Argus and Tai Dachel?"

Max's chest constricted and a new pain radiated across his chest and down his left arm. "Stop! I don't know anything. I kidnapped Argus because I think there's a connection between him and Lenox. That's all. Please stop." He gritted his teeth as sweat rolled down his face.

Jampara took his hand away and the pain stopped in an instant. "You administered drugs to Argus. Your selfish, stupid attempt to build a case against the boy could have killed him. Do you have any idea how important those boys are to Ramtala?" his voice was louder and deeper, angrier.

"No, I don't. I told you I don't know anything." Max swallowed. He knew Jampara wasn't going to let him go. Jampara admitted he and the Dachel brothers were aliens. That wasn't the sort of thing you'd tell someone if you were going to let them go.

"I can hear your thoughts, Mr. Jackson. I will release you if you tell the truth. How many people in your organization know about Ramtala, Lenox, and the Dachel brothers?"

Max shook his head and felt wires jiggle. The probes? Shit, can this guy read minds? "Nobody. My boss wants proof of aliens on Earth but doesn't have any faith in me that I'll find any. I don't want to hurt anybody. I want to keep my job."

"Is your job worth causing the loss of an entire species? We have been on this planet for fifty thousand planetary years, nurturing our kind. We belong here as much, if not more, than you do."

Really? Fifty thousand years? How could that be? Max swallowed again, but his sore throat made him wince. When Jampara moved away, more like floating than walking, Max checked out the room. Stainless steel cabinets, like the table he was strapped to, and white concrete walls with no windows.

Cold, clinical, with bright lights overhead. An operating room? He trembled again. Like the room Lenox was in when they were going to do brain surgery? No, no, no. He had to get away.

Jampara came back holding what looked like a hand-held auger or drill. What the hell was he going to do with that? Max couldn't breathe. He sweated more even though he was naked, and the room was cold. Was he going to be tortured more or worse, killed? Why would Jampara kill him? He mostly told the truth.

"Yes, Mr. Jackson, you mostly told the truth."

The auger or drill was right in front of his eyes now, getting closer and closer. Max felt sick to his stomach, his vision faded, and a blackness crept in all around. He was about to pass out.

Chapter 35

The blinding morning sun shone right into Argus's room because he'd left the curtains wide open. It was only seven. He sat up, stretched, and thought about the right words to say to Aunt Celeste so she'd let him visit Lola before they left for the Citadel. He got out of bed, amazed at how much better he felt, and took a quick shower.

After drying off, he got dressed in his favorite pair of jeans and a black tee shirt and headed to the kitchen. He didn't want to come right out and ask to go and see Lola because Aunt Celeste would almost certainly say no. What would Tai say to convince her? He always had a way of twisting things around.

"Morning, bro," Tai greeted from a stool at the breakfast bar. "You look good."

"Yeah, I feel good. Where's Aunt Celeste?" Argus sat next to his brother.

"Packing. Why?"

Argus lowered his voice, "I want to see Lola and I need something Tai-like to say to get Aunt Celeste to let me go."

"Tai-like? Ah, okay, let me think. Oh. Tell her that Mom would have wanted you say goodbye to your friends, so you want to drop by and see Lola, and Dave of course so she's not suspicious. Since she's our Guardian, she really should honor Mom's wishes and since Mom's not here because Aunt Celeste couldn't save her, you want to do what Mom would have wanted." He smiled. "Tai-like enough for you?"

"Damn. Yeah. But I don't know if I can guilt her like that though." Argus was amazed at how fast Tai came up with that.

"You can. It's basically the truth. She's coming." Tai grabbed a magazine and pretended to read.

Aunt Celeste came into the kitchen, her hair loose, not in its usual ponytail. "Argus, you're up. I thought you'd sleep later."

"I guess I had enough sleep. Can I ask you something?" He glanced at Tai who subtly winked.

"Of course." She raised an eyebrow expectantly.

Word for word he repeated what Tai said and then waited while Aunt Celeste tilted her head slightly like she always did when she considered a question or proposition. She looked over at Tai and back at Argus.

"I cannot allow you to leave. It's dangerous. My orders are to bring you both to the Citadel. We leave in a matter of hours. I understand that you want to say your goodbyes to your friends, but you'll have to call them instead." She took the magazine away from Tai. "Do you agree, Tai?"

"Oh, gosh, ah, well, not really. Look Aunt Celeste, New Breeds like us, well, we need human companionship. We bond with the humans and being away from them will be, ah, painful. I think Argus should go and spend a little time with Lola. And Dave."

She sighed. "I suppose you didn't know anything about this, did you, Tai?"

He shook his head and grabbed the magazine again. Argus looked at his brother, his twin brother, and replayed the words "New Breeds like us" over in his head. Tai wasn't a New Breed anymore, he was more Ramtalan. He still seemed like the same Tai, but in truth, he wasn't. Argus turned away for a moment to collect himself.

"Argus, are you upset at what I said?" Aunt Celeste came to him and placed her hand on his shoulder.

This might work after all. Argus nodded. "Yeah, I am. I thought you'd be pleased that I fit into human society so well and have two friends after only a week." His sadness washed away, and he now had to hide a smile.

"All right. You can go. But only until 10:00. I will track the Camaro and come and get you if you don't come back by 10:00. I could also bring your friends here to say goodbye."

"I'd really like to drive our car, maybe for the last time. I won't get into any trouble. I promise." Argus glanced at Tai, who still didn't look up.

With a sigh, Aunt Celeste said, "I understand. You want to be alone with your friends without me around. Remember, the plane leaves at 2:00 we still have to get to Los Angeles and battle traffic at LAX. That means leaving here no later than 10:30. You only have a couple of hours." She reached into her pocket and took out a twenty. "Take Lola to breakfast."

Argus smiled and thanked her, texted Lola, and jumped into the Camaro. He drove down the driveway as Lola texted him back. He stopped and read the text. She was already awake and couldn't wait to see him. He thought of her green eyes and her messy wavy hair and the gold heart she always wore around her neck.

At such an early time on a Sunday, the streets were practically deserted, and he pulled up to Lola's house in no time. She was sitting on the front stoop wearing a red sundress and sandals. He'd never seen her in a dress before. He couldn't take his eyes off her when she walked to the car. The dress was short, and her legs were long. How could her legs be so long when she was only about five foot four?

"Hi, Argus," she said cheerfully when she got to the car.

He jumped out and opened the passenger door for her. "Hi. You look amazing."

She got in and put her seatbelt on. "Thanks. My mom and I went shopping. My dad wouldn't let me wear dresses."

He shut her door and jumped into the driver's seat. "I'm glad he's gone then. You want to get pancakes?"

She shook her head. "Not really. You know what I want to do?"

"Nope. Tell me." He smiled. That dress had crept up her thigh a little more.

"Go kayaking. We never went." She looked down and played with the ends of her hair.

"What a great idea." It was. Spending an hour alone in a kayak with her would make traveling to the Citadel a bit more tolerable. "I have twenty dollars, is that enough to rent a kayak?"

She shrugged. "I think so. I hope it's not too early."

"Let's go and see." Argus pulled out of the driveway and drove to the end of Elizabeth Lake where Ramtalans didn't practice because of the houses nearby.

It wasn't too early, because there were several cars in the parking lot and a couple small boats already on the water. When they were there during the week it wasn't crowded at all. At the kayak rental kiosk, however, he had to do some fancy talking to get the guy to agree to let him rent one because he was under eighteen and didn't have a hundred dollars or a credit card for a deposit. But after explaining, in Tai-like fashion, that his girlfriend was moving away and he wouldn't see her ever again, the guy said he understood about young love, and rented them a bright yellow two-seat kayak.

Lola giggled and slipped into the front seat. "I guess I shouldn't have worn a dress. I've never been in a kayak before, Argie."

"There's nothing to it. You just paddle." He got into the rear seat and waited until the kayak stopped rocking before picking up his paddle. "Ready?"

"Yep." She took her paddle and plunged it into the water with a splash.

It was slow going at first until they got into a rhythm, but once they did, they cruised around the lake enjoying the warm sunshine and each other. Lola told him how well she and her mom were doing without her father and that he was paying child support. She was happy and that's all Argus cared about.

He saw a small cove and they paddled over to it. "Let's stop here for a minute, Lola."

"Okay." She put her paddle in the kayak and traced her fingertips along the top of the water, leaving little sparkling ripples.

He took a deep breath. "I want to tell you something, but I don't really know how." He couldn't tell her the entire truth, but he wanted to let her know that he might not come back. How could he tell her that without explaining about Max and Ramtala? "We're not really going to visit friends."

"Oh?" She turned around. The sun lit up her eyes.

He shook his head. "It's complicated." So complicated that he didn't know where to start.

"Tell me, Argie."

"Well, you know my brother and I are different. We need to go and meet some people, in another country."

She made a little gasping sound. "Another country? Is it something to do with your medical issue thing? You don't look sick."

"No, I'm not. Neither is Tai. We don't have any blood disease or anything. We're...not from around here...originally."

"Oh. Well, I'm not from Palmdale either. I was born in Tampa, Florida."

Argus returned the wave of a fisherman as he went by in a motorboat. "I don't mean like that, Lola. We were born here, but, um, my ancestors...I mean—"

"Argie, I don't know what you're talking about. What are you trying to tell me? Are you trying to make up an excuse why you don't want to hang out with me?"

"No, that's not it at all."

Before he had the chance to say anything more and tell her that she was all he thought about, he heard the underbrush about twenty feet away on the shore rustle like crazy. Maybe a deer? There was a faint whistle and a slight thump right near him. He heard a groan and saw that Lola was slumped forward and had slammed her head against the kayak. And there was an arrow through her shoulder. An arrow?

"Lola!" He wriggled free from his seat and gently eased her upright. "Lola!" She was unconscious.

The brush rustled again, this time moving along the shore. The shooter was getting away. Oh, no you don't! Argus kept his eyes on the path of the shooter and felt for a pulse on Lola's neck. Strong pulse. An upwelling of anger coursed through his entire body. He stood, keeping the kayak as steady as he could, and dove into the water.

In only a few seconds, he was at the shoreline. He pulled himself onto the land by grabbing branches from overhanging shrubs and trees. He didn't feel in control of his body at all. His movements seemed automatic. The rustling sound wasn't too far. Good. The underbrush was heavy, making the shooter's getaway difficult.

Argus stormed through the bushes, shoving everything out of his way. He stopped every now and then to listen. He was close to the shooter, like he could feel the person was nearby. A tree about six inches across blocked his way. The fury inside him built up even more. His heart was raced. He grabbed the tree trunk and effortlessly yanked it from the ground, tossed it aside, and continued on his way. Nothing would stop him.

Eventually he came to a clearing and saw a guy running into the bushes, wearing a red plaid vest, with a bow slung over his shoulder. *Oh, no you don't.* Argus couldn't let him get away.

"Stop!" Argus shouted, his voice booming.

The guy turned. It was Justin Jones. He dropped the bow and held up his bandaged hands. "Man, I'm sorry. I didn't mean to hit Lola."

Argus stomped toward Justin, his body on fire with anger. "You were running away. You coward. You could have killed her. Who were you aiming at, Justin? Me? You hate me so much that you want to kill me?" He stopped a few feet from Justin.

"It's your fault I hit her. With these bandages, I couldn't aim right. It's your fault." Justin lowered his hands. "What's wrong with your eyes?"

Argus ignored the comment. He already knew his eyes were black and he didn't care. He lunged at Justin, grabbed him around the throat with one hand and lifted him off the ground a few inches. Argus squeezed his fingers and it felt so good pressing into Justin's flesh, tighter and tighter.

"You should be removed like Max Jackson. You don't belong in society. You don't belong anywhere." Argus trembled with energy, tingling all over, an electric burst rushing through him.

Justin gurgled and thrashed about but couldn't break free.

"Arg! Stop! Put him down!" Tai came around from behind Argus. "*Argus.* Put him down."

Argus glared at Tai. "Did you see what he did?" He squeezed his hand a little tighter.

"No, I didn't. My shared-sight only saw you crashing through the bushes and then grabbing him. Put him down, Arg." Tai put his hand on Argus's arm and pushed. "Put him down."

Argus opened his hand and let Justin fall to the ground. "You're not worth the effort." He spat on Justin.

Justin rolled on his side and gasped for air.

Tai stepped away from Justin. "So what did he do that got you this worked up? And what the hell are you doing at the lake?"

"How are my eyes?" Argus turned away from Justin.

Tai peered closely. "Black as coal, bro. We should call Aunt Celeste."

"No. If she finds out about this, we'll never leave the Citadel. I've got to get back to Lola. Justin shot her with an arrow. Can you help me?" Argus crouched near Justin. "If you mention this to anyone, I'll come for you."

Tai went to Justin and kicked him in the ribs. "You shot Lola? Asshole. You don't talk about my brother or me to anyone. Understand?" He gave him another kick.

Argus stood and ran across the clearing with Tai. There was no hiding which way he'd come because all the trees and shrubs were flattened like a bulldozer had come through.

Tai whistled. "I guess you didn't control your strength this time. Wow, you really can create devastation when you're pissed off."

"Drop it, Tai. We need to help Lola."

"I know."

They ran down the now-cleared trail, dove into the water and swam to the bobbing kayak. Lola was still unconscious, which was probably the best thing at this point. Argus climbed into the back seat while Tai managed to get onto the kayak in front of Lola and straddle it without tipping it over. They both paddled as hard and fast as they could and got back to the dock quickly.

The rental guy rushed out with his mouth gaped open. "What happened?"

Argus grabbed the dock and pulled the kayak alongside. "Some idiot with a bow and arrow."

"Jesus, Mary, and Joseph. I'll call an ambulance." The guy yanked a cell phone out of a holster on his belt.

"Don't bother. It'll be quicker if I take her to the hospital myself." Argus waited until Tai was on the dock before getting out.

"What's wrong with your eyes?" asked the guy, staring. "Are you okay?"

"Yeah, it's nothing. Contact lenses." Argus waved his hand dismissively. Why hadn't he thought of that as an excuse before?

With Tai's help, he lifted Lola out and did a quick assessment. She looked so frail lying on the dock in her pretty sundress. The arrow went in from the front, about three inches from the top of her shoulder and poked out the back about two inches. Damn Justin. Damn him to hell. There wasn't much blood, only a little around the entry and exit wounds.

Argus carried Lola carefully while Tai ran ahead and unlocked the Camaro. Placing her in the rear seat was tricky, he couldn't put her flat, so he had to wedge her on her side, using his wadded-up jacket behind her so she wouldn't fall against the back of the seat and push the arrow through further.

He accelerated slowly at first so he wouldn't jolt her, then sped up and zoomed through town and up the hill to the hospital. To hell with the speed limit. Tai got a wheelchair and brought it to the car.

Tai grabbed him by the sleeve. "Hey, Arg, Aunt Celeste is going to know we're at the hospital."

"Oh, damn. I forgot about the tracker." He pushed Lola to the triage station. "Help us, please. My girlfriend's been hit with an arrow."

The nurse, a short, plump woman in her forties or fifties, hurried around the counter. "Come with me." She pressed the button on the wall to open the ER doors and ushered Tai and Argus in. "We'll go to room 3." She pointed to the same room they were in before when Tai was bitten by the snake.

"Ah, what do we do?" Tai looked at the nurse. "How do we get her onto the bed?"

The nurse leaned out the door and shouted, "Need a doctor, stat!" She came back in. "Don't worry, we'll move her. Can you tell me what happened?"

Argus glanced at Tai. "Ah, we were at Elizabeth Lake when my girlfriend was shot with an arrow. I didn't see who did it. Please help her." He held Lola's hand.

The nurse gave a comforting smile as the doctor, the same gray-haired doctor as before, came in. She nodded to the doctor and placed her hand on Argus's shoulder. "I need her name and her parents' names. I'll be with you as soon as I can, but you need to go to the waiting room so we can take care of her. Okay?"

Argus gave the nurse Lola's mom's phone number.

The doctor stared at Tai for a moment, appearing a bit confused. "Don't I know you?" He pointed to Tai. "You were in here before. Snake bite. You left against medical advice."

Tai rolled his eyes. "Forget about me, take care of her." He motioned to Lola in the wheelchair.

"Of course." The doctor turned his focus on Lola.

Two other people in scrubs rushed into the room.

Tai tugged on Argus's sleeve. "Come on, bro. Let the doc do his thing."

Reluctantly, Argus followed Tai to the waiting room. He took a couple deep breaths. Obviously his eyes had flipped back to normal since nobody said anything. His cell phone vibrated in his pocket. He already knew who it was without looking. He took it out and clicked on messages. Yep, Aunt Celeste.

Why are you at the hospital? What's wrong?

He really didn't want to deal with Aunt Celeste right now, but if he didn't answer, she'd come to the hospital. The clock on his cell phone said it was 9:55. He didn't want to leave Lola. He hadn't even called her mother yet. How could he go to the Citadel when she needed him? He wanted to be there when she woke up so he could tell her how sorry he was that she was injured because of him. He typed a return message:

Please don't worry. It's Lola. She got hurt, but she'll be fine. I'll be home in a while.

He shut his phone off and hung out in the hallway near Lola's room as the doctor and several nurses or techs or whatever where hovering over her, fussing around with an IV and what looked like gardening pruning shears. He looked at his reflection in the glass doors of the room. What was he doing? He was pretending. Pretending to be a normal kid with a girlfriend. Because of him Lola was hurt, and Justin was hurt, and Max had been kidnapped. *You're a freak, Argus Dachel, you'll never be a normal kid.*

The triage nurse noticed him and came over. "She's going to be fine. We have parental consent and her mother will be here soon. Only a few stitches. We'll get some x-rays to make sure, but it doesn't look like anything vital was damaged. She'll be sore for a week or so."

Stitches? Sore for a week? It was like a lead weight settled in his stomach. He was supposed to protect her and now look what he did. He wasn't a protector. "Thank you".

He should call Lola's mom and explain what happened, but he didn't want to turn it back on in case Aunt Celeste tried to call. He couldn't deal with her yet. There was a phone on the wall in the hallway, he'd use that. He dialed their home number and held his breath.

"Hello?"

"Um, this is Argus Dachel."

"Argus, what happened?" She sounded worried. Of course she was. "Were you with her? The nurse said someone shot Lola with an arrow. Was it you?"

"No, of course not. It was an accident. But she's going to be okay. We're at the emergency room and they're taking the arrow out I think. It's in her shoulder."

"I'll be right there. I was halfway out the door when you called." She hung up.

Tai came him. "We need to leave before she gets here, bro."

"I can't leave Lola." He put the receiver back in the cradle. "You go. I'll stay."

"You will both leave," it was Galena's voice. She was approaching with two tall men in black suits walking a few feet behind her.

"Oh, no," Tai mumbled. "This doesn't look good."

Argus instinctively backed away. The men had flat expressions and walked stiffly. They had to be well over six feet tall, with ripped muscles bulging against their jacket sleeves. What were they going to do?

Galena strode to Argus and shook her head slightly. "I knew I shouldn't have left you in the charge of Celeste. She doesn't know how to control you. Allowing you to wander off on your own is not how a Guardian should act. You will both come with me now. I have a jet at the Palmdale airport." Galena stepped over to Tai. "You have recovered nicely."

"I guess." Tai moved closer to Argus.

Argus figured he might as well try to explain to Galena that he was responsible for Lola's injury and wanted to stay with her and that Tai had nothing at all to do with it. "It was my fault. Aunt Celeste and Tai had nothing to do—"

Galena cut him off, "I know what happened. The only mistake you made was allowing Justin Jones to escape. He could have injured *you* if his aim was better. We cannot risk you or Tai getting hurt. We will take care of Justin Jones."

Argus shook his head. "What? No. No, I don't want you to do anything. He won't say anything, I know he won't." He'd seen the fear in Justin's face back at the lake. He wouldn't talk. "I have to stay here with Lola."

Galena frowned. "You do not." She turned and motioned to the men behind her. "Take them to the jet."

The men nodded in unison and walked their stiff walk, one stopping at Tai and the other at Argus. They were huge, like bodybuilders. There was no chance of getting away from them. Argus looked toward Lola's room but couldn't see inside. There had to be a way to get away from Galena.

"Galena?" it was Aunt Celeste striding down the corridor, her eyes burning brilliant blue.

"Guardian 647, you are hereby relieved from duty pending further investigation into your reckless and incompetent attempt at keeping the Dachel brothers safe. You are to go directly to the Citadel. I am finally taking charge of the brothers."

Galena stood still. Argus could tell she was challenging Aunt Celeste. What would she do?

"You cannot relieve me. Only Commander Jampara can do that." Aunt Celeste got to within a couple of feet from Galena and stopped.

Galena raised her arm slightly. "I was given full authority to do whatever is necessary to bring the brothers safely to the Citadel. I've been waiting for this moment for a long time. Good thing I monitored you and the boys, or I wouldn't have known about how close Argus was to being killed."

Aunt Celeste turned to Argus and whispered softly, "I trusted you. I honored your mother's wishes by giving you freedom to make your own choices. And this is what you do." She looked down at the ground for a moment and then back at Galena. "Do as you will." She stepped aside.

Galena lowered her arm. "You have made the right decision, Guardian. Boys, we're leaving."

Argus wanted to apologize to Aunt Celeste, admit he'd been craving freedom, but would that make a difference to her? He'd betrayed her by acting irresponsibly and trying too hard to be like any other kid. His whole body was heavy, like a weight pressed down on him. It was guilt. Aunt Celeste's eyes glowed a dark blue. She was angry. And defeated. He'd never seen her like that. She was always strong and in control.

"Excuse me," the nurse said, waving. "Which one of you is Argus?"

He raised his hand. "I am."

"Your girlfriend is asking for you. You can come and see her now." The nurse looked at the large men in suits. "Are you all right, young man?"

Argus nodded. He was tempted to say *no*, but that might irritate Galena even more. The nurse didn't seem too convinced but returned to Lola's room anyway. He glanced at Aunt Celeste who looked up but made no effort to tell him if he should go or if he should stay. She stood there, glaring sideways at Galena, and said nothing. When he took a step toward the nurse, the man by him reached out and grasped his arm so hard that it hurt.

In an instant, Galena turned to the man, and he let go. She shook her head. "Not so rough. Argus, you will come with us now."

Aunt Celeste addressed Galena, "I'll see you at the Citadel, Galena." She turned to Argus and Tai. "And I'll see you there as well." She spun around and strode quickly down the hallway and through the ER's double-doors.

A crushing sadness hit Argus. He was about to be taken away from everything he'd ever known and there was nothing he could do about it. Worst of all, he knew damn well it was all his fault. He'd been selfish and thoughtless and now look what had happened.

He went up to Galena. "I want to see Lola."

Galena had a barely perceptible smirk on her face. "I am your Guardian *pro tem*. There is no time for you to see anyone. A black limousine is out front, boys. We will not be returning to your home. Everything you need and desire will be provided. You will want for nothing." She marched off down the corridor, looking very satisfied with herself.

The large men waited until Tai and Argus followed Galena, then walked behind them. Argus looked back toward Lola's room. Galena had no idea what he wanted or desired. Everything he needed was in that room. Lola is what he wanted.

Chapter 36

Max woke up on a bare mattress, tired, exhausted, and scared. He wasn't in the surgery room any longer but in a small dark cell complete with bars all the way around. He reached up and touched his head. No wires or probes. There were several little bumps where the probes must have been and one larger bump at the back of his head, but they didn't hurt. He was still naked, with only a blanket around him, and there were thick red marks around his wrists and ankles where the metal restraints were. At least he was out of that damn room. Even a cell was better than being strapped to an operating table.

The image of Argustine Lenox strapped down on an operating table at Edwards flashed into his mind. Lenox must have felt the same terror. Max drew in a deep breath and wandered around the cell, maybe ten by ten feet. How the hell did he get into this mess? He was doing his job, that's all. Would Stone come looking for him? Probably not. He wouldn't care.

"Oh, I've got to get out of here," Max mumbled.

He checked the rest of his body and was pleased to see Jampara hadn't done any surgery or used that weird drill thing, unless that's what made the larger bump at the back of his head. What was that thing anyway? Was it really a drill or something to scare Jampara's victims?

There had to be a way to escape and get back to AURA. With the information he'd gathered, Stone would have to take notice and listen. It was incredible to know for sure that aliens existed and that the Dachels were Ramtalan.

He grabbed the bars and shook them. Firm. What was he thinking, they'd simply break, and he could walk out? *Get a grip, Max.* No, he'd probably have to fight his way out. But how? He didn't have gun, or even his clothes. He looked through the bars. From what he could see in the low light, the cell was in the middle of a large room. He sat down on the mattress wrapping the blanket tighter.

He'd been sitting there for who-knows-how-long when a series of overhead lights flicked on one after the other, letting him see that he was indeed in the middle of an empty room, except for the cell. A woman wearing white scrubs, flat shoes, and a stark white lab coat came to the cell.

She was holding a tray covered with a white cloth. "Time for your treatment, Mr. Jackson."

He felt completely helpless. "Treatment? What treatment?"

She tilted her head as if she didn't understand what he was saying. "It's time for your treatment."

"I heard you the first time. What treatment? And where are my clothes?"

She removed the cloth from the tray revealing several syringes lined up in a row. "You don't need clothing, Mr. Jackson. It would only get soiled if you should vomit after I administer your treatment."

What? What was she going to do? What sort of "treatment" was this? Whatever it was, he wasn't going down without a fight. With only her in the room, it was one on one. He was bigger and stronger than her. Unless she was an alien with weird powers. But he hadn't witnessed any powers from the Dachels other than Argus's black eyes and some sort of burst of light from Celeste that knocked him senseless. If this alien used something like that, he'd be powerless.

"What is this treatment? Why are you doing this?" He jumped up and grabbed the mattress, placing it in front of him for protection.

"Mr. Jackson, Ramtalans are forbidden from killing humans. This treatment is for your own protection."

"Protection?" Who was she kidding? They'd stuck probes into his brain, tortured him, stripped him naked, and put him in a cell. He wasn't falling for any mind games at this point. "Don't come in here or I'll be forced to defend myself."

She stood at the barred door and sighed heavily. "My orders are to make you comfortable, Mr. Jackson. I can't do that if you put up a fight."

"You want to make me comfortable? Then give me my clothes and let me out of here."

"That's not going to happen. At least not yet. Depending on how well you perform after I administer the treatments, you may be allowed to return to Los Angeles. But I must administer the treatments first before that conclusion can be drawn."

"No." He could resist because she said Ramtalans wouldn't kill a human. He had nothing to lose.

"I can subdue you and administer the treatments by force if you'd prefer." Her eyes glowed bright blue. "It's your choice. It would go easier and probably be less painful to you if you wouldn't resist."

Painful? Great, more pain. Why hadn't he stayed a teacher instead of joining AURA? "Okay, wait. Tell me what these treatments are first."

"Certainly. You won't remember anyway. Commander Jampara implanted a neurosynaptic reprogramming device into your medulla oblongata with neuro-stimulating probes into the cerebellum and the frontal and temporal lobes of your brain. The treatment entails erasing your memory of all events dealing with Celeste Apodaca and the Dachel brothers. Human brains are easily manipulated. Oh, and we have also located your cohort, Gretchen Manheim."

Oh, what the hell? Erase his memory. And they have Gretchen? "You kidnapped Gretchen? What have you done with her?" How did they find her? She could hide her trail better than anyone he'd ever known.

"Inconsequential, Mr. Jackson. Commander Jampara always finds the information he needs. There is only one outcome to the scenario put before you. I will administer the treatments and you will not remember any of this. You will not suffer any long-term effects and you will blissfully continue your life as before."

Blissfully? There wasn't anything blissful about any of this. They'd won. There wasn't a choice. Submit or go through more torture. He'd found evidence of aliens on Earth only to be captured by those aliens to get his memory erased. He didn't have a pen and paper, or his phone to take notes. Nothing at all. All the time he'd spent was about to be erased.

"I won't fight." He dropped the mattress.

"Good." She unlocked the cell and came in carrying the tray. "These injections will not hurt, but the reprogramming can sometimes cause discomfort and vomiting due to the stimulation of the different areas of the brain. Please sit down."

He fell onto the mattress and closed his eyes; he didn't want to see anything. Silently, he kept repeating the words, *Argus Dachel is an alien from Ramtala*. Hopefully some small part of the sentence would hide deep in his brain somewhere. *I won't forget you, Argus. If it's the last thing I do, I'll find you again.*

Chapter 37

Argus sat across the aisle from Tai in an eight seat Citation jet. He'd never flown in a plane before and would have been excited in any other circumstance, but at this time, he was depressed. His whole world had crumbled. Been taken away from him in a blink. He stared out the window at the dry, brown Mojave Desert below as the jet climbed and banked steeply.

Lola was down there, lying in a hospital bed, wondering why he hadn't come to her when she'd asked for him. No matter what, he had to get back to her. He closed his eyes and swore a silent oath that he'd see her again.

"Arg," Tai said quietly. "How are you doing?"

Argus opened his eyes. Tai didn't look upset. "I don't know. I screwed things up. Why couldn't I have done everything Aunt Celeste said? I want to go back home."

"Well, I'm no angel either. Look at it this way, we're in this predicament now, so maybe it'll be a cool experience. We're going to see the Citadel. We're the longest surviving New Breeds of our generation. They'll treat us like kings, you know that, right?"

"I don't care. I wish I wasn't Ramtalan at all." He slumped in the seat. "Aren't you concerned at all about Aunt Celeste?"

Tai shrugged. "She'll be all right. We'll see her at the Citadel. We're almost eighteen. I don't think we need a guardian now anyway. She can take care of other kids."

"Really? She's like our real aunt. I don't want to never see her again." Argus resumed his window gazing. They climbed up higher until the plane cut through wispy clouds. The patches of ground that showed through the gaps in clouds looked more like a drawing with differing shades of desert sand, and an occasional body of water breaking up the scene. He never realized there were so many rivers and lakes in the desert. He put his hand on the cold window and wished he could jump out and float among the clouds and be free.

After a while, Galena came walking down the aisle. She stopped and held onto the seat backs for support as the plane buffeted slightly. "Do you boys want anything?"

Argus was tempted to say "yes, I want to go back", but thought better of it and simply shook his head instead. He was sulking like a child, he knew that. Who could blame him though? Tai asked for food and a drink. He was smiling, and it irritated Argus. Galena nodded and went back up the aisle.

"How can you be happy about any of this?" Argus snapped.

"Easy, bro. We don't exactly have a choice. Can't you make the best of it? Lola's going to be fine, Aunt Celeste is coming as well, and Max Jackson is...well, I don't know what's going on with him. We're on a private jet at thirty thousand feet and we're half-alien. Think of it, Arg, this is an adventure no matter which way you look at it."

It wasn't the sort of adventure he wanted. Why couldn't Tai understand that? He'd only just started feeling like a normal teenager; going to school, making friends, being the quarterback on the football team. And now he was on his way to an alien stronghold, removed from everything he'd ever known.

He leaned back and closed his eyes, thinking of Lola. She was so pretty and funny and those green eyes of hers, they drew him in every time. There was so much he wanted to say to her, so many places he wanted to go with her. His mind took him back to the lake and the arrow and her lying on the hospital bed in the ER.

He heard a sound like someone crying and opened his eyes. What happened? Was it a dream? He wasn't in the plane anymore but standing in a sterile hallway. A hospital. It wasn't a dream. Oh, no, this wasn't good. The room near him said 202. He was on the second floor, not the ER. And he wasn't weak at all from using his ability. Okay, that was good, but dissolving away from Galena sure wasn't.

"Oh, ah, Argus, right?" came a voice behind him.

He turned around so fast he almost fell. It was the ER nurse approaching. He smiled and nodded. "Yes." He wasn't invisible this time.

"Where'd you go? We admitted your friend for an overnight stay. She's down the hall in 209. It's past visiting hours, but I'll let you stay." She winked.

"Thanks." He hurried down the hall to room 209 and knocked.

"Come in," Lola said, her voice catching in her throat.

He opened the door. She sat in bed in a blue hospital gown, her eyes teary and her cheeks wet. "Lola," he whispered, coming closer. "I'm so sorry. I'm so sorry."

"Argus, what are you doing here? I thought you'd left for your trip. I didn't think I'd see you again. How did I get shot with an arrow?" She dabbed her eyes with a tissue.

"It doesn't matter." He sat on a chair beside the bed. "Please don't cry. I couldn't leave without seeing you. Are you all right? Are you in any pain? I can call the nurse if you are."

She shook her head and sniffed. "I'm okay. Better now. My mom left to get a change of clothes. She's coming back to spend the night with me. The doctor said the stitches can come out in about a week. It's not that bad, really. Sore when I move."

Thinking of her in pain broke his heart. He'd gladly take the arrow if he could go back and change things. They sat for a while, not saying anything. He could stay like that forever, being close to her with no one else around, the sound of her breathing to keep him company. It was exactly where he wanted to be.

Lola reached out and took his hand. "Argie, you were trying to tell me something in the kayak."

He looked into her eyes. He never wanted to keep secrets from her. "I was. So much has happened this week, I don't know where to start, or even if I should. I'm not normal. I mean, I'm not crazy or anything, but I have...it's my DNA."

"Your DNA? Your blood disease, right?"

He squeezed her hand slightly. "Not exactly. Remember how you said you can do things with your mind?"

She nodded. "I haven't done it lately though."

"Well, I can do things like that, too." He watched her carefully to gauge her reaction. *Please don't get freaked out.*

Her eyes widened. "Really? So it's not only me? I bet there's a chemical or radiation in the water supply."

"No, I don't think that's it. It's not you that...you can't really...I told you my ancestors weren't from around here originally. That's the truth. We're..."

The door burst open, and Aunt Celeste stood there, breathing hard, her hair loose and mussed, and her eyes crystal blue. "Argus!"

He jumped up, still holding Lola's hand. "How did—?"

"Tai used shared-sight when you disappeared in front of him, and Galena called me. You must come with me immediately. I was on my way to Los Angeles and had to turn around. If we take a helicopter from the Palmdale airport, we'll make our flight." She looked past him to Lola. "I'm glad to see you're doing all right, Lola."

Argus kept holding Lola's hand. He didn't want to let her go. "Aunt Celeste, I'm not going. I want to stay here with Lola." It was worth a try.

"Absolutely not. Now, Argus." She held the door open and motioned him out.

He turned back to Lola and lifted her hand to his mouth and kissed it. "I have to go, Lola. I'll call you or text you. We'll be together again soon."

She smiled and wiped her eyes again. "That's the second time you've kissed my hand."

"Yeah, that's right. That's kind of lame, isn't it?" He leaned down and kissed her damp cheek. "Is that better?"

She blushed and nodded quickly. "Much better."

"Argus," Aunt Celeste said firmly.

"I'm coming." He held Lola's hand to his heart. "I'll miss you every second we're apart."

"Me too," her voice was barely audible as she started to cry again.

"Bye, Lola." He turned and jogged out of the room, not wanting to look back.

In the hallway, Aunt Celeste grabbed him by the back of his jacket. "Are you stupid? How could you do something like that in front of Galena?"

Wow, where'd that come from? She'd never called him stupid. "It was an accident. I didn't mean to do it. And Galena wasn't in the cabin anyway."

"You know what I mean. Argus, I know all of this is very hard for you to accept, but you must comply. We all must. Galena is building a case against me continuing as your Guardian." Her attitude softened. "I have a helicopter on standby. Try to understand how important this is. Think of it this way, it's your first ride in a helicopter. It can be an exciting experience." She didn't look like she believed what she was saying.

Exciting? No, there was nothing exciting about riding in a helicopter that was taking him away from his home. "I don't care. Isn't there some way Galena can take out my Ramtalan DNA? I want to be all human."

"You know there isn't. You must accept who you are. Everyone is unique in one way or the other and you need to embrace your particular uniqueness. Being a New Breed is an honor. You should realize that. I will always be here for you, even if they remove me permanently from being your Guardian." She brought him in close and held him tight.

It was the first time she'd ever given him a hug. It felt good and made him feel like he was really loved. It was weird that a simple hug could do that. She held him for a little bit longer, then let go, and motioned for him to follow her. Reluctantly, he trailed behind her to the parking lot and got into the SUV. She drove fast to the airport where a red Jet Ranger helicopter waited with its rotors turning.

The helicopter was cool with soft seats and headsets so he and Aunt Celeste could talk to each other. After getting buckled into the back seat beside Aunt Celeste, he suddenly felt exhausted. The pressure of everything wore him out. His mind twisted and turned in a hundred different directions, not able to focus on any one thing. He already missed Lola. He shut his eyes and listened to the hypnotic whoomp-whoomp of the rotors. No matter what anyone said, there was no way he was staying at the Citadel, no way.

Chapter 38

Max's hands were coated in a sticky substance when he woke. He held them up and gasped. Blood. Why were his hands covered in blood? And where was he? He was lying on plants. Those succulent green iceplants to be exact. The plants that were all over in California.

He moved slightly and saw that he was on a bed of highway landscaping about ten feet off the side of the road. How the hell did he get there?

A shrill siren stung his ears as a police car screeched to a stop. He forced his body to a sitting position and looked around. His car was upside down, half off the road. He'd been in a rollover. And he'd survived.

"Sir, are you all right?" a police officer asked as he knelt beside him.

Max nodded a little, but even that hurt. "I think so."

"You've been in an accident. Did you lose consciousness at all?"

"Yeah, I think I did." Max reached up and touched his head. "Am I bleeding?"

"Yes, sir. Looks like you've got a nasty cut on your scalp. An ambulance is on its way." The officer unfolded a silver emergency blanket and draped it over Max's shoulders. "Do you remember the accident, sir?"

Max tried to think, but his mind was blank. He couldn't even remember where he was; what city, what state. What day was it and what time? "I can't remember anything."

"That's okay, sir. Relax, we'll get you help." The officer unwrapped a roll of gauze pad, balled it up, and pressed it against the back of Max's head. "Can you hold onto this? Apply pressure."

Max held the gauze to his head. "Okay. Hey, where am I?"

"Las Vegas."

Las Vegas? What was he doing in Las Vegas? He worked in...where did he work? Los Angeles? Yeah, that was right, he worked in Los Angeles. For...the

Astronomical...Urgent Recovery Administration. AURA. He shivered. Wasn't being cold a sign of shock?

The officer came back. "Sir, have you been drinking?"

"No. Wait...I don't think so." Max shielded his eyes from the blazing sun.

"We found some open containers in your vehicle, and I can detect the smell of alcohol on your breath. Considering your condition, I'll administer a sobriety test at the hospital."

Why did the word "administer" ring a bell? Someone said they were going to administer something to him. Didn't they? When was that? He felt his head again. There was a bump at the back where he was bleeding. Well, that would explain his loss of memory. He probably had concussion. "Did I hit anyone? Is anyone else hurt?"

"No, sir. Solo incident. Looks like you lost control."

Wasn't he drinking with a couple of guys? But where was that? Guys in uniforms? No, that couldn't be right. The ambulance came and the medics worked efficiently to bandage his head and stabilize his neck with a brace. They loaded him onto a gurney and whisked him away. His head throbbed and he felt slightly sick to his stomach. He was going to lose his job over this for sure.

Chapter 39

After the short helicopter ride to LAX, Argus followed Aunt Celeste through the airport to security screening. With only her single carry-on bag, they went through with no delay and got to the gate in plenty of time.

Argus stayed with the bag while Aunt Celeste went into a nearby shop to buy a few magazines. An elderly lady with her purse stuffed with gift bags sat down next to him. She groaned and put the purse on the ground.

"You're not traveling alone are you?" she asked in a British accent.

"No, with my aunt." He didn't feel like talking but didn't want to be rude.

"Oh, that's nice. Most young people don't want anything to do with grown-ups. I'm heading back home to Sherborne. Do you know where that is?"

He shook his head and looked around for Aunt Celeste. "Ah, no, I don't. Sorry."

"Well, it doesn't matter. I'm Mary McCalvin." She extended her hand.

He shook it to be polite. "Argus."

Before he knew what was happening, a man ran in front of the chair and flashed a badge. "Argus Dachel, you're under arrest for assault with a deadly weapon."

"What?" Argus looked around but didn't see Aunt Celeste anywhere. "I don't understand."

Mary McCalvin picked up her bag and got out of the seat. "Sorry, lad. Got fifty dollars to find out who you were." She shrugged and wandered off.

The man with the badge motioned for Argus to stand up. "I'm Detective DeAlba. Where is Celeste Apodaca?"

Argus stood. "I...what's going on? I didn't assault anyone." Except Justin Jones, but Justin wouldn't say anything, not after the threat at the lake.

The detective continued, "You are accused of burning Justin Jones with acid."

Argus groaned. At least it wasn't about the arrow incident at Elizabeth Lake.

Right then, Aunt Celeste returned, looking flustered. "What's this?"

"You're Celeste Apodaca, booked on a flight with Argus Dachel to Labrador." Detective DeAlba nodded to a security guard who was waiting about twenty feet away. "Mr. Dachel is under arrest for assault on Justin Jones."

Argus wanted to run. He had an overwhelming urge to use whatever force was necessary to get out of the situation. His adrenaline spiked and he knew his eyes would flip black any second. Control was necessary, like he'd learned, but deep down, he didn't want to control his rage. He was angry, infuriated, and wanted to let his built-up energy go.

Aunt Celeste frowned at him and shook her head ever so slightly. He regulated his heart rate like she taught him and cleared his mind. He relaxed.

Aunt Celeste stood so close to Argus that her body was touching his. "Excuse me, Detective, but do you have any proof that Argus did anything to Justin?"

DeAlba nodded. "There are witnesses and a sworn statement from Mr. Jones. Took a while to locate you."

She turned and looked at Argus, keeping her body pressed against his. "Listen to me, Argus," she whispered. "You are protected by me right now. Do not move."

Detective DeAlba waved the security guard over. "Ms. Apodaca, I need you both to come with me."

Aunt Celeste put her hands together in praying position and pulled them apart slowly, creating a wavering pale blue light that extended from each palm. Argus held his breath. What the heck was that? Was it her energy source or something else? He wanted to ask, but that'd have to wait. Detective DeAlba's brow pinched. He took a step back.

"What are you doing?" he asked, taking another step backward. "Stop that right now."

When her hands were about four feet apart, she put her hands over her head and then to her sides so that the light covered them both like a veil as it fell right to the ground. Argus saw through it, although everything looked bluish. He let out his breath and stood as still as he could. It was quiet inside the veil thing, muffled.

Detective DeAlba looked from side to side and yelled out. "Where'd they go? Did you see where they went?" He reached out. His hand went right through the blue veil and seemed to go right through Argus as well. "They couldn't have disappeared. Find them."

"Aunt Celeste?" Argus whispered. He started to take a step.

"Don't move. You can neither be seen nor heard at the moment. Stay close to me so our bodies touch. When DeAlba leaves, we can go, and I can release the energy field. We can no longer take the plane to Labrador." She kept her hands lowered, palms up. "I can only maintain the field for a few minutes." It seemed to be draining her. Her breathing was slowing.

"Aunt Celeste, are you all right?"

"I will be as soon as he leaves. This field uses my energy source to dissociate the molecules in my host body, which makes it non-existent on this plane."

What did that mean? Argus watched Detective DeAlba walk away, scanning the area as he went. "I don't understand. What about me? This isn't a host body, it's *my* body."

She drew in a breath. "That's why I said body contact is important. Your body and mine become one and the effects of the field can pass into you as well. Your body won't be harmed. I've got to close the field now." She was gasping for air.

She brought her hands up to eye level and brought them together. As soon as her palms touched, the field was gone. She wobbled for a few seconds. "We must leave here right away."

No kidding. Argus kept an eye out for the detective and the security guard. It didn't seem like any of the passengers around the gate had resumed reading or fumbling with their luggage and hadn't noticed them reappear again. This was too weird. Tai would get a kick out an invisibility energy field for sure.

Argus looked around. "Where do we go? They'll probably have the entrances blocked."

"Yes, they will." She shook her head. "I can't believe I didn't consider the incident with Justin Jones. Of course there'd be an investigation," she mumbled.

"What do we do?" Maybe going to the Citadel wasn't such a bad idea after all. Being arrested and put in juvie was not even on his list of things to do in his lifetime. But if he came back to Palmdale after going to the Citadel, he'd have to deal with it then. Which would be better? Living at the Citadel as a virtual prisoner or getting thrown in juvie? What a screwed-up mess.

"We initiate an emergency exit strategy." She took out her communicator and pressed a few buttons, waited, pressed a few more, used the touch screen like she was drawing something and put the phone away. "We have our exit."

Argus shrugged. "Okay. What does that mean?"

"It means we're being rescued. Now hush." Aunt Celeste sat down. "Sit. Try to act normal."

Act normal? He'd wanted to be normal ever since he found out he wasn't. He sat beside her, not sure what he was waiting for and did his best to appear like a seventeen-year-old human. He picked out a magazine from the paper bag Aunt Celeste dropped on the floor when she created the energy field and flipped through the pages. It was a car magazine and there was an article about Camaros. He missed that car. Where was it? At the hospital? The detective probably had it impounded.

An announcement came, "Howard and Kristie Fuller please report to Gate 4. Howard and Kristie Fuller report to Gate 4.".

"That's us," Aunt Celeste whispered.

How did she know that? So what, now they had aliases? He got up and followed her to Gate 4. There was no sign of Detective DeAlba or the security guard. When they were at the gate, a woman in a dark blue skirt and white blouse waved to them. Argus felt a little sick to his stomach. Wasn't this illegal?

The woman smiled. "Are you Howard and Kristie Fuller?"

"Yes." Aunt Celeste strode forward. "Sorry we're late."

"No problem. Getting your purse stolen can really create havoc in your life, but your company faxed over a copy of your passports and your driver's license. The American Consulate has issued you a temporary passport that I guess they'll have waiting for you in London. There's a brief stop in Labrador first for refueling. This isn't the sort of thing that security generally allows, but I guess your company must have some pull. Anyway, enjoy your flight." She handed Aunt Celeste two boarding passes.

"Thank you." Aunt Celeste smiled sweetly and motioned for Argus to follow.

Passports, American Consulate? How did all of that get arranged so fast? Obviously it was the Citadel, but still. Did they have people on stand-by for this sort of thing? Argus walked up the ramp and onto the plane, the second plane he'd been in, and was surprised to find that they were seated in first class. This plane was a lot bigger than the private jet and first class was very nice.

He settled into the window seat and put on his seat belt. As much as he didn't want to go to the Citadel, at least he'd see Tai again. Within a few minutes, the cabin doors closed, and the flight attendants gave instructions about emergency procedures. He sighed. Emergency procedures? The whole flight was an emergency procedure arranged by aliens.

He turned away and looked out the window and saw inside the terminal building. Detective DeAlba was staring out the plate glass window right at the plane. Did he know they were on it or was he merely suspicious? Argus pulled the window shade down and flipped through the magazine again.

He stopped at an article about restoring Camaros. There was a photo of a blue Camaro, but it wasn't as nice as their car. He noticed the author's name was Jackson. Of all the names, did it have to be that? Now he was thinking about Max Jackson and what had happened or was happening to him. What if they were experimenting on him? Would Ramtalans do that?

"Argus, what are you smiling about?" Aunt Celeste nudged him.

He hadn't realized he was smiling. That wasn't right, he shouldn't smile. He didn't want anything bad to happen to anyone, not Justin or Max. Or did he? Back at the lake he wanted to kill Justin and in Max's motel room he would have done whatever was necessary to get away. Was he becoming like Tai? No, that wasn't possible. Tai was more Ramtalan.

He looked at Aunt Celeste. "I'm really confused. I used to know what sort of things I believed in and how I felt about things, but now I'm not so sure. Everything's turned upside down and mixed up. I don't even know who I am anymore."

She leaned back against the seat. "That's a part of growing up. Remember, you're only half Ramtalan. Your human half has more emotions and those will develop more as you grow older. Don't let it worry you. In time you'll find a balance. Argus, I would like to express something to you."

What else could she possibly have to say? Was he ready to hear something else? "Ah, okay."

She lowered her voice, "I think of you boys as more than my New Breeds. I truly feel like I'm your aunt. I've been with you since you were born and have watched you grow. I have true feelings for you and Tai and I'm very proud of you both."

Wow. That was quite a revelation. Argus didn't know what to say. He always felt like she was his aunt, even when he found out she wasn't. She and Tai were his family, all the family he had. "You are my aunt. I don't care what anyone says. You're my aunt."

The smile on her face made her look happier than she'd ever looked. "That makes me feel...warm. I have to ask you, Argus, what outcome from the tribunal will make *you* warmest?"

Why was she asking that? He shrugged. "You mean what do I want?" He paused, trying to work out what he wanted. Of course he wanted to be with Lola, but if he went back to Palmdale, he'd be arrested, and that wasn't a very warm thought. Then there was Tai. Tai didn't seem to care if he stayed at the Citadel or not. Could he live without seeing Tai? No, he couldn't. Without Tai around, he felt lost. So what outcome would be best? "I have to think about it."

"Take your time. I will make my best case at the tribunal depending upon what you decide." She faced forward and began reading a science magazine she'd bought.

There were video monitors in the back of the seats, so he switched to a channel that tracked their progress across the country. The projected route was over the eastern portion of Canada to Labrador and then across the Atlantic to London. Not that they were going all the way to London. One day he'd love to travel all over the world and see different countries and cultures. Were there New Breeds in every country or only some? He suddenly felt lonely. He and Tai were the only New Breeds over sixteen. They were unique. Yet another thing that set them apart from everyone else.

After he watched a movie and finished the car magazine, dinner was served. Roasted chicken and potatoes with white asparagus, his favorite. Tai hated white asparagus because he said it was unnatural and that asparagus should be green. Argus smiled at the thought and finished the food. Anyone who joked about airline food should fly first class. When the tray was cleared away, he took a short nap and woke as they were descending into the Labrador airport.

Aunt Celeste fiddled with her hair, making sure it was tied back neatly and then straightened her clothes. It was unsettling to see her so anxious. The strong, no-nonsense Aunt Celeste was who he was used to.

They got off the plane and followed the other passengers to the customs line. How were they going to get through without any passports? Even he knew you needed a passport for customs.

"Aunt Celeste?"

"It'll be all right." She wasn't anxious at all anymore.

A tall man with slick black hair and wearing a heavy gray overcoat approached them. "Celeste Apodaca, it's good to see you again. It's been many years."

Were all Ramtalans tall? Argus hadn't seen a single short one, not a single one. Of course that was their host body. That reminded him, he still hadn't asked Aunt Celeste how they got their host bodies. He had so many questions to ask but it was never the right time. He stayed close to her, feeling uncomfortable when they stepped out of the customs line, and everyone stared at them.

The tall man had a circular emblem on the left side of his coat, below the collar with what looked like a depiction of a spiral galaxy in the center. He smiled. "You must be Argus. Very nice to officially meet you." He had amazingly white teeth and the friendliest smile.

Argus nodded. "Nice to meet you too, sir."

"Oh, no need for sir. I'm Aridesian Stargaard. Ari for short."

"Hi." Cool name. Argus liked Ari right away. He looked like he was in his twenties or maybe early thirties.

Ari took them away from the customs area without anyone apparently noticing or caring and straight outside to a waiting heavy-duty SUV, pure white with tinted windows. Ari must have used mind control on the customs agents. There was a thin layer of snow on the ground and the temperature was very cold. Argus shivered. His thin jacket was nowhere near warm enough. He'd probably freeze to death before he made it to the Citadel.

He and Aunt Celeste got into the back of the SUV while Ari got into the passenger seat up front. The driver didn't turn or say anything, simply pressed down on the accelerator and pulled onto the road. Ari twisted around in his seat and looked at Argus.

"Argus, this is your first *real* trip to the Citadel, so I should orient you a little, if Celeste hasn't already."

She shook her head. "No, I haven't told him anything."

Argus stared at Ari. Why did he say first real trip? What did that mean?

Ari grinned. "Fine, then I'll be your tour guide. First of all, New Breeds do not follow Ramtalan protocol, you do not need to offer greetings or explanations to any Ramtalans. Well, except to Commander Jampara. You always greet him with a simple hello and always answer him when he speaks to you. The Citadel is a subterranean facility, located three hundred meters below the surface of an island we call L-1, Labrador One. We have three other ancillary facilities on neighboring islands, but you don't need to know about those. Any questions so far?"

Any questions? Argus had about a million questions. "Yes. Um, can you tell me what happened to Max Jackson?"

Ari raised an eyebrow. "He was questioned and released. That's all I know about that. Anything else?"

So Max wasn't killed. That was good news. Argus let out a breath, relieved to hear some good news. "Am I responsible for Aunt Celeste being called to face the tribunal?"

Ari glanced quickly at Aunt Celeste. "Not at all. Celeste must report periodically to the Citadel, as all Guardians do. But due to the incidents in Palmdale over the past week, Commander Jampara simply wishes to meet with her in person to get a, ah, how do humans put it, a blow-by-blow account."

"Oh." Argus knew it wasn't as simple as that but decided to accept Ari's explanation so as not to make waves. "And my brother, is he already here?"

"Yes. He's a feisty one, very curious. Of course, that's understandable considering Galena's handiwork. Sorry, perhaps I shouldn't have said that. I know he's your twin and having him genetically altered must be hard."

Yeah, no kidding. Argus glared at Ari. How could he say that like it was nothing? Galena's handiwork? She'd changed Tai's DNA, that's not exactly handiwork.

Ari turned around and looked out the front window. "Oh, we're here."

"Where?" Argus peered out his window but didn't see anything except a field of snow. What were they supposed to do, hike through the snow? He didn't even have boots or gloves.

Ari snickered. "We're at the hover-port, Argus. We take a small hovercraft to the island. It's hard to see anything with all the snow and ice." He pointed to the right.

Argus pressed his nose to the window and finally saw the outline of a white building about the size of a gardening shed. They were taking a hovercraft? Really? He'd seen one on TV once.

The car stopped and Ari hopped out, came around and opened Argus's door first, then went around and opened Aunt Celeste's.

As Argus stepped out, a blast of freezing air took his breath away. Ari came back and handed him a down-filled white parka, with the same galaxy emblem, and puffy gloves. *Okay, now we're talking.* Argus put it on and zipped it all the way up to his chin. The gloves were so padded that he could hardly bend his fingers, but it kept out the cold.

He squinted at the shed and saw an odd-looking open boat perched on the shoreline right in front of the shed. It had wing-like structures protruding from the sides and a circular fan at the back. It was almost exactly like the one he'd seen on TV.

"Hop in," Ari said with a grin. "Might want to put your hood on. It's a little chilly."

Argus climbed into a seat in the middle of the six-passenger boat and put on his hood, pulling the drawstrings tight. Couldn't they have a closed boat? Tai probably loved the hovercraft. He never minded the heat or the cold. He said it was good to feel extreme temperatures, it made him feel alive. *Well, Tai, I hope the hovercraft made you feel alive.*

Aunt Celeste got in next to him. "How are you doing, Argus? I know this is all very strange."

All bundled up, Argus didn't feel cold at all. "I'm fine. Did my mom and dad every come to the Citadel?"

She nodded. "Your father was here once when Galena interviewed him and your mother was here three times. The first time was when she was a baby and the second was when she wanted to marry your father."

Wow, his parents had been to the Citadel. They were probably scared like he was. Or maybe not. Maybe they were both braver than him. But he'd never know. His life would probably be completely different if he'd grown up with parents. "And the third time?"

"When you and Tai were born. She brought you two here at the request of Commander Jampara. He likes to meet and examine each New Breed. But since you and Tai had a human father, he was especially interested to meet you both." She seemed to think for a moment. "Galena was there, too."

Oh, so that's why Ari said it was his first *real* trip to the Citadel. "So I was here before."

"Yes, but you were only three months old." Aunt Celeste reached under the seat and took out a thick woolen blanket. "Here." She draped it over his shoulders. "If you catch a chill, I'll never hear the end of it."

Ari got into the driver's seat and started up the hovercraft. It was noisy but lifted off the ground a few inches effortlessly. They glided over the land and into the ocean, actually above the ocean. It was a little weird to be floating above the water.

Argus gripped the seat only to let go a moment later. It was fun. He'd expected to be terrified, but he wasn't. He twisted and turned to see everything around him. The shore soon disappeared in the distance and all that remained was ocean surrounding them on all sides. The water was slightly choppy, but the hovercraft zipped along smoothly.

The trip lasted only a short time, maybe twenty minutes or so. Ari steered the hovercraft up and onto a sloped ramp that led to an elevated concrete platform about the size of a basketball court. He shut it off and it settled down onto the concrete.

"Here we are," Ari said as he got out.

There was nothing but the concrete slab. No buildings, no trees. Nothing but flat, frozen ground surrounding the slab. Argus climbed out of the hovercraft and walked over to Aunt Celeste. She motioned to the right with her head. He hadn't seen it before, but there was a trapdoor-like contraption built into the concrete. Ari walked over to it and pressed a button on a watch around his wrist. The trapdoor slid open, and a glass elevator rose up and stopped. It was enclosed on three sides with the entrance completely open. They were supposed to go in that thing? It didn't look safe.

Aunt Celeste took his hand and led him into the glass box. Even the floor was transparent. It was like standing over a bottomless pit. When they were all inside, the elevator descended quietly into the blackness. As it continued, a bluish light below grew brighter and brighter until it filled the elevator. Argus gripped Aunt Celeste's hand harder. She glanced at him and smiled.

"Almost there, Argus," Ari announced.

The elevator slowed and stopped. The blue light came from recessed lights in the floor and from the walls of a large room. Aunt Celeste let go of his hand and stepped into the room with Ari. Argus shook. Now he felt cold, although he wasn't. It was fear of the unknown.

He glanced back at the elevator. He wanted to go home. When Aunt Celeste urged him out, he saw a doorway at one end of the room and several computers on countertops against one wall. It looked like some sort of control room. The door at the far end of the room slid open and Tai and Galena came in.

Tai opened his arms wide. "Arg!" He ran forward and gave Argus a brief bear hug. "This place is something, huh? What did you think of the hovercraft? I want one so bad. And that glass elevator thing. How cool is that?"

"Yeah, cool." Argus watched Galena walk over to Aunt Celeste and hand her a folder. Galena had the same spiral galaxy emblem on her shirt. Well, at least Tai didn't seem any different. Funny how much he'd missed Tai after only a few hours apart. *Oh, grow up, Argus, you can't be with him every minute.*

"Come on, bro, I'll show you our rooms." Tai grabbed him by the sleeve of the parka. "You won't need that coat in here. It's temperature controlled to 75 degrees."

Argus turned to Aunt Celeste. "Can I go with Tai?"

She nodded. "Of course. Get oriented. Tai, show him around."

Tai hesitated and looked at Galena, who nodded as well. "Yes, Tai, you may go."

What was that? Argus raised his eyebrow to Tai. Tai shook his head and tugged on his sleeve until they were through the doorway and into a large semi-circular lobby area where there were three corridors evenly spaced apart leading to who-knows-where.

"Okay, Tai, what's going on? You have to ask Galena's permission now?" He pulled free and unzipped his parka. Tai was right, he didn't need a coat.

Tai frowned. "No. Don't be ridiculous. She's looking out for me. Anyway, that first corridor on the left leads to the eating facilities, the pool, and the gym. The one in the middle goes to the control rooms and some other places that Galena said I don't need to know about, and the third corridor on the far right is where the sleeping quarters are. This place is like a small city. Wait until you see the sleeping quarters. Our room is like a five-star hotel, maybe better. Aunt Celeste's room is next to ours. They connect to each other with a door. Our room is huge. I mean *huge.*"

"Bigger than at our house? Our house is really big." Argus defended their home, and he didn't know why. Could be because Tai was acting like this was their home now. It wasn't. It never would be.

"Big. We can have anything we want here. Galena said if we want clothes or to see TV shows or movies, we only have to ask."

Argus took off the parka when he started to sweat. "*Galena* says? We don't even know Galena, Tai. You sound like you want to stay here."

"Well, why not? What's so great about Palmdale? Think about it. We can have anything. Do you know that we're the only New Breeds here? They treat us like kings." He smirked. "I'm going to like it here."

"This isn't our home. You're saying that because you have nothing back home." That was rude, but Argus didn't care.

Tai rolled his eyes. "I know you miss Lola, but come on, you didn't know she existed a week ago. She's the first girl you met in high school. You're infatuated, that's all. Get over it, Arg. Oh, and the best part is that we'll be trained in using our abilities and how to develop them more or discover new ones. Galena said abilities can be perfected better at the Citadel and New Breeds usually get more later. You can't deny how cool that is."

It wasn't cool that they were trapped underground on an island that was inhabited by Ramtalans. Argus looked around the lobby. "Aren't you worried about Aunt Celeste? She's going to meet with the tribunal. They might not let her be our Guardian."

"She'll be fine. Galena told me that the worst that'll happen is she'll have to stay here as a monitor unless she chooses to go back to Ramtala." Tai pointed to the third corridor, the one on the right. "Let's go to our rooms."

Argus frowned. Tai wasn't thinking of anyone but himself. He didn't even care if he'd ever see Aunt Celeste again. Would it make a difference to him if he knew that Aunt Celeste said she felt like their real aunt? Probably not. It seemed like Galena had him brainwashed.

He followed Tai down the corridor, which was painted a soothing bluish green with lights or something that made the paint move like undulating waves. They came to a door marked *Tai and Argus Dachel*. Next door was another door marked *Celeste Apodaca, Guardian 647*. Tai opened their door with a swipe of his hand over a flat silver panel about six inches square on the left of the door. The door swished open like an elevator door.

"Welcome to paradise." Tai stepped inside and turned around in a complete circle. "Now tell me this isn't cool."

Okay, Tai was right, the room was incredible. It had to be over forty feet by forty feet with a sunken living area in the center with couches and a humongous TV mounted on the wall. On either side of the sunken area were two spiral metal staircases that led to a loft area up above. There was even a kitchenette with every conceivable appliance on the countertops.

"Oh, wow. Wow. Holy hell. This is...amazing. The beds are up there?" Argus pointed to the loft.

"Yep. Galena said if you want your own room, she'll arrange it. I don't mind bunking with you if you don't. That loft is roomy. And there are screens you pull down from the ceiling that separate the beds if you want."

As much as he didn't want to be excited, Argus couldn't help it. He wandered into the kitchen and stopped dead. "Is that a brick pizza oven?"

Tai jogged over and slapped him on the back. "Yep. And a popcorn maker, cotton candy maker, and soda dispenser. They thought of everything, Arg."

"Not everything." Argus placed the parka on the counter. "We don't have any friends here."

"Oh, come on. Who needs friends? We got along fine without friends at home. You'll make new friends here." Tai opened the double-door refrigerator. "Fully stocked. Want a Coke? Water?"

"Yeah. Coke's good. Tai, as great as this place is, we'd have no freedom if we stay here." Argus peered into the pizza oven.

"Freedom? We can do whatever we want. And we get to learn the full potential of our abilities. You don't call that freedom?"

Argus shook his head. "That's not freedom. What does it matter if we have more abilities or learn to use the ones we have? We can't do anything with them. They're using us, that's all. We're prisoners, guinea pigs. You know that. You hated the thought of staying here when Aunt Celeste first said it might be a possibility."

"That was before I got here and saw this place." Tai smirked. "This is a win not matter how you look at it."

"Okay, what about college? You wanted to go to college. And the Camaro. You love that car. What about the cheerleaders?" Argus took a can of Coke from Tai and popped the top.

Tai was quiet for a bit. "Stop trying to warp my mind. This is where we belong. It feels right."

"Is this what Mom wanted for us? What do you think she'd say if she knew we'd ended up here?" Argus took a sip and went to the sunken living area and sat down on the soft couch. "Mom wanted us to be raised like humans."

Tai came over and sat down on the couch beside Argus. "Don't bring Mom into this. That's not fair." He pouted. "Listen to what you said. Raised *like* humans. We're not humans, and we're not livestock."

There was a knock on the door and without waiting for them to say, "come in", Galena entered. "What do you think, Argus?"

"It's nice," his voice was cold. He didn't mean to sound like that, but oh well.

She tilted her head to the side. "Nice? That's a fairly low opinion of this grandeur. You'll learn to appreciate all we have to offer."

Did that mean she was assuming they would want to stay or was it already a done deal? And was that an indication that Aunt Celeste's case was a foregone conclusion? Maybe the tribunal was a way of getting them to the Citadel.

"Can I see Aunt Celeste?" Argus asked, getting off the couch.

Galena came further into the room. "I'm sorry, Argus, she's preparing for the tribunal. In the morning, we will begin your testing."

"Testing?" Argus glanced at Tai for an explanation. He must know exactly what Galena was talking about.

Instead, he shrugged. "What testing, Galena? Arg has to know everything."

Galena gave a brief smile. "I thought you understood that you were to be tested so we can find out why you two have survived longer than the other New Breeds. We start early, so you should get to sleep soon. I will send Ari to get you in the morning. We will run a few tests first and then breakfast. Testing will continue until we have conclusive results." She turned and headed to the door. "Goodnight," she called over her shoulder as she went out.

Tai stared at Argus. "What...why...I swear I didn't know about..."

"I knew she couldn't be trusted." Argus slumped onto the couch.

"I feel like a dick. I guess I got swept up in all this." He motioned around the room with his hand. "I love this place, but I wonder why Galena never told me about the testing."

"Because she wanted to get us here. If she told you about that, would you have come? We've got to find a way to see Aunt Celeste. She'll know what to do."

Tai nodded. "Agreed. But first we have to find out where she is. I don't think she's in her room next door."

"Neither do I. I'm up for a little adventure, how about you?" Argus made a fist and held out his hand.

"You know it, bro." Tai fist bumped Argus's hand and let out a breath. "We're in alien territory, Arg...literally."

Typical Tai, nervous joking. First they had to rule out that Aunt Celeste wasn't in her room. Tai handled that by opening the connecting door on the far end of the room. As expected, it was empty. They went into the corridor and backtracked to the lobby where several Ramtalans were gathered talking.

Argus remembered what Ari said. They didn't have to greet anyone if they didn't want to, and since he didn't feel like engaging anyone in conversation, he walked along and kept quiet. The Ramtalans smiled and resumed their discussion. Tai pointed to the first corridor, but before they took a step, someone called out to them.

"Argus and Tai Dachel, where are you going?" came the voice.

Argus turned and saw a ghostly blue figure across the lobby. It had big black almond-shaped eyes, a thin, narrow mouth, and long translucent arms and legs. It floated along instead of walking on its legs. There was no clothing, but the spiral galaxy emblem was somehow embedded within the glow. And there weren't any visible genitals. What the hell was this?

It floated closer. "You must always respond to me. I am Commander Jampara. Now, where are you going?"

Chapter 40

After being admitted into the hospital in Las Vegas, Max lay in bed waiting for the doctor to show up to go over the results of the head x-rays. He wasn't feeling too bad overall, only a bit of a nagging ache from the bump on the back of his head.

The TV set didn't work, so he occupied his time playing memory games, hoping he'd recall what happened. Not much luck, although he did remember speaking to his boss about traveling out of town somewhere to do something. But the details were gone.

It was night by the time the doctor came in with a chart. "Mr. Jackson, how are you feeling?"

"Okay, I guess. Considering I flipped my car, I'd say I'm in good shape."

The doctor nodded thoughtfully. "Yes, you were very lucky. The radiologist made his report and said there's nothing major on the x-rays, except for several minute puncture wounds of unknown origin in your skull. He thinks they may have been caused by flying glass shards. Other than that, there's nothing else wrong. No internal injuries or broken bones. Not sure how you managed that. You did have a blood alcohol level of 0.28. Pretty high. Vegas catches most people off guard."

"I don't even remember drinking. Hell, I don't even remember coming to Las Vegas."

"Not surprising. I'd say you have a case of alcohol-induced amnesia. We'll keep you overnight and you can be released in the morning."

"Good." Max sat up.

"I'm afraid it might not be so good for you. The police are waiting to take you into custody for DUI."

"Oh. Custody?" He'd get fired for sure. Stone was always looking for an excuse to fire him.

The doctor wrote in the chart and left. With nothing else to do, Max decided it was time to call Stone. He picked up the landline phone by his bed and dialed Stone's cell number since it was past seven. This was going to be ugly.

On the third ring, Stone picked up. "Stone."

"Mr. Stone, it's Max Jackson."

"Jackson? Do you know what time it is? Why are you calling me this late? I'm in the middle of dinner."

"I'm sorry, sir. I wanted to let you know that I've been in a car accident." If there was any sympathy in Stone, surely he wouldn't get angry.

"In the pool car? You crashed the pool car? That's coming out of your salary."

No sympathy. Max wiped a trace of sweat off his forehead. "I was almost killed and all you care about is the car?"

"The car's more valuable than you are, Jackson. Did you at least dig up any information to make the loss of a pool car less distasteful?"

Information? About what? What was he working on? "Mr. Stone, I can't remember what I was working on. Can you help me out?"

There was a groan on the other end of the phone. "You are the most incompetent agent I've ever worked with. Tell you what, if you don't deliver me a complete report of your findings in Palmdale by morning, you're fired." He hung up.

Well, that's terrific. At least he found out he was working in Palmdale. But how'd he end up in Las Vegas? With any luck his memory would come back before morning so he could prepare a report.

He leaned back against the pillows and shut his eyes. What was he doing in Palmdale? Had he ever been to Palmdale before? He knew how to get there; take the I-5 north from LA to the 14 and there you go, Palmdale. But what the hell was in Palmdale? Oh, wait, it was close to Edwards Air Force Base.

Ah, now he was getting somewhere. Palmdale and a military base, a military base and Palmdale. What was the connection? Was there a connection? He opened his eyes and looked around the room. His clothes were in a neat pile on a chair by the bathroom. He got out of bed, a little woozy still, and found his wallet and cell phone in his pants pocket. Clues, clues, he needed clues.

His license was in the wallet, as well as his credit cards and old photo of him and his ex-wife. Why did he keep that? Hmmm, there was a motel key tucked into the wallet. And his teaching credential ID card. What was that doing in there? He hadn't taught anything in years, not since joining AURA. He plucked out the ID card and the motel key. Now he had clues.

Chapter 41

Argus was at a loss for words. He didn't want to lie to Commander Jampara about looking for a way to avoid the tests, but then he also didn't want to tell the truth. The Commander's body was freaky and fascinating at the same time. Is that what Aunt Celeste looked like without her host body?

"I'll ask you one more time. Where are you going?" the Commander asked. His severe black eyes widened slightly.

Tai shrugged. "We're going to the eating facilities for a snack. Is there anything wrong with that?"

Commander Jampara looked at Argus. "Is that true, Argus? You are hungry?"

Argus nodded. "Yes. I asked Tai if we could walk around a little and get something to eat. I'm sorry if I overstepped my—"

Commander Jampara floated backward a few feet. "You did not. Of course, you can go wherever you please. You are guests here. I must say, it is nice to meet you again after seventeen planetary years." He turned and glided across the lobby and down the middle corridor.

"That was about the weirdest thing I've ever seen," Argus whispered. "Is that what Ramtalans look like without a host body?"

"Yeah, I guess. I've never seen one. His eyes are like yours. Well, when yours change. I've always wondered something. What are the host bodies? Do they make them?"

Argus looked around. They were alone. "I don't know. I wanted to ask Aunt Celeste when she first told us about everything, but I wasn't sure if she wanted to talk about it. It seemed, I don't know, personal." He pointed down the middle corridor. "I have an idea."

"What idea?" Tai smirked. "Tell me."

"You said the middle corridor led to the control rooms and other rooms. What if Aunt Celeste is in one of those other rooms? Galena said she was preparing for the tribunal. What if there's a meeting room or something? We can try to find her and tell her we want to go home."

Tai nodded. "Good thinking. My deviousness must be rubbing off on you."

Maybe it was. Argus tried to calm down, his heart was racing a mile a minute. The only way they'd get to leave is if Aunt Celeste helped them. "We'll have to watch for the Commander." He took the lead and walked casually down the middle corridor, although he wasn't feeling very casual inside. He was sweating like crazy.

The corridor was long with unmarked doors about every twenty or thirty feet. How would they know what any of the rooms were? After passing by a few more doors, Tai tapped Argus on the shoulder.

"Stop for a second." Tai waved his hand over the silver panel by the nearest door. Nothing happened. "Worth a try."

Argus pressed his ear to the door and heard voices. He waved Tai over. "Listen."

Tai listened and shrugged. "I can't tell who that is in there."

"Yeah, me either. What do we do now?" Argus sighed. "How can we find...wait. I can try to go invisible."

"Right here? What if someone comes by." Tai glanced around.

"No, of course not here. In our room. All I have to do is concentrate on Aunt Celeste."

Tai grinned. "Cool. And I can use shared-sight so I can dissolve and find you if you're in any trouble."

They ran to their room, ignoring the stares of a few Ramtalans. Argus sat on the couch, closed his eyes, and concentrated on Aunt Celeste. He had trouble at first because he couldn't clear his mind, but after a few attempts, he focused and saw her in a small room. She was standing in the center of the room and there were...one, two, three...ten people sitting in chairs around her. Everyone was wearing the emblem. Commander Jampara wasn't there.

He concentrated harder and opened his eyes when he heard Aunt Celeste's voice say, "I have been their Guardian since birth". Yes. He was standing in the room. He walked around and saw that one of the people sitting was Ari. Everyone had a computer tablet on their lap. Argus got closer and saw that the tablets contained lists of questions.

Aunt Celeste had her ponytail around the front and was fiddling with it. "The boys are growing. They require independence. Their behavior is not unusual for teenagers."

Ari spoke, "Trust me, I know. But Argus and Tai aren't like other teenagers, Celeste. In fact, they're not like other New Breeds either. We all know that. In only one week Argus and Tai were in a fight, Tai was bitten by a rattlesnake, Argus threw his friend's father to the ground, almost strangled a human, and discovered invisibility, which we know is a very rare Ramtalan trait. And then there's Tai. He's a defender and a good one at that. There's never been a record of any New Breed who turned out to be a defender, or a protector like Argus for that matter. Can you explain how two New Breeds have become a protector and a defender at the age of seventeen?"

"No, I cannot." Aunt Celeste shifted her feet. "These boys have incredible qualities. I have begun training them and they've already learned some basic control techniques. They learn fast."

Ari stood and nodded. "That's great, Celeste. You're making your point. But, the tribunal won't be concerned with how well they're learning, they'll want to know what measures you've taken or will take to keep them safe and out of harm's way. Max Jackson kidnapped Argus and you didn't know. That's inexcusable."

Argus came forward. "It was me. I didn't tell her the truth about where I was going." Damn it. They couldn't hear him.

"Argus!" Ari shouted.

"Argus? Is that you?" Aunt Celeste spun around. "Where are you?"

"You can hear me?" He walked over to her. "I'm right in front of you."

Ari groaned. "Okay, Argus, you obviously heard what we were talking about. Turn visible right *now*."

He thought of pain like he'd practiced and appeared. "I'm sorry for...intruding."

Ari shook his head. "All right, Celeste, now I have a better understanding of what you've gone through with these boys." Ari waved at Argus. "Good to see you again."

It was so embarrassing to have everyone stare at him. "Aunt Celeste, how did you hear me this time?"

"This is the Citadel, Argus. The collective Ramtalan energy in here makes us all extra perceptive. It will influence you as well. Why are you here?" She flipped her hair so her ponytail snaked down her back.

He glanced at Ari and then back at Aunt Celeste. "I wanted to talk to you. Alone. In private."

"Oh." She looked into his eyes. "Do you remember what I said when you didn't want me being so intrusive?"

Intrusive? Oh. She told him that if he didn't want her reading his thoughts, he only had to say to stop. Now she wanted him to give her permission.

"Aunt Celeste, go ahead." He winked back.

Her eyes flashed bright and instantly dimmed again. "Done."

Argus knew he wouldn't have long before they became suspicious, so he thought about everything Galena said and how they didn't want to stay at the Citadel to be tested like a couple of lab rats.

Aunt Celeste nodded and placed her hand on his shoulder. "Argus, you need to return to your room and go to sleep. No more snooping around into matters that don't concern you."

"Yes, ma'am. Sorry." He nodded to Ari and hurried out when the door slid open. Damn, that was close.

The corridors were deserted, so he jogged all the way back to his room, but the door wouldn't open when he waved his hand over the panel. He knocked and Tai answered.

"Why didn't you come in, bro?"

"The door wouldn't open." Argus pushed past him. "Tai, I found out something interesting."

"Cool. Does that mean you found Aunt Celeste?"

Argus nodded. "Sure did. She was going over questions for the tribunal. Ari was there. Get this, they heard me while I was invisible."

"How? I don't like this, Arg. I feel nervous and jumpy, like something's not right. Remember how Aunt Celeste said to always listen to our intuition and instinct? Well, my instinct says to get out of here." Tai paced around the room, back and forth from the kitchenette to the spiral staircases.

"I know, me too. But listen, the...ah...collective energy here makes everyone extra perceptive according to Aunt Celeste. Which means we'll have to watch ourselves. Why are you pacing so fast?"

"Why are you talking so fast?" Tai stopped. "You sound all hopped up on caffeine. Do you think it's the energy here?"

"I guess. I didn't realize I was talking fast." Argus drew in a deep breath and forced himself to slow down. "Aunt Celeste did say it'll affect us, too. Anyway, I told her what's going on through telepathy."

Tai nodded. "Okay, so what does that mean? Is she going to help? Are you sure nobody else read your mind?"

Argus groaned. "No, I'm not sure. I don't want to be here. I feel trapped."

"Yeah, same here. While you were gone, I thought about what it would really be like here. You were right, I got sucked in by the cool stuff and wasn't thinking about what was going to happen down the line. I actually like school and *Marco's* and walking in the desert with the hot sun beating down on me. I don't really like rattlesnakes anymore, so those I can live without, but I don't want to stay here. What can we do? The tribunal is going to make the decision about our lives, and we have nothing to say about it."

Argus sat on the couch. "But Aunt Celeste will try to convince them that we should stay in Palmdale. She asked me before what decision would make me happiest, or warmest as she put it. Now she knows and she'll work extra hard at convincing them to let us go back home."

Tai came over. "You're forgetting about Galena. She seems to have more authority than Aunt Celeste, and she wants us to stay. I didn't want to say anything before, but she treats me like I'm her pet. I have to ask her permission for everything, and she *tells* me what I can and can't do. Why does she control me like this? She's not as bossy with you. Because she healed me from the snake bite doesn't mean she owns me." He slumped onto the couch. "I thought we were supposed to be treated like kings, but somehow it's not really that way. I want to go home, too."

Argus put his arm around his brother. Should he tell Tai what Galena did to him at the hospital? How would he react to that news? He might want to stay if he found out he was more Ramtalan than New Breed. No, best to keep it a secret. "We'll find a way to leave here. They let Max go."

"Yeah, but we're New Breeds. He's a human."

Argus got up and wandered around looking at the shelves of movies and video games to distract him from dealing with Tai's genetics. None of the material stuff mattered. The floor could be made of solid gold and it wouldn't matter. He looked back at his brother. For a change, he was sad and brooding.

"I'm going to try to get some sleep." Argus went to the spiral staircase on the right and gripped the banister. "I'm so wound up though, not sure if I can sleep." He took one step up and almost fell over when the banister broke free. "Oops. Guess I was holding it too tightly." It had to be the extra energy giving him even more strength.

"Easy, bro. Remember your control techniques." Tai ran up the other staircase and looked down from the loft at Argus coming up. "That one's my staircase since you broke yours." He chuckled.

Argus charged up the remaining steps and pretended to fight Tai. They goofed around for a few minutes, then lay down on their beds, full size with the softest mattresses ever. The ceiling above the beds glowed with a scene of the Milky Way Galaxy. One star on the tip of one of the spiral arms glowed brighter than the rest. Argus knew it had to be Ramtala. That made him remember the telescope he had at home. It would be cool to look at the real Ramtala.

There was no way he could settle down with so many thoughts running through his brain. The arms of the galaxy on the ceiling moved like a slow-motion interstellar dance. He watched the stars and planets in the galaxy twinkle and glow and imagined that his parents were still alive. As a family, they could take off in a spacecraft to visit Ramtala.

He closed his eyes and pictured what the craft would look like; the Space Shuttle on the outside and a comfy motor home on the inside with bunk beds for him and Tai. Lola would be, of course, invited along. She'd stand with him at a large viewing window as distant stars seemed to zoom by.

He imagined his dad coming up beside him, pointing out the window, but then he turned with a serious expression and said, "We will all be together again, boys. We must be together, I need you."

Argus's eyes flew open, and he sat up, temporarily disoriented. He glanced over and saw Tai sitting on the edge of his bed, gripping the comforter in his fist, and breathing hard.

"Tai, did you have a weird dream?"

He nodded. "Yeah. Dad was there. He said we'd all be together again. But I couldn't see his face."

"That's the same dream I had." Argus got up and sat beside his brother. "That sure as hell wasn't a normal dream. We need to get out of here."

Chapter 42

From his hospital room, Max bought an airline ticket to Los Angeles and reserved a rental car. He called for a taxi and waited. Answers were in Palmdale, so that's where he had to go. He dressed and peeked outside the room. A cop hung around the nurses' station, waiting to haul him off to jail. Damn, damn, damn.

Without checking, he already knew the windows were locked. A hospital rule to stop patients from jumping out. Not for the patient's sake, but for liability reasons. The hospitals didn't want to get sued by the distraught family members. He used to think it was a good idea, but now he wished the windows were unlocked. The only way out was past the cop.

He went to the bathroom and smoothed his hair, washed his face, and managed to tear the hospital bracelet off after a few tries. He looked in the mirror. He could pass for a visitor, but only if the cop didn't see him coming out of the room and couldn't see his face clearly.

He peeked out the door again and saw the cop in the same place, flirting with a young nurse. That gave him an idea. He worked up a few tears and went into the corridor. With his hands over his face, he sobbed and rushed down the corridor past the nurses' station.

"Hey." the cop barked. "Hey, you!"

Max kept going, crying harder, ignoring the cop. He made it to the elevator and heard the nurse say, "Give the guy a break, he's upset." He pressed the down button a dozen times and looked through his fingers to see the cop chatting with the nurse again. The ruse worked. The elevator door opened, and Max rushed in. He was alone in the elevator and so close to freedom he wanted to shout out a victory cry.

The door opened on the main floor, and he hurried out straight to the front of the hospital where there was a taxi waiting. He got in and let out a relieved breath, smiling to himself. That really wasn't all that hard.

"Where to?" the driver asked.

"Airport. Domestic flights." Max hunkered down in the seat. Secured to the back of the seat was the taxi driver's ID card in a plastic sleeve. There was something odd about his last name. No, not odd, familiar. Why? It's not like he had any friends named Ramatana. So why was the name familiar? He shrugged. Maybe he'd heard it in a movie.

The trip lasted only a few minutes. He paid the fare and gave the driver a five buck tip, then hurried into the terminal. His flight was scheduled to leave at midnight. But he wouldn't feel safe until he was through security and in the plane.

A large clock on the wall said it was 11:37 pm, which had to be the reason the security check line was short and why the terminal was practically deserted. Only a few people catching the red-eye back home after losing their hard-earned money at the casinos. He hated gambling, so why did he go to Las Vegas of all places? It didn't make sense. And drinking so much that he rolled his car? That wasn't like him. He needed answers.

He made it to the gate as the passengers were boarding and got in line. He found a window seat and buckled up. As the flight attendant went about her routine of securing baggage and giving the emergency instructions, he took out the motel key. The Palms Motel. Didn't ring a bell. Obviously not a high-class establishment because it was an actual key, not a security card key like in most places. It was frustrating having a fragmented memory. And what was with that cab driver's name; Ramatana? It was bugging him. Why did that trigger something in his memory?

Ramatana, Ramatana, Ramatana. He repeated it over and over. Rama...Tana...Ram...Tala...Ramtala? That was it! What the hell was Ramtala? It was familiar, tickling the back of his mind as if he used to know who or what it was. At least his memory was coming back.

Hopefully the motel clerk would remember him and give him some information about when he'd checked in and if he was with anyone. He leaned his head against the seat. It was a short flight, but longer enough for a nap. If there was any reference to Ramtala in Palmdale, he'd find it.

Chapter 43

Argus couldn't sit still and paced around the kitchen. How could he and Tai have the same dream? Was that possible? And what was with their father talking to them?

"Arg, we've got to get out of here. This place is making me feel weird." Tai nervously tapped on the side of a can of soda. "And we have to tell Aunt Celeste or Galena or Ari or someone."

Argus shook his head. "Not Galena. If we can get close to Aunt Celeste, she can read our thoughts. That's the only way we can communicate with her right now. We can't let Galena know or she'll make sure we never see Aunt Celeste."

"I was thinking, the increased energy here probably made us dream the same thing, you know, like a connection between our minds or whatever. Obviously it wasn't really Dad reaching out from the grave." Tai downed the rest of his soda and opened another one. It fizzed and bubbled over, spilling onto the countertop. "Damn it."

Argus wiped up the spill with a paper towel. He opened the fridge, closed it, wandered around, and finally sat on the couch. "I can't put my finger on it, but there's something weird going on. It's like that dream really was trying to tell me...us...something."

A thought flashed into his brain. What if the Commander wiped away Max's memory? That'd be the only way they'd let him go. He glanced at Tai. What if the testing Galena spoke of was to remove parts of their memory about Palmdale so they wouldn't care about staying at the Citadel?

"What are you thinking about, Arg? You've been staring at nothing for five minutes."

Argus got up and told Tai about his theory, which upset Tai even more. His eyes glowed bright and he flung the can of soda across the room.

"Tai, stop. We can't lose control now. Why don't we ask someone if we can see Aunt Celeste? What have we got to lose?"

"Oh, I don't know, our freedom, our lives, our memories. Maybe we can take the elevator up to the surface and steal the hovercraft." Tai raised an eyebrow.

"Seriously? We'd get caught before we got out of the elevator. Besides, I don't know how to drive a hovercraft."

Tai drummed his fingers on the countertop. "How hard can it be? Come on, think about it. We can go back to Labrador or to another island or anywhere."

Tai wasn't thinking right. Argus pretty much felt the same way but knew stealing the hovercraft wasn't a good plan. The only way they were getting home was if Aunt Celeste convinced the tribunal that it would be the best thing for them. But Galena would certainly speak out against her. Aunt Celeste would need extra help. What if he and Tai were allowed to talk to the tribunal?

"Tai," Argus grabbed him by the arm. "I've got an idea."

"That's weird, Arg, I sort of heard what you were thinking. And I agree. Let's go find the Commander or Ari or anybody and ask them, no *tell* them, that we want to stand with Aunt Celeste at the tribunal."

Argus frowned. "Don't read my thoughts, Tai."

"Like I can help it. I didn't even know I could until now."

It had to be the extra energy, or because Tai was.... "Yeah, okay. Let's go." Argus went to the door and stopped. "Remind me to ask why the door won't open for me."

They went to the lobby and down the middle corridor to the room where Aunt Celeste had been. Argus knocked. The door slid open, and Ari stood there with his arms folded across his chest.

He smiled. "I was wondering when you two would show up."

"What do you mean?" Tai glanced at Argus like he was expecting him to explain.

Argus didn't have any answers. "Were you expecting us?"

Ari shook his head and stepped aside. "Not me. Galena."

There was Galena, standing behind him, wearing a long black cloak and holding a stick about six feet high with a blue orb at the top. The orb had that same spiral galaxy winding all around it.

She took a step, lifted the stick, and thumped it gently on the ground. "I knew you both would show up. It's against protocol for New Breeds to attend a tribunal, but under these special circumstances, I will allow Tai to be present."

Argus felt the blood drain from his face. He knew what the special circumstances were. She was talking about Tai being more...was Tai still reading his thoughts? Did that mean she was going to tell him? Argus had to stop her. Tai wasn't ready to hear that sort of news.

Tai glanced at Argus. "What news? I can't hear everything you say, only some stuff. What news, bro?"

Argus shook his head and spoke up, "We should both stand with Aunt Celeste. She raised us both." Argus watched Tai. It looked like he was trying to work things out.

Galena took another step, lifted the stick, and brought it to the ground beside her. "I cannot allow that, Argus. Tai can attend or you can both stay in your room."

Argus took a step into the room, but Ari shook his head and motioned him to step back out into the corridor. He did as he was told and stood at the threshold. "I want to speak with Commander Jampara." He figured it was worth a try.

"No." Galena extended her arm, keeping the stick on the ground, but leaning it forward. "I am the head of the tribunal and I hold the Wand of Ramtala. My word in this matter is law. The Wand has been activated and attuned to the energies of the Tribunal. No New Breed may enter the court chambers. Make your decision, Argus."

Tai held up his hand. "Wait. Don't I get a say in this? Why can I attend and not my brother? I'm a New Breed."

Galena looked at Argus with a slight smile. "Well, Tai, I'm glad you asked. Perhaps I should explain why. I've been waiting for the right time to tell you—"

Argus interrupted, "Okay. Tai can go." Why was she playing these games? It sure looked like she enjoyed it.

"Good." She brought the wand back beside her. It was almost like a judge's gavel, her symbol of office and authority. "The tribunal starts at midnight in the court chambers. That's the blue door at the far end of the hall. Don't be late, Tai." She nodded to Ari who pressed a button to close the door, leaving them standing alone in the corridor.

"What the hell's going on, Arg? Didn't I tell you she treats me like I'm her pet? I'm getting sick of this. She gives me permission to come, but not you. That's not right. And what did she want to tell me? Is she messing with my brain because she saved me? Come on, let's steal the hovercraft." Tai leaned against the corridor wall and pouted.

"She's asserting her power and trying to get us on her side. You've got to go to the tribunal and help Aunt Celeste. With Galena in charge, Aunt Celeste needs all the help she can get. If you can get her alone, tell her about the dream." Argus motioned toward the lobby. "Why don't we get a snack while we wait? I'm starving. You can show me the cafeteria."

Tai smiled. "It's way more than a cafeteria. It's like a five-star restaurant, well, like what I'd imagine a five-star restaurant to be like. There aren't any waiters though, you order from a computer inlaid into the tabletop. It's awesome."

"Cool. So if there aren't any waiters, who brings the food? Do we get it ourselves?"

"Nope. It's...kind of a robot or a hovercraft thing. A moving pedestal with a stainless-steel tray with the food on it comes to the table. It hovers above the ground, that's what I meant by hovercraft. These people...I mean, Ramtalans...sure like hovering things."

"Well, the Commander sort of hovered. Maybe it reminds them of home."

They walked to the lobby and then went down the first corridor on the left. The smell of food got stronger as they went. It was late, but someone had to be eating.

The eating facilities were inside a very large room without any doors. It was the size of a large grocery store. There were quite a few people already eating, some looked up, smiled, and nodded, then went back to their food.

The Citadel must have graveyard shifts. Argus and Tai walked right in and sat down at a round table as far away from the other people as they could.

The table was glass and the computer Tai talked about was flush with the tabletop. Argus scrolled through the various menu items, which took about ten minutes since there were so many and chose a hamburger and sweet potato fries.

Tai clicked his tongue. "That's all you're getting? Where's your sense of adventure?" He scrolled through the menu and stopped at Fresh Maine Lobster. "Now that's what I call a snack."

"Lobster? Really? At this hour?" Argus teased. "Order me one, too."

Tai pressed the "order now" button and added a couple glasses of ice water as well. After a few minutes, Argus turned around and saw a robotic stainless steel serving tray on a pedestal float to the table. How they cooked lobster in a few minutes was anyone's guess. They got their plates off the tray and started eating. The lobster was delicious.

The distraction of eating didn't last long because at about five minutes to midnight, a chime sounded and everyone in the room got up and headed into the corridor, nodding to Argus and Tai as they left.

Tai pushed his plate away. "I don't want to go without you, Arg. What do I say?"

"Oh, come on, you talk a good game even when you don't have to. You'll have them eating out of your hand." Argus followed his brother to the court chambers where a line of Ramtalans were filing in. "Don't be nervous. Use those persuasive words you're so good at." He tried to peek inside, but the doorway was blocked with the throng of people. So, this was it. The verdict that could possibly change their lives. Argus wiped sweat off his forehead.

"I'll try my best." Tai took several deep breaths. "Damn it, I'm nervous. Why don't you go invisible and come in, too?"

"They can hear me, so if I made any sound at all, they'd know. I don't want to make it look worse for Aunt Celeste. Tell her I'm with her in spirit." Argus knew that sounded silly, but it was too late now. "You better get in there. I'll wait right out here."

Tai held his fist up and Argus bumped it. "See you soon, bro." He went in when the line halted to let him.

As soon as the last person entered, the door slid closed with a click. A lock? Argus pressed his ear to the door but couldn't hear a thing. He slid to the ground in front of the door, hoping to catch a word or two when they started. There was a faint knock and then silence again. It could have been a gavel or maybe Galena's wand thumping on the floor. The fact that she was running the show wasn't good.

Time passed slowly; ten minutes, twenty minutes, an hour, two hours. What were they doing in there? Wasn't it only questions and answers like he'd heard in the other room? He stood and stretched, paced for a while, did a few push-ups, jogged in place, and slumped back against the door. He really wanted to know what Aunt Celeste and Tai were saying and had to resist the urge to turn invisible and sneak in.

Another hour ticked away before the door made a loud click that startled him. He jumped up, stiff from sitting so long and stood to the side, waiting. The door slid open, and Argus finally had a view inside. It was almost like a courtroom in TV shows and movies, except the judge's bench and witness stand were in the center of the room on a round platform with seats surrounding it in a complete circle. The platform was like a giant Lazy Susan, designed to rotate by the looks of it.

Tai and Aunt Celeste were standing on the platform at the base of the judge's bench with Galena. The audience members were all getting out of their seats and heading for the door.

Galena held her wand and was still wearing her cloak, but she didn't look happy. Not at all. Her lips were pressed together tightly, and her eyes were smoldering bright blue. Tai made eye contact with Argus and smirked.

Yes! It had to be good news. Argus shrugged and raised his eyebrows expectantly. He saw Tai glance at Galena and when she looked away, he gave the OK sign. Aunt Celeste was unreadable as usual, although she was standing straight, gazing sideways at Galena. She'd won and was obviously trying not to let her gratification show.

Once the court chambers were empty, except for Galena, Aunt Celeste, and Tai, Argus stepped inside. It was a cavernous room with hardwood flooring and a ceiling that glowed blue. Blue must be a favorite color for Ramtalans.

Tai went to him and kept his voice low, "That was an ordeal. I'll tell you all about it later. The verdict was voted on and Aunt Celeste gets to stay our Guardian and we can go back to Palmdale the day after tomorrow."

"Awesome. Can't wait to get the low-down. Is Aunt Celeste okay? Galena looks...I don't know...disturbed." Argus watched how Galena interacted with Aunt Celeste; stiff, formal, and not friendly.

Tai nodded. "She's fine, believe me. It was intense for a while. I thought Galena and Aunt Celeste were going to go at it. Remind me to tell you about that orb on the wand."

"Okay." Argus couldn't wait to hear about the entire proceeding.

Galena strode out of the court chambers, holding the wand off the ground this time, and acknowledged Argus with a brief nod when she passed. Aunt Celeste waved them over and visibly relaxed a little as soon as Galena was gone.

She brought her ponytail to the front and sighed. "I'm glad that's over. Tai, you did very well, very articulate. And Argus, thank you for not intruding. It wouldn't have gone well for us if you had."

Argus nodded. "I was tempted. Thank you for getting them to let us go back home. Galena didn't look happy."

Aunt Celeste stepped off the platform and glanced out the doorway. "This still may be an issue. I believe Galena might go to Commander Jampara to make a plea to keep you both here."

Tai raised his voice, "What? Can she do that? After the tribunal agreed with you?"

"According to Ramtalan law, she can't go against the tribunal when it comes to New Breeds. But..." she stopped and looked at Argus. "But there's something else that she can use."

Now was not the time to tell Tai the truth about his DNA. Argus jumped in, "She'll let us go, I know she will. Come on Tai, let's go to our room and you can tell me everything. Aunt Celeste, are you coming?"

She nodded. "I'm exhausted. We must stay here tomorrow while the tribunal documents the events and the results, but then the following day we can leave." She didn't look too certain.

They left the court chambers and said goodnight to a few people gathered in the lobby discussing the tribunal. Galena was nowhere to be seen. Argus didn't trust her at all, especially after what Aunt Celeste hinted at. Why couldn't she leave them alone?

At their room, Argus turned to Aunt Celeste, "Why can't I open the door? It won't work for me. Tai waved his hand over that panel, and it opened."

She looked at the door. "It should. Unless it's because Tai is...you know. I'll check into it in the morning. Now I don't want you two staying up all night. You need your sleep. Goodnight, boys." She waved her hand over the panel beside her door and went inside.

Tai did the same with their door and went right to the refrigerator. "What did Aunt Celeste mean about me opening the door?"

"No idea."

"Hey, I'm starving."

"Really, Tai? You had lobster for dinner, how can you still be hungry?" Argus headed for the broken spiral staircase that was now designated as his but stopped and waited for Tai. How long should he hide the truth from his brother?

Tai shrugged and didn't seem like he heard Argus's thoughts. "I was locked in that court chambers listening to those aliens argue about what was best for us like we couldn't answer for ourselves. Made me mad and made me hungry." He rummaged through the fridge and took out a loaf of bread and peanut butter. "I'm going to make a sandwich and I'll be right up. Wait until you hear about that orb!" He waved the bread in the air. "Want a sandwich?"

"Yeah, okay." Argus was feeling a bit hungry after all. Maybe because it was almost morning and he'd been up all night.

Tai finished with the sandwiches and raced up his staircase, getting to the top at the same time as Argus. They sat on their beds, cross-legged, and started in on the sandwiches.

When he finished, Tai cleared his throat and began his story. He explained how he and Aunt Celeste had to stand before the judge's bench first as the audience came in and sat down. When Galena entered, the orb on the wand glowed and threw off little sparks. She took her seat at the judge's bench and thumped the wand on the ground four times, which must have signaled the beginning of the tribunal.

Galena started first, telling every little thing that happened in Palmdale, and saying how it was all Aunt Celeste's fault for not controlling the situation better. She even brought up how their parents were killed and how Aunt

Celeste should never have allowed their mother to be put in a situation where she was in danger.

Argus jumped off the bed. "That's ridiculous! She didn't know Mom was in any danger."

"I know, but Galena was doing everything she could to discredit Aunt Celeste. When I tried to talk, Ari got up from his seat in the front and shouted "silence!". I tell you, bro, it was Galena's show. She went into detail about how the other New Breeds weren't surviving, so you and I had to be protected and tested to see what it was about us that made us survive." Tai got off the bed and paced around the bedroom loft. "I'm still really wound up."

"Good, because I want to hear the rest of the story." Argus sat back down on the bed. "Continue, brother."

Tai smiled. "Yes, sir. Anyway, when Galena finished, it was Aunt Celeste's turn. Here's where it gets interesting."

"Like it wasn't already?" Argus was as wound up as Tai. He couldn't settle and got up again.

Tai took a breath. "Galena came down and pointed the wand at Aunt Celeste. The orb sparked more, like a 4th of July sparkler, and then this curtain of light or whatever covered Aunt Celeste like a veil. Galena said it was energy from Ramtala and would prevent her from lying and would record her answers. Aunt Celeste would never lie, but I guess Galena didn't believe that."

Argus wrung his hands. "Figures. What happened? How did Aunt Celeste convince everyone?"

"She told everyone how she was Mom's Guardian right up until she died and then became our Guardian by default. She said how she had our house built far enough away from the city to keep us safe and rigged it with the security system and never left us alone for more than an hour or so at a time."

"That's true." Argus gazed at the starry ceiling. "That's so true."

"Tell me about it. Aunt Celeste went on about school and how we were getting settled in when Max appeared and caused all the trouble. Oh, you'll love this. When Galena accused Aunt Celeste of being careless, Aunt Celeste lifted off that veil thing and dropped it on the ground. It floated up and went right back into the orb. That's when Aunt Celeste really poured out her heart about how she thought of us as her family and would gladly give her life for us."

Argus stopped pacing. "She said that? Wow."

"I know. The other Ramtalans gave her a standing ovation. That really cheesed Galena. Galena even tried to say it wasn't true because Aunt Celeste took off the energy of Ramtala veil thing. Nobody listened and they kept applauding saying that Aunt Celeste's sense of duty and love was inspiring. When it came down to the vote, Aunt Celeste had everyone's vote."

"And Galena's?" Argus couldn't believe that Galena would ever do anything positive for Aunt Celeste.

Tai shook his head. "She didn't vote. Not allowed to. But I've got to tell you, the look on her face was scary."

"Wait, didn't you speak?" Argus wanted to hear everything, every single word.

"Oh, yeah. I got my chance right before the vote. Galena put the veil on me. I don't know how light has weight, but it did. It felt like a blanket. I could see through it, although everything was tinted blue. I guess Galena was hoping I'd say something bad about Aunt Celeste, but I didn't. I couldn't. There is nothing bad about her. That's basically what I said."

Argus sat on his bed. "Cool. Very cool. Did Galena say anything to you?"

"Nope. She took the veil off and that's when they did the voting. I think her plan to have me speak backfired on her."

Something didn't seem right. Argus looked over at Tai. "Hang on. That took three hours?"

"Three hours? No, more like one."

"Tai, I waited out in the corridor for three hours. Trust me, I know. I practically counted every minute."

"It was one hour. They recorded the time the tribunal started and when it ended. It was one hour." Tai yawned. "I'm going to sleep all day tomorrow so when I wake up, it'll be time to go home."

"Sounds like a plan." Argus yawned, too, and climbed under the covers. The time difference of the tribunal bothered him. He knew for sure it was three hours. Very weird. In the morning he'd ask Aunt Celeste about it. She'd have the answer. In the meantime, he planned on sleeping all day like Tai, and dreaming about Lola. They'd be back home in no time.

Chapter 44

Max paid the cab driver and stood outside The Palms Motel office, room key in hand, and straightened his wrinkled jacket. It was 2:45 a.m. No one was at the front desk. Might as well check out the room since he still had the key.

When he found the room, the curtains were drawn. That didn't necessarily mean it was occupied by new guests. He put the key in the lock and turned it slowly, then eased the door open. The faint scent of perfume or aftershave drifted out. Damn. Steady snoring let him know the occupant or occupants were asleep. Good, so long as the snoring continued, he was okay. They'd never know if he came in. No harm done unless he woke them.

He pushed the door open more and crept in, careful that he made no noise whatsoever. Snore, take a step, snore, take a step. The scant light that filtered in through the curtains was enough to see there were two people in the bed, two small suitcases near the closet, and a pile of clothes on the dresser.

It wasn't their stuff he was interested in. He got down on his hands and knees and peered under the dresser and under the bed hoping to find a clue that the maid might have left. Anything. Unfortunately, the room was spotless.

The snoring paused and Max froze, tempted to get up and run for the door, but when the snoring continued, he let out the breath he'd been holding. Okay, time to get the hell out of there. He went as quickly as he could through the door but closed it too fast and it slammed.

"Who's there?" came an angry male voice from inside.

Max high-tailed it out of there and stopped at the front desk. He hit the little metal bell several times. After a moment, a sleepy man in a shabby tee shirt and hair that stuck out in all directions came to the desk.

"Can I help you? Do you have a reservation?" he asked with a yawn.

Max placed the key on the desk. "Ah, no. Hey look, I stayed here—"

The man looked at the key. "You! Well, returning to the scene of the crime, eh?"

"What are you talking about?"

The man smiled sarcastically. "I charged your credit card for the damages and made a police report."

Max stared, unable to say anything as he processed what the man said. So, he did stay there. But what damages? What had happened? Obviously something to do with the accident in Vegas. Did he get drunk and then trash the room? He'd never done anything like that before.

"Did I leave anything in the room?" Max tried to grab the key back when the man snatched it up. "Anything at all?"

"This." He reached under the counter and brought out a small suitcase. "Everything's in there. Now get out of here before I call the cops." The man reached under the counter again. "I've got a gun."

"Okay, okay, relax. I came back because I can't remember anything. How long was I here?"

"Damn black-out drunks," the man mumbled. "You were here for a week. A substitute teacher at Highland High."

How did he know that? "A sub? Me?"

The man rolled his eyes and frowned. "A couple teachers came looking for you. Guess you went on a bender, eh? They said they couldn't reach you and this was the address you gave."

Okay, now he was getting somewhere. Subbing at a high school? But why? What was he working on? Stone hadn't given him anything to go on. Maybe Stone didn't know.

The office door opened and a sleepy guy about fifty came in, stared at Max for a second and then turned to the man behind the counter. "Someone was in my room. Room 8."

Max took the suitcase and looked away from the sleepy clerk. Should he play it cool or run? The last thing he needed now was to draw more attention to himself. The man behind the counter looked at Max's key. Oh, no, he knew it was the same room. Okay, truth time, with a little spin of course.

Max put on his best apologetic face. "Sorry, that was me. I stayed in that room and opened the door without thinking. When I realized it was occupied, I closed the door right away. Really sorry, didn't mean to scare you."

"Asshole." The guest spun around and went to the door but stopped and turned around. "This yours?" He took a wadded-up paper bag from his jacket pocket and tossed it to Max. "Found it under the dresser when I was looking for my slippers."

Max caught the bag before the man behind the counter did. He looked inside. It was a smashed OEED. How did it get broken? Okay, he was a sub, and he had an OEED. "Yeah, thanks. It's mine. Again, sorry I woke you."

The guest waved his hand in the air as if to say, "never mind" and stumbled back to his room. Max rolled the top of the bag down and started for the door, but the man behind the counter wasn't done.

"Hey! What's in the bag? Whatever's in that room belongs to me."

"It's mine." Max put his hand on the door, heard a click like the hammer of a handgun being cocked, and stopped. Sure enough, when he turned around, the man had a gun pointing at him.

"Give me the bag."

Max shook his head. "I told you it's mine. A broken radio. I want to see if I can fix it. It's got sentimental value. You can't use it or sell it if that's what you're thinking." Max opened the bag and tilted it so the man could see inside. "Just broken pieces."

The door opened again, and Max jumped. Two uniformed military guys stood there, staring at the gun in the man's hand. One of them immediately drew a pistol. The man behind the counter put the gun down and raised his arms.

The military guy, Air Force by the uniform, slipped his gun in a holster. "We cool, man?"

The man behind the counter nodded and stood back from the counter, probably so they wouldn't think he was going to go for the gun.

The Air Force guy scratched his head. "So, what's going on here, Max? Geez, we've been looking for you everywhere and then we find you with a gun pointed at your head."

Max glanced behind to make sure the guy was talking to him. "Me? You know me?"

"Come on, Max, don't screw around. It's me, John. John Franklin." He stepped into the office, followed by the other guy. "Remember? You disappeared that night from the bar. Angel and I have twenty-four hour leave and went to every bar in town looking for you." He chuckled. "I don't remember much about that night, but I do remember you're the first AURA agent we've ever partied with."

The man behind the counter cleared his throat. "Why don't you get outta here? And don't come back!"

"Fine with me," Max said. What a great opportunity to get reacquainted with the Air Force guys and find out what they knew. The clues were coming fast but putting them in place was going to take a little work.

The other Air Force guy, Angel, held the door for Max. "We found a cool bar on the other side of town when we were looking for you. Open twenty-four hours. They got free buffalo wings and pizza. You in?"

Free food? Who'd say no to that? Max nodded. "Sure."

John pointed to a Jeep in the parking lot. "Hop in the back."

"No problem." Max followed them, squeezed into the back seat, and crammed his suitcase next to him. He opened the paper bag with the broken OEED. The motel clerk didn't mention a laptop, so now he'd have to find a computer to log into the main server at AURA headquarters in LA to see what data he'd collected on the OEED. What happened to his laptop anyway? If someone stole it and tried to hack into it, it would delete all of the information stored on there. He yawned. No time for sleep. He had detective work to do.

Chapter 45

Argus rolled over and opened his eyes. There'd been no dreams of Lola, but that was okay, he'd see her soon enough. Tai was still asleep. No point waking him up yet. He checked the time; 10:30 a.m. He'd never slept in so late. He got out of bed, dressed, and climbed down the staircase, careful not to make any noise, and went to the kitchen. He didn't feel like making anything or eating cold cereal.

The restaurant had to be open. It seemed like it was always open. He glanced up at the loft. Knowing Tai, he'd sleep for a couple more hours at least. Argus got to the door, and it silently slid open. At least it opened for him so he could get out.

There were a few Ramtalans walking around who nodded to him and continued on their way. It really was a strange feeling knowing how they considered him special. He'd never felt special before. Well, maybe when the coach made him quarterback. And when Lola said he was hot. That made him feel awesome. He frowned when he remembered her in the hospital with Justin's arrow through her shoulder. He stopped in the lobby and clenched his fists. He felt hot, angry. Damn it, Lola got hurt because of him.

"Argus?" it was Ari, coming out of the middle corridor. "Are you all right? Your eyes."

"Oh. I'm still learning to control my anger."

"You're angry? There's nothing to be angry about here. Hey, I understand. I had a similar problem, but my face turned blue when I was upset." Ari shrugged.

What was he talking about? Did he mean his host body turned blue? "Excuse me?" Argus unclenched his fists and drew in a deep breath.

"Oh, didn't you know? I was a New Breed like you and Tai."

What? How come nobody said he was a New Breed? "Was?" Argus felt cold now.

Ari nodded. "Sure. Galena saved me, too. I'm one hundred percent Ramtalan now." He winked. "Not a pure-form though, I still have my human body. Where are you headed?"

Argus couldn't speak. He stood there, staring like an idiot. It was impossible to make New Breeds Ramtalan, that's what Aunt Celeste said. Impossible. Why was Ari saying he was Ramtalan? Maybe he meant *more* Ramtalan than New Breed, like Tai.

"Breakfast," was all that came out of Argus's mouth. He wanted to say, "what are you talking about" and "how can you be one hundred percent Ramtalan", but he couldn't bring himself to say it. Maybe because he didn't really want to know. What if Galena made Tai a full Ramtalan?

Ari smiled. "All right. Enjoy your breakfast. Oh, I'll be in the gym in a while if you want to join me. You can practice your abilities if you like. The collective energy here at the Citadel will help you when you work with your abilities."

"Okay, maybe." Argus did his best to smile politely. He looked back to the hallway leading to their room. He should go back and see Aunt Celeste.

Ari shook his head. "She's not there. She and Galena are meeting with Commander Jampara."

"Please don't use telepathy on me, Ari."

He laughed. "I can't. I can see you're concerned and figured you had a lot of questions to ask her."

"Oh." Now he felt stupid. "Sorry."

Ari smiled. "Don't be. I can imagine how strange it must be for you to be the only true New Breed here. Go and get something to eat and join me in the gym." He hurried off down the middle corridor.

Argus stood for a moment. Ari said the only *true* New Breed. Did that mean Tai wasn't considered a true New Breed anymore? Aunt Celeste said he still had human DNA. That meant he was still a New Breed. He really needed Aunt Celeste. What sort of meeting was it with the Commander? Hopefully it was about going back to Palmdale and didn't involve Galena trying to change things.

His stomach growled. He might as well go and eat, although he didn't feel like sitting alone in a restaurant being served by a robotic waiter. What would Dave or Lola or even Justin think if they saw the Citadel? Or saw the

Commander? Maybe one day he could bring Lola. What was he thinking? Of course he couldn't. She wouldn't even want to be his friend if she found out he was half alien.

"Get a grip, Argus," he mumbled.

He wandered to the restaurant and got hungrier when he smelled the food. Most of the tables were taken, but when a couple of Ramtalans saw him, they hustled out of their seats, nodded to him, and left. The thought crossed his mind that this sort of thing probably happened to famous people, rock stars and movie stars, all the time. But this was different. Way different. He wasn't famous. He was a teenager with messed up DNA, who could turn invisible and change his eyes to black.

He sighed and sat in the seat that was vacated for him. After scrolling through the computer menu, he chose scrambled eggs and pancakes with fresh squeezed orange juice. Who squeezed it? The robot? He snickered a little and furtively checked out the other patrons. Some were eating, some were ordering, and some were sitting and talking over a cup of coffee. He listened, pretending he was still scrolling through the menu.

A couple of guys a table over were talking about the tribunal, keeping their voices hushed. Maybe they weren't supposed to talk about it. If that was the case, he really wanted to know what they were saying. He caught a few words.

"Tomorrow."

"That soon?"

"That was the ruling."

"And the other boy?"

"Both of them. But Galena..."

They must have noticed him listening in because they stopped talking and got up, giving him a fleeting smile as they left. Damn it, why couldn't they have finished what they were going to say about Galena. He felt awkward by himself. He took out his phone and opened a game where he had to save the world from aliens. It used to be fun, but now it was like he was shooting his family. He shut off the game and decided to text Tai.

Hey, are you up yet? I'm in the restaurant. I'm bored.

The robotic waiter floated over with his food. It smelled delicious, but he still wondered about the orange juice.

"Hey, Robot, you squeeze this juice yourself?" He chuckled and picked up the glass of juice.

"No. It comes that way," the robot replied in a mechanical voice.

Argus dropped the glass on the floor. "You can talk?"

"Only when spoken to."

Argus leaned over to pick up the glass. "Wow. That's amazing."

"I will clean the spill." The robot backed away a few feet. A retractable arm came out from beneath the tray and grabbed the glass. "I will bring another orange juice."

"Thank you." Argus watched the robot float away into the kitchen.

His phone chimed.

I'm coming, bro!

He ordered Tai the same breakfast and by the time the robot returned with another glass of orange juice, Tai jogged in and sat down, almost running into the robot.

Tai pouted when he saw only one plate on the table. "Where's my breakfast?"

"I already ordered it. Give the robot a second to bring it." Argus took the orange juice off the tray. "Thanks, Robot. This is my brother."

The robot floated back a foot or so. "I know. I will return with his food." It turned and zoomed away.

Tai pointed to the robot. "That thing can talk?"

"Yeah. Cool, isn't it? I guess I'll miss some things about this place." Argus took a gulp of juice.

Tai grabbed a pancake and took a big bite. "Me too. Tomorrow we'll be back in the desert among the lowly humans."

Argus tried to spear the pancake dangling off Tai's fork. "Hey, that's my food. And what do you mean by *lowly*?"

Tai finished the pancake. "Kidding. Where's your sense of humor? And where's Aunt Celeste? I knocked on her door, but she didn't answer."

"Ari said she's in a meeting with Galena and the Commander. Oh, I'm going to the gym after breakfast. Ari said I can practice my abilities before we go. Want to come?" Argus protected his other pancakes when Tai reached over. "Hands off my food."

"I'm hungry. Oh, here comes mine." Tai rubbed his hands together. "Yeah, I'll come with you. I want to see if I can develop my abilities more before we leave."

Argus finished his breakfast and had to wait while Tai ate a second helping of eggs. They decided to go for a walk to let their breakfast go down before heading to the gym. They ran into Ari again in the lobby.

Ari was typing into a tablet computer, but quickly stopped. "Are you both coming to the gym? That's where I'm going right now."

Argus shook his head. "Not yet. We just ate. We'll see you there in a bit."

"So where are you going?" Ari pried.

Tai patted his stomach. "For a walk. Got to let this food settle."

"Well, don't wander off. Galena wants to talk with you, Tai." Ari glanced at Argus. "She wants to do a quick health check to make sure he's recovered from that snake bite."

Yeah, right, that wasn't what she wanted to talk to him about. Argus faked a smile and tugged on Tai's sleeve. "We'll meet you at the gym in a few minutes, Ari."

Ari seemed to believe him. "Fine, fine. See you there." He wandered off.

Tai pulled free. "Let go of me. What was that about? Health check? There's nothing wrong with me. This is getting weird, Arg. I told you we should have stolen the hovercraft."

"I'm starting to think you were right about that. I can't wait to get home and go back to school and put all of this behind us."

Tai rolled his eyes. "That's because you're the quarterback and have a girlfriend." He glanced around. "Maybe I can find myself a nice Ramtalan girlfriend. That blue color is so sexy." He smirked.

"And you'll have a houseful of blue alien babies!" Argus laughed.

Tai laughed as well. "Papa, Papa, I'm feeling blue today!" He laughed harder.

"Glad you think this is funny." Aunt Celeste stomped toward them. "None of this is humorous."

Tai groaned. "We're only kidding around."

She seemed nervous. "I want you both to go to your room and stay there." Her mouth was held tight. Something was wrong.

"Aunt Celeste, we are leaving tomorrow, aren't we?" Argus asked.

"Yes, yes, of course." She didn't sound too certain. "Go to your room and wait for me."

"But we were going to hang out with Ari at the gym." Tai sounded disappointed.

Aunt Celeste shook her head. "Later, Tai. Galena is...she's...go and wait for me in your room. Don't open the door to anyone, not Ari and especially not Galena. I need to take care of a few things." She pointed down the third corridor. "Go."

"Yes, ma'am." Argus nudged Tai. "Bet I can beat you to the room." He took off and heard Tai close behind him.

They made it to the room at the same time. Tai waved his hand over the panel and ran in first when the door slid open. Argus hurried in and bumped right into Tai who'd stopped one step inside the room.

"Damn it, Tai." He walked around him and froze. There in the sunken living area was a wavering image of their dad. Exactly like the photos they had of him.

Chapter 46

Argus took a step backward. It was their father. He stood there, transparent, swaying like a palm tree in a breeze. The TV could be seen right through him. What was going on? Was someone playing tricks? If they were, it wasn't funny.

Tai grabbed onto Argus's arm. "What is this, Arg? Are we dreaming again?"

"Damned if I know. Dad?" Argus moved a few steps forward.

"You must not go with Celeste," their dad said, sounding distant, hollow.

"What? Is that really you?" Argus ran and stood directly in front of his dad. He reached out, but his hand went through. "Can you hear me?"

"Find Ari and he will protect you. Allow Galena to be your Guardian. You must do this, my sons, if we are to be together again." The image wavered and disappeared.

"What the hell." Tai went to the spot where the image was and walked around with his arms extended, reaching into the air.

Argus checked out the rest of the apartment, but the image was gone. And it was not a dream this time. Why did he say what he said? "Tai, we need Aunt Celeste. Now." He pulled out his phone and texted:

Help, now! In our apartment. Dad appeared!

A reply came almost immediately:

Do not leave the apartment. I'm coming.

"Tai, Aunt Celeste is coming. You have no idea how much I want to be home." Argus wandered around, not sure if he wanted to sit, to stand, to throw something across the room. His life had been turned upside-down in a week. It was almost too much to take. He started to shake.

"Bro, your eyes." Tai slapped him on the back. "Calm the hell down." He paced around the apartment, clenching and unclenching his fists. "This sucks."

Argus nodded. That was an understatement. He sat on a stool at the breakfast bar, his feet tapping on the foot rail. He slid a shiny aluminum toaster over and looked at his reflection. His eyes were coal-black. So what. He didn't have to hide his appearance here, everyone knew who, or what, he was.

The door opened and Aunt Celeste rushed in, scanning the area. "Where was the apparition?"

Apparition? It was their dad. Argus pointed to the sunken living area. "There. Um, we both saw him in a dream last night, too. He said we'd be together again."

"Argus, you need to relax. Practice your control techniques." She jogged to the spot where their dad had appeared and turned around slowly, her arms waist level, palms up. Her brow pinched and her lips pressed together. She was upset or maybe even angry. It was the same look she had whenever Galena was around.

"What is it, Aunt Celeste?" Argus asked quietly.

"Shhh," she whispered.

Tai sat on the steps leading down to the sunken area. "Is it Galena?"

"I'm not sure." Aunt Celeste lowered her arms. "Tell me exactly what happened."

Argus explained about the dream, the message, and the recent appearance. She listened, nodding, and put her finger to her lips. "Do not talk about this to anyone. Understand? Galena and Ari are involved somehow. I don't know if they created the image of your father to get you to stay here or not. But whatever is going on, you can bet Galena is involved."

They both nodded. Argus wanted to ask her more about the "apparition" but it was obvious that she didn't want to talk about it right now. But why not? What did it mean? He'd do whatever she said at this point because he didn't want anything to jeopardize their leaving tomorrow. The Citadel was cool at first, now though, it was a prison.

Aunt Celeste pointed to the loft. "If you have anything to pack, pack it. I'm going to arrange for us to leave right away."

"Can you do that?" Argus walked toward his staircase.

She nodded. "I'm still your Guardian, Argus. If I can convince the Commander that it's for your benefit, he'll permit it."

For their benefit? What benefit? Not allowing their dad's ghost to haunt them or allowing Galena to take them as prisoners? Argus hesitated at the staircase. "Aunt Celeste, I want to ask you something about Ari."

"Not now, Argus. I have more important business to attend to. We'll talk later. Take care of anything you need to do and be ready to leave at a moment's notice." She gave a very brief, fleeting smile, and walked quickly to the door. She turned. "Be ready."

She left and the door slid closed behind her. Argus looked at Tai who shrugged and ran up the stairs to the loft. Whatever was going on had concerned Aunt Celeste enough that she wanted to leave the Citadel immediately and not wait for tomorrow.

Argus sat on the bottom step and closed his eyes, concentrating on his dad's image. A thought crossed his mind; the image he saw looked like his dad from a photograph at Lake Elizabeth. But that was seventeen years ago. He wouldn't look the same now. Plus, he was human, so there was no way he could have any abilities. It was a trick. It had to be Galena.

He opened his eyes and gasped. He wasn't in the apartment anymore. It was dark, but not too dark to see. It was an empty expanse, a room, stone walls, about ten feet by ten feet he estimated. The ceiling was low, maybe six and a half feet tall, and looked like wood planking. It felt damp, warm, humid. It was repressive and claustrophobic. His heart thumped and his body trembled. Where was he?

"Argus?" croaked a voice from the darkness.

"Who's there? Dad?" Argus turned but didn't see anyone. "Who's there?"

"Argus? Is that you?" A faint light, a red light, began to glow from the far corner. "How did you find me? You must not see me like this." The light faded until it was gone.

"Dad! Is that you? I thought you were dead. Dad!"

No answer. Silence. Crushing silence. The ceiling felt like it was pressing down. A deep rumbling filled the room as everything shook and knocked Argus off his feet. He squeezed his eyes shut and thought of the apartment at the Citadel. He imagined Tai in the kitchen, the spiral staircases, the loft. Each time he focused, the shaking got worse and broke his concentration.

"Dad!" Argus shouted.

He crouched on the ground. Dust from the ceiling drifted down over him. He coughed and covered his head with his hands and tried to block out the sound of bricks falling and wood splintering. He had to get back to the Citadel.

"Argus!" it was Tai shouting. "Where are you?"

"Here." Argus stood and saw Tai holding onto the wall as the room continued to shake violently.

"Where are you? You're invisible, bro!"

"Damn it!" Argus ran to Tai and grabbed his sleeve. "Dad was here. How are we going to get out of here? I don't even know where we are." He was about to think of pain when a brick slammed into his shoulder and made the pain real.

"Okay, I see you now. You okay?" Tai stepped back.

"My shoulder." Argus winced. "We have to get out—"

"No kidding. You've really got to figure out how to dissolve in reverse. Hold my hand." Tai's eyes looked even bluer in the dim light. "I told Aunt Celeste that you disappeared. She told me what to do to get you back."

"Okay. Hurry." As soon as Argus grabbed Tai's hand, he tingled all over and felt light, like he wasn't standing anymore, but his shoulder still hurt like hell.

"Hold on, Arg, Aunt Celeste said this might hurt the first time."

Hurt the first time? What was Tai about to do? The room went out of focus, shimmering, fading away. The rumbling and shaking stopped, replaced by a blinding white light. Argus had to close his eyes, but even that wasn't good enough. The light shone through his eye lids. It stung and made his eyes ache. No words came out of his mouth as he tried to talk. He gripped Tai's hand tighter until he was whisked away in a swirling current of air. He reached out but felt nothing but the cyclonic air around him. Then it came. Pain. Like his bones were breaking and snapping like twigs. It was unbearable.

Relief eventually came. The wind dissipated, the light was gone, and his body was limp. He gasped for air. He lay on the floor in the middle of the apartment at the Citadel. Someone was beside him, breathing hard. It was Tai.

"Tai?" his voice was hoarse.

"Yeah. You okay?"

"I think so. What the hell was that?" Argus sat up, carefully moving his fingers and legs, but when he tried to work his shoulder, pain shot through his arm.

"It's called a molecular shift. Aunt Celeste gave me a two-minute lesson. I don't ever want to do that again."

Argus remembered when she did the protection thing at the Palmdale airport, she said they had to maintain contact. The molecular shift must work on the same principle, whatever that was. Maybe that's how the dissolving ability worked as well. "Tai, I hurt my shoulder."

Tai got to his knees. "Aunt Celeste! We need help."

She ran down the spiral stairs and crouched by Argus. "What happened? Where did you go? I told you not to leave."

Argus groaned. "I don't need a lecture right now, Aunt Celeste. I didn't mean to dissolve. A brick crashed down on my shoulder." He caught his breath. "It hurts. Dad was there. I couldn't see him, but he was there. He said I shouldn't see him like that. I think he was hurt or sick or something. Is he really alive? You said he and Mom died."

Aunt Celeste touched his shoulder. "They did, or at least I thought they both did. I thought when you saw the apparition, it was a trick at first, but now I'm not so certain. If it really is your father, then I need to find out where he is and why he's still alive. Galena investigated him at the Citadel before he married your mother, like I told you. She's involved, I know it. First though, you need to be taken care of."

Tai stood. "Hurry up, he's in pain. What do you want me to do?"

"I'll have the medical team come here. Well done, Tai, well done. You need practice to perfect the molecular shift, but you did it well enough to save your brother." She placed a call on her communicator. "I need medical assistance to the Dachel brothers' room immediately."

She helped Argus to his feet and onto the couch. Tai handed him a glass of water and sat beside him.

Argus sat carefully, but he still moved his shoulder too fast and groaned in pain. "Aunt Celeste, what's a...ow...molecular shift?"

She paced in front of him. "It's used to transport another settler Ramtalan, or in this case, a New Breed, from one location to another. Remember the energy field I used at the airport? It's like that. I had to stay here to make sure nobody came in. Tai had to maintain contact with you so that as his molecules shifted and dissociated, so did yours. The dissociation allows the body to move through space."

"Oh." Argus wasn't sure he completely grasped the concept. But he knew he didn't want to go through it again, that's for sure.

"Arg, when I used shared-sight, I saw a red light. What was that?"

Argus took a long drink of the water. "I don't know. I think Dad, or whatever, was hiding in the light. As soon as he left, the room shook. What caused that, Aunt Celeste?"

She shrugged. "It could have been an energy burst...but that only happens with pure-forms. It's possible that the apparition isn't your father and is an Invader."

A screwed-up thought popped into Argus's head. Max asked about Argustine Lenox and if they were related, and Aunt Celeste said Lenox was an Invader. Could the apparition be Lenox?

There were three knocks on the door. Aunt Celeste let two men in white coats inside and pointed to Argus. They came over and stared at him for a moment. They each took a roll of gauze out of their pockets and asked Argus to stand. He did.

"Argus," Aunt Celeste said calmly. "Take off your shirt. Tai, help him."

It wasn't easy because his shoulder hurt so much, but with Tai's help, he got the shirt off. His shoulder was bruised, black and blue, with an indent where the brick hit. It made him queasy to look at it.

The men worked fast, wrapping his shoulder, arm, and chest in the gauze. The wrap vibrated as soon as they were done. It was soothing, not painful at all, like tiny invisible fingers massaging him ever so gently. He was lightheaded and had to sit down again. Tai said something, but the words were muffled and made no sense. It didn't matter. Nothing mattered at the moment. Everything was peaceful and beautiful.

"Unconscionable!" screamed a voice that broke through the peace.

Argus's mind cleared and he recognized it was Galena's voice. He struggled to sit up straight, amazed that his shoulder felt perfect again. He touched the gauze and it disintegrated, revealing a completely healed shoulder. Incredible. He looked up and saw that Aunt Celeste was near the couch, eyes glowing, her legs apart and her arm raised with the palm aimed toward the front door.

He got off the couch and stood with Tai. Galena's eyes shone bright blue and her arm was raised as well. What was this, a show down? A power struggle?

"Stop it!" Argus yelled. "Come on, stop it. Everyone is fighting because of me and Tai. Why isn't anyone listening to what we want? Don't we have a voice? We're seventeen, almost legal adults. We want to go home."

Tai jumped in, "Exactly. You can't tell us what to do, Galena. If you try to keep us here, we can dissolve and go anywhere we want. You can't stop us." He strode forward and moved next to Aunt Celeste with his arm raised. "It's two against one, Galena."

That was Argus's cue. He stood with them. "Three against one."

Of course, he didn't have the ability to shoot photometric pulses, but maybe she didn't know that. Galena kept her arm raised, a scowl on her face. The two medical guys in white coats hustled out of the room without looking back. Who could blame them for not wanting to be in the line of fire.

Galena lowered her arm a little. "Don't ever challenge me, boys. You will not win."

Aunt Celeste mirrored Galena and put her arm down the same amount. "You can't threaten them, Galena. It's forbidden. No harm to any human or New Breed. Ever."

Galena glared with such intensity that Argus turned away. "I know the law, Guardian. Don't presume to tell me what I can and cannot do."

"We're leaving now, Galena. I've arranged for the hovercraft and a flight back to Los Angeles. I am within my rights to do this per the tribunal's decision. Do not stand in my way." Aunt Celeste raised her arm again. "Get out of this apartment."

Argus watched Galena again. She made a low growl sound deep in her throat and spun around. She stomped out to the hallway and the door slid closed behind her. Aunt Celeste lowered her arm and drew in a deep breath.

"I apologize that you had to witness that behavior, boys." She placed a hand on each of their shoulders. "We must leave now."

"You're bad ass, Aunt Celeste." Tai smirked. "I like this side of you."

"Not a good time for joking around, Tai," she cautioned.

He rolled his eyes. "Yeah, yeah. You're still bad ass."

Argus put his shirt back on. "Is she going to let us leave?"

"She can't stop us. Commander Jampara declared the final authorization for us to return to Palmdale and resume our lives. He will monitor us for thirty planetary days. If nothing significant happens, he will release me to continue as your Guardian permanently."

Argus fist-bumped Tai. "Okay, great. Then let's go." He wasn't about to bring up the issue about his dad, or the Invader or whoever it was, even though he wanted desperately to find out more about it. It was more important to get home as fast as possible and put as much distance between them and the Citadel as they could.

There was another knock on the door, but Aunt Celeste didn't seem nervous. She opened the door and Ari came in.

"The hovercraft is ready, Celeste. Boys, get your parkas. There's a storm outside." He smiled and stepped back into the hallway.

Tai ran up the spiral staircase and came down with the white parkas. He tossed one to Argus and they put them on.

Argus zipped up the parka. "Aunt Celeste, don't you have a coat?"

"I don't need one. We won't be out long enough to cause damage to my host body. Are you ready?" She stood at the doorway and motioned them out.

Argus nodded. "Oh, yeah."

Ari led the way to the lobby and to the glass elevator. Once they were inside, it smoothly ascended to the concrete platform outside. Ari was right, there was a blizzard. Snow blew and swirled, and the wind was so freezing cold that it took Argus's breath away. He put up the hood and pulled the parka collar over his mouth.

Ari shouted above the sound of the whistling wind, "Keep your heads down and follow me!"

Argus found Tai ahead of him and grabbed the back of his parka, blinking against the stinging wind. Ari helped them into the hovercraft and started the engine. It lifted off the ground a few inches and edged down the ramp leading to the water. The weather was horrible. It was hard to see and even harder to breathe. Argus couldn't even see Aunt Celeste or Tai in the hovercraft because of the white-out. He hunkered down, covering his face with his arm.

To pass the time, he counted the minutes. At twenty-nine minutes, he felt the hovercraft rise higher and settle down. They must have landed on the mainland of Labrador. The blizzard wasn't as bad. He looked up and saw Aunt Celeste in a seat ahead of him, a blanket draped over her shoulders, her head drooped down. So she did get cold.

Ari tapped him on the shoulder. "Okay, we're here. Need any help getting out?"

"No." Argus climbed out and stood shivering while Ari pulled the blanket off Aunt Celeste.

She straightened right away and looked around. "No!" she shouted as the wind whipped her hair around. "You put a shield over me?"

Argus took a step toward the hovercraft. Where was Tai? He wasn't in the craft, and he wasn't on the land. What was going on?

Aunt Celeste sprung from the hovercraft and grabbed Ari by his jacket. "Where is he?"

Ari shook his head and pulled free. "You know where. There's nothing you can do. Galena is still technically Tai's Guardian." He jumped into the craft and took off.

Aunt Celeste stood at the shoreline. Argus watched as the hovercraft floated over the water and accelerated into the storm. He felt sick. Tai wasn't with them. He ran to the water's edge and considered diving in. He had to get back to the Citadel and get Tai. He leaned forward and was about to jump when Aunt Celeste grabbed him and pulled him back. This couldn't be happening. Tai was gone. Galena had won.

Chapter 47

The dark sky of Palmdale was alight with twinkling stars. From the back of the Jeep, Max felt confident as his new Air Force buddies drove to the bar. If they opened up about what they knew, he'd have more than enough clues to put his memory back together.

They went into the near-dark bar and sat at a small table. Max still had his AURA credit card and ordered a couple pitchers of beer and three shots of Tequila. That'd loosen them up. Drinking was a risky move since he'd already had a wreck after a drinking binge he couldn't remember. And Stone would have a cow when he saw credit card charges for booze, but so what?

"So," he started, "What did we talk about last time?"

The one named John poured a glass of beer and downed it in about five seconds. "Aliens. At least I think that's what we were goofing about. I was pretty hammered."

Angel nodded. "Yeah, that Argustine dude." He tossed back the Tequila.

"Aliens?" Max couldn't believe his luck. Now he couldn't wait to see what data he'd downloaded from the OEED. "What about aliens?"

"Oh, man, you really must have got toasted, too." John laughed and poured another beer. "I told you about the Jared XTRA-A1 file. That extraterrestrial bomber project in the sixties. It's Top Secret though, so no chance you can get into it. I saw a few unclassified reports once. Wild stuff."

Max sipped on a beer. He didn't want to get drunk. "You guys ever hear of Ramtala?"

Angel put his beer down. "Ramtala? That's the planet. You know, the alien planet. I don't know anything about it. Top Secret." He licked his lips. "I got a question for you, Max. What does AURA do? I mean really. To tell you the truth, I don't believe in all this alien crap. I guess you do, huh?"

Max shrugged. "Not sure. The jury's still out. That's what AURA does, look for evidence. My boss is ragging on my ass for proof. And I don't have any. Can you guys help?" Max passed his shot of Tequila to John.

John held the shot glass but didn't drink it. "You repeat what I'm going to tell you and I'll mess you up, man."

"Okay. My lips are sealed." Max leaned forward.

"Do some research on an incident about 25 years ago when Palmdale had this weird blue cloud over it. Don't you remember I told you about it before? Anyway, the Air Force got blamed for it and the people said it was a toxic cloud of gas. It wasn't. All the tests Edwards did came up negative, like it didn't exist. But during the 24 hours that the cloud was over Palmdale, there were blackouts and energy surges that knocked out telecommunications for miles." John drank the Tequila.

"Interesting." Max sipped more beer to be sociable. "I like hanging out with you guys." His cell phone vibrated in his pocket. "Hang on." He took it out and checked an incoming email.

To: Maxwell J. Jackson

From: L. Stone, Chief

Subject: Immediate termination

Per this notification, you are hereby terminated from the Astronomical Urgent Recovery Administration (AURA) effective immediately due to incompetence, insubordination, and misuse of expense account.

Your desk has been cleaned out and your personal belongings sent to your home address. Your final paycheck will be issued and sent to your home address.

L. Stone

Chief of Operations, AURA

Max reread the email several times. It was three in the morning. Didn't Stone sleep? He must have monitored the credit card, waiting for the opportunity to send the email. Great. No job, no memory. But there was booze. And right now, that was good enough.

He waved to the cocktail server. "Bring me another pitcher."

Chapter 48

The flight home was incredibly depressing for Argus. He sat and stared out the window, wondering what Tai was doing. He hadn't even had the chance to say goodbye. What was Galena going to do to him? How could she take him like that? Tai was trapped and there was nothing that could be done.

As Aunt Celeste explained, Ari had used an immobilizing chemical woven into the blanket to keep her subdued during the hovercraft trip. Whether Galena had taken Tai before they actually set off or once they landed was anyone's guess. The fact was that Tai was gone and the only thing that could be done was for Aunt Celeste to make a formal complaint against Galena and request another tribunal. But what if that didn't work?

He'd asked why they couldn't go back to the Citadel and find Tai, and all Aunt Celeste said was that it couldn't be done, and she'd explain why later. That wasn't what he wanted to hear. He wanted his brother back. It was like a big piece of him was missing. He was empty inside. Even the thought of seeing Lola wasn't good enough to shake the emptiness.

"Argus, try to get some sleep." Aunt Celeste handed him a blanket.

He shook his head and pushed her hand away. "I don't want to sleep. I'm going to dissolve and go and find him."

"You can't. Galena has a security shield around the Citadel. I can detect it. It won't allow anyone, not New Breeds or Ramtalans, to penetrate it."

"How can she do this? You said the Commander gave his authorization that we could go home. Is she going against him?"

Aunt Celeste ran her fingers through her ponytail. "No, there's no way she could. He's very powerful. No one can go against him. She must have subverted his authority in some way. I would expect that she convinced him that since Tai now has more Ramtalan DNA, that she should remain as his Guardian."

"So why did she do it like this?" Argus had a lump in his throat. "This is such bullshit."

"Language, Argus. She knew I'd fight if she tried to keep Tai. She had to disable me to get to him. I am so sorry, Argus. I never imagined she'd stoop to this level. And Ari, too. I'll find out if she's involved with the apparition of your father. As soon as we're home, I'll begin the complaint process." She looked away. "We'll get him back."

Argus turned back to the window and wiped away a tear. How could he go on like everything was all right when his brother was gone? How long would it take to get him back? Would he be different? Would Galena change him even more? What if she made him all Ramtalan, like she'd done with Ari?

He wanted the old Tai back. The Tai who dissolved and went for walks in the desert, called him "bro" and rolled his eyes and pouted when he didn't get his way. Nothing would be the same now, nothing.

The rest of the flight seemed to take forever and the drive from LAX to Palmdale took even longer, even though Aunt Celeste rented a fast car. Every mile that brought him closer to home reminded him that Tai was gone. Home wasn't home and it wouldn't be until Tai was back.

By the time they pulled into the driveway it was ten in the morning, Monday. Aunt Celeste said he didn't have to go to school anymore, but he wanted to. He needed to. If he stayed home, he'd be surrounded by reminders of Tai. School might be the only thing that'd save him from going crazy.

He spent the day in Tai's room watching stupid TV shows as a distraction. He was tempted to call Lola and let her know he was back, but he couldn't bring himself to do it. Not yet anyway. He needed time to mourn and adjust to the loss of his brother. When night fell, he was exhausted and must have drifted to sleep right away because when he woke, it was morning.

He felt like the robot in the dining hall at the Citadel, going about his morning routine mechanically, not feeling anything. He couldn't eat, he wasn't hungry. It was lonely sitting at the table by himself, sipping on orange juice without his brother beside him making some wise ass remark or dumb joke.

"Argus, do you want me to drive you to school?"

He got up and put the juice glass in the sink. "No, I'll drive."

"You don't have to do this."

"Yeah, I do. Tai would want me to go on like everything was okay."

He slung his backpack over his shoulder, fully healed now thanks to the weird gauze strips. That reminded him of the brick room. He didn't want to bring it up. Aunt Celeste had enough to think about. But what would it mean if his dad was alive? What if Argustine Lenox was their dad? Was that possible? Aunt Celeste said their dad had been checked out at the Citadel and he was human. Then again, it was Galena who did the investigation of him. Galena was at the heart of everything.

"All right. Be careful and text me if anything at all happens. When I was at the Citadel, I inquired about Max Jackson. Commander Jampara said he wasn't one hundred percent certain the memory erasure had taken. There appeared to be an unusual energy force that may have given Jackson some type of protection. I believe it was from the photometric pulse I shot at him. That could have given him a small amount of Ramtalan protection. Be cautious if you see him anywhere. And if you hear or see your father's image, get back here immediately. Understand?" She raised an eyebrow. "Immediately."

"Yes, ma'am." He'd dissolve and go home now that he had better control.

The Camaro waited for him in the driveway. Tai would have jumped in first, and screamed down the road, showing off for the girls.

"Get your head straight, Argus," he muttered as he started the engine.

He drove to school and trudged to physics a few minutes before the bell rang. Lola was there. She looked so pretty in a yellow tee shirt and tight jeans. New clothes obviously. Her hair was wavy, and her green eyes lit up when he walked in.

"Argie! I didn't know you were back."

"Yeah. Yesterday. Short trip. How are you? How's your shoulder?" Wow, what was it with shoulders?

"It's fine. I only had to stay overnight. They put me on antibiotics, and I have some pain pills, but it's really not too bad. Mom said I should stay home for a few more days, but I didn't want to miss anything. I'm so glad you're back." She leaned close. "I missed you so much." She played with the gold heart around her neck.

"Yeah, me too." He felt his eyes tearing up and pretended to root through his backpack. He couldn't get his mind off Tai.

"Okay, class, pop quiz," announced a familiar voice.

Argus looked up and felt a cold chill creep up his spine.

Max took out the roll book and called out names. When he got to Argus Dachel, Argus kept quiet and shrunk down with the backpack blocking him.

"Argus Dachel?"

Lola nudged him. "Argie."

He reluctantly raised his hand. "Here."

Max saw him and made a checkmark in the roll book, but then looked up again. "Argus Dachel?" he repeated. The way he looked at Argus seemed like he didn't recognize him. "Argus Dachel," he said again.

Argus lowered his head and practically hid inside the backpack. What did Max remember and what didn't he? He obviously figured out that he'd been subbing at the school, although now he was teaching physics instead of math. And the way he tested out the name, there was still some memory there. There had to be.

Max finished roll. "Take out a piece of notebook paper and put all your books and backpacks on the floor. And no phones on your desks."

"This shouldn't be hard, Argie." Lola dropped a new backpack on the ground. "But you can cheat off me if you want."

Max came by and placed a one-page quiz on his desk. Their eyes locked. "Good luck, Mr. Dachel."

Argus didn't respond. Did he remember? Max's eyes narrowed a tiny bit, as if he was thinking. He blinked and continued passing out the quizzes. Argus let out a breath.

In a whisper, Lola asked, "*Marco's* after school?"

"Sure."

He closed his eyes and thought of Tai. Where was he, what was he doing, was he all right? There was nothing there. The connection they once had was severed. Argus picked up his pencil. Tai would be back soon and then everything would be okay. In the meantime, life had to go on. That's what Tai would want and that's what Argus wanted, too.

For one day, he would be a regular teenager without any connection to Ramtalans, New Breeds, photometric pulses, Argustine Lenox, AURA, or

Galena. Today, he was simply Argus Dachel, quarterback, and high school senior in the desert town of Palmdale, California. He wasn't anything special.

END

The story continues with:
The Ramtalans, Heritage: Book Two

Acknowledgments:

A huge thank you to friends and family who supported me as a writer, allowing me the endless hours to construct this story. A special thanks to the critiquers who generously provided their views to improve the book and characters. And of course, I acknowledge the readers who take the time to sit down with my books.

Additional books by Sofia Diana Gabel:
War and Money, Book One
Neanderball

Don't miss out!

Visit the website below and you can sign up to receive emails whenever Sofia Diana Gabel publishes a new book. There's no charge and no obligation.

https://books2read.com/r/B-A-GPBBB-OXSZC

BOOKS 2 READ

Connecting independent readers to independent writers.

www.ingramcontent.com/pod-product-compliance
Lightning Source LLC
Chambersburg PA
CBHW020908200626
46814CB00001BA/233